A Note from Fran Rizer

A very special thanks to all the readers of my previous books, the cozyesque Callie Parrish mysteries, which are not quite cozies, but have no overt sex, profanity, or described brutality. Callie has had some youthful readers, whom I appreciate.

KUDZU RIVER is different.

It's a much grittier book about three women whose lives become entangled as a serial killer leaves a trail of murdered teachers up and down the coast of South Carolina. In a few places, the writing goes beyond gritty to raw. It is not meant for children. This is a tale that could not be told in cozy style, but it's a story that I feel compelled to share.

I cannot think of better words to describe the differences between Callie's books and KUDZU RIVER than these:

KUDZU RIVER *is to cozies what a great white shark is to a guppy.*

Richard D. Laudenslager
Author of *Wounded*

KUDZU RIVER

A NOVEL OF ABUSE, MURDER, AND RETRIBUTION

Fran Rizer

ODYSSEY SOUTH

ODYSSEY SOUTH

Copyright © 2015 by Fran Rizer

All rights reserved, including the right to reproduce this book or portions thereof in any form whatsoever. For information, contact odysseysouthpublishing.com

To bring Fran Rizer to your live event for an interview, reading, or book talk, contact her directly at franrizer@gmail.com or through FranRizer.com

Partial lyrics to "Maggie May," as recorded by Rod Stewart, are quoted in KUDZU RIVER. The song was written by Rod Stewart and Martin Quittenton, and the copyright is held by Rod Stewart, Unichappell Music, Inc.

Cover design by David Smoak Graphic Design

ISBN-13: 978-0-6922-8754-5
ISBN-10: 0-6922-8754-X

STORMY SUNDAY

"I'M SORRY, SO SORRY. I should have told you. Let me go. No one will ever know. You'll never see me again. I'm begging you. Please, please let me go!"

The fearful pleading had no effect on Shug, nor did the sheer terror on Carly's face. Shug no longer wanted to be parked in a tiny sports car with Carly — much less during a horrific storm — but his maniacal rage was directed as much at life as it was toward Carly and the weather. Shug closed his eyes and slapped himself frantically, repeatedly pounding his hands against his face, wide-spread fingers beating against ears that couldn't stand hearing Carly's words.

Lightning streaked through the darkness and into the car, illuminating Carly's anguished face and naked body. Screaming unidentifiable words, Shug pulled a .38 from under the driver's seat.

"No! Oh, God, no!" Carly shouted and grabbed at the

door handle, but it wouldn't work. Tried the window control. Still no way out. Hammered at the glass with clenched fists – desperate to escape.

"Bye, bitch," Shug said and pulled the trigger.

Once. *Keerack!* Twice. *Keerack!* Three times. *Keerack!* The harsh stench of gunpowder filled the car.

Torrents of crimson gushed from the crater in the back of Carly's head. Gobbets of bloody tissue spattered on the shattered glass.

A monster was loose in the small coastal town of Tanner, South Carolina.

"Dead as hell."

Those words echoed in Shug's mind as his trembling hands clenched the steering wheel, trying to hold the battered old Ford on the road. Wind whipped against the vehicle and rocked it from side to side. Worn wipers battled against rain sheeting the windshield. He gave up on reaching his destination – a wooded area on the other side of town – and stomped the brakes. The car slid across the empty street before skidding to a stop beside the gutter.

"Damned sure dead as hell," Shug whispered while looking into the rear at Carly's naked remains. "Not she . . . it. That dead body is an *it*," the killer thought. Its arms now ended in bloody stumps, and the smooth legs bent awkwardly, obscenely. Shug stepped out into the rain and opened the back door. Streaming water splashed the corpse as he struggled to pull it from the Ford. His muscles burned from the strain. Carly's body felt heavier than when he'd moved it from the sports car to Carly's battered old Ford. The carcass plopped in the gutter.

Just as well. The front of the head was a big mess of bloody tissue and bone—leaving no clue to what the victim had looked like. This pleased Shug and brought more shrill laughter from his lips. No face, no clothes, no hands. The appearance had lied just as the garments had. Carly didn't deserve to be identified

The .38 lay on the front seat. Shug reached across for it and dropped the gun onto the pavement before slipping back into the car. Soaked to the bone, he shivered. The full quotation returned to his mind as he drove away from the abandoned remains and weapon.

"The guy was dead as hell."

They were the opening words of an old Mickey Spillane novel Shug had sneaked out of Father's private bookcase and read as a child. A recent issue of one of Shug's literary magazine subscriptions had stated that Charles Dickens's "It was the best of times; it was the worst of times" in *A Tale of Two Cities* was the finest opening sentence ever written. Screw that. "The guy was dead as hell" was much better.

"Darn! Darn! Darn!" Rain pounded the windshield so brutally Katie Wray couldn't see the lines on the superhighway, even when lightning brightened the night sky. She'd almost run off the road when she exited I-26 onto I-95. Now she could barely distinguish the exit to Walterboro. Best get off the highway and find a room for the night.

As she swerved onto the exit lane, the car hydroplaned into a spin. Katie forgot everything she'd ever known about handling skids and screamed as she lost control of the vehicle.

Miraculously, the movement stopped with the passenger side of the car slammed against a retaining wall. Katie patted herself to see if anything were broken or bleeding. She'd probably have some bruises from the seat belts, but at least the air bags hadn't inflated. She shook herself and lost some of the anger she'd been carrying against the rental agent for not having a compact available and forcing her into their most expensive rental — though probably one of the safest — a Mercedes.

The loss of that fury made room for Katie's rage at her sister Maggie. A long day of delayed flights had left Katie worn out and eager to be off the plane when it landed after eleven o'clock that night. All summer long, her sister Maggie had used Katie's apartment and new Fusion free of charge — while promising to meet her at the Columbia Metropolitan Airport when Katie returned to South Carolina.

Katie realized that she should have planned to come home for a few days between her summer job and returning to work at Tanner Elementary School. "Weary." It was an old word, but it described how Katie felt — totally exhausted. She'd looked forward to sleeping during the three-hour ride to her hometown, Tanner, South Carolina. Instead, she was battling a horrific rainstorm in a rental car at three in the morning because sister Maggie had let her down as usual. Katie didn't even consider that Maggie might have forgotten. They'd spoken by phone right before Katie boarded the plane. Like so many times before, Maggie had chosen to do something else instead of meeting responsibility.

Katie stumbled as she walked around the car to look at the damage. No tires had blown, and nothing seemed to be seriously bent though there was definitely some cosmetic damage. The Mercedes appeared drivable.

Whoosh! An old Ford came out of nowhere and nearly hit her. Katie didn't see it before it sped around her. She felt assaulted. The car hadn't touched her, but the driver hadn't stopped to check on her either.

Water dripped all over the fancy leather upholstery when she sat down in the driver's seat. The transmission slid smoothly into reverse. Katie carefully backed onto the exit. A long streak of lightning lit up a motel vacancy sign just beyond the end of the ramp. Her thoughts jumped back to her sister. Perhaps Maggie's failure to meet her in Columbia was because she'd had an accident in this storm. Was she lying at the bottom of a ditch in the Fusion somewhere hidden by the trees and kudzu vines?

"Please, God, don't let Maggie be hurt," Katie prayed silently. "And please don't let my car be wrecked," she added.

"Damn!" she exclaimed aloud. She rarely cursed beyond "heck" and "darn," but Katie felt the word was defensible tonight. Her emotions jumped violently from fear to anger and back again until fear filled her mind, then d ropped to her stomach. She swallowed it, and the nausea passed for the moment.

Katie arrived at the motel and parked under the awning over the registration window. She took a minute to try calling Maggie. No answer. She texted her again, "Plse call or txt where u r."

"Nice place," Katie thought with sarcasm. "They don't trust their customers enough to let them into an office, and the open space at the bottom of the window is barely big enough to slide a paper through under closed blinds."

"Hi there," the skinny young man behind the window said with a big grin as he opened the covering. "I'd 'bout given up on anybody else coming along tonight. How ya been doing? Ain't seen you 'round much lately."

"I think there's some mistake," Katie said. "I don't believe I know you."

The night clerk roared with laughter. "Doan even think about tryin' that. You remember me and you know it. What'cha need? A double for the night?"

"Just a single will be fine. How much will that be?" She held up her debit card for him to see through the glass. He mumbled a reasonable rate and pushed a registration form and pen through the opening at the bottom. "I'll have to get the tag number," she said. "I'm driving a rental."

"That's pretty obvious unless you married a rich man since last time I saw you." Katie swiped her card through the machine and covered the keypad with her left hand as she entered her pin number. She completed the registration form except for the car tag number and shoved it
it back to the clerk. "Don't worry about the license number," he said. "I put you in the room next to the office, so you don't even have to move your car. Just leave it where it's at. I'm locking up in a minute." He slid a magnetic key card to her.

Katie said, "Thank you," and turned away, but the clerk called her back. "Katherine? That's not your name."

"I'm telling you. I'm not whoever you think I am."

"Maybe not."

The thought lit up Katie's mind like a lightbulb over a bald man's head in a cartoon.

"Maybe you know my sister Maggie. We look a lot

alike."

"That's the name—Maggie! I thought you were my friend Maggie. I wondered why you were being so standoffish."

"Have you seen Maggie lately?" Katie asked as she accepted the room key.

"Ain't seen Maggie all summer. You tell her Dewaine asked about her. If you leave before ten in the morning, just leave the key card in the room. I'm not gonna open early."

He ended the conversation by slamming the window and closing the blinds.

Katie ended the evening by crawling into bed wrapped in a damp towel. She'd used it to dry her body after shedding her wet clothing, but there was only one towel in the room and the sheet and spread were thin. She tried Maggie once more, but Maggie's cell went directly to voice mail again. Katie pulled the covers over her head to muffle the sound of thunder.

Linda dreamed. With the shades closed, the old house was as dark as a tomb, even with the lightning outside. Linda whimpered as she tossed and turned on the filthy love seat. She dreamed noise. Earsplitting, persistent sound that had covered the roar of the thunder and now its rumble as the storm finally moved away. She struggled to wake, to escape, but the visions flashed and locked her mind in the nightmare she'd endured for more than twenty years.

She dreamed of pounding, *loud* pounding on the door.

Wishing the sound would stop, Linda cringed against the far wall in her dream. With hopes of starting over, leaving the past, going back to college to become a teacher, Linda had run away to a rented room hundreds of miles from Bert. She was positive he couldn't find her this time, but she trembled with fear even when the noise dwindled to a knock. Linda tiptoed across the room and pressed her ear against the door.

"Who is it?" she asked.

The muffled answer sounded like, "Management. I've brought you a message from the desk." That didn't make sense.

"Just call and read it to me on the telephone," Linda answered.

"It's not working."

Considering the communication was probably from her mother, would *have* to be because Mama was the only one who knew where she was, Linda tried to control her panic by taking long, slow breaths. Leaving the chain on, she opened the door. Just a sliver.

The door frame splintered. The chain popped like thread. Bert stepped on Linda's feet before she even had time to gasp. He was a big man. She flailed against him, but his shoes nailed Linda's feet to the floor like spikes. Bert balled his broad hand into a fist and slugged her, first in the left eye, then on the side of her head. Linda crumpled to the floor, unconscious, chewing her tongue in a concussion-induced seizure.

Linda felt something warm. Wet heat. She coughed, spluttered, and came awake from the convulsion, but not from the dream. For a moment, Linda thought Bert was trying to revive her. She tried not to inhale — to avoid each excruciating breath. Besides, that water in her face could drown her. She opened one eye and then closed it.

12

Bert Disher stood on his wife's chest. The warm liquid cascading onto Linda came from him. Her husband bounced his two hundred twenty-seven pounds on her breasts while he pissed in her face. In real life, Linda had passed out again, but in the dream, her mind jumped to blackness that wasn't unconsciousness.

Where was she? Linda attempted to sit up, but movement was excruciating and brought waves of gagging nausea. She tried to open her eyes for a clue to where she was. All she saw was darkness. Had Bert blinded her?

"It's okay, Mrs. Disher," a female voice consoled. "Now that you're awake, I'll take the bandages off your eyes."

Soft, cool hands touched Linda's aching face. Even when the wrapping was gone, she could barely see. Her vision was blurry, but the woman's clothing told Linda where she was right away. A hospital, obviously. The man standing beside her wore a uniform. Not white or scrubs, but tan. Some division of law enforcement. "Would you like a sip of water?" the nurse asked.

Linda tried to nod, but it hurt too much. The other woman held a cup with a straw up to Linda's mouth. As Linda attempted to suck the straw, the woman said, "Mrs. Disher, do you remember coming here?" Silence. "Mrs. Disher, you were brought in by your husband. He said you had an accident. Said you fell down. Do you remember that?" Linda shook her head no.

"Mrs. Disher, Officer Weedon is here to speak with you. Will you talk to him?"

The man didn't wait for an answer. He moved closer to the bed. "Can you tell me what happened?"

"No."

"Do you have any idea how badly you're injured?"

"How bad?"

"You have four broken ribs and a massive concussion." He paused. "Are you willing to sign some papers?"

"I can't."

"Look at this." Officer Weedon held a pocket mirror in front of Linda's face. Though nearly closed from swelling, her left eye looked like something in a horror movie. A crimson blood ball surrounded a cornflower blue iris, and a large hematoma rose from the top left side of her head. Most of her face was bruised and swollen. Bits of black thread protruded from cuts that had required stitches.

"I don't think you fell, Mrs. Disher. Someone hurt you."

"I fell."

"Isn't there anything I can do to change your mind?"

"No. There's nothing anybody can do about anything."

"I can help you put an end to this," the officer promised, "but only if you sign."

"I can't."

Officer Weedon turned abruptly and spoke to the nurse. "If she changes her mind, call me, but until she's willing to work with us or they change the laws, I can't do a thing." He walked out of the room, and the nurse followed.

In her dream, as she had in real life, Linda lay silently in the hospital bed. The door to her room squeaked, and she painfully squinted her eyes, trying to focus. With her blurred vision, Linda saw only a large shape with a big patch of red, but she recognized Bert's confident voice and words before he reached her bedside with his armful of roses.

"I didn't mean to, baby. It's just that you make me so mad. No other woman has ever had that effect on me. If I didn't love you so much, I wouldr.'t get like that. Why'd you try to leave me? You *know* you can never leave me."

In her family home in the little coastal town of Tanner, South Carolina, Linda screamed herself awake. She thrashed around on the love seat. It was the first day back to work for Blair County teachers, but Linda's dreams of teaching had never come true. Tennessee Linda had no dreams left. Only nightmares.

Katie Wray's nightmares were just beginning.

MONDAY MOURNING

CHAPTER 2

". . . EMBARRASSING THAT I'M required to remind professional teachers that these are matters not just of what is right and wrong, but also matters of law. I . . ." Katie Wray heard not a word. Her mind lurched between fear and rage. Why hadn't her sister shown up to meet her at the airport as planned? *Where* was Maggie? Almost every news broadcast reported a missing female or a woman murdered by her husband, boyfriend, or a stranger. Was Maggie's failure to meet her sister beyond her control or had she simply found something she'd rather do? Katie was more comfortable with anger than fear. Why in hell had Maggie abandoned her three hours from home with no car?

Glancing down, Katie smoothed a wrinkle out of her skirt and felt relieved that she'd packed some professional outfits for the summer. Getting up early enough to drive from Walterboro to Tanner in time for the opening meeting was hard enough. Katie hadn't had time to go by her apartment.

The sounds of a door opening and steps across the floor of the media center snatched Katie to the present—the first teachers' in-service fall meeting at Tanner Elementary School.

She looked up just as an irate voice suddenly blared over the principal's words, "You have the right to remain silent, and . . ."

A uniformed Blair County sheriff's deputy and a shorter man in a suit and tie stood directly in front of her. Katie could *feel* the eyes of everyone, including the principal, burn into her.

Other teachers sat in their jeans and sneakers or sundresses and sandals, busying themselves with cutting out pictures for bulletin boards and whispering summer gossip to each other. Their occasional glances toward the principal had been meant to give the appearance they were paying attention to him. Now they stared at Katie. Even her best friend, Samantha, gaped at her. Coworkers' whispers blurred together like a swarm of bumblebees buzzing over succulent nectar.

Every teacher's interest riveted to the men standing in front of Katie. A deputy was reading the Miranda rights to Tanner Elementary School's Teacher of the Year.

"Katherine Elizabeth Wray?" asked the shorter man in a quiet tone with a drawl exaggerated even for low-country South Carolina.

"Yes." Katie's heart hammered. She stood—her throat suddenly dry. "What's happened to my sister? Are you arresting me? What's going on?"

The man who'd asked her name opened his mouth to

reply, but the taller one stepped toward Katie, his toes almost touching hers, and interrupted. "Anything you say can and *will* be used against you in a court of law," he said—his tone harsh. And loud. So loud everyone in the room could hear. Probably could be heard by anyone in the hall or office.

"Can it, Corley," the shorter man snapped.

"But Chief..."

"Call me sheriff, damn it! Can't you remember anything?"

Katie recognized him then. The shorter man was Wade Jolley, Sheriff of Blair County. She'd seen him on television during his last campaign. He'd seemed taller on TV. "Wonder if he was standing on his campaign promises?" she thought, then mentally reprimanded herself for such a silly idea at such a serious time.

"We just need to talk with you, Ms. Wray. Can we go somewhere more private?" the sheriff asked.

For the first time, Katie noticed Aimee Martin, the school secretary, standing behind the men. She must have led them into the room and pointed out Katie. A quick anger rose, but Katie shoved it down. Aimee should have discreetly called her into the hall, but Aimee was young and had probably been intimidated by the two officers.

"I'm sorry," Aimee whispered, tears in her eyes.

Had the sheriff already told Aimee what had happened to Maggie? Regardless, Katie didn't want her business announced in front of the faculty and staff. She looked toward the principal, who stood silently glaring at her.

"We'll be in my classroom if you need me," Katie said. She turned and walked to the door.

"Certainly, Ms. Wray." The principal cleared his throat

and attempted to shift everyone's attention away from Katie. "Let's get back to the meeting. We have a lot to cover this morning.

In the hall, the shorter man held out his ID card and badge. "Ms. Wray, I'm Sheriff Wade Jolley, and this is Detective Corley." Katie looked at the sheriff's identification, then turned expectantly toward the deputy. After a minute of silence, the deputy also offered his credentials. Katie pretended to read, but she couldn't have told anyone what it said — not if her life depended on it.

"I'd prefer we speak in private. Please follow me." The only sounds Katie heard on the way to Room 202 was the gentle click of her very sensible mid-heel leather pumps and the thudding of her heart.

When they reached her classroom, the professional Ms. Katherine Wray resumed control from the frightened Katie. She'd rather hear what happened to Maggie here than standing in the hall. This was her turf. The room she'd taught in for over ten years.

A thick covering of dust on the classroom furniture stacked by the windows irritated Katie. The room must not have been cleaned all summer. She placed two second-grade chairs in front of her and motioned the men toward them as she sat in her adult-sized oak seat. A power move and probably not a wise one, but it was rather pleasant to see the grown men sitting in the little chairs. Katie smiled inside at the sight of the deputy, his long legs folded like a giant insect. The sheriff stretched his feet out in front of him, crossed at the ankles. "Payback," Katie thought, "payback for being here to tell me something horrible's happened to my only living relative. Proof, too. Proof that even grown-ups respond to teacher authority."

"What happened?" she asked in her most professional tone.

The deputy snapped, "You don't ask the questions. We do, but first, I need to finish your Miranda rights. You have the . . . "

"Corley, we're not arresting her. We've just come for an interview," the sheriff sounded exasperated.

"But Chief, don't you want me to read her the rights before you interrogate her?"

"This isn't an interrogation. I'm just going to ask Ms. Wray a few questions, and I'm tired of telling you I'm a sheriff, not a police chief." Jolley turned from Deputy Corley. "Ms. Wray," he said, "do you own a .38 Special Colt Cobra six-shot revolver?"

"Oh, damn!" Katie thought. "Has Maggie shot someone or, even worse, committed suicide?"

The sheriff and deputy stared at her. Finally, Katie forced herself to answer, "I'm not sure about the kind, and I don't really own it, but I do have a .38 my ex-husband lent to me."

"Where is that weapon now?" Corley demanded as he stood and stepped toward her.

"At my apartment."

"Where were you last night between ten and midnight?" Corley demanded. He leaned across the desk, invading Katie's space with his eyes locked on Katie's.

"Why do you want to know?"

"You're the last known person to have possession of the murder weapon," the deputy accused.

"Corley," the sheriff snapped, "you seem to be getting ahead of yourself. Sit down and let me handle this."

"What murder weapon?" Katie's voice rose. "What

happened to my sister?"

The deputy's face flushed bright red, and he glared at the sheriff. He looked like a two-year-old who might erupt into a temper tantrum at any minute. "But you said . . . "

"Yes, I said this would be your case, but I'm doing the questioning here," the sheriff drawled.

Corley didn't sit down, but he did back away from Katie.

Thankful for the sheriff's intervention, Katie slid back and crossed her legs. Adjusting her skirt over her knees, she took a deep breath. Her voice didn't betray the fear that returned even on her own turf.

"What's this about a murder weapon?" she asked.

"Before that, Ms. Wray, why did you ask if something has happened to your sister?" the sheriff said.

"I spent the summer teaching on a reservation out west. My sister Maggie was supposed to meet my plane in Columbia last night. The flight was delayed, several hours late, but Maggie wasn't at the airport when I arrived, and she never answered when I kept phoning and texting her. After midnight, I finally rented a car and headed back to Tanner, but I was so tired that I stopped and spent the night in a Walterboro motel. I've been calling Maggie all morning and still get no answer at home or on her cell."

"Have you been by her house?" asked Sheriff Jolley.

"No, I was running late, came straight to work in the rental car. At lunchtime, I'll go to the apartment and see if she's there."

"You don't seem too worried that she might be sick or injured." The deputy smirked. "Not especially concerned that she might have fallen and can't get up."

"It's more likely she took off on an unplanned vacation," Katie said. She laughed self-consciously. "It wouldn't be the first time Maggie forgot a commitment or found something more fun to do."

"We didn't come to talk about your sister, but I'll be glad to have a deputy swing by and see if she's home," the sheriff said. "Could be simply that her phones are out. We had a rough storm last night."

"The apartment landline *and* her cell?" Katie asked. Her eyebrows arched with doubt.

"Tell you what, Ms. Wray. When we leave here, we'll go to check on her. Do you have keys to her apartment?"

"It's *my* apartment. She's been living with me the past year."

"Does she have a car?"

"She had my Ford Fusion for the summer while I was in North Dakota."

"Is your sister a teenager?" Deputy Corley interrupted with another smirk. "She may have run off with your car when she knew you were coming back. Teenagers do that kind of thing."

Katie straightened her shoulders and gave the deputy a hard look. "My sister is thirty-seven years old, hardly a teenager."

"Where's the .38 now?" Corley demanded.

"I left it at my apartment. Since 9/11, the airlines don't smile too kindly on passengers carrying nail clippers, much less guns. I didn't want to be arrested as a possible terrorist."

"Is the weapon at the same apartment where you've been trying to contact your sister?" Corley snapped.

"Yes, what's this all about? I thought you'd come to tell me something about her, but you seem to know less than I do."

"Ms. Wray." The sheriff stood as soon as he began speaking. Katie had wondered how long it would take for him to realize how ridiculous he looked in that chair. "Last night," Jolley continued, "a white male was found shot to death on Payton Street."

"What does that have to do with me?"

"A .38 Special Colt Cobra six-shot revolver presumed to be the murder weapon was found beside the body. That gun is registered to Charles M. Wray, and Mr. Wray tells us that you, his ex-wife, borrowed it from him last year claiming you sometimes heard noises and were afraid."

The sheriff placed his hands on Katie's desk and leaned toward her, but he wasn't as threatening as when the deputy had done it. "We won't be positive the Colt is the murder weapon until we receive ballistics reports, but it probably is. Your husband says you had it."

"*Ex*-husband," Katie corrected before adding, "the gun Charles lent me should be in the drawer of my nightstand."

"Totally impossible!" the deputy growled. "That gun is in the Blair County Sheriff's Department's evidence compound, and . . . "

The door opened, and a high-pitched feminine voice called, "Katie! Katie! What did those cops want? We're free for lunch. Do you—"

The extremely slender, blond woman in jeans and Nikes stopped in the doorway when she saw the two men.

"Samantha," Katie said, "I'm speaking with the sheriff right now. We'll get together later."

"Sorry, Katie. I really need to talk to you, and we have more meetings after lunch."

"How about an early dinner?"

"Okay, I just *gotta* talk to you!" Samantha started out, then turned, and said sweetly over her shoulder to the officers, "Sorry for interrupting."

Sheriff Jolley smiled. When the door closed, he said, "Tell you what, Ms. Wray. Why don't we kill two birds with one stone? We'll follow you over to your apartment right now and check on both your sister and the weapon. This could all be a mistake."

"Not likely," the deputy muttered.

Katie saw the irritated look on the sheriff's face, but it was directed toward Corley, not her. This wasn't the time to worry about the sheriff's expression. Fear and anger spoke in Katie's mind. Fear: "Is my sister safe?" Anger: "What has Maggie done *now*?"

Katie keyed the door and stepped into her cool sanctuary. She felt guilty that she didn't really live "green," even though she taught eco-friendly practices to her second-graders. Katie paid large utility bills for a small, one-bedroom apartment, but she liked her home almost frosty. Maggie hardly ever kept the air-conditioning so low. She must have lowered the thermostat in preparation for Katie's arrival home. Why hadn't she shown up at the airport?

Pausing for a moment, enjoying the chill with Sheriff Jolley standing a respectful step behind her while Deputy Corley leaned over her shoulder, Katie looked around the living room. It took a moment to register. She gasped and her stomach lurched. The computer, stereo, TV, and landline telephone were gone.

"What's wrong?" Jolley asked in reaction to Katie's sharp intake of breath.

"Some of my things are missing."

Deputy Corley began filling in forms on a clipboard he'd brought in. Both men followed her into the kitchen where she discovered her microwave and individual pod coffeemaker had disappeared. The television and telephone were no longer in her bedroom.

"Where's the gun?" Corley snapped.

Katie opened the bottom drawer of her lingerie chest beside the bed. She pushed delicate undergarments out of the way and reached to the back of the drawer for the revolver. Nothing but flimsy, soft fabrics. She frantically tossed everything out of the drawer. Bras, panties, and sheer gowns surrounded her.

"It's not here," she whispered in amazement.

"Yeah, sure," snarled Corley. "Where'd you hide your things so we'd believe the weapon was stolen? When did you call in this burglary?"

"I didn't report anything. I haven't been here in over two months. If there's a report, it would have been made by my sister Maggie."

"Maggie Wray?" the deputy asked, hurriedly writing.

"No, Wray is my married name. I kept it when I divorced because the children at Tanner Elementary knew me as 'Ms. Wray.' My sister uses our maiden name. She's Margaret Magnolia Halsey. We call her Maggie."

The deputy giggled.

Katie didn't feel it necessary to comment on her parents' choice of names for their other daughter. She was thankful that her middle name was Elizabeth, not Camellia, Azalea, or some other southern flower.

"The Charleston Halseys?" the sheriff drawled calmly.

"Our father was from Charleston. Our mother was from

25

Beaufort. Maggie and I grew up here in Tanner after our parents divorced."

"Is your sister a teacher, too?" Jolley asked.

"No, Maggie hasn't found her calling. She attended Coastal Carolina University, but she quit before she finished."

"Was the gun here when you left for the summer?" The sheriff changed the subject.

"I think so, but I can't really say."

"When's the last time you actually *saw* the revolver?"

"It hasn't crossed my mind for months," Katie answered.

"You kept it with your underwear?" Corley questioned sarcastically. "How could you not think about it every time you went into that drawer?"

"I don't see where it's any of your business how often I go into a particular lingerie drawer!" Katie's eyes flashed. She wanted to slap that deputy, but she'd never physically hit anyone in her life, and she wasn't about to start with a law officer. Instead, she socked him verbally with her own brand of sarcasm.

"What if I told you I kept the gun in the drawer with my special occasion stash? Will you write that down?"

"Stash? What are you on? Meth? Pot? Crack?" Detective Corley wrote frantically.

"My stash of Victoria's Secret for special occasions!" Katie grinned.

The sheriff laughed, and his blue eyes sparkled. The detective didn't crack a smile.

"Did you keep the gun loaded?" Sheriff Jolley asked. His tone was serious, but his eyes still twinkled.

"The revolver was loaded when I borrowed it from Charles."

"Was it loaded with hollow-point bullets?"

"Yes, I asked Charles for the gun last year when there were burglaries around here. He knew I'd never be able to load it in an emergency, and I don't shoot well. He put hollow points in it so that if I actually hit something, it would do some real damage."

"You know, we could take you downtown right now." Corley's expression matched his tone.

"But we're not," Sheriff Jolley assured Katie before asking, "You hadn't thought about the gun in a while?" Katie nodded. The sheriff asked, "When's the last time you actually saw it?"

If this were good cop, bad cop, these two didn't need any practice. Katie answered, "I saw it at the beginning of the summer when I showed it to Maggie before I left town."

"So it could have been removed at any time between then and the burglary or during the theft of your other belongings, couldn't it?" asked the sheriff.

"Yes." Katie barely whispered her answer.

"Do you have any idea who might have taken your gun or burglarized your apartment?"

A sick feeling washed over Katie. A tear filled one eye and spilled down her cheek. She hated to cry, especially in front of anyone. She replied, "Probably."

Surprisingly, Deputy Corley didn't snap at her. The two men waited for Katie to continue.

"My sister or her friend," she finally said.

"What friend?" The sheriff's voice was gentle.

"It could have been the man she told me about. He's gone."

"What do you mean? Why do you think he's gone?"

Katie replied, "His name is Frankie Barker. Maggie said

27

that he'd spent most of the summer staying here with her, but she was making him leave night before last. She was afraid he'd be angry even though she'd told him that he had to leave before I returned. He may have taken my belongings out of spite." She paused. Her voice trembled. "Maggie is missing, and I've been ripped off. I'm scared this man has done something to my sister."

Deputy Corley wrote feverishly, but he paused to ask, "What's this man's address and telephone number?"

"How should I know?"

"Don't know!" Deputy Corley didn't need more than those two words to express his contempt.

"Maggie never mentioned where he was from. He spent the summer with her in my apartment. She talked to me almost every day, and she babbled on about how much fun he was, but she definitely planned to put him out before I returned. She said they were together all the time except on weekends."

"Where'd he go on weekends?"

"He had a bass guitar case. She told me he was in a band and had to play on weekends."

"Didn't she go watch him?"

"No, Maggie and I both like rock 'n' roll, but she said he was playing modern, alternative rock. We don't like any of the new stuff. Just old, classic rock our mom listened to." Katie hesitated before adding, "Besides, she said he never invited her. Maggie called me on weekends to discuss Frankie because he wasn't here then and I didn't want her with him. She was miffed, but it also gave her a chance to talk without his hearing what she said. During the week, he was like a kid, trying to distract her every time she was on the phone. She told me that when she suggested going to hear his band, he said she'd make him nervous."

"Where did she meet Frankie Barker?" the sheriff quietly changed the subject.

"On the Internet? In a bar? Or through a singles column?" the deputy added to the sheriff's question before Katie could answer.

Katie bristled. She wasn't proud of some of Maggie's past and the facts surrounding her meeting Frankie Barker, but she resented the deputy's assumptions about her sister. "She said she met him in the book section in the back of the all-night drugstore the first week after I left for North Dakota."

"When did she next see him?" Jolley questioned.

"That night. They talked for a long time, then came to the apartment for coffee." The deputy's new expression annoyed Katie even more. She busied herself folding the flimsy garments as she talked. The deputy was in her face, but the sheriff walked around the room, looking, but not touching.

"It's not like you think," Katie continued. "He stayed for the night, but she said they talked all night. It turned into a relationship later." The expression in the deputy's eyes showed what he thought. Katie didn't look at the sheriff. She didn't want to see what might be there.

"And you don't have his number or address?" the deputy repeated while continuing to write.

"It was a summer romance. Maggie said she knew that from the beginning, but I doubt that you'd give your brother the name and address of a new girlfriend even if the relationship was serious, would you?"

"I guess not," the deputy conceded.

"I'm worried that they fought when she pushed the issue of his having to leave before I returned."

"Fought?"

"I hope they just argued. She told me he didn't want to leave, but she was going to make him. I should have told her to wait until I got home, and I would put him out."

"Ms. Wray, do you know what Frankie Barker looks like? Did your sister ever describe him?" the sheriff asked.

"Over and over. She talked constantly about him when she called me."

Katie repeated Maggie's excited words from their telephone conversations. The way the deputy echoed Katie's comments as he wrote them irritated her.

When Katie finished, the sheriff reached over and took the clipboard from Deputy Corley. "Ms. Wray," he said. "This is the description you've given us. Listen and see if you can add anything to it. White male. About five feet, eight inches. Twenty-eight years old, or at least, that's what your sister told you. Corley, change that to between twenty-five and thirty. Thin build."

"How old is your sister?" Of course, it was Corley asking.

"Maggie's thirty-seven. I've already told you that, and no, I don't know if she usually dates men that much younger, but she calls herself a cougar," Katie defended her sister while apologizing for her at the same time.

"Are you a cougar, too?" the deputy asked Katie.

She answered without thinking, "No, I'm forty-two, and I prefer men my age or older."

"Corley," the sheriff reprimanded the deputy, "that's not relevant at the moment." He turned back to Katie. "Anything else you can think of about Barker?"

"She said he was lean, not skinny."

"Okay. Dark auburn hair, shoulder-length, but no pigtail or ponytail. Any facial hair?"

"He had a beard when she met him. He shaved it a week or so later. Said he felt cooler clean-shaven during the summer months."

"Green eyes?"

"She said green, but I think she meant hazel. Maggie said they looked green, but sometimes they seemed brown." Katie glanced at the deputy's notepad. He had one of the worst handwritings she'd ever seen. "Darn!" Katie thought, "if that's not a schoolteacher thing, I don't know what is. This is serious, and I'm grading this creep's handwriting."

"No significant scars, tattoos, or anything?"

"Not that she ever mentioned, and believe me, she spent hours talking about this man when she called me on weekends."

"And so far as you know, his name is Frankie Barker? Do you know if it's really Frank, Francis, or Franklin?"

"Frankie's all she ever told me."

"Ms. Wray," the sheriff said, "I'll have your apartment dusted for fingerprints. I think Barker may be your thief and is probably involved in the homicide. We don't have an ID on the victim yet. He's a white male about Barker's size, so Barker could be the victim as easily as he could be the doer. If he's the killer, he burglarized you. If he's the victim, whoever murdered him apparently has Barker's key to your apartment."

The sheriff turned to Corley. "Call forensics to dust for prints here." He looked back at Katie. "We usually wait to issue an all-points bulletin on a missing adult with a vehicle, but Deputy Corley will fill out the forms for you to sign to report your sister and your car missing since there's suspicion of foul play. You should replace your house telephones and have new locks put on your doors. We'll need an inventory of anything else that's missing, but I'd prefer you wait until the techs have finished here to make that."

"Yes, sir," Katie replied.

"Corley, wait here until forensics finishes and be sure the place is locked when you leave." He faced Katie again. "Take your key with you unless you want to stay."

"I will," Katie said, thinking, "Kinda like locking the barn after the horse is stolen, right?" but she kept her thoughts to herself.

A cheap no-tell motel. Cash up front. No ID required. Just sign a name, any name, and pay. No questions asked. The room was small and shabby, but the water was hot. Shug showered, and showered, and showered. What did Lady Macbeth say? "Out, damned spot, out!" Well, the steaming water wasn't helping. Blood had splashed on him, but some of those splatters and swipes were washed off by the pouring rain when Shug pulled Carly's body out of the car. Still, he felt a need for cleansing, and no matter how hot the water, his skin felt contaminated, stained in places no blood had touched.

Finally, exhausted both physically and emotionally, Shug wrapped a towel around water-pruned skin and flopped on the bed. The no-tell didn't supply fancy robes with its accommodations. Eager to bathe, he hadn't turned on the room AC when he came in. He reached across the bed and flipped it on. The one-room unit blew barely cool air at him, but he still felt hot and sticky. He tossed off the towel and lay nude on the too-soft mattress. The room felt no cooler with or without the cloth covering his junk.

Shug reached for the remote control on the bedside shelf. He pressed the power button, and some half-hour comedy show blasted from the TV. He liked cartoons, but this was real people acting out some stupid sitcom. Channel-jumping didn't lead to anything better. Then—the news. The cops had already found the body.

"If you have any information about this victim's identity or any other aspect of this case, please contact . . ."

Shug didn't hear the number. Damn straight. One phone call could clear up this "brutal murder here in Tanner." His shrill laughter echoed off the walls of the small rental room. Gotta stop doing that. Crazy laughter wasn't a smart idea. When life got funny, a quiet, well-modulated chuckle would attract less attention in public.

Against rational thought, Shug tossed the remote control. Threw it against the television screen, expecting an explosion, but instead the control bounced back on the bed.

He jumped up and dashed back to the bathroom. The shower was still wet from the last time, but he stepped back in and turned the water on full-force. He'd used up most of the soap before when he'd sudsed up over and over. When the water turned cold, he stepped out, pulled on jeans, a tee, and flip-flops. Within five minutes, the no-tell motel room was empty, and the killer was speeding up the coast on Highway 17. Screw Tanner.

CHAPTER 3

AFTER A TRIP to Walmart, Katie had two new landline telephones on the seat beside her in the rented car and a raging hunger in her stomach. She'd skipped breakfast and had no lunch. The dashboard clock showed 3:30. Teachers at Tanner Elementary School could leave the building at 3:45. Some would stay late working in their rooms, but Katie assumed Samantha would walk out at 3:44.

Katie pulled into the faculty parking lot near Sam's ten-year-old Hyundai, which had needed both a paint job and air-conditioning repair for longer than the past year.

Spanish moss draped motionlessly from the twisted oak limbs over the asphalt pavement and filtered out some of the bright August sunlight. Katie thought the shade was an illusion. The parking lot was as hot as an open field. She sat listening to old rock 'n' roll on 102.7, engine and air conditioner running to keep out the sweltering heat of coastal South Carolina.

Samantha, the petite, extremely slender, blond teacher who'd interrupted Katie, the sheriff, and the deputy earlier, beamed when she spotted Katie. "When did you buy the new car?" she asked as she slid in beside her friend. "You just bought that new Fusion before school ended, but this is a step up from even that."

"I didn't. This is a rental. Maggie has my car."

Although Samantha Branham and Katie Wray were good friends during the school year, they hadn't written or telephoned during their two-month vacation. "Thought you were going to trade cars this summer yourself," Katie continued and motioned toward the Hyundai.

"I thought so, too," Samantha answered. "Don't ever, ever marry a lawyer!"

"More important, don't ever divorce one!" Katie said. She and Sam giggled like nine-year-olds. Samantha had supported her husband Marc through law school by teaching fourth grade and now first grade. Their understanding was that when his practice was established, he would put her through grad school for her master's and doctorate. What Samantha really wanted to do was teach on the college level. Instead, when Marc's law practice was barely on its feet, Marc left Samantha for his new law clerk, a little blonde, even shorter than Samantha, who "laughed more" and "didn't take life so seriously." Of course, Marc's law clerk wasn't in debt up past her painted eyebrows for anything he'd needed or wanted but had financed in Samantha's name while she was the only one working.

"Seriously, how's it going?" Katie asked.

"Awful!" Samantha replied. "My attorney claims there's

35

nothing I can do. No kids, no child support. No alimony because Marc never supported me. I've been the breadwinner, and Marc had no income. According to the law, I'm even stuck with making the payments on all those expensive furnishings in his office!"

"Why don't you at least take possession of his office furniture?" Katie asked.

"Listen to you, Katie. 'Take possession!' You sound like you were married to a lawyer yourself."

"I did work in a legal office one summer years ago. No kidding, if I had to pay for it, I'd sure take it."

"Why would I want furniture he's probably grubbed around on with that little mouse of his?" A hearty, belly laugh erupted from the tiny woman.

"I'm glad you can see the humor."

"If I didn't laugh, I'd cry, but . . ." Samantha paused dramatically with a big grin on her face. "I was dying all day to tell you. I've met a man!"

"Well, congratulations! I told you the best way to get over a man is to replace him. One nail drives out another. Tell. Who is he?"

"He's an advertising executive and he's divorced and he's wonderful! We go riding in his classic Jag, then stay up all night in his hot tub."

"Oh." Katie raised an eyebrow. "He's got a hot tub?"

"Yes, in his backyard under the stars."

"Does he have a name other than Mr. Wonderful?"

"Don't laugh. You'll have to call me Samantha when you meet him. His name is Sam, too. Sam Campbell."

"Sounds like a perfect match. Sam and Samantha. This could be serious."

"I hope so, but my divorce isn't final, and he says he

hasn't been divorced long enough for commitment yet. What about you? What did the sheriff want? Are you dating him?"

"Samantha, you and everybody else heard that deputy start reading me my rights. Why would you even ask if I'm dating the sheriff? I just got back last night, and I'm not seeing anyone special."

"I was kinda hoping if I said that, you'd tell me what the business with the sheriff was all about," Sam answered.

Katie desperately wanted to talk to Sam about what was happening, but she said nothing. She'd shared too many of Maggie's mistakes with friends in the past. Perhaps Maggie had pawned the computer and telephones and gone off with Frankie Barker. Maybe that body had nothing to do with Maggie and Frankie, but then, what about the gun? Better for Katie to keep her mouth shut until she knew what was going on.

"Are you gonna tell me?" asked Samantha.

"No," Katie said. "I came to see if you want to get something to eat now. I know I suggested dinner and it's late for lunch and early for supper, but I'm starving."

"Me, too. I worked in my classroom during lunch break. I don't like to eat more than one meal a day because my stomach pooches out if I do."

"I skipped breakfast. How about breakfast for lunch?"

"Waffle House?" asked Samantha.

"No. Pancakes. How about the Downtown Diner?"

"Sure, I love that place, and they have breakfast, lunch, and dinner twenty-four hours a day."

Katie laughed, "So long as we ride in this air-conditioned car."

"You got it!"

The Downtown Diner by afternoon was like it was around the clock—crowded, brightly lit, and noisy. Katie and Samantha sat in a booth at the back, and the waitress eventually stopped beside them. "Hello," she said in a bored tone, "my name is Courtney, and I'll be your server today." Sam ordered a small salad. Katie requested grits and scrambled eggs with cheese.

Samantha looked surprised and said, "Thought you wanted pancakes."

"Actually, I *think* pancakes a lot , but I hardly ever *eat* them. I could read the menu in here for an hour, and I'd wind up ordering grits and eggs."

Samantha grimaced and wrinkled her nose in distaste. "I hate grits."

"That's 'cause you're from up nawth," Katie responded with a comical, exaggerated drawl, which made her think of the sheriff.

"Give me a break, Katie. Just because we're in South Carolina, you're going to call me a Yankee because I'm from North Carolina?"

"I happen to like grits, and you don't have to smother, cover, or chunk 'em to make them edible." The waitress chuckled as she walked away, but Samantha became serious.

"Marc and I used to eat pancakes and waffles a lot when he was in law school in Columbia because they were cheap."

"Still not over Marc, are you?" Katie asked.

"No, I really thought our marriage would last and we'd start a family when he finished law school. My whole life was planned out, and he left me for another woman as soon as he didn't need me to support him. Now, my lawyer tells me I'll get nothing. It's like Marc just used me, and I think attorneys have this thing they call 'professional courtesy.' They don't try real hard against each other in personal divorce cases."

The waitress placed glasses of iced tea in front of them. Sam took a small sip to be sure hers was unsweetened before adding Splenda. Katie glanced toward the door and smiled. "Well, if it isn't Tennessee Linda. Last time I saw her was last spring, but Maggie said she and Frankie saw her sitting on her front porch a few weeks ago." Katie waved, but the older woman didn't seem to notice. She seemed oblivious to her surroundings.

Samantha looked toward the entrance. "Tennessee Linda?" she questioned.

Katie nodded. Tennessee Linda appeared to be in her sixties. Her small, round stomach pressed out against hot pink polyester stretch pants, but her arms and face were thin. Her slacks and lime green striped knit shirt were picked as fuzzy as an angora sweater. Her cheeks were flushed, and vivid lipstick slashed bright red on her mouth. Pencil-drawn eyebrows swooped over each eye. Her gray-streaked tangled mass of hair fell to her waist.

The woman carried an empty, dingy beige pillowcase that occasionally touched the floor as she shuffled to the counter on the opposite side from where Katie and Sam sat. Although her gait wasn't steady and one shoelace in her Keds was untied, she had no difficulty climbing onto a stool near the cash register at the counter.

"Oh, is she a street person?" Samantha whispered sympathetically.

"No, Tennessee Linda grew up right here in Tanner. She lives in that big, dilapidated house with the columns a few blocks over on Oak Street. I know you've seen the only house on an entire fenced block of trees and weeds in the business section. When I was a little girl, I begged my mom to take me there to play because it looked like a park with pretty trees and flowers, but it's been overgrown for years."

"Did your mother ever let you play there?"

"No, Tennessee Linda's dad kept everything fenced to keep people out. He died a while back, but the place had gone downhill long before that."

Samantha stirred another packet of Splenda into her tea as she asked, "If she grew up here, why do you call her 'Tennessee' Linda?"

"That depends on who you ask," Katie responded. "I've heard stories about Linda Pearson all my life. She went to school with my mother. She'd get drunk and climb up on tables and dance."

"What's that got to do with her name?" Sam took a sip from her iced tea and reached for a package of Equal to add to the Splenda.

"My aunt used to say they called her Tennessee Linda because she's straight out of Tennessee Williams, but my mother said they called her Tennessee way back in school because she'd get so drunk on Jack Daniel's. The joke was Linda could drink Tennessee dry. She was married once and left town for years, but she came back not long before her mother died. She took care of her father until he passed on a year or so ago. Now she lives by herself in the old family home. She used to come to see my mom once in a while, but that was a long time ago. Maggie said she looked the same as always when she and Frankie saw her sitting on her front porch not long ago."

"How is Maggie and who's Frankie?" Sam asked with a grin. "Is your sister settling down?"

"Who knows?" Katie's cryptic answer was totally accurate. She had no idea where Maggie was or what she was doing.

"But who's Frankie?" Samantha repeated.

"Frankie's a guy Maggie dated during the summer. She told me he seemed fascinated with Tennessee Linda's story. Wanted to know all about her and the house and that jungle surrounding it."

"Jungle?" Samantha emptied her tea glass and began sipping water. "I'd call that a small-town block of deciduous forest with lots of undergrowth, not a jungle."

"You're right," Katie said. "I can't help it if you taught fourth-grade social studies, and I forgot it. Next you'll be describing the characteristics of the deserts and rain forests."

"When I first looked up, I thought she was comical, but actually she looks pathetic." Sam changed the subject from regions of the Earth back to Tennessee Linda.

"Are you talking about the lady in pink and green?" Courtney Mack asked as she set their plates in front of Katie and Samantha.

"Yes, does she come in often?" Katie answered a question with a question.

"Once a day, every day, rain or shine. Different time each day, but she always sits on that same stool. If this place was empty except for one person and that person was sitting on her stool, she'd stand back and wait until they left. Always eats the same thing: one waffle with four packs of jelly. No syrup or butter. Never drinks anything except ice water. What did you say her name is? She told

41

me her name is Miss Possum."

"Her name is Linda Pearson," Katie said and laughed softly. "I wish I could tell my mother about that. She would have gotten a big kick out of Miss Possum. Mama told me Linda was fun and really smart in school but always a little strange."

"She looks a lot more strange than fun and smart these days," Samantha commented. Courtney nodded.

As they headed across the parking lot toward the car, Katie realized she didn't want to go back to her apartment alone. She asked Samantha, "What are you doing tonight? Want to come over and work on lesson plans?"

"I'd love to, but let's make it another time." Samantha lowered her eyes demurely. "Sam said he'd come by to hear about my first day back to work."

"Sounds serious to me. Definitely serious."

"Oh, it's gonna be. I just know it is!"

Katie was almost to her apartment before she remembered the e-mail. She called the Blair County Sheriff's Department on her cell phone.

"I'd like to leave a message for Sheriff Jolley," she told the operator.

"Just a moment. He's in." In a few moments, Katie heard that drawl.

"Wade Jolley here."

"Sheriff Jolley, this is Katie Wray. I just remembered that Maggie e-mailed me a picture of her and Frankie Barker back at the beginning of the summer. Since my computer's been stolen, I can't check to see if I downloaded it on the hard drive, but there's a chance that I didn't delete it from my g-mail. Do you want me to stop by the library and check on it?"

"Better yet, swing by my office and you can access your account on my computer," Jolley answered. "You know where the sheriff's department is, don't you?"

"Sure." Katie was glad to have a reason not to go back to the apartment where she knew she'd do nothing but worry about Maggie. She kept telling herself that Maggie had probably left in the Fusion with Frankie Barker. Still, thoughts of how many women disappeared only to be found dead or never heard from again filled Katie with fear that Maggie wasn't just being irresponsible this time.

At the sheriff's office, a deputy, not Corley, but one who seemed nicer, ushered Katie into Sheriff Jolley's office. Katie's g-mail account revealed that particular e-mail from Maggie had been deleted.

"I hate to ask you to do this," Jolley said, looking everywhere except at Katie. "But," he continued, "I'd like you to look at the body and see if you recognize the man. Maybe if it's Barker, seeing him will help you recall the details of the photo. If not, it might be someone else you and your sister knew. We can't prove it, but it appears he was killed with your gun."

"My *ex*-husband's gun," Katie corrected.

"I spoke with the coroner a short while ago. He's probably still at the morgue."

"If you want me to meet you there, I'll have to follow you. I have no idea where the morgue is." Katie said.

"Ride with me. I'll bring you back for your car."

Sheriff Jolley's cruiser was clean and neat. No McDonald's wrappers or empty coffee cups. It smelled like Armor All. The ride was short and comfortable with very little conversation.

Katie had never considered whether the town of Tanner

had a morgue, but she wasn't surprised that they didn't drive to a municipal building. The sheriff parked in the rear of Jennings Funeral Home. Katie had been to funerals there, and though viewing bodies in caskets wasn't one of her favorite activities, she thought she could handle this. "I know it's not like attending a funeral or going to a viewing in the chapel, but a body's a body, isn't it?" Katie laughed nervously. Sheriff Jolley didn't respond. She wondered who she was reassuring, the sheriff or herself.

Jolley guided Katie through the back door and introduced her to tall, gray-haired Mike Hawkins, the coroner, who led them down a hall, into a room even colder than Katie liked. Overhead fluorescent lights hung from the ceiling brightly lighting the stark, bare room. It didn't look at all like the areas where funerals were held at Jennings. No carpet or overstuffed furniture. No soft music to soothe mourners.

Katie, who was very conscious of smells, was surprised that the air had no odor, not even a chemical one. Katie had mentally anticipated an unpleasant scent there even though an overhead exhaust fan was on. An avid reader of mysteries, she thought she knew exactly what to expect.

"Before we do this," Sheriff Jolley said to Katie, "you need to know that the victim was shot in the back of the head three times with hollow-point bullets. They all exited in front. You won't be able to identify his face at all."

The coroner nodded solemnly.

"Okay," Katie answered quietly as she wondered, "then why am I here?"

The gurney rattled as the coroner pulled it to the center of the room. Katie wanted to turn away from the mound encased in its zippered bag. She mentally braced herself.

"The body is unclothed," said the coroner.

"I understand."

"There are no significant scars, marks, tattoos, nothing to aid in identification. An amazingly unmarked body for an adult male," the coroner continued.

Sheriff Jolley smiled. "If this is who we think it might be, it seems he made his living doing easy work."

Katie reeled as though he'd slapped her. Her sister had never said so, but Katie had suspected that Maggie was paying for everything while Frankie Barker stayed with her. Maybe the sheriff meant being a musician was easy work, but she thought he meant being a gigolo wasn't difficult. Katie couldn't think of any good response. The sheriff had insulted her sister. This thought prompted her fears about Maggie to resurface. She vowed not to shed tears, but her lip trembled even as the thoughts registered.

The three of them stepped closer to the gurney. Katie was aware that the sheriff's attention was totally on her. Katie asked herself if he feared she'd pass out or if he was observing her so intently for other reasons. She felt the sheriff take her arm with just the barest touch. "This won't be easy," he said. Then the coroner unzipped the bag and spread it open. The smell that rose from the refrigerated body was worse than Katie had expected.

Her sudden gasp reflected both shock and relief. Shock: the reality of the naked male corpse on a steel gurney compared in no way to the neatly dressed bodies Katie had viewed in their satin-lined coffins surrounded by flowers—nor to anything she'd seen in movies. Relief: she didn't think it was Frankie. She stared at the unnaturally light flesh under the stark fluorescent lights. "A whiter shade of pale." The words of one of her mother's favorite old songs drifted uninvited through Katie's mind. She averted her gaze from the top of the body as the coroner placed a napkin-sized cloth over the head and another over the pubic area. Small paper bags covered each of the victim's hands.

"No," Katie whispered with breath too short to get out a a normal tone, "I don't think that's Frankie. At least, not from my memory of the photograph."

"Are you sure?"

"The body build is similar, but in the picture Frankie had a dark tan. The skin is lighter and . . ."

"Postmortem lividity," interrupted Coroner Hawkins, "makes skin look lighter. When the blood settles after death, the . . ."

"I've read about that," replied Katie in a stronger voice, "but I don't think it's the same person who was in the photo my sister e-mailed to me."

"Are you sure?" The sheriff's voice sounded business-like, yet gentle. "How do you know?"

"This man is probably near the same height and weight, but the body is shaped differently. Maggie and I are both about five feet, eight inches tall. In the photo, Frankie and Maggie looked the same height, but the man had longer legs than Maggie. This man has a longer torso and shorter legs than Maggie and me, and his arms and legs seem skinny. Frankie looked slender, but not skinny."

"A body looks different stretched out like this," commented the coroner.

"I've never seen a picture of Frankie lying down, but let me see his hair."

Katie didn't miss the fact that the sheriff immediately looked toward the body's cloth-covered pubic region, but she didn't comment that the authorities would need her sister Maggie to identify the body based on its more private areas.

Coroner Hawkins lifted the edge of the cloth covering the head and held out a swatch of hair. To her own shock Katie almost reached out to touch it, but instead she pronounced emphatically, "It's not Frankie. His hair is more auburn, and it wasn't that long in the photo."

"Hair grows, and the color you saw on the photo could have been distorted on the computer," the sheriff said.

"Do you want to see the whole head?" asked the coroner.

"That won't be necessary," the sheriff said immediately.

Since their arrival, Katie had bounced back and forth between the vulnerable Katie and the professional Ms. Katherine Elizabeth Wray. Her mind was Katie, but her voice was Ms. Wray. "I'll look at the head if you want me to," she said. "I'd rather face it now than decide later that I should have looked."

The coroner removed the cloth. Katie stared in shock at the horrific sight. A veteran fan of Stephen King and horror movies, including a few blood, gut, and gore spectacles that had won special-effects awards, Katie discovered immediately that nothing on the screen had prepared her for this. There was literally no face at all. Where it should have been was a gaping waste of tissue and bone. The hair looked a little shorter and brighter seeing it attached to what was left of the head.

Sheriff Jolley stood silently beside her. Both he and the coroner stared at Katie's face. Finally, Jolley interrupted the silence with one word, "Well?"

"Now I'm not sure. The body looks different from my memory of the picture, but I'm not positive. Won't you be able to tell by comparing this body's fingerprints with what they get from my apartment?"

"No," the coroner replied. "See." He lifted one of the corpse's hands and opened the bag. The last joint of each fingertip was missing. Dark brown, dried blood crusted the knuckles where the fingertips should have been. "We won't get any fingerprints here. No trace evidence beneath fingernails either."

Sheriff Jolley added, "What we hope to get from fingerprints at your apartment is an identification on Barker regardless of whether this is his body or not. I believe he took your revolver. That definitely ties him into this case. We'll send prints from your apartment through the databanks and hope your sister's boyfriend had his fingerprints taken at some time in the past."

Katie cringed at the sheriff's calling Frankie "your sister's boyfriend," but that was exactly what Maggie had called him—her boyfriend.

The sheriff continued, "We'll also print you so we can eliminate your prints on the search. You can tell we'll get nothing from teeth here, but we should know more about this man after the autopsy in Charleston." He looked over at the coroner expectantly.

"They're picking the body up sometime tonight for the trip to Charleston. 'Course, there's all sorts of new stuff and new tests. Depends on the case as to what all they'll do, but one thing's for sure, we ain't never had anything like this in Tanner before," Hawkins said.

"What about DNA?" asked Maggie.

"Got to have something to compare the body's DNA with," said the coroner, "but the postmortem will provide samples for future use with identification. We'll just have to wait and see. Hold on a minute. Let me put him back and I'll walk you out."

The gurney squeaked as the coroner pushed it from the room. Sheriff Jolley smiled at Katie. "You did better than I thought you would," he said.

Katie mentally compared him to Deputy Corley. The sheriff was a lot nicer, and his drawl didn't sound as bad as she'd first thought.

She looked at Jolley and suggested, "Why don't you show me the clothes and shoes he was wearing? There's a slim chance he was wearing what he had on in the picture."

"Because he wasn't wearing any clothing when we found him."

"They left it like this?" Katie asked Sheriff Jolley angrily when she opened her apartment door. As he'd predicted, the technicians were gone when they returned after stopping by the sheriff's department for Katie to be fingerprinted and to pick up her rented car. Jolley had walked in with her. Katie stood in shock and looked at her home in disbelief.

"There's usually some dusting residue." He did have the good grace to say it apologetically.

"Some residue? It's a mess! It's everywhere!"

Sheriff Jolley looked at his watch. "I've got to go now." He picked up a paper from an end table and handed it to Katie. "Here's your copy of the theft report. You'll need to finish filling in serial numbers. Don't forget to let us know if you discover anything else missing when you go through your things."

"You're leaving with this mess all over?" Katie's tone

was indignant, though she knew the sheriff couldn't be expected to clean up after the technicians.

Jolley ignored her outburst and continued, "We'll need serial numbers for the stolen items too." He handed her his business card. As he pulled the door shut, the sheriff advised her to have her locks changed and keep the dead bolts set.

Katie sat on the cream-colored daybed couch in her living room and asked herself, "Is that Frankie's body? Where's Maggie?" She looked around at where the television had been, where the stereo had been, where the computer had been. She wanted to call Samantha and just talk, but Samantha had said her new man was coming by.

Walmart had supplied Katie with what she considered the essentials: telephones with caller ID, one with a built-in answering machine for the kitchen, and a coffeemaker. She'd have to wait for insurance money or dip into savings to replace her other belongings.

As soon as she locked her front door, Katie plugged in her new telephones and set the answering machine. They weren't used that night. Regardless of how worried Katie was, telling anyone that Maggie was missing would be embarrassing. Maggie had dropped out and run off for a good time in the past, only to resurface. Katie needed a personal pity party. She couldn't believe Maggie had actually allowed someone who would steal into her home, into her bed.

Katie spent most of the evening cleaning her apartment, even the areas that had no black dust. She wanted to scrub Frankie Barker out of her space. She realized her early supper of grits and eggs was gone. She was hungry for something warm and comforting.

She heated a can of vegetable beef soup in a pot on the stove, since she no longer had a microwave. She hand-washed the bowl, spoon, and saucepan and decided a long, soaking hot bath would help calm her nerves.

The bathtub had been the deciding factor when Katie leased this particular apartment. Though only a single bedroom with a tiny living room, the unit's one bathroom was larger than its pullman kitchen. Katie had surrounded the oversized, step-up garden tub with aromatherapy candles and baskets filled with containers of pastel bath oil beads. Though attractive, they weren't just decoration. Katie used the candles and oils regularly and replenished her supply every payday. Clear acrylic containers displayed seashells she'd gathered on the beach at Fripp Island. Apparently, Maggie had used up all of the bath oils during the summer months.

Though a wraparound curtain encircled the tub, Katie showered only in the mornings. Long, hot, soothing baths were her evening luxury. Pouring the remains of two almost empty bath oils into the water, Katie tried to reassure herself that it would all work out. Maggie and Frankie had probably gone on a trip. It would be just like Maggie to forget about picking her up at the airport. Or, after Maggie explained that when Katie returned, the bedroom would be hers and Maggie would be back sleeping on the single daybed in the living room, Frankie might have taken her to his place. They could have already been gone before the apartment was burglarized. If Maggie would just turn up okay, life would go on. Insurance would replace Katie's belongings, and heaven knew what kind of predicament Maggie would get into next.

Katie dropped her clothes on the floor and slid into the warm, slippery water. She immersed her body until only her face showed. She told herself that Maggie had made Frankie sound okay, then reprimanded herself. Maggie always made the men in her life sound fine, and until now, every one of them had proved to be losers. Not that Katie could brag about her own relationships. She'd thought Charles was the most wonderful man in the world until she'd married him. Was Maggie's Frankie the homicide victim over at Jennings and his murderer the person who had burglarized her home? Too much coincidence. Then again, Frankie could have stolen the gun and been the killer.

Suddenly, Katie lifted her head from the water. She heard something. Once again her stomach knotted, this time in fear. She hadn't called to have the locks changed. How could she have forgotten that? Locks were more important than phones and a coffeemaker. She rose and stepped out of the tub as quietly as possible. Pulled on her terry-cloth robe. She thought of the .38 Charles had lent her, but she knew it wasn't there. No ammunition either. What did that matter? What good would ammunition be without a weapon?

Katie picked up a heavy brass figurine from the top of the bureau and silently opened the bedroom door. No one was in the living room. In the kitchen, Katie removed a large knife from the butcher's block. Checked the door and dead bolt again. Locked. She went back to her bedroom and looked through the top dresser drawer until she found an old, long-sleeved flannel nightgown she hardly ever wore except during an occasional bout with the flu in winter. She pulled the garment over her body, slipped into the brass bed, put the knife and the figurine on the bedside lingerie chest, and pulled the covers up to her chin. Some women had comfort foods; Katie had a comfort nightie.

She lay absolutely still, thinking about calling the sheriff, but he wouldn't be the one to respond, and she hadn't heard any noise for a long time. She snuggled down in the warm nightgown under the covers. Nothing could overcome the haunting thoughts of Maggie. Safe or in trouble?

How many red flags had Maggie ignored from Frankie Barker? How angry had Frankie been when Maggie told him he had to leave? Where was Maggie? Would Frankie come back to the apartment? Or was he lying in a cold drawer in Charleston, awaiting autopsy? She snuggled down deeper under the covers.

The white Battenburg comforter still smelled of Maggie's perfume and perhaps a slight odor of a masculine cologne. Was it the scent of a dead man?

TUESDAY TERROR

TENNESSEE LINDA felt like she'd pass out any minute. The sun and heat made her head pound. Rivulets of sweat poured down her face. She was so empty of energy she could barely cross from the Shop & Save to the Downtown Diner. She pushed on the door as she always did and wondered if she were too weak to open the door. Then, as usual, the voice in her head said, *Look at the door, Linda Louise. The decal says PULL.* Linda tugged the heavy door open and entered the noisy, wonderful coolness.

"Thank you, Mama," Linda muttered as she shuffled over to "her" stool and climbed up. The waitress, Courtney Mack, surprised to see Miss Possum so early in the day, slid a glass of iced water in front of Linda.

Don't gulp that, Linda. It'll make your head hurt worse if you drink it too quickly.

"Yes, Mama," Linda mumbled and took a delicate sip.

"Ready to order?" asked Courtney, already knowing

exactly what Miss Possum would request as always.

"See, Mama, I didn't drink it fast, and my head still hurts like it did when I came in," Linda said. Courtney pocketed the order book in her maroon apron and moved down the counter to top off a customer's iced tea. She'd observed Miss Possum talking to herself many times, and Courtney handled it as she always did—by ignoring her until the customer finished her conversation, even if the conversation was with herself.

Soon the mumbling stopped and Miss Possum called, "Miss Coatney. I'm ready to eat!"

"Yes, ma'am, will you be having waffle and jelly?" asked Courtney.

"Of course, Miss Coatney."

"Will you be having something to drink with your waffle?" asked Courtney, knowing word-for-word what Miss Possum's answer would be.

"Certainly not, Miss Coatney. I have my water here and Mama always tells me not to drink before bedtime. Since my bedtime is nine o'clock, I shall wait until then to drink, except for this wonderful cold water!"

When she'd finished her water and her waffle with jelly, Tennessee Linda slid down from the stool and shuffled toward the door. Instead of leaving, she returned to the register. "Miss Coatney," she said, "can you tell me where I can purchase some of those birthday napkins and hats? I believe he'd like some of those."

"Yes, ma'am. You can buy birthday things at the party shop over on Magnolia Drive, but it's awful hot for you to walk so far this afternoon."

"Mama always says exercise is good for you."

Miss Possum tried to pull the door, but she finally

figured out that she had to push to get it open now that she was on the reverse side.

By the time Tennessee Linda returned to her house, the pillowcase was full of party supplies. She also brought two helium-filled balloons with their strings tied to her wrist, allowing them to float above her head. Though she was soaking-wet with sweat, Linda knew that she would have to unload the pillowcase and go out again for her evening shopping for beer and cigarettes.

As she approached the house, Linda admired its beauty. The peeling columns, which had once risen in bright white splendor, now supported a sagging roof in a condition as bad as the columns themselves, but Linda saw them freshly painted and sturdy, exactly as they'd been forty years ago. She had to step carefully to avoid falling through several cracked and broken boards of the porch floor, but Linda was so accustomed to walking around these that she no longer noticed they were there.

During Linda's childhood, the house had been close to town. Now the house was *in* town. As Tanner had grown around the Pearson property, various developers had attempted to buy the house, but Linda's father had fiercely held on to his family estate. Most people assumed it was stubbornness or devotion to the old home place. Actually, Linda's father had been holding out until the price reached its maximum. Instead, the price had peaked and then begun to fall as the developers simply built around the old house. By the time Pearson understood the offers would not be going back up, they had stopped.

Now it was possible to walk from Linda's front door to the franchises that had once offered her father good money before buying other properties after his repeated refusals.

Pearson had sold some of the land in the early stages of negotiation. This had resulted in the house occupying much smaller acreage than it had originally, but the Pearson place still sat on a square block of wooded land right in the middle of Tanner. Rumors were that the first sale of property had fueled the greed that made Pearson's expectations so high. It was also rumored that the old skinflint had frugally invested that money so it earned enough interest for Linda to live, but he'd kept the money locked up in trusts so there was none for house repairs, luxuries, or frills.

Occasionally, some of the townspeople expressed their opinions that the sheriff should force Tennessee Linda to clean up the property, especially the yard immediately around the house. It was a mess. It did not, however, have that scourge of trashy southern yards—not a single junked car. Those same townspeople sometimes urged the sheriff to do something about Linda herself. After all, shuffling around town in her fuzzy, thirty-year-old polyester clothes, carrying her dirty pillowcase, gave Tennessee Linda a distinct visual kinship to the homeless and derelict.

When a citizen became concerned enough to mention Linda to Sheriff Jolley, his reply was always the same. "So long as Ms. Pearson cares for herself and is no danger to others, I cannot and will not take any action to force changes on her." He had thought out his "broken record" reply, worded it carefully, and quoted it verbatim whenever necessary.

Wade Jolley had once spent a Saturday morning trying to rid Linda's yard of the kudzu which had climbed the walls of the old Pearson garage, started around the house, and begun creeping over the porch railing on the north side. Linda had asked him to stop, so though he'd considered sneaking in one night and putting out weed killer, Jolley hadn't bothered Ms. Pearson or her yard since then.

Except for those horrible years Linda thought of as the "Bert Years," this house had been home to Linda Pearson since birth. Thoughts of Bert always upset Linda. She shivered in the blistering heat and felt sharp pains in her stomach as though she were being stabbed with a shard of ice. Linda stood still and listened to the silence until the freezing, piercing pain eased.

"Yes, Mama," she said softly, "I know he won't hurt me anymore."

Tennessee Linda entered through the front door directly into the parlor and put her pillowcase of purchases on a huge, Queen Anne mahogany table. Although the table sat twelve, its matching chairs stayed in the dining room. Linda hadn't bothered to move any of them. She lived in the parlor and kitchen with its adjacent half bath, going beyond these rooms only rarely when she went to the full bathroom in the back to bathe. The kitchen had never been remodeled and still had worn black linoleum countertops. In the parlor, Linda had pushed everything except one love seat, a ragged La-Z-Boy recliner, the tremendous table, and one chrome and plastic kitchen chair against the wall.

The primary object in the room was a television at one end of the table. It was an expensive forty-eight-inch Sony, purchased by Linda's daddy while he was still competent back when TVs were heavy, cumbersome objects and high definition was unknown to the public. The recliner was pulled up to one side of the table, and Linda's chrome kitchen chair sat directly opposite it. The table's mahogany surface was piled high with crossword puzzle books, and beer cans covered the floor beneath it. An ashtray in front of the chrome chair overflowed with cigarette butts. Their stale smell mingled with the stink from those rare few drops of beer left in the cans.

Tennessee Linda turned toward the vacant La-Z-Boy and grinned.

"Guess what, Daddy? Today's your birthday! See? I bought balloons for you." She tied the balloon strings onto the wooden lever on the side of the chair, and the balloons ascended into the air to their limits, swaying back and forth above the chair. "I didn't get hats or napkins because they only came in packages of eight. We'll celebrate when I get back, but I have to go out to do my evening shopping first." Linda stood silently for a moment.

"Yes, Mama, I will. I'm sorry I forgot," she said softly, then turned up the air conditioner, which was anchored in a piece of plywood fitted into the front window. Tennessee Linda picked up a pair of eyeglasses from the table and placed them on the arm of the La-Z-Boy. She turned on the television and adjusted the volume very loud. "Bye, Daddy," Linda called. She waved at the empty recliner and went back out into the midday heat. She was concentrating so hard that she forgot to close the front door. Television and air conditioner sounds escaped into the front yard. Heat entered the open door and defeated the valiant efforts of the small air conditioner.

Sitting in yet another faculty meeting, Katie was almost happy to be summoned by Aimee Martin. The secretary waited until she and Katie were in the hall before confiding, "It's the sheriff again." Fear shot through Katie as she wondered if he had come to tell her bad news about Maggie.

Sheriff Jolley walked up beside Katie before they reached the office. With mid-heels, Katie stood perhaps an inch taller than he did. Barefooted, they probably were about the same. Katie remembered a risqué rhyme Maggie had told her that ended with, "toes to toes, nose to nose." Though Katie felt it would be a long time before she even considered another man in her life, the poem brought a smile. Jolley noticed and smiled back, totally unaware of what prompted Katie's pleasant greeting.

"We haven't been able to locate anything on a Frank, Francis, Franklin, or Frankie Barker," Jolley began. "There's a chance that's not even the man's correct name. Have you heard from your sister?"

"No. Nothing."

"Stupid" was a word Katie neither used nor allowed her students to say, but it was the perfect description of how she felt about her sister at the moment.

The sheriff interrupted Katie's thoughts. "Ms. Wray, I know we took you away from your meetings yesterday, but I'd really like for you to go with me and look at some photographs now. See if we have a picture of Barker in our mug shots."

When the faculty of Tanner Elementary School dismissed for lunch, Samantha hurried to the teachers' lounge. She wanted to be first to reach the telephone. Quickly she pressed the digits of her home number and listened to her own voice, instructing her to leave a message. Samantha hit 1-2-4 to retrieve whatever messages she'd received.

Sam Campbell had promised to call Samantha this morning before she left for work, but now it was noon, and he still hadn't called. She'd convinced herself that her cell phone wasn't working right. That could be why she hadn't heard from him. She'd tried his house, but there was no answer.

Next, Samantha worried that he could be ill or had been injured on his way home from her house last night. After all, it had been very late and that soft-top Jag was fun, but it wouldn't be much protection in an accident.

Samantha wondered where Katie had gone. She needed someone to talk to about Sam, someone to reassure her that he was fine, wherever he was. She felt panic. She had no idea where Sam was or why he hadn't called like he'd promised, and now she didn't know where Katie was either. Samantha decided to skip lunch and work in her classroom through the break.

She thought the afternoon would never end. She'd really expected Katie to be back at school after lunch. The older teacher never missed work. Sam had asked the secretary, Aimee Martin, what happened, but she'd replied she didn't know. Sam really needed to talk to her friend.

Samantha hoped the rest of the faculty didn't think she was having stomach problems. Some of them had looked at her a bit strangely after the third or fourth time she'd left the afternoon meeting. She knew they thought she was going to the bathroom, but really she was checking her home answering machine, hoping for a message from Sam.

Finally, it occurred to her that if Sam had become ill or been injured, he wouldn't be at work, so though he'd told her it was best not to contact him at the agency, she called and inquired if Mr. Samuel Campbell were in, hoping the receptionist would say he was out today and why.

"He's here, but he's with a client. May I take a message or have him call you?"

Samantha responded in her most businesslike voice. "No, I'm not going to be in my office. I'll contact Mr. Campbell tomorrow."

There was nothing wrong with Sam. It was just another one of those times when he didn't bother to call after he said he would. How could anyone be so wonderful, so much fun, and so attentive almost always, yet so negligent and rude at other times?

When Samantha arrived home, she locked her cell phone in the glove compartment of her old Hyundai and unplugged her house phones. She knew she wasn't strong enough to ignore a ringing phone when the caller ID said Sam was on the line. She knew that all it would take was a message on her machine to make her forgive him once again. If he went a few days without being able to contact her, it would only make him more eager. It was like behavior modification. Samantha had spent a lot of time with Mr. Sam Campbell, and she knew that he was one who enjoyed the chase. She'd simply do whatever it took to keep him coming back to chase some more.

Tennessee Linda returned to her house with her pillowcase not quite so full as from her first shopping trip, but it was heavier. She called out, "Hey, Daddy, I'm back," as she entered the parlor. The television still played loudly to the empty La-Z-Boy, blaring into the room, and the eyeglasses remained on the chair. The balloons danced above the recliner in a rhythm dictated by the blower of the air conditioner.

Linda took her bag into the kitchen and unloaded a six-pack of cheap beer into the refrigerator. She set a single pack of generic cigarettes on the counter beside the refrigerator and placed items from the counter into the pillowcase. She filled two Bugs Bunny jelly glasses with water from the tap, carried them to the parlor, and set them on the table, one in front of her chair, one in front of the recliner. She returned to the kitchen and brought her pillowcase back to the parlor.

"Look, Daddy, I fixed our water in matching glasses because it's your birthday!"

Don't forget the cake.

"I didn't forget, Mama. I've got it right here." Linda removed two Piggly Wiggly cupcakes from the pillowcase. They were a little smushed, and the wrapper was torn, but Linda didn't notice as she placed one in front of the chrome chair and one in front of the recliner. She opened a pack of tiny candles and stuck as many as she could into the cupcake in front of the recliner. Linda lit all the candles, though some were burned down to the cupcake before she'd finished lighting the others.

Tennessee Linda stepped back and admired her work with pride and pleasure. "Happy birthday, Daddy," she said and burst into a lively, off-key rendition of "Happy birthday to you, happy birthday to you, happy birthday dear Daaaaaaaadeeeeeeee, happy birthday to you!" Then she blew out the candles.

Did you remember to get your daddy's gifts?

"Yes, Mama, I've got them right here." Linda turned to face the recliner. "See, Daddy, I got you some presents for your birthday. I'll get them for you." She pulled two gift-wrapped boxes from the pillowcase and placed them beside the cupcake, which had candle wax all over it. "I'll unwrap them for you."

She eagerly tore open the package covered in SpongeBob SquarePants gift wrap and seemed pleasantly surprised to find two pairs of men's socks. "See, Daddy. A man can't have enough socks, now can he?" She placed the socks beside the cupcake and ripped the paper from the other present.

"See, Daddy. Handkerchiefs. A man can't have enough handkerchiefs, now can he? Guess what I bought me for your birthday. A crossword puzzle book." She took the book from the pillowcase and waved it in front of the recliner. "I didn't have it wrapped because that costs extra money, and it's your birthday, not mine. But Mama said I could have a gift too, just like I always do when it's your birthday."

Linda Louise, are you going to give your Daddy a birthday kiss?

"No, Mama, don't make me. I don't want to," Tennessee Linda whined.

Linda Louise, you know good girls do what their mommies and daddies tell them to do. I want you to give your daddy a big birthday kiss. You'll hurt his feelings if you don't, and you know it's his birthday!

"Yes, Mama." The tone was fretful. Tennessee Linda walked around the long table, leaned over, and kissed the rear of the recliner. Then she quickly ran back to her own chair.

Linda Louise, it's your daddy's birthday. Why are you being so difficult? You know your daddy likes you to sit on his lap to give him a kiss. You're still your daddy's little girl. It doesn't matter how old you get to be, you'll always be Daddy's little Lindy Lou.

"But Mama, I bought the cake and the presents. I even got the balloons and put the water in matching glasses. I'm all grown up. I don't want to sit on Daddy's lap. I don't want to ever sit on Daddy's lap again."

Linda Louise!

"Yes, Mama." Linda trudged around the long table. She sat in the recliner sideways with her back against the right arm and her legs draped over the left arm of the chair. She kissed the back of the La-Z-Boy with a loud smack, stood, went to the half bath by the kitchen, and brushed her teeth. She rinsed and spit several times. When she walked back into the kitchen, she filled a large glass with tap water and rinsed and spit again and again.

Good girl, Linda Louise. You're a very good girl. Why don't you work some crossword puzzles now?

"Yes, Mama."

Shug grew up hating country music. Father had listened to it, but the son despised it, especially the old stuff. Not only did the whiney sounds of that so-called music make him want to blow chunks, busy Highway 17 on a bright sunshiny day shouldn't have brought lonesome highways to mind anyway. But it did, and he sang along with Hank Williams, Sr., in his mind, before settling into Willie Nelson's "On the Road Again" as he drove toward Myrtle Beach.

Thinking back to Father's country music during Shug's childhood made him think of his mother. She'd originated his nickname by calling him "Sugar Baby" when he was little. Gradually, it had been shortened to "Sugar," then "Shug." Thank God it wasn't "Bubba!" Shug wiped his eyes. He'd never admit to tears, but thoughts of his mother brought back the bad times after he'd been caught with the teacher and that horrible day after the court case when he'd found his mother. Shug shook his head and sang louder, trying to drown out the memories.

The old car couldn't go as fast as his own vehicle, but he knew his beautiful sports car was a goner. He didn't want it back after what had happened, and sooner or later, the cops would haul it away. For now, he was contented to sing to himself and stay slightly below the speed limit. He'd seen on television how Ted Bundy and other serial killers had been caught when pulled on routine traffic stops. Not that he considered himself a Ted Bundy. He'd only murdered one person, and Carly had deserved it.

After escaping the no-tell motel in panic, the killer had driven until he'd calmed down, stopped at a top-dollar motel, and slept several hours.

He felt pretty good even though he'd rather be playing or even listening to *real* music instead of the crap that filled his head today. He smacked the on-off button on the car radio, but nothing came from the speakers. He slammed his hand against the radio itself again and again, hoping an electrical short was causing it not to work, hoping one of his slaps would jar the wiring enough to fix it. The radio didn't play and wasn't going to work in this piece-of-shit car, so he had to settle for what he heard coming from his mind.

Did he dare buy a newer car? Something nicer than the Ford but not as flashy as his sports car? Screw cars. This one was getting him where he wanted to go. He needed to tend to other things before getting another vehicle so long as this one kept running. The killer dared not use his cell phone—the law might be trying to pinpoint his location already. He wanted another gun, too. A pistol gave him control—absolute control. "Dirty hands: Pontius Pilate, Lady Macbeth, and me," he thought. "What great company! I'm going to have fun today."

Ka-pow! The sound exploded as the car dipped toward the shoulder like some mighty giant had slapped it. The steering wheel jerked violently, and for a moment, the killer thought he would crash into the vehicle in front of him or even flip, but he wrestled the car to a stop beside the highway. Other cars sped by as he got out and walked around to the shoulder of the road. The front passenger-side tire had blown, and smoke rose from the few shreds left on the rim.

All the happy thoughts of a good time in Myrtle Beach dissolved along with the smoke and smell from the ragged remains of the tire. Anger erupted into rage. He kicked the passenger door several times, then stomped to the back, and lifted the trunk lid. At least there was a jack and one of those May-pop spares that came with instructions not to drive on it at high speeds or for much distance.

The damned car slipped as he jacked it up. The killer jumped back and spewed forth almost every curse word he'd ever heard. Son-of-a-bitchin' car could've fallen on him. Crippled or killed him. Screw Myrtle Beach. He was near Charleston. One of his old girlfriends lived there. He finally succeeded with the spare tire and drove cautiously to a tire dealership.

While a punk kid installed four new tires on the Ford, the killer walked across the street to a drugstore and bought a prepaid cell phone. He called his Charleston girlfriend while jaywalking back to the car place. At first, she complained that he'd mistreated her when they broke up, but the killer turned on his "I'm sorry" charm, and she agreed to meet him for dinner.

Next stop—a pawnshop. Convincing the bitch to see him had changed his mood, but he wanted some power back—the power of a loaded gun.

"No, Corley, I do *not* think we need to have forensics luminol Katie Wray's apartment." Sheriff Jolley was definitely irritated.

"But Chief . . ."

"I've told you, Corley. I'm a sheriff, not a chief of police. Now, if you can't keep that straight, maybe you need to go back to a bigger town and work for a chief of police, but if you're going to keep working in Tanner, you're stuck with a sheriff. Can you get that in your head?" Sheriff Wade Jolley leaned back in his chair, but he didn't prop his feet on the desk though he wanted to.

"Sir, I came to Tanner because I want to work in a small town with a sheriff like yourself. I was tired of the big city, but because of my time there, I believe I have more experience with this type of crime than others in the department." Throughout the discussion, Corley paced back and forth.

"If you mean others excluding me, that's why you're in charge of this case, but if you're including *me*, I advise you to remember that I *am* the sheriff, and you work for me." When Sheriff Jolley became angry, his drawl decreased, and his speech accelerated.

"Yes, sir! But that whole theft thing might be a setup.

It's obvious the victim was dumped and not found at the scene of the crime itself. Ms. Wray may have shot him in her apartment. She admits she had the weapon until she claims it was stolen. Why not luminol her apartment? It would show up the least trace of blood and we'd know."

"First, Corley, you don't have to tell me what luminol does. Second, we don't even know if the deceased is this Frankie Barker that Ms. Wray's sister was with all summer. Third, Katie Wray doesn't fit the profile of a female perp."

Corley's tone was argumentative, but respectful. "We don't even know if the sister has the car. Ms. Wray could have come home and gotten so mad that she killed both of them. The car may be hidden somewhere with her sister's body inside."

"I don't believe Ms. Wray is anything like her sister, and we don't really know that her sister did anything beyond having a summer romance with this man. I seriously doubt your scenario. I acknowledge Tanner hasn't had a murder like this one, or at least not since I remember, and I was born ten miles from here. That's why I've called in the State Law Enforcement Division. I think your problem, Corley, is that you resent my calling in SLED. You don't want the state people on the case. My problem is that I should've called them in at the scene. This is definitely a case that has to include state agencies. My point of view is that we need their help but we also need to cover our butts! You're going to have to work with the state men from SLED, like it or not."

"Yes, Chief—I mean Sheriff Jolley. I see your point, but will you consider the luminol?"

"I'll keep that option open, but I want forensics and postmortem results first, and I want confirmation that the

.38 we found is the murder weapon. You know the coroner and I may both already be in deep shit for having Wray view that body before state forensics got it." Jolley scowled. "Will you please sit down? You're wearing me out with all that walking." He paused. "Corley, have you thought about the amount of blood there had to be at the scene? We know Wray was at work early Monday. I see her as a real long shot anyway, but if she did him, I don't think it was in her apartment. Luminol would probably be a waste of time and money there."

Corley sat on the very edge of a chair facing Jolley's desk. "That .38 was loaded with hollow points except for three empties we found lying beside the body."

"Still could've been a defense weapon. I want physical proof, and I want this department to solve the case, *not* SLED, even though I had to call them in."

"I'm planning to talk to Katie Wray again," said Corley. "It seems she could tell us more about Frankie Barker than she has. I mean, he lived with her sister for three months."

"Listen, Corley, you're not going to get anything from Wray. She doesn't like you."

"What do I care what some slut thinks about me? I just want to solve this case, and I think I can make her confess and wrap this up before we even get the autopsy report. She got into town earlier than she's telling us. Something happened that sent her ballistic. She shot Barker, maybe her sister, too. That theft business is just to cover her ass. Dumped the body knowing she'd be asked to identify it. Of course, she says it's not Barker."

As Corley became more excited, he stood and began pacing again. He talked faster and louder.

When he paused, Jolley drawled, "My turn to talk?"

Corley nodded and the sheriff continued, "Back up then. Where do you get off calling Ms. Wray a slut?"

"Just look at her sister. She picked up a man and took him home with her the same night."

"That was Ms. Wray's sister, not her. Besides, from what I've heard you're not exactly Mr. Abstinence yourself. Aren't you the deputy who called me one Saturday morning to bring him a uniform at some gal's apartment because you were on duty and couldn't come to work without your britches? What was your story? I believe you picked up a woman at Kenny B's and let her go out early the next morning to do her laundry with your pants in her clothes basket."

Corley had the good grace to look a little embarrassed. He said defensively, "That's different."

"Why? Because you're a man? It takes two, Corley. The Wray woman's sister is single, and this could have been a once-in-a-lifetime thing, but it doesn't really matter. Katie Wray isn't who spent the summer with Frankie Barker, but I wouldn't be offended if she did. We're looking for a murderer, not somebody who's had sex. Personally, I would describe Ms. Wray as spirited."

"What about her attitude? She's not exactly a shrinking violet, is she? I mean think about her tone and how she kept interrupting. I don't want to be disrespectful, but sometimes you're the most naïve officer of the law I've ever known."

"Well, this naïve sheriff wants you to either sit down and continue this discussion in a civilized manner or get the hell out of my office and do some work. Don't bother to interview Wray again. I'll do it myself."

"Yes, sir!" Jolley almost expected Corley to do a salute

and heel click, but the detective just walked away.

Tennessee Linda worked crossword puzzles until exactly nine o'clock P.M. "Mama, it's nine. Beer time!"

Yes, Linda, and you've been a good girl all day. You may have your beer now.

"Mama, do you think I could have a real drink tonight since it's bedtime and it's Daddy's birthday?"

No, Linda Louise, you may not have any hard liquor, but you may have your beer now.

"Thank you, Mama."

Linda went to the kitchen and came back to the parlor carrying the six-pack of beer and the cigarettes. She sat in the chrome chair and smoked one cigarette after another as she drank one beer after another. She added the butts to the overflowing ashtray and tossed the empty beer cans under the table on top of the others. When she'd drained the last drop from the last can, Linda went to the love seat and curled up on it. She was asleep almost as soon as her head hit the dirty, grimy throw pillow.

The television shut itself off at midnight. After that, the only sound in that big house was the humming of the air conditioner and Linda's periodic shrieks of "No! No! Don't!" as she once again reentered the nightmare of her worst reality.

WORRIED WEDNESDAY

CHAPTER 5

"IN CONCLUSION . . ."

The principal had talked all morning, and none of the teachers in the faculty meeting thought that "in conclusion" meant he wouldn't talk a whole lot more before the children began the new school year.

"In conclusion," he repeated. Katie thought he must have lost his place in his notes. "Please remember that I'm totally serious about this. Most of the cases have involved teenagers, but there have been a few younger students involved. Do NOT touch your pupils. You must communicate your care and concern for the little ones through spoken words, facial expressions, and an occasional treat. Zero tolerance for touching. Not even a pat on the shoulder is allowed. Also, we suggest that you not become socially involved with students' families."

He harrumphed and then continued with a totally unexpected announcement, "You may leave the building for lunch if you like. Be sure to sign back in by one o'clock. You will have the remainder of the day to work in your rooms."

Samantha raised her hand. Katie always wondered if adults in the business world raised their hands before speaking at meetings or if this were just a school thing.

"Yes, Mrs. Branham."

"Will we have the rest of the week in our rooms also?"

"Half days on Thursday and Friday. This afternoon, you'll receive textbooks in your rooms. Friday morning is in your rooms to prepare for the first day, then we have a meeting following lunch. Rooms will be inspected Friday afternoon to see that everything is in order and that lesson plans for next week are on teachers' desks. Are there any other questions?"

"No, sir."

As the faculty rose from their hard fiberglass student seats in unison, Katie asked Samantha if she wanted to join her for lunch. Sam readily agreed.

Over quiche and salad in Theresa's Tearoom, Samantha once again told her friend about wonderful Sam Campbell. She described how romantic he was, how he chose the nicest restaurants, and how great it was to spend an evening under the stars in his hot tub. She was expounding on the freedom she felt riding around in the Jag with the top down when Katie interrupted.

"Sam," Katie said with direct eye contact. "You've told me how great he is over and over. You're trying pretty hard to convince me. I think you're trying to persuade yourself more than me. What's wrong?"

Samantha rubbed her hand across her eyes. "I guess you're right. I just need to tell somebody, and I suppose

I've been hoping you'd ask. You know, I get so tired of teachers talking about their personal lives at school and crying in the hall over some squabble, but I really need to talk to someone about it."

"Go right ahead. If you take long enough, we might just have to order dessert so you'll have time to finish your story." Both women laughed, knowing Samantha wouldn't order dessert.

"When I'm with Sam, he acts like I'm the greatest woman he's ever known. He brings me little gifts. Not big things. Sometimes flowers he's actually picked from his yard, sometimes nothing more than a Snickers bar, but he's so sweet when he does things like that."

"Yep, those little things do kinda get to you," the older woman agreed.

"He's only been divorced a year and my divorce isn't even final, so we certainly can't be thinking about marriage or anything like that. In this town, I don't think it would help my reputation to live with him."

"Has he asked you to live with him? I know some teachers who're living with significant others instead of spouses. The fact that you're a teacher shouldn't dictate your life," Katie said while thinking, "Maybe Maggie would be better off if she went back to college to teach and *did* let it influence some of her actions."

"No, Sam hasn't mentioned my living with him, and when I talk about commitment, he changes the subject or brings up my divorce not being final. We could have an exclusive relationship without marriage, but when I bring it up, he always says, 'It's too soon for us to think about marriage, but that time will come, and when it does, it'll be Sam and Samantha.' I just can't understand why he won't even discuss commitment when everything's so great with us."

"Sounds to me like it's going all right. Maybe you're pushing it. Why don't you just relax and enjoy what the two of you have and see what happens?" Katie smiled wistfully. "You do realize that my track record doesn't qualify me as an expert on relationships, don't you?"

"But you're so smart. I know that what I should do is exactly what you say, but it makes me crazy when he says he'll call or come by, and then he doesn't and there's no answer at his house. The other night, I actually got out of bed, dressed, and drove by his house in the middle of the night to see if he was home."

"Was he?"

"No, and he wasn't there early the next morning, either."

"But you said you're both free to see other people."

"I don't understand why he'd even want to see other women. I don't want to be with anyone else."

"You don't know where he was," Katie consoled before motioning Theresa over and asking, "What's for dessert today?"

"Raspberry cream cake or fresh peach cobbler. My son went up to Gilbert for peaches over the weekend. Peaches peaked in July, but they're still wonderful. The cobbler's really good, especially if you let me top it with homemade ice cream for you. Shall I send out two cobblers?"

"Yes." Katie grinned. "I think that may do more good to our psyches than it does harm to our waistlines."

A quick, unpleasant, repulsed look flashed across Samantha's face. "Not for me, Theresa," she said. "I'm already too full."

"Is it going to bother you to watch me eat it?" Katie

teased. She was very familiar with Sam's eccentric eating habits and had noticed that Samantha hardly ate a bite of her salad or quiche. Sam frequently just shoved her food around on the plate while others ate.

A soft smile preceded Samantha's next comment. "Not at all. I'd watch you eat anything as long as you'll sit here and let me talk about Sam. I know I'm probably rushing it. I think that maybe since Marc went straight out of our apartment to a house with Miss Mousie Law Clerk, I may be overeager for a relationship."

"That was months ago. You weren't in any big hurry to start dating until you met this Sam."

"It's just that he's so perfect. I don't want any old relationship. I want a relationship with Sam."

"Except sometimes you don't know where he is and sometimes he promises to call and doesn't."

"Yeah." Samantha looked as though she might cry.

Katie's dessert arrived—a huge bowl of cobbler with flaky crust and a warm cinnamony smell, topped not with vanilla ice cream, but homemade peach. Samantha looked at it and grimaced. "Only in the South," she mumbled.

"You said it!" answered Katie. "I should've skipped lunch and started with this. Sure you don't want some? You know, you've gotten downright skinny, Sam. An occasional sweet won't hurt you." She spooned warm cobbler and ice cream together, then once again broke the silence. "What are you doing when these things happen? Are you screaming at him or telling him calmly how it makes you feel? What are your reactions when he doesn't do what he says he'll do? Did you actually have a date and he didn't show up?"

"No, he hasn't stood me up for a real date. You know, if

he says we're going out to eat or to the movies or over to Kenny B's to dance and names a day and time, he shows up. He hasn't stood me up for a definite date, but sometimes he'll say he's stopping by the next night, and he doesn't."

"And what do you do?"

"I figure screaming and fussing will just drive him away, and I know he loves the chase, so lately what I do is unplug my phones. I make it hard for him to find me for a day or so, and when I plug the phone back in, he calls and things get better."

"Sounds to me like you're playing games." There was a slightly critical edge to Katie's voice.

"I guess I am, and that bothers me. I don't want to be a game player, but you can't possibly understand how much I want this to work. I see myself with him for the rest of my life. Babies, the whole nine yards!"

Her friend sighed. "I remember feeling like that. Now I don't want the emotional strain of it all anymore. I don't know if I ever want another seven-day-a-week man."

"That's cynical even coming from jaded Katie Wray. We've spent the whole time talking about Sam and me. What's been going on with you this summer?"

"I spent the summer in North Dakota, but you'll have to wait to hear about it. We need to get back." A tear slipped from Katie's eye.

"Is something wrong? I'm here if you need to talk to me. I'd ask you over tonight, but I'm cooking dinner for Sam."

"We'll get together soon. I probably should talk to someone about what's going on. It's Maggie again, but I'm not ready to talk yet, Sam."

"Let's change the subject then. What do you think of all

these rules that teachers at Tanner are not to ever touch students or socialize with their families? First-graders need a hug sometimes."

Katie grimaced. "You know what this is all about, Sam. Teachers who get pregnant by middle school students. Teachers who convince teenaged lovers to kill their husbands for them. Teachers who flaunt affairs with seventeen-year-old students in front of spouses who kill the teenagers. Years ago, I read a list of rules for teachers from the eighteen hundreds. It was ridiculous. Teachers couldn't even date. I don't believe in that. Teachers are people, too, but I still believe educators should be role models."

"But who's going to have an affair with a six-year-old? My students need affection."

"It's a shame that all students have to suffer and all teachers bear the stigma of what only a few do. Personally, I think teachers should have to go through psychological evaluations before they're hired. Like policemen. There's something mentally wrong with an adult who wants to have sex with a teen, and so far as a six-year-old is concerned, don't forget about the pedophiles."

"You said most of the students are teenagers."

"Still has to be something wrong with them. Besides, look at the double standard. Male teachers are punished. Female teachers are joked about with dirty old men chortling, 'Wish they'd had teachers like that when I was in school.' Then there are the defense attorneys who say their clients are 'too pretty' to go to jail."

"Wow! I sure got you wound up."

They continued the conversation on the way to the car.

"I'm sorry to jump on my personal bandwagon," Katie said. "So far as I'm concerned, women can be pedophiles just like men. It's one of my major griefs that a woman molesting a boy doesn't carry the same stigma as a man with an underaged girl. Boys and young men can be emotionally damaged, too. Personally, I'd like to hang anybody who abuses anyone else — physically, sexually, or mentally!"

"Amen!"

Tennessee Linda opened one eye and determined that the degree of light in the parlor meant midday or early afternoon. She stretched. As always, her arms and legs felt tight and kinked after she'd slept on the love seat. Her neck was cramped, too, and, as she did whenever she woke, Linda thought she should get a real pillow off one of the beds instead of just using the throw pillow. Linda would forget about pillows of any kind before she finished her evening beer that night.

"Good morning, Daddy," Linda said when she stood.

Linda Louise, it's Wednesday, and you haven't changed clothes in a week. I want you to bathe and change today.

"Oh, Mama, I don't want to. I need to go out. I'll do it later."

Make sure it's today, and don't forget to turn on the TV. You know Daddy doesn't like to be left alone. He thinks someone's here with him if you leave the television on when you're out of the room.

"Yes, Mama."

Linda went to the kitchen and removed her ATM card from its hiding place beneath the sugar canister. She took a tube of lipstick and eyebrow pencil from the cutlery drawer and slid color across her face. She picked up her pillowcase and went out the door dragging it behind her. She'd reached the gate when the sound thundered in her head.

Linda Louise! Turn around right now. Go back and turn on that television for your daddy! You know he can't get up and do it for himself!

"Yes, Mama," Linda said, then mumbled, "he could at least try to use the remote control."

Don't get smart with me! You know good little girls do what their mommies and daddies tell them to do.

"Yes, Mama."

Wherever Katie looked, she saw another speck of black fingerprinting powder. She had already gone over everything thoroughly, but it would take the whole evening to remove residue that was left on what she'd previously cleaned. The cold of the apartment felt good when she stepped in. The first thing she did was take off her shoes. Her second task was to check the answering machine which flashed "2."

"Ms. Wray, this is Sheriff Wade Jolley. I'd like to talk to you again. Please call me." Katie pressed "delete."

The second message sounded like a young female trying to be very businesslike. "Please don't hang up. This is Susan Barker, and I'm callin' about Fred Barker. You may know him as Frankie. Fred called me Monday and said he was coming home. He ain't home and I haven't heard from him since then. The caller ID showed your number. I really need to talk to you. I'm calling from Columbia." The voice lost its formal, rehearsed sound and faded into tears. After a few moments, she added through the sobbing, "Please call me at 803-555-1673. Please call. I'm scared something's happened to Fred."

Katie pressed "save" and phoned the sheriff's office. She expected to be asked to leave a message and was surprised to be told he'd be with her in a moment.

"Sheriff Wade Jolley here," came his exaggeratedly slow answer, which sounded rather pleasant to Katie today. She asked if he'd learned anything about Maggie. When he said no, she explained that she was returning his call, then told him about the message from Susan Barker. Jolley asked her to wait until he could come to her apartment before calling Columbia. He closed with "I'll be there in fifteen minutes. Please don't erase that woman's message."

Katie looked into the mirror as she finished touching up her makeup and thought, "Now why am I doing this? I don't usually even like short men." She was surprised that her heartbeat accelerated slightly when the doorbell rang.

"Who is it?" she asked through the door.

"Sheriff Jolley." No mistaking that accent.

When she opened the door, he was leaning against the door frame. He had on jeans and a light blue shirt that matched his eyes. His sandy brown hair was tousled, and he looked very different from their last encounter. "Pardon my attire," he drawled, "but I'm officially off this afternoon and had just stopped by the office to check up on a few things when you called."

"Come on in," Katie replied. "I guess you want to hear the message."

"Yes, will your answering machine record? I'd like to save the conversation when you return the call. We'll have to tell the woman we're recording, but I do want a copy of what she says. Do you have to pay for long distance? If so, we can charge it to the department."

"No extra charge to call Columbia. Let me play her message for you now."

Jolley listened intently and had Katie play it twice. When they tried to return the call, there was no response, not even an answering machine or voice mail.

"That's strange," Jolley commented. "She says they have caller ID. Most folks with that also have some kind of answering device."

"Maybe she's got a computer and has dial-up without an extra line for the Internet," Katie suggested. "That can make the line ring like no one's there even with an answering machine. Mine used to do that."

"I don't think anybody does that anymore," the sheriff said.

"I'm sorry. I should have remembered that." Katie's expression was sheepish.

"It's okay."

Katie gave him a real smile. "I'm sure you've got a lot more on your mind right now than my theft. What were you calling me about before I got the message from that woman?"

"Just had a few thoughts cross my mind about your sister's friend Barker, and I wanted to ask you about a few ideas. I don't have to tell you this is an unusual case for Blair County. The murder itself was execution-style. If we assume your husband's revolver was taken by Barker, there's a connection between him and the murder since the gun was found beside the body. You said Maggie told you that he just hung around except on weekends. She said he had an electric bass guitar case, but she never saw the instrument. Did she ever say he seemed nervous about the case?"

"You know how musicians are. He didn't want her touching it."

"He never opened the case in front of her? What I want to know is did she ever actually see the musical instrument he said was in the case?"

"Not to my knowledge. She said he never practiced, but he took the case with him every weekend when he said he was going off to play with the band."

"Do you know the name of the band?"

"Platinum Posse." Katie pronounced each word precisely and glanced away from the sheriff. "Look, could I get you a beer or something? I'm dying of thirst myself."

"A Pepsi would be great. I don't drink on duty."

"I thought this was your day off." Katie's eyes and tone teased.

"It is, but I might be back on duty at any minute. Depends on what this woman in Columbia tells us."

Katie went to the kitchen and returned with two Cokes. "Sorry, no Pepsi. I'm a Coca-Cola person." She handed him a can. I guess you're back on duty right now since you're over here talking to me."

Jolley took a long swallow from the Coke can. "Make no mistake, Ms. Wray, I would happily talk to you on my own time. Unfortunately, until this case is cleared, that would be totally inappropriate. So far as the band is concerned, I've heard of them. It won't be hard to check out."

Katie sat with her legs curled up under her on the couch, tucked her skirt around her knees, and asked, "What do you think Frankie may have had in the case? You don't think he had a bass guitar in there, do you?"

"That'll depend on what we find out from the band. In the old days, gangsters sometimes carried weapons in musical instrument cases. We need to know if he's been playing music on weekends, and if so, what was he doing during weekend daylight hours. The night your sister met him in the bookstore, how was he traveling? Did she ever say what kind of car he had?"

"Maggie said Frankie didn't have a car. They used my car when they went out."

"Did they spend much time together between that night they met and the day of the burglary?"

"He was with her always except weekends."

"Neither of them went to work? What about your sister? Does she have a job?"

"Not often."

"Can you remember any details about his being gone on weekends?"

"She said he left about lunchtime every Friday. He'd leave walking. Turned down her offers of a ride. Said the band members were picking him up down the street."

"She said he wouldn't let her go hear the band?"

"That's what Maggie told me."

"That's strange. The musicians that I know are always begging everyone they see to come out to hear them."

"Maggie and I both like old, classic rock music. He told her that the band played hard alternative and that most of their gigs were dives. Plus they were always playing away from Tanner—Charleston a lot, Columbia sometimes. Occasionally even Greenville or Charlotte. It wasn't like they were playing Joe's bar on the corner. Maggie couldn't run down to hear them and go home if she didn't like it."

"What about clothes? Was he carrying a suitcase when your sister met him at the bookstore?"

"Maggie said he was just carrying his instrument case."

"Did he wear the same clothes all summer or did your sister buy him new threads?"

Katie hackled like a cat. "I'm getting a little tired of the insinuations. Yes, my sister lived with him, and no, she never said he paid rent or bought gas, but he did help buy groceries, and he paid sometimes when they went out. He liked to go hear local bands. Maggie wasn't paying him to live with her, and she didn't buy him clothes."

The sheriff rubbed his chin thoughtfully. "So where did he get clothes?"

"The best I remember, Maggie met him in the book department in back of the all-night drugstore on a Thursday night. She was very depressed because she still hadn't found a job and her boyfriend dropped her the previous weekend. Also, it was the anniversary of her first divorce. Frankie left Friday and came back Sunday night. I may as well be honest with you. When she told me on the phone Friday night that he'd be back Sunday, I thought he'd lied to her and she'd had a one-night stand. I didn't believe she'd ever see him again, but she called on Monday telling me that he came back Sunday night with a suitcase full of clothes and a large pizza."

"You were surprised Barker came back. Was your sister in the habit of going out and picking up men for one-night stands?"

"Don't you think some of this is personal, maybe private?" Katie tried to ask the question without sounding critical or offended though she felt both.

"Ms. Wray, this is a homicide investigation. A lot may

be personal, but nothing is private. So Frankie Barker came back on Sunday with a supply of clothing, obviously planning to move in?"

"He didn't actually move in. Maggie explained to him that he could stay awhile, but that the apartment is really mine and he'd have to leave when I returned the end of the summer. She told him there could be no future for them. They just had a summer fling."

"Is that what you and your sister do for school vacation? Have a summer romance each year? Is that what you went to North Dakota for?"

"No, I went west to teach summer school on a reservation for the summer. Maggie's romances come and go with no regard for season, but I can't see where that has anything to do with your investigation."

The sheriff responded to the slight edge in Katie's voice by changing the subject. "Do you have any idea where your sister might be now?"

Tears filled Katie's eyes. She wiped them away with the back of her hand, then said, "Excuse me," stepped across the room, and retrieved a box of Kleenex from the small table by the door. After patting her eyes with a tissue, she said, "I have no idea where she is. She said she'd told him he had to be gone before I came home. She'd promised to pick me up at the airport. I'm worried that Frankie may have hurt her, even killed her, if he's who killed the man on Payton Street."

"Let's hope not."

"I never met Frankie, never even talked to him on the telephone, but I didn't trust him."

"Looks like your mistrust was well founded. When he disappeared, so did some of your belongings, including a gun that's a murder weapon. Let's try the phone number again. I'll be listening on the extension. If she answers, be sure to tell her the call's being recorded."

Katie chose to use the bedroom extension and left Jolley on the living room phone. This time a woman answered.

"Hello." The voice was young, and background sounds included cartoons and a baby crying.

"May I speak with Susan Barker."

"This is Susan."

"This is Katie Wray in Tanner. You left a message on my machine about Frankie Barker."

"Yeah, well, actually my message was about Fred Barker, but he calls himself Frankie sometimes. Is he there?"

"No, he hasn't been here since Monday, but before we talk anymore, I need to tell you that I'm recording this call."

"Recording the call? Why?" She sounded frightened.

"There's been some trouble down here."

"Oh, no. What's he done this time?" Maggie heard tears in Susan's voice.

"There's a possibility he was involved in a theft. Has he been in trouble before?"

"Fred has these problems. Are you a schoolteacher?"

"Yes, I teach second grade."

"I figured as much."

"What do you mean?"

"Fred has this thing about teachers. When I married him, I didn't know he has mental problems. He's been in the nut ward at the hospital and in the state psychiatric hospital. Sometimes he just kinda flips out and goes off. He always winds up shacked up with some teacher. Usually, he gets tired of it and comes on home."

Katie reeled inside. One thing she and Maggie agreed on was that getting involved with a married man was insane. Aside from the morality of adultery, there was no future in a relationship with a man who had a wife to be home with on the holidays. Besides, as the two sisters had said many times, "If he'll cheat *with* you, he'll cheat *on* you."

"I'm sorry," Katie said softly. "We didn't know he was married. When you said you were Susan Barker, I thought you were probably his sister."

"I don't blame you. This has happened before. The last one that lasted more than a few days was in Charleston last summer, but he got tired of her after a few weeks and came on home."

"Do you mean you just let him go off and stay with other women and then let him come back to you?" The sheriff came into the bedroom and stood beside Katie as she asked the question.

"That's no worse than you letting a married man live with you," Susan defended herself. At first, Katie thought she'd screamed something, but then she realized what she heard was a child crying out.

"Oh, I didn't mean to sound critical of you. He wasn't with me. It was my sister, and now both of them have disappeared," Katie explained.

"What do you mean disappeared? He's sick and he's out of meds. I had the prescriptions filled last week, but he hasn't picked them up. They're still here in the medicine cabinet. I love him and we have two children. I keep hoping he'll get well or at least take his medicine. When he called me, he said he was coming straight home, but that was several days ago."

Katie was silent for a minute as she interpreted the

sheriff's hand signals that he wanted to speak on the telephone.

"Are you there? Did you hang up?" Susan sounded frantic.

"I'm here, but there's someone else who wants to talk to you," Katie answered and handed the receiver to Jolley.

"Ms. Barker, this is Blair County Sheriff Wade Jolley." He could hear the gasp on the other end of the line. "Now, don't be frightened. We want the same thing you do. We just want to find your husband and make sure he's all right. Can you answer a few questions for me?"

"I'll try. Is Fred in trouble?"

"We really don't know, but if he's sick like you said, he needs help. Let's concentrate on finding him and helping him. In the past, if he took up with someone and stayed with her, where did he go when he leaves the woman he's been staying with?"

"He comes home to his family. He calls and says he's sorry. Then he comes home. I cooked all his favorite foods Monday. He said he was sorry again and he was coming back to me and the kids."

"Has he ever stolen anything when he was away?"

"He's in trouble, isn't he? I knew it." She began sobbing.

"We don't know that he stole something. I just want to help you find him." Jolley comforted as he repeated, "Has he ever stolen things while he was away?"

"He stole jewelry, but we gave most of it back, and his dad paid for what was missing. Fred just wanted to bring something nice to make up for what he'd done. After all, it's not just Fred's fault. Those teachers shouldn't take up with a married man, but we gave everything back except a couple of pieces Tori broke, and that woman got paid for those. Fred's dad always pays for Fred's mistakes."

"Mrs. Barker, I need a picture of Fred. Can you fax or e-mail me one? Better yet, what if I come up to Columbia tomorrow and get it?"

"Sure. I've got lots of pictures of Fred."

"Do you think you might have a hairbrush with some of his hair in it?"

"I don't know but I'll look around. You're not going to put him in jail, are you? Fred's just mixed up sometimes."

Sheriff Jolley reassured Susan Barker he wanted to help her husband and made arrangements to see her at one o'clock the next day. When the conversation finally ended, he asked Katie if he could take the message device out of her machine to have the conversation copied. She agreed. Katie locked the door behind him.

"Who've you been talking to?" Samantha asked when she called right after the sheriff left. "I've been calling and calling you. If you're going to have such long conversations, you need call waiting."

Katie laughed. "Did you phone me just to fuss?"

"No, I called to ask what to do with caviar."

"Caviar? What are you doing with caviar?"

"I don't *know* what to do with it. That's why I called you. I decided to really splurge tonight. I bought caviar and filet mignon steaks. I'm doing twice-baked stuffed potatoes and wilted salad. I even bought two bottles of expensive champagne."

"Oh, and I suppose this is all in honor of Sam."

"Yes, a candlelight dinner with my mom's best china."

"I didn't know you have your mom's dishes."

Both of Samantha's parents had died before she finished

high school. She'd lived with her elderly Aunt Sadie until college. The aunt had died the previous year, leaving Sam with no relatives except a soon-to-be ex-husband.

"Sure do! Aunt Sadie saved those things for me. Actually, I have my aunt's china, too. I'd invite you over to see how pretty my table looks, but Sam's coming early. Tell me what to do with the caviar."

"Just chill it and serve it with crackers and cream cheese. Put a few lemon wedges on the plate, too."

"Great! I bought cream cheese to make a cheesecake, but I changed my mind and stopped at the bakery. I just bought an éclair for Sam. I've got lemons in the fridge for iced tea. I'll tell you all about it tomorrow at work."

Once again, Katie found herself alone and feeling sorry for herself. It wasn't that she didn't want Samantha to be happy. She just wanted a little happily ever after for herself, too.

At eight o'clock, Samantha called again. "Well, Katie, everything's ready, but he's not here yet, so I thought I'd talk to you. Are you busy?"

"No, I've been working on some bulletin board things for school, but I'm not busy. What time do you expect Sam?"

"He said around seven, but I think he might have had to work late." Samantha sounded downright pathetic. "Don't you think he probably had to work late?"

"Yes, that's why he hasn't arrived. He'll be there soon. What are you wearing for this romantic dinner?"

"Oh-h-h-h, you'll have to see it! I bought a gorgeous lounging outfit, and guess what, Katie! It's a size three! I thought I'd be stuck in fours forever!"

"Size *three*? I didn't know they made below a five!"

"Specialty shops carry zeroes. That's my goal."

"Sam, that sounds awful. You don't need to be any smaller than you are. A zero? That's like being nonexistent."

In Katie's poor-pity-me mood, she didn't really want to talk to Samantha too long about size zeros. Katie herself struggled to stay in tens and twelves. At five feet, eight inches, Katie could carry more weight than Samantha, but a three? A zero?

Katie said, "Listen, Sam, unless you've got call waiting, you'd better hang up in case he's had car trouble and tries to call you."

"Don't worry. I have call waiting. Got it this summer after I met Sam so I'd never have to worry about missing him when he calls. Of course, I have caller ID, too, but I still unplug the phone sometimes. You can't ever tell who it is if he calls from someone else's cell phone."

Katie found herself praying for Sam to hurry and get to Samantha's apartment. Samantha bemoaned his being late, made up excuses for him, cried, then started all over again. At nine-thirty, she stopped crying. "Katie, I know you haven't eaten because I've had you on the phone all night. Come on over. We'll eat this meal ourselves. It'll make us feel better." Katie resisted slightly, but since she was starving even though she'd had lunch and that giant dessert and Samantha's apartment wasn't far away, she finally agreed. She thought, "I'll bet he shows up just when I get there, and I'll have to come home still hungry," but there was no sign of a man when she arrived at Sam's apartment.

Samantha had really pulled out all the stops. Fresh flowers filled a crystal vase centered on antique lace. The table was set with real linens, china, silver, and lead crystal flutes for the champagne. Sam had finished cooking while Katie drove over. They set out the appetizers and brought the meal to the table at the same time. Samantha lit the candles and turned off the overhead light. She filled the flutes with champagne and passed one to Katie.

"A toast," Sam said and held out her champagne. "Here's to friends, because they don't let you down like lovers!"

"Amen!" said Katie.

The food was delicious, and Katie enjoyed every bite. Sam just shuffled things around on her plate as usual. She did taste the caviar, and Katie had an idea it was her first time eating it. "I hope you like this," she said to Katie. "It doesn't taste worth what I paid for it. Eat a lot. I don't even know if Wookiee will like it."

"It's made out of fish, Sam. Your cat will definitely eat what we don't."

When Katie finished eating, they left the dishes right on the table, picked up the candles and champagne, and moved to the living room. They drank champagne by candlelight and shared women secrets. Sam told Katie about the abortion she'd had while Marc was in law school. Katie told Sam about Maggie and Frankie. By the time they'd almost finished the second bottle of champagne, they stopped confessing to each other and got the sillies. A little after midnight they exchanged toasts.

"My favorite toast," said Sam, "is one to men. I don't practice it. I just think it's funny. Are you ready?" Katie nodded yes. "Friends may come and friends may go," Sam said in a sing-song rhythm. "Friends may peter out you know. But we'll be friends through thick or thin, peter out or peter in."

"What do you mean you don't practice it?" Katie giggled.

"When I've been intimate with someone, it's hard to put it on a platonic basis. Like Sam, if it doesn't work out between us, I don't think I'd want to turn into just his friend."

"Is that how you feel about Marc? You don't think the two of you will ever be friends?"

"After what he did to me? Don't make me laugh! No! Do make me laugh. What's your favorite toast?"

Katie answered, "Here's to you, as good as you are. Here's to me, as bad as I am. But as good as you are, and as bad as I am, I'm as good as you are, as bad as I am."

"Where'd you learn that?" asked Sam.

"My sister Maggie taught it to me." Her smile faded at the thought of Maggie.

"Don't look sad," Samantha said. "You and I both know that Maggie can take care of herself."

"But why haven't I heard from her?"

"You will."

In their champagne glory, they told more schoolteacher jokes. Finally, Katie told Sam to go to bed and locked the door on her way out.

On her way home, Katie drove right past the Pearson place, but she had no way of knowing that Linda Pearson lay inside on the love seat, screaming in her sleep. Linda had finally remembered to close the front door, and the sound remained captive inside the old house.

THURSDAY THUNDER

KATIE'S HEAD HURT so bad she could hardly hold it up the next morning. "Nothing worse than a champagne hangover," she thought. "Unless it's a champagne hangover from a night spent nursing another woman's heartache." She wondered if Samantha would get to work at all, much less on time, but when Katie drove the rental car into the faculty parking, there were two cars waiting for her: Sam in her Hyundai and Sheriff Jolley in his tan Taurus. "What now?" Katie thought as they both hopped out of their vehicles the minute she pulled in.

Samantha reached Katie first and jumped into the front seat beside her. Jolley stood politely by his car. "Katie, you've gotta help me! Sam is furious. He thinks I had another man at my place last night. I told him I'd set the table for him, and you came when he didn't show, but he insists I wouldn't have used all that good stuff for a woman. He just won't listen!"

"And when did 'Mr. Wonderful' finally come over?" Katie asked sarcastically.

"This morning, and it was all just a big mix-up. He thought I'd invited him to dinner for tonight. He tried to call but couldn't get me. He stopped by Kenny B's for happy hour with a couple of friends. By the time he got away, it was too late to call or come by."

"Do you believe that, Samantha?"

"Yes, I believe him, but he doesn't believe me! I just want everything to be okay. He's so hurt. He thinks I had some other man to dinner last night."

"You did have someone else—me. But only because he stood you up. How could he not get you on the phone while you talked to me if you've got call waiting?" Samantha said nothing. Katie continued, "I thought you said you're both free to see other people anyway."

"That's what he said, but he's furious. He just doesn't think you and I drank all that champagne. When he saw the good china and crystal still on the table, it just made him crazy. Will you tell him it was you, Katie? Please say you'll talk to him. I'll get him on the phone for you."

"I think that's kind of adolescent, Sam, but if it's all that important to you, I will. Not right now, though. I believe the sheriff over there wants to talk to me. Why don't you go on in?"

Samantha was about to close the car door when Katie asked her, "How's your head?"

"It hurt something fierce when I woke up, but I feel great since I've seen Sam."

Katie walked from her car to the cruiser. "Good morning, Sheriff. Are you waiting for me?"

"Sure am. I need to talk to you. Do you want to get in

or should I go inside with you?" He sounded worried.

"I'll sit in your car if you keep the air-conditioning on."

"No problem." He walked around and held the door open for her. "Where'd you go last night?"

"Over to my friend Samantha's house. Why?"

Katie was conscious again of the clean smell of his car – a combination of Armor All and some pleasant men's cologne she'd smelled before but couldn't identify.

"I tried to call you and got no answer. Couldn't leave a message. He reached into his pocket and pulled out the recording from her machine. "Here's a replacement for your answering machine. I'm glad you bought one that will record."

Katie put it into her purse and said, "Thanks."

"What I want may be difficult for you today," Jolley said. "I know you need to be at work, but is there any way you can take off and ride up to Columbia with me? I have to talk with Susan Barker. You handled her quite well on the phone last night, and I think you'll get a better response than one of my female officers. It will really help if you can be there to see the photograph and tell me whether it's the same man who was in the picture your sister sent you."

"Difficult is an understatement," Katie said. "Not only do I need to work, I'm not eager to meet Frankie's wife."

"I can't legally make you go. All I can do is ask you to. There's been a new development. We've got a body with a similar MO in Charleston as of this morning. Do you remember Mrs. Barker saying her husband stayed with a teacher in Charleston for a while? The victim found this morning is a fifth-grade teacher named Mary Ellen Shealy.

"Priorities now are to find out if Fred Barker of Columbia

is, indeed, your sister's friend, Frankie, and whether Mary Ellen Shealy is the teacher he was involved with in Charleston last summer. I'm betting I'm right on both counts. I'm also hoping we can get something from Susan Barker that will enable us to compare our John Doe's DNA with DNA from Fred Barker and from forensic evidence at the Charleston crime scene. I still don't know whether to believe Fred Barker is the John Doe or a suspect in his homicide."

"Let me go in and tell them I'm leaving. I'll go with you, but I *have* to work tomorrow or I won't be ready for my students Monday."

Jolley stopped at the Downtown Diner for take-out coffees before they headed out of town. Katie went inside with him and was surprised when Courtney Williams recognized her.

"Good morning," Courtney said. "Where's your little friend today?"

"Working, like I should be," Katie answered. "Seen Miss Possum lately?"

"Every day, rain or shine."

"Miss Possum?" asked the sheriff as they got into the car.

"Linda Pearson," Katie answered and explained the waitress's confusion.

"A sad story," Jolley said as he maneuvered through the morning traffic. "That's one woman who's had more than her share of trouble." He didn't say any more, and Katie didn't feel comfortable questioning him.

Soon they were on Highway 21 headed for I-95. Katie always enjoyed the stretch of 21 between Tanner and I-95. She didn't think she'd ever tire of the beauty of this part of

South Carolina where old trees arched over the road dripping Spanish moss with the sunlight peeking through, creating little kaleidoscope patterns on the pavement. Katie opened her eyes and realized she'd been asleep. She looked over at Jolley.

"You wakin' up?" he asked with a smile.

"I'm sorry. I didn't mean to doze off."

"It's okay. Now, let me know if you want to stop or anything. We're about halfway there. We'll be in Columbia in less than two hours." He motioned toward her cup in the holder. "I doubt your coffee's even warm."

"I'll drink it anyway. I like cold caffeine. Can you tell me anything more about the teacher found in Charleston? Is it all right for you to talk about it?"

"It won't hurt to tell you. What I know is already in today's *Charleston Courier*. Lady's body was found in an alley not long after midnight. Face shot away and fingers chopped off. Remains have already been identified by a birthmark and metal implant in her hip. Her kids had reported her missing when she wasn't home to prepare dinner. Too early for an official report, but the officer the children called was a family friend."

"She had children?"

"Divorced mother with two young teenagers she's been raising by herself."

They rode silently until Jolley exited off I-95 onto I-26 toward Columbia. "If we have time, we might stop in Charleston on the way back. Hank, the Chief of Police, is a good friend of mine. I spoke with him this morning, and he wants to know what I learn in Columbia."

"What do you think? Is Frankie a victim or did he murder that man and this teacher?" Katie asked.

"No way for me to know yet. I sure wish you could've identified the remains one way or the other. Do you feel any more positive now than you did when we saw the coroner?"

"Not at all. I don't think that body is Frankie, but I can't swear to it." Katie finished her cold coffee and returned the empty cup to the holder.

"By the way, Ms. Wray, don't mention the possibility that Frankie might be dead while we're talking to Susan Barker."

"I don't plan to say a word."

The sheriff drove skillfully. Katie saw him glance over at her several times. She watched the trees and fences zip by. There wasn't any Spanish moss now, but kudzu draped and covered some of the trees and abandoned buildings. Its thick vines created gigantic topiaries. Jolley kept glancing from the road. He almost seemed to be staring at her.

"Ms. Wray," he said, "I don't want to speak out of turn, but you're a very attractive woman. If your sister looks at all like you, she can do better than some psycho hanging out in all-night stores."

Katie's first reaction was offense and anger, but a desire to explain replaced those feelings. "Sheriff, you may mean that as a veiled compliment, but it's insulting. It's not something I've ever done, and I don't believe my sister does that regularly either. Considering how life's been recently, I may never go out with any man again!"

"Now, I wouldn't go that far. I apologize if I made you mad, but I've been thinking about it all morning."

"Ah," Katie thought, "so you were thinking about me." She said aloud, "It would be your word—inappropriate."

They rode on into Columbia silently. Jolley suggested lunch before they went to see Susan Barker. That was fine with Katie who would have liked to put off seeing anyone related to Frankie forever. The sheriff was obviously more familiar with Columbia than Katie. He took her to a family-type restaurant called Lizard's Thicket. Katie was interested in how the restaurant had been named, and the cashier explained that the owners heard the term "Lizard's Thicket" while living in Alabama years before and thought it was so country it would be perfect for their southern home-cooking restaurant. Before long, Katie and the sheriff were back on the highway.

The Barkers lived in an upscale subdivision called Briargate about ten miles north of town just off I-26. Katie was impressed when they passed through the massive brick entrance to the housing development. The houses were all large homes with double garages and immaculately landscaped yards.

Jolley had called Mrs. Barker to tell her they were in Columbia before leaving Lizard's Thicket. She opened the door on the first ring. Katie had heard the expression "barefoot and pregnant" her whole life; now she saw it personified. Susan Barker stood in the doorway with one baby on her hip and a toddler clinging to the edge of her stretched T-shirt. A third heir was obviously soon to be born. Under better circumstances, Mrs. Barker may have been pretty, but her honey-colored hair hung limply over red-rimmed eyes. Her face and body language both showed weariness far beyond her years.

"Come on in. I ain't cleaned up much lately. Been too worried about Fred not coming home." There were toys on the floor, but otherwise, the great room was clean. The toddler still clung to her mama, and Mrs. Barker pulled her up onto the couch beside her when she sat down. The sheriff and Katie sat in large, overstuffed chairs facing the sofa.

"Mrs. Barker," Jolley began, and once again, Katie detected a soft, soothing tone in his voice. "Mrs. Barker, I want you to know that we've come all the way up here to help you find Fred. I have some questions to ask but first, I really need a photograph of your husband. Do you have a picture we can look at?"

"I'll get you a picture. Where is Tanner anyway? I never heard of it before Fred called me from there."

"It's a very small town down near the coast."

"Near Myrtle Beach?" Mrs. Barker asked as she patted the baby's back.

"No, near Beaufort."

"I just wondered because Fred really likes the ocean. We talked about moving to the beach, but his dad said we need to stay here. Fred's got lots of medical problems and can't work regular, so his dad gave us this house. He sends us money every month, so me and Fred can't hardly just pick up and move if his daddy don't want us to. I thought maybe if we lived near the water, Fred might stay home more." She stood. The toddler rose too, still clutching on her mama's shirt. "I'll get that picture for you."

While Susan Barker was out of the room, Katie looked around. The furnishings and accessories weren't elaborate, but they were in good taste and obviously not discount merchandise. A large studio portrait over the mantel showed Susan with a man and a baby. The man was the person Katie had seen in the photo with Maggie.

She motioned toward the fireplace. "That's him," she whispered to the sheriff.

Susan returned, carrying several pictures. She pulled one out and laid it on top as she handed them to Jolley. "This is the best one. You can take it with you if it'll help. We got the whole package, and we don't even know that many people. I've got lots of them," she said, indicating the top photo. It showed Barker wearing the same suit he had on in the family portrait. "It's about two years old, made right after Tori here was born." She patted the toddler when she said the name "Tori," and the pudgy little blonde looked up at her mom and grinned. Katie noticed that she had hazel eyes like her father's were in the picture.

"Why, would you just look at me?" Susan said, "Hardly anybody ever comes to the house. I plumb forgot about my manners. Can I get y'all something to drink? I got Cokes and Mountain Dew and sweet tea."

Jolley said, "No, thank you," but Katie sensed that to turn down Susan Barker's hospitality might insult her.

"Yes," Katie said with a smile. "A Coke would be great."

Susan brought two canned Cokes from the refrigerator in the kitchen, which could be seen from the great room. She poured part of one into a baby bottle and handed it down to Tori. The little girl popped it into her mouth, held the nipple between her teeth, and used both hands to clutch again on Susan's shirt. "Do you want a glass and ice?" Susan Barker asked Katie.

"Not if it's cold."

When Susan handed the can to Katie, she looked at her long and hard. "Are you the woman I talked to yesterday?" Katie nodded yes, wondering if Mrs. Barker might react in anger, but Susan's demeanor remained calm as she sat back on the couch.

"Mrs. Barker," Sheriff Jolley began. "You mentioned that your husband spent last summer with a teacher in Charleston. Can you tell me about that?"

"Well, I told you Fred's got these mental problems. I didn't know that when I met him. Me and my girlfriend was out at this club dancing, and Fred was just the best dancer I ever seen." She turned toward Katie. "Did Fred ever take you dancing?"

"No," Katie said, then felt compelled to add, "I just want to apologize to you for my sister. She's who was seeing Fred. I'm sorry about what happened."

"It's these mental problems. I'm sure he didn't tell her he's got a wife and two and a half kids." She grinned and rubbed her stomach. "He sure didn't tell me he'd been locked up for bein' crazy when I met him."

"How long have you been married?" Jolley interrupted.

"Tori's two. We been married about two and a half years. I guess it's all right to tell you, what with you being the law and all. We got married after I got in the family way. His dad had fits. Wanted me to have an abortion, but I told him that ain't the way my family raised me. His dad's been real good to us since then, and he just loves these babies. He'll be up here when this next one's born, I know. He loves the girls, but this one's a boy."

"Does your husband ever work?"

"Not really. Oh, he gets jobs, but it seems they always start to pick on him and he quits. Then, just about every couple of months, he disappears for a day or so, and every summer he winds up at the beach and lives with some woman." Susan Barker looked at Katie, nodded her head, then added, "I don't mean to insult you, ma'am. That's just the way Fred is. I hope he didn't break your sister's heart or nothing." Susan Barker shifted the baby's position--moved from jiggling on her hip to rocking the infant on her arm.

"I'm just sorry it ever happened," Katie said.

Jolley's drawl seemed slower than ever to Katie. "Mrs. Barker, does your husband ever get really angry with you? Does he hit you or the babies? What's his general disposition?"

"Oh, he loses his temper lots, but he's never hurt me or the babies. His daddy told me if that ever happens, just get the babies outta the house and call him. Usually, Fred's just as nice as he can be. He loves to dance. Sometimes we dance right in the kitchen if Fred gets upset. Since the babies came, we don't go dancing a whole lot. Now we usually just go out to eat so we can take the babies with us."

"What did Fred tell you when he called?"

"He said he was tired of where he was and he was coming home. He said cook meat loaf, 'cause that's his favorite. I cooked the meat loaf and waited and waited, but he never came. That was Monday. When he wasn't here yesterday, I called the number on the caller ID."

The baby had fallen asleep, and Susan Barker put her down on the couch. Tori finally let go of her mama's shirt, lay on the sofa beside the baby, and began sucking her bottle of Coke, holding it straight up, perpendicular to her tiny face framing those beautiful, hazel eyes.

"How does Fred travel?"

"What do you mean?"

"Does he have a car?"

"Sure does! He's got a new Alfa Romeo. His dad gave it to him for his birthday. So now I got his red Firebird to drive."

"Can you give me the tag number?"

"For the Firebird?"

"No, for Fred's car."

"Yes, it'll be around here somewhere on the insurance papers."

"Do you think you might have a brush or comb with some of Fred's hair on it? If you could get me that and the tag number for his car, I'll do my best to find him for you. I'd like to have the telephone number for his father too."

"I don't think there's anything here with Fred's hair on it. He's real particular about me and the babies not using his comb or brush. One time Tori was just playing with his hairbrush and he threw it away and bought another one even though that one was just a few weeks old. He buys new toothbrushes every month, too. Fred would never use my comb or brush, and he's got his with him." She smiled apologetically.

"How about his dad's phone number?"

"He lives in Florida. I'll give you his regular number and the eight hundred one. It's a business line, but he won't care if you use it as long as it has to do with Fred."

"That's okay. We don't pay any long distance charges anymore. I just want to talk to him about Fred's medical problems. Do you know if your husband was ever in the military service or has ever been arrested?"

"Not that I know of, but his dad will know. Why?"

"I'd like to have his fingerprints."

"Shucks! I can give you Fred's prints. We had the babies fingerprinted down at the mall when they did Printakid.

You know, where they make up IDs for children in case they ever get lost or anything. Fred and I were just horsing around about wanting identification cards for ourselves, and the salesman made 'em for us. I've got Fred's card with his picture and his prints, but the picture's not near as good as the picture I just gave you."

"Great," Jolley said, "by the way, does Fred play bass guitar?"

"Not that I know. He loves music and he sings sometimes, but he mainly likes to dance. I'm really glad you're gonna look for him. I been worried sick." Susan looked down at the two little girls on the couch. "If you'll watch them a minute, I'll get his dad's numbers and that identification card. I'll find the tag number for his car too." She paused. "I know you probably think I'm crazy for putting up with Fred's ways, but I believe he really loves me."

CHAPTER 7

"A REMITTANCE MAN," Jolley said when the cruiser was back on I-26, out of Columbia, and headed for Charleston.

"What?"

"A remittance man. That's what Fred Barker is."

"What do you mean, a remittance man?"

Jolley laughed, "So, the schoolteacher doesn't know her Faulkner nor her Buffett."

"Explain, please."

"The first place I ever heard of a remittance man was in William Faulkner's writings. In the Old South, when a son was not someone the family wanted around, he became a remittance man. It might be that the son was a ne'er-do-well, or an alcoholic, or had been to jail. Didn't matter. If he was undesirable and the family could afford it, they paid him an allowance or paid his bills with the understanding he was to stay away." He glanced toward

Katie. "Don't look so surprised. I read Faulkner when I was a student at Coastal Carolina University. I think Barker's father is supporting his son's family to keep his mentally ill son away from where he lives."

"What's that got to do with Jimmy Buffett? I assume you mean him."

"Yeah, he recorded a song called 'Remittance Man.' I'll have to play it for you sometime. Were you a Parrot Head?"

"Sure was." Katie looked out the window. They were passing a heavy patch of kudzu vine, climbing trees and power lines, covering them and creating monster shapes. "You know what my mama told me one time?"

"No, what did she tell you?" Wade smiled.

"She said if you watch kudzu vines for two hours, you'll see them grow. The tendrils just creep out all twisted up."

"I've heard that kudzu can grow as much as a foot overnight, but I never watched it to see. I do know it's a bitch to get rid of once it gets a foothold, but I've read they experimented with making paper and cow fodder out of it."

"I don't think it'll ever be good for anything except creeping across the land and hiding secrets," Katie said softly. "I used to think of it as the Kudzu Highway, but I decided that's wrong. Now I think it's the Kudzu River."

"That vine certainly can hide things, but why a river instead of a highway?" Wade asked.

"A highway has a beginning and a definite route to an ending. A river meanders, sometimes changing its path, and a river can swell up over its banks and flood the area, covering the land completely, attempting to hide the sins of the South. Kudzu hides a lot in the South."

"That's a cynical attitude," the sheriff drawled.

"I guess I'm feeling cynical. As each moment passes, I'm feeling more and more worried about Maggie and angrier at her for getting involved with Frankie, I mean Fred, Barker. I feel sorry for that woman he married and those babies, too. How old do you think his wife is? She hardly looks like more than a child herself."

"She does look young, but that's not your problem. The thing we need to do now is find both Barker and your sister. I could fax these photos to Charleston, but I'm going to detour by there. I'll buy you dinner."

"You've already fed me lunch."

"I'll count that as business and let the county pay for it. This one will be on me. I know a place in Charleston with the best she-crab soup in the world."

"It might surprise you to know that I make pretty good she-crab soup myself."

"Good. You can cook for me sometime."

They rode in silence until Jolley asked, "Is there anything your sister said about Barker that we should know but haven't asked?"

"No, I feel like I've bared my soul to you already."

"If you think of anything, let me know. I'm hoping to get the autopsy report on the John Doe body by tomorrow. I've been thinking we've got Barker's body, but if the deceased in Charleston turns out to be the woman he was with last summer, I'll be inclined to think different."

"Sheriff," Katie said, "may I ask you a question?"

"Yes, you *may*, Teacher!" Jolley replied.

"I'll say, 'Can I ask you a question?' if you won't call me 'Teacher' again," Katie responded seriously.

"Okay, Ms. Wray. You ask your question and I'll answer

if you'll tell me why you don't want me to call you 'Teacher' again."

"Maggie said Barker called her 'Teacher' sometimes. Knowing Maggie, she probably told him she was a teacher. She's lied to men before. The more I find out about Frankie, I mean Fred, Barker, the less I want to hear anything that makes me think of him."

"Okay," now the sheriff was using what Katie thought of as his "comforting" voice with her. "What's your question?"

"Why didn't you read the Miranda rights before you talked to Susan Barker?"

"Susan Barker isn't a suspect," Jolley said matter-of-factly.

"Am I? Your deputy read the warning to me."

"A suspect? Not to me, you're not."

"I'll bet your Deputy Corley thinks I did it all — including faking the robbery!"

"He probably does." Sheriff Jolley laughed.

Tennessee Linda spent the afternoon at the library. She'd filled in all the crossword puzzles in the book she'd bought for her daddy's birthday. As usual, she still needed to shop for her beer and cigarettes for the night.

Now that South Carolina's blue laws had changed, she could buy her evening beer and cigarettes on Sunday afternoon. Before that, Linda had to buy Sunday's supplies on Saturday. This had been a real problem because if she had Sunday's provisions on Saturday night, she frequently drank and smoked them all that night and had to do without on Sunday. Now she simply shopped daily, but there were still Mama's rules.

Except for special occasions, crossword puzzle books were only purchased on Saturdays. If she bought one on Thursday, she knew Mama would be furious, and Linda hated for her mother to be angry with her because she would nag her even more.

Linda Louise, you've been here long enough. I don't see why you want to spend all your time reading books and working crossword puzzles anyway. Why don't you go home and watch television with your daddy?

"Oh, Mama," Linda said aloud, but softly, "I'd rather read."

I never saw anything like it. That's all you wanted to do as a little girl, too, just read.

"I wanted to be a teacher, Mama."

Well, you shouldn't have run off and got married so young. Your whole life could've been different.

"Yes, Mama, I know. I wish it had been."

Well, it's certainly not your daddy's or my fault you ran off with Bert.

"I don't blame you, Mama."

I should hope not. Hurry and finish that book! It's gonna rain before the afternoon is done.

By the time Linda left the library, a storm had come up. Thunder rumbled all around, and the rain was blowing hard against her as she dragged her pillowcase along the wet sidewalk.

See, Linda Louise, I told you it was gonna rain. You need to go on home and not shop today.

"No, Mama, you know I've gotta do my shopping. It'll only take a minute."

Child, I just don't think I'll ever understand you. What would you do without me?

"I don't know, Mama. I really don't know."

The Piggly Wiggly was near the library, so Linda Pearson stopped in there for her beer and cigarettes. As she headed for the exit, a tiny woman reached out and touched her. Linda jumped back as though she'd been slapped. "I didn't mean to frighten you," the woman said. "It's just I know you always walk, and the weather's too bad to be walking today. I saw you in the Downtown Diner, and my friend Katie said you used to visit her mother. My friend—Katie Wray? You know her, don't you?"

Linda smiled, and Samantha was surprised that behind the awkward makeup, the face had, no doubt, at one time been extremely pretty. "Teacher Girl? I know Katie, the Teacher Girl, and her sister Maggie. I went to school with their mama."

"Well, I'm her friend Samantha, and I'd like to give you a ride home. My car's not much, but it's better than walking in the rain."

"Why, that would be real nice of you. I believe I'll accept your kind offer."

Katie sat in the Charleston Police Department drinking coffee out of a Styrofoam cup. The sound of rain invaded the commotion of law enforcement going on around her as she waited for Wade Jolley. "Ms. Wray," a uniformed officer said to her, "Sheriff Jolley asked me to bring you to the chief's office. Follow me, please."

She was surprised. She'd understood from Jolley that she'd wait and when he finished business, they'd have dinner, then head for Tanner. The sheriff stood when Katie entered the room. The other man looked shocked.

"Ms. Wray," Jolley said, "this is Charleston Chief of Police Henry Legrand. He's working the case we talked about. We've talked to Fred Barker's father in Florida. Mary Ellen Shealy was the woman he paid off last summer to keep her from pressing charges against Barker for stealing the jewelry she inherited from her grandmother. Apparently after he'd lived with Shealy for several weeks. I've explained to Hank that you've identified the photographs of Fred Barker as the man your sister called Frankie."

"That's right."

"I don't want to upset you, Ms. Wray," the chief interjected. Katie was surprised that, although "Legrand" was an old Charleston name, the chief's accent was not pure Charlestonian. In fact, his accent and drawl were identical to Sheriff Jolley's. "But do you have relatives in the Charleston area?"

"My father was a Charleston Halsey, but I don't know of any relatives here. Why?"

"We obtained a photograph of Ms. Shealy from her family to run on the news. You know, to see if anyone saw her last night, to see if we could find out who might have been with her. I want you to look at the picture and tell me if you know this woman."

"Sure." Katie leaned across the desk and reached for the paper he was handing her. She gasped. The dead woman stood in the color photograph with a young teenaged boy on each side. She appeared to be tall, not fat, but certainly not really thin. This matched Katie's build, but what amazed her was the woman's head. The face and hair were like looking into a mirror. She had Katie's even features, dark eyes, and brown hair almost, but not quite, touching her shoulders. She looked as much like Katie as Maggie did.

"No, I don't know this woman."

"It appears that Barker has a type, and you fit it."

"So does my sister." Katie thought for a minute. "What about his wife?" Katie turned toward Jolley. "Mrs. Barker doesn't look at all like me or this woman."

"Wives don't count," Legrand said. "His wife's not a teacher either, but his father said he's got a hang-up about teachers. He also said to tell you that if you send him an itemized list of the items you reported stolen, he'll reimburse you for them. He didn't seem to doubt that his son stole them. Right now, Wade here's told me your story, but since you're in Charleston, I'd like to get a formal statement from you about Barker. It shouldn't take long, and I'm officially off duty in two hours, so I'll take you and my old pal here out to dinner."

Katie went through the story once again. At least Chief Legrand refrained from snide comments or insinuating looks like Corley had used to interrupt her. When they'd finished, he and Jolley agreed where to meet for dinner.

The sheriff spent the next hour driving around Charleston in the rain. The slap of the windshield wipers smacked even harder against Katie's nerves. Finally, he pulled up to the curb on a back street. Katie looked around and saw where he was looking — a hole-in-the-wall bar with white chaser lights bordering the edge of its one window. Pink neon over the door flashed "The Pink Elephant." A hand-lettered piece of poster board in the window read "Live Tonight! Platinum Posse!"

"I want to see if anyone's in there," Jolley said.

"You're not leaving me out here by myself," Katie

exclaimed as she opened her door and stepped out across a mud puddle and onto the curb.

Katie had been at happy hours at Applebee's with other teachers, and she'd danced an occasional Saturday night away in clubs during her undergraduate days. The Pink Elephant was, however, a new experience.

It was dimly dark and had a sour smell. The room was deep and narrow. A single row of small, round, ice cream parlor tables and chairs stretched the length of the room. The bar extended from the rear to the front on the other side. Rickety, backless stools were crowded up to the bar. Katie wondered how they would ever accommodate customers since the chairs and stools touched even when empty. A tiny bandstand projected from the back corner beside a door labeled "JOHNS & EMERGENCY EXIT."

The only person inside was a sparsely bearded man with a long, wispy ponytail. He sat behind the bar reading a paperback book and didn't even look up when Katie and the sheriff entered. Katie wondered how the man could see. The only light came from electric beer signs hanging over the bar.

"Excuse me," Jolley began.

"We're closed," the man interrupted. "Since it's raining, you can wait inside, but I can't serve you until we open in twenty minutes." Katie thought this was a strange comment. The sheriff was dressed in uniform and certainly wouldn't expect the guy to break the law. Even after Jolley showed his badge, the bartender was little help. He said Platinum Posse would be playing that night, but he didn't know when they'd start. "As soon as there's a good crowd," was his comment. When the sheriff asked what time the band would come in to set up, the bartender answered, "Who knows? Whenever they get here, they're here."

About halfway through dinner, Chief Legrand looked at Katie and smiled. He said, "Ms. Wray, I realize that Wade and I are officers of the law and you're involved in an investigation, but I feel a little awkward with me calling him Wade, him calling me Hank, and you calling us Sheriff Jolley and Chief Legrand. I guess you've figured out that Wade and I go back a long way. We grew up on farms right up the road from each other in Tanner. This is a social dinner, not part of the investigation. How about you call me Henry or Hank?"

"Okay, Hank, and you call me Katie, if you like."

"I like."

"In that case, I'm Wade," Jolley said.

They spent the remainder of the meal laughing and talking about all the ways Wade and Hank had gotten into trouble back in school. "It's a wonder we didn't wind up behind bars instead of putting other people there," Hank said as they left the restaurant.

"I hate to tell you this," Katie told Wade as he pulled out into traffic. "I'm not cooking you any she-crab soup. Theirs is better than mine."

Wade avoided comparison by asking, "Do you know why it's called *she*-crab soup?"

"Not really."

"Years ago, Charleston aristocracy used only large male crabs to make a chowder-type soup. During hard times after the war, one of the male cooks bought the less-desired female crabs to save money. Determined to use every part of the crabs, he added the female roe to the soup. That was the beginning of she-crab soup."

"Who put the sherry in it?"

"I don't know, but it sure tastes good, doesn't it?" He didn't pause for an answer, but continued talking. "I'm going to stop and try to talk to those band members, then we'll head back. I know you have to work tomorrow."

Apparently, what the band considered a "good crowd" didn't fit Maggie's interpretation of the term. There weren't a dozen customers, but the band was already playing. It was very loud, heavy alternative rock.

Wade seated Katie at a table and asked what she wanted. There were no servers, so he went to the bar himself. He came back with a beer for her and a Pepsi for himself. There was no way Frankie could have been a band member in Platinum Posse. The four musicians were all tall. All shapely. All obviously very well endowed in the bosom department. Each had long, straight, platinum blond hair and perfect cheekbones. During the first intermission, the sheriff stopped the lead guitarist and spoke to her as they exited the stage. The four musicians came over, pulled up chairs, and crowded around the tiny table.

The lead guitarist smiled and introduced herself and the others. She was Ann. The others were Nan, Jan, and Fran. Holding the photograph of Barker in front of them, the sheriff asked, "Do any of you know this man?"

"Why?" asked Ann.

"I'm on a homicide investigation. It will help if you just tell me what you know."

Nan, the bass player, shrugged her shoulders. "Yeah, we know him. He used to follow us around. He'd show up wherever we played. Said his name was Frankie and he liked our music. Haven't seen him in, oh, probably six months." She looked at the others with a questioning expression.

"About that long," Fran, the drummer, confirmed.

"Why are you asking us this when you've got his woman here with you?" questioned Ann.

"This woman's never seen you before. I think you're talking about someone who looked a lot like her."

"She sure did. I thought it was her for sure when you two came in," Ann confirmed.

"Can you tell me anything about either of them? Did he ever play onstage with you?"

"Are you outta your mind? We don't let amateurs onstage with us!" Fran's expression was incredulous.

"How well did you know him?"

"Pretty good. Oh, we never saw him outta the clubs, but he was always wanting to buy us drinks. We sat with him a lot during breaks. He talked about music. Said he wanted to sponsor us and get us a recording contract. He threw a lotta money around."

"I'm going to leave you my card," Wade said. "If you see him or think of anything else, get in touch with me. I'm eager to talk to him." The sheriff gave a card to each of them. "Sorry we can't stay for your second set. You sound real good."

"Thanks. If we think of anything, we'll call you," Ann said and motioned to the others to return to the bandstand.

In the car, Katie asked, "Were you just trying to stay on their good sides by telling them they sound good?"

"No, that's not my favorite kind of music, but I like just about all kinds. For what they're playing, it's good."

"They certainly look great. That's about the four best-looking women I've ever seen."

Wade looked at Katie quizzically. "Katie," he said, "you're kidding, right?"

"Oh, maybe not Frankie's type but I wouldn't mind looking like any one of them. Why are you staring at me?"

"Katie," Wade repeated, "you've gotta be kidding."

"Why? What's wrong?"

"Katie, those are cross-dressers. There's not a woman among them. They're all men."

"I should've pawned all that damned stuff from Maggie's apartment," Shug told himself. "Don't know why I smashed it and hauled it to the dump." He laughed and added, "Of course, I know why. To spite her, just to spite her." He rolled over in the king-sized bed in his expensive hotel room, grabbed the remote, and shut off the television.

"Hell, if I'd pawned that shit, I'd have a little more money. Can't cash a check or use a credit card while the cops are looking for me. If I call my father, he'll probably notify the authorities. Good thing I drew out some dough before my picture hit the news or I'd be sleeping on the streets."

Hunger gnawed his gut, but he didn't want to go out. Someone might recognize him. He hadn't been very hungry since Mary Ellen Shealy. She'd been sweet, and he'd liked her sons before, but he'd found more pleasure in what he'd done to her than he would have from staying with her a few days. A twinge of guilt nipped at him. What would happen to her two sons? Would losing your mother to a murderer be any worse than it had been for him to find his own mother after her suicide?

A quick check of the literature on the desk led to businesses that delivered pizza and other foods. There was also a room service menu, and though it was more expensive and money was beginning to run low, he thought he might be less noticeable if he ordered from inside the hotel.

The cost for a sandwich would buy a full-course dinner at some better restaurants, but the killer called room service and ordered a Reuben sandwich, an order of home fries, and a large root beer. Reubens had been his favorite sandwiches since he was a little boy. His mom had made them for him.

Waiting for his food, Shug reconsidered going out. Screw caution. He'd hit the streets after he ate. He leaned against the pillows against the headboard of the bed, closed his eyes, and remembered the look on Mary Ellen's face when he'd pulled the gun from his pocket.

"What are you doing?" she'd cried in a shrill voice.

"Easing your pain," he'd said.

"Don't hurt me," she'd begged. "What about my kids? You know their dad won't take them. They'll wind up in some institution."

"I've been in a few institutions myself. Turn around."

"Why? If you're going to hurt me, look me in the eyes while you do it."

"Time's up for you telling me what to do. Tell you what—you turn around, and I won't hurt you."

The stupid bitch had turned her back on him.

A knock came at the door just as the killer's memories reached the point of firing the gun—the part that excited him. For a moment, he thought the law might be knocking, but the voice said, "Room service."

FRIGHTFUL FRIDAY

CHAPTER 8

CORLEY WAS FIT TO BE TIED. "Sheriff, I can't believe you took that Wray woman with you to Columbia and Charleston! It's my case. Why didn't you send me?"

"First, it's *our* case. Second, I'm the sheriff, not you. Third, I wanted to see if Katie made the identification on Fred as Frankie. Not only did she ID him from the photo, we got a positive match on prints from Katie's apartment.

"Katie?"

"Ms. Wray to you. Has the John Doe autopsy report come in?" Jolley was dressed in uniform again today, and he straightened the nametag on his shirt. Corley looked down at his own, but it looked straight enough. Sheriff Jolley was as fussy as the military about uniforms being absolutely correct when worn.

"Not to my knowledge."

"Check on it. You need to read everything on the Charleston case too. Hank faxed additional papers in."

"Okay, Chief! I mean Sheriff." Corley grinned like a kid.

"That's better," thought Jolley as Corley left his office. Sometimes Corley irritated him, but the sheriff liked him and thought Corley would be a fine officer when he matured. He hardly expected the deputy to be back in less than five minutes.

"Chief," Corley began, "we've got a report of a bloody car abandoned by the old burned-out church over on Rutledge Road.

"Let's go," said Jolley, grabbing his hat as he went.

Katie's mind wasn't on school as she wrote students' names in textbooks Friday morning. She kept thinking of Mary Ellen Shealy, murdered and left in an alley. She wondered if Frankie had called the dead woman "Teacher" and told her the same lies he'd told Maggie. Was the dead body Katie had seen Frankie? If so, who killed the teacher? If it wasn't, did Frankie kill the man and the teacher in Charleston? Katie was also worried about Samantha, who had come to work ecstatic that Sam had "forgiven" her for Wednesday night.

The church had burned almost a century before, and all that was left standing were the columns and stone steps, but the centuries-old cemetery and the beauty of the ancient azaleas around the place drew tourists. This morning, the solitude had attracted two high school kids looking for privacy on their last morning free from classes. Both of them had been carrying cell phones, and they'd called law enforcement from the scene. When Jolley and Corley arrived, the teenagers were sitting on the stone steps of the church ruins. The boy had a helpless look as he patted the girl's shoulder while she sobbed loudly.

"That's right, son," thought Jolley. "Ain't a damned thing you can do for a crying woman except hold her and pet her."

The boy explained that when they pulled in and saw the sharp Alfa Romeo, they'd started to leave, but he'd never seen a car like that except in magazines. He didn't spot anyone around, so he decided it would be okay to park and just walk over and check out the vehicle. "Dude! When we saw all that blood and smelled that stink, I knew we needed to call the law!"

The sheriff thought he'd grown immune to the odors of crime long ago, but the stench from the car was as bad or worse than any he'd ever encountered. He could understand why the boy said he'd been sick over in the trees. The girl continued to cry loud, racking sobs. Corley circled the car while the sheriff talked to the teenagers. The deputy went over to the patrol car, then joined Jolley with the kids. "I think we found some of what's left of our John Doe's face. Forensics is on the way here, and the tag's registered to Frederick Barker in Columbia."

"Good. I knew whose car that is when we pulled up. That's the car Barker's father bought him for his birthday," the sheriff answered. The girl mumbled something, and Jolley turned back to her. "What'd you say?" he asked gently.

"Can we go now?"

"Tell you what. Let Detective Corley here see your identification, and you can leave and go down to the department to make your statements."

"To the sheriff's department?" the girl screeched. "You mean you're going to take my name and I have to go to your office? I don't want my dad to know I'm here. He thinks I'm at the library. He'll kill me!"

Jolley's tone remained gentle. "Then go make the statement now. If you don't show up, I'll have to send someone to your house to get you."

"You'll arrest me?" The screeches turned into a whine.

"No, just come get you to tell us what happened."

"We already told you," she whimpered, but she pulled out her student ID. After Corley recorded information on both teenagers, the boy patted the girl's back some more and led her to his car. He waved at the sheriff and deputy as he drove away.

Now it was Wade's turn to circle the Alfa Romeo. He gave it a wide berth. There were shattered pieces of bone and tissue mixed with glass in the slushy mud outside the passenger door. The passenger window had shattered, but even after last night's storm, bloody smudges streaked the exterior on that side. He leaned carefully into the driver's open window. The interior was fully drenched, but the rain had not washed away what had happened inside the car. Jolley checked the area for tire tracks, but found none except the teenaged boy's old clunker and Corley's cruiser. "Damned rain," he muttered, then added, "at least the top wasn't down.

Samantha stayed in Katie's room and helped until lunchtime, but when Katie said she was skipping lunch to finish setting up her classroom, Sam left. She was back at the end of the day, after the last faculty meeting, just as Katie opened the lesson plan book on her desk to leave everything prepared for Monday.

"Whatcha doin' tomorrow, Katie?"

"Nothing. I plan to spend the whole day resting."

"Come with me to Summerville."

"Summerville? I was about fifteen minutes from there yesterday. Why are you going to Summerville?"

"You've heard of Sally Brown, haven't you?"

"The psychic?"

"One and the same. I called her. She's willing to see us Saturday morning at eleven."

"Us?"

Katie had just slipped into a tub full of bubbles. A glass of Chardonnay sat on the ledge beside her, and the CD player was loaded with Janis Joplin and old Z Z Top. "Time for a little R&R. After all, it's POET'S Day," she thought. During the first couple of years of her marriage, she and Charles had always celebrated POET'S Day. It was an acronym for "Piss on Everything; Tomorrow's Saturday."

"At least back then I had a date every Friday night," she thought. "For the first few years anyway." She squirmed down and stuck her feet up out of the water. "How long since you polished your toenails?" she asked herself.

Katie was more than half through her glass of wine and singing along with "Tush" when the phone rang. "Let it ring," she thought. "Probably Samantha to tell me Sam's late or he's there or they're at his house getting in the Jacuzzi." Katie slipped down into her favorite tub position with only her face out of the water.

"Katie? Katie?" At first she thought the sheriff was in her living room. Then she realized he was talking on the answering machine. She scrambled out of the tub, grabbed a towel, and foolishly dashed to the bedroom, nearly slipping on the wet bathroom tile.

"Yes—I mean hello," Katie said as she grabbed the

receiver.

"Ms. Wray?" the sheriff drawled. Now why was he back to formal last names? He'd called her Katie before she got to the phone, and they'd been on first-name terms in Charleston.

"Yes, this is Katie."

"Sheriff Wade Jolley here. I wanted to check on a few things. Thought I'd drop by if you're not busy."

"Come right on."

"I'll be there in five minutes."

"Make it fifteen. I'm stark—I mean—I'm just out of the shower."

"Fifteen it is," Jolley answered.

Katie quickly towel-dried her hair, slapped on lipstick, then pulled on a pair of jeans and a tank top. Wade didn't give her fifteen minutes. He was there in ten, and Katie answered the door barefooted. The sheriff stood in the hallway with a big grin and a sack in his hand.

"You don't look like Ms. Wray, the schoolteacher I saw earlier this week."

"Well, it's Friday." Katie glanced down at her bare feet and wished she'd polished her toenails. As a matter of fact, she thought it would be nice if her hair was done and she had on different clothing. The sheriff was really kind of cute when he grinned.

"Would you like a Pepsi?" Katie asked through those distracting thoughts.

"Aren't you a Coke person?"

"I am, but now I've stocked some Pepsi, too."

Wade grinned, then said, "Actually, I'm technically off duty and brought a six-pack. Do you like imported beer?"

"There may be one brand in the whole world that I don't

like, but chances are slim that you'd choose it. Would you like a mug or a glass?"

With a frosted mug of beer in his hand and a chilled glass of the same in hers, they made small talk. Wade inquired politely if Katie had completed her preparations for the first day of school Monday. He spoke about the weather. He sipped one beer and then another. Finally, he said, "We found Barker's Alfa Romeo today."

"Where? Did you find Frankie?"

"No, we didn't find Barker. At least, we don't know if we found any part of him. The car was abandoned over by the ruins of the burned church on Rutledge Road. There's evidence a shooting took place in the car at that location."

"Is that what you came to tell me?"

"Actually, I came to ask you something."

"Ask."

"Susan Barker couldn't locate a brush or anything that might have Barker's hair on it. I happened to think that since he has longish hair, maybe he used your sister's brush sometime. Mrs. Barker said he wouldn't share his hairbrushes, but sometimes a man will do things with other women that he doesn't do with his wife." After the sentence was out of his mouth, Wade realized it could have a different meaning. Katie didn't seem to think anything of it, so he simply continued, "Maybe there's something around here that might have one of his hairs on it."

"I don't have any idea if he ever used Maggie's brush. There are several on my dressing table, but since we all have brown hair, I don't know how you'd tell them apart."

"We can DNA you to know whose is whose."

"Well, you're welcome to my hairbrush, but I think the

only hair you're going to find will be mine."

"How about your bed? Have you changed your sheets since you came back?"

Katie bristled. "The sheets looked fresh Monday when I came home. I assumed Maggie changed them, but no, I haven't changed my sheets this week."

"Are you angry?" Wade drawled. "I didn't mean to upset you. It's just I'd really like to get a positive ID on this John Doe body we've got or at least eliminate the possibility that it's Barker. We're checking with the hospitals he's been in to see if we can get any X-rays they may have taken. We can DNA one of his children if it comes to it, but that's a last resort in my opinion." He took another swallow of beer, reached in his pocket and pulled out a pair of tweezers and several plastic Ziploc bags. "Could I see your bed?"

"Oh, crap," Katie thought, "it's not made up." That's what she thought, but she said, "You can see the bed if that's why you came over."

"Why do I get the feeling you're irritated with me? I know this whole thing is awkward and unpleasant for you, but I assure you I'm trying to keep it from being any more difficult than it has to be." Wade sounded annoyed himself.

"I guess it's just sinking in. It's been a really hard week with a lot of shocks and unpleasantness. Frankie and Maggie both missing. The robbery. The body. Finding out Frankie's married. The victim in Charleston looking like me isn't exactly reassuring either."

"Tell you what. Let me look at your bed, and I'll take you out to dinner."

Katie looked down at her bare feet and thought about

her hair. "That's nice of you, Sheriff Jolley, but I'm really too tired to go out."

"Have you eaten?"

"No, but I honestly don't feel like going anywhere. You can look at the bed though."

"How about pizza? Do you like pizza? I haven't eaten. We can order a pizza."

"Okay. There's the phone. You order a pizza. Then I'll show you the bed."

Wade laughed. "Katie, are you putting me on the telephone so you can go in the bedroom and make your bed? I guarantee you it doesn't matter to me whether your bed is neat or not. I know mine's not made at home, and if you make yours right now, I'll just have to undo it."

It was Katie's turn to laugh. "Now, how did you know that was bothering me?"

"I'm the sheriff. I'm supposed to be able to figure out things like that. What do you want on the pizza?"

"Whatever you like."

"How about everything except anchovies? Does Domino's deliver to this address?"

"Sure," Katie answered, remembering all the times Maggie had told her that Frankie had ordered pizza from there during the summer.

After the sheriff called Domino's, they went into the bedroom. Wade carefully searched both pillows and collected several hairs he sealed in bags. Katie wasn't surprised to find that standing in the bedroom while he picked hairs off her pillows was embarrassing.

When they returned to the living room, Wade sat on the couch and Katie sat in a chair. "I'm sorry we can't watch television. I haven't had time to shop for replacements for some of the things that were taken."

"That's okay. I'm enjoying the music."

"That's my personal portable CD player from my classroom. I brought it home so I'd at least have some way to listen to music until I replace the stolen items."

When the pizza came, Katie went to the kitchen and came back with plates. "No, not for pizza," Wade said. "They sent a handful of napkins. Let's just use those. Unless you've got paper towels."

"Of course I have paper towels. They don't have much resale value, so nobody stole them," she snickered.

"I'm glad you can still laugh. I realize this has been hard on you."

They finished Wade's imported beer. Katie was beginning to get a slight buzz when Wade stood and said, "I guess I'd better move on out of here and let you get some rest."

Katie stood, too. "Yes, it's been a long day," she said. "Thank you for the pizza and beer."

"And thank you for letting me enjoy my job for a change."

At the door, Katie could have sworn he wanted to kiss her. It was just a feeling she had, strange under the circumstances, but the sheriff simply told her good night and left. She stood there until he drove away, then went to bed. She tossed around about an hour before giving up. Katie got out of the bed and changed the sheets. The ones on the bed had looked clean, but there was no way to know if Maggie had changed them for her sister's homecoming. Maggie was known for not always doing the "right" thing. In fact, Maggie was usually known more for making poor choices and taking incorrect actions. Had she changed the sheets for Katie's return? No way to know, and the thought of sleeping on sheets where a suspected killer had spent the night brought shivers to Katie.

After putting on her old flannel nightgown, she crawled between the fresh sheets. When she finally went to sleep, Katie dreamed about hairs growing out of her pillows.

Tennessee Linda would have gladly exchanged dreams with Katie. A few hairs sprouting from pillows would be nothing to Linda. Bert haunted her sleep. She moaned pathetically and screamed in horror and pain as she relived days and nights with him. When nightmares of Bert finally ended, her mind took her back even further, back to the tortures of the man in her life before Bert.

PSYCHIC SATURDAY

CHAPTER 9

"KATIE, IF YOU GET TIRED of driving, just let me know," Samantha suggested.

"No way. You're too excited to drive. I didn't know you were really into all this psychic stuff. Do you call the friendly psychics on the phone or track them down on the Internet?"

"Heavens, no! But this is Sally Brown we're going to see. She's legitimate! She's the real thing! I've seen her on the local news, and I've heard her on the radio. Sally Brown really has the gift."

"I sure hope so. A hundred dollars is pretty steep for one question, but I guess that's what friends are for, to tag along on trips like this."

"You're not tagging along. You're driving!" Sam's exuberance showed itself by the way she bounced on the seat even though her seat belt was fastened.

"Well, you didn't think I'd ride in your oven of a car, did

you?" Katie teased. She drove silently for a while, watching the side of the road. "Look at those old trees. This part of the drive is so pretty. It's like riding through an arch of moss the way the trees lean over the road." Samantha didn't respond. After a few more miles, Katie asked, "Sam, is something wrong?"

"It's just that I want this to work so much." Her mood had totally changed.

"Well, you said you believe in Sally Brown. It'll work."

"I don't mean the psychic. I mean Sam. It seems like when I'm with him, everything's okay, but when I'm not, I wonder about it all."

"Give it time, Sam. Do you have the directions?"

Samantha pulled a piece of paper from her purse. "Yes, we turn off soon. There'll be a sign. Then we take a right. Go six and two-tenths miles. We'll see the house on our left."

"Well, this is it." They pulled off the highway and turned right onto the dirt road. It would have been impossible to miss the turn. A large billboard sign announced, "Turn Left to See the Future with Sally Brown, Psychic Renowned!"

The house was small and covered with vinyl siding that wasn't quite yellow, but wasn't really white either. A drive circled the entire house, and the yard was swept clean, not a blade of grass or ground cover. There were a few shrubs in the yard, but most of it was just smooth, brushed dirt. Katie parked, and the two of them stepped up onto the front porch and rang the bell. Nothing happened. Katie rang again. Still nothing.

"Are we early?" Katie asked. "Maybe she's gone shopping or something."

"No," Samantha replied, "we're right on time. She agreed on eleven when I talked to her."

Katie rang the bell again, this time really leaning into it. The door opened, and the biggest woman Katie had ever seen stood in the doorway. She wasn't plump, fat, or obese; she was enormous. Her bleached blond hair was slicked back smooth into a ponytail tied with a fluffy red ribbon. She wore a sleeveless cotton print muumuu of gold and red cloth. She was barefooted. Katie noticed that even the woman's feet were humongously fat. She also noticed that Sally Brown's toenails were painted bright fire engine red.

"Well, come right on in. I don't guess you ladies had any trouble finding me?" Her tiny, little girl voice surprised Katie coming from such a large body.

"Are you Ms. Brown?" asked Samantha.

"I'm Sally Brown, but it's Mrs., not Ms." The large woman laughed, and the sound had a tinkling quality. "I'm certainly not the receptionist, if that's what you thought. Follow me."

Katie and Sam walked behind her through a hallway to a room where she motioned them to sit. The room had two maroon velvet couches, a square coffee table covered with magazines, and several stands overflowing with lush, green plants.

Sally Brown looked at them and pointed daintily toward Katie. "You're Ms. Wray, right?"

"Yes, and this is Ms. Branham," Katie replied.

"You don't have to tell me. I know that you each have a question." She nodded toward Samantha. "Is it okay if we start with Ms. Wray since she's the skeptical one? She might back out if I leave her here thinking while I talk to you." She laughed again, and Katie found it even harder to reconcile that high-pitched girlish sound to the woman in front of her. "Ms. Wray, please follow me to the reading room and I'll answer your question."

The psychic led the way through the doorway. Katie wasn't surprised that the walls were hung with heavy, black drapes. The round, wooden table in the center of the room was bare except for an old-fashioned portable cassette recorder. Several different-style chairs were pulled up to the table. "Have a seat and relax," the psychic instructed. Then she pressed the button on the recorder and lowered her tremendous bulk into the largest chair. "I can work however you like. I have a crystal ball. I have tarot cards. I have tea leaves. But, Ms. Wray . . . "

"Just call me Katie."

"Okay, Katie. I feel that you are very skeptical and think you are wasting your money. I also believe that you know as well as I do that whatever knowledge I have comes from within and not from a crystal ball or any other artifact. Do you want me to use an object or shall we just talk?"

"No gimmicks, please, and you're right. I'm very skeptical, and I'm not overly impressed that you sense my skepticism. I'm certain you're an excellent people reader."

"Did your friend explain my charges?"

"Yes, and I have the money here in cash as you requested."

"You must decide now whether to go back into the waiting room or to give me the hundred dollars. If you give me the money, I will give you a reading. At the end of the reading, you may ask me one specific question, which I will answer. I make no money-back guarantees.

Once money crosses my palm, it is mine. No returns."

Katie counted out five twenties across the table into the woman's pudgy hand. Then she sat back, trying to look more comfortable than she felt. Sally Brown examined the cash before slipping it into her muumuu in a pocket that Katie hadn't seen until the money disappeared.

"I see that your concern is about a man, Katie Wray," the tinkly voice began, "and you're thinking I say that to all women who come to me, but you might be surprised. Most of my female clients come to me in search of something. A ring, a necklace, or if not jewelry, sometimes a recent widow comes to ask where her husband's will might be found. You are also seeking something, but it's not jewelry and it's not paper." Sally Brown stopped.

After a few minutes of silence, Katie said, "Please don't be offended, but not only am I skeptical, I'm also smart enough to know that the more I talk, the more you pick up from me. I've paid you. I do not intend to say anything else until the end when I ask my question."

Sally Brown laughed so hard her huge stomach rolled like a giant watermelon beneath the muumuu. "No problem. I do not need you to talk. I see that you work with children but you have none of your own. That will change within the next two years. You do not need to seek love. It will find you, and when it does, your child will come into your life. You will also change your home soon. All of these are good things that will come in your future, but none of them are what brought you to me. You came to do your friend a favor, but you also have a question.

"The question has to do with a man, but he is not the man for you. This man has serious problems, and they will accelerate. You must avoid him."

The tiny voice paused, and the only sound in the room was the breath of the two women. "I cannot urge you strongly enough to stay away from him. Flee from him. Do not ever allow yourself to be with this man." Sally Brown reached across the table and took Katie's palm-up hand in her own. The fat lady turned it over and stroked the back.

"I do not wish to read your palm. I don't need that with you. I needed to touch you to read your health. Your health is good. Your career will go well though it will change. The future is good—if you succeed in avoiding the man you came to ask about. Now, what is your question?"

Katie laughed nervously. "I must confess I'm confused. My question is, 'Where is my sister?' "

"Your sister is where she chose to be. That is all I can say about her. Because of that, you may ask me one more question—a question about a man."

"What I really want to know is about my sister. If I must ask about a man, I must word my question wisely."

Sally Brown laughed that tiny laughter again and said, "Use wisdom anytime you pay for something. I saw your intelligence before I opened my door to you. Word your question well. An extra question after this will cost you another hundred dollars."

"Please don't answer until I tell you that what I say is my question. I need to think carefully. I could ask if the man in the future is the sheriff. I could ask if the man I should avoid is the sheriff, but I don't think it is. This is my question: Is the man's body I saw at the morgue Frankie Barker?"

"That's your question, right? Is the body you saw at the

funeral parlor Frankie Barker? You're sure that's correct?"

"Yes. That's my question."

"No, the body you saw is not Frankie Barker," the tinkly voice almost whispered.

"Then Frankie Barker isn't dead?"

Sally Brown grinned. "Are you buying another question?"

"Oh, no!" Katie sat up straight and laughed.

"There is so much doubt these days. So many people who do not believe, and so many people who leave and do not remember correctly. I close each reading with two things. First, I must ask you if you would like to be on my meditation list. For only a hundred dollars more, I will put you on my meditation list for three months."

"I really don't think so, but just what does being on your list do?"

"I spend time each day thinking of the people on my list and encircling them with good thoughts and white light so they may look forward to continued prosperity."

"No, thanks. What's the other thing you do?"

"I give you the tape of the session, so that you may listen to it in privacy and better understand what's been said. You may also share your tape with your friends. I do not hide anything. That's why the table is bare. There are no tricks here." Sally Brown removed the audiocassette from the tape player and handed it to Katie. She leaned her hands on the table heavily and began to rise from her chair. "I'm not going to ask if you think you got your money's worth, but you will think so later. I assure you of that."

Katie followed Sally Brown back to the waiting room and sat down as Samantha stood up to go to the reading room.

She had just begun thumbing through a copy of *People Magazine* when she heard Sam's voice. At first, she couldn't actually understand what Samantha was screaming. She could only hear that Sam was getting louder and louder and more and more upset.

"What do you mean you won't do a reading for me?" shrieked Samantha. Katie stood and was going into the reading room to see what was happening when Sally Brown came through the doorway, huffing and puffing as though she'd never catch her breath.

The big woman's face turned bright red. She panted, "Please, please take your friend and go," thrusting a handful of cash at Katie. "Take back the money. Take it because I will not read for her. Take your money, too. Just get your friend out of here."

Katie pushed past Sally Brown into the reading room. Samantha sat at the bare wooden table. "What's wrong, Sam?"

"I found her. I made the appointments. Now she did your reading, but she says she won't do one for me. I've come all this way to find out if Sam and I are going to stay together, and she's refusing my money!"

"Take her away!" screeched Sally Brown in her shrill little voice. "I told her to forget the man! Forget the man! Don't ever see him again! It's free. My advice is free. I never give free advice. I never do readings without pay. Take your money. Go back to your husband. Go to California. Go anywhere, but get away from the man!"

"You promised me a question," Samantha shouted. "I came all the way here because you promised me a question. I'm not moving from this table until you answer my question."

"No, I'm giving you free information. Forget the man!"

Katie tried to calm them. "Both of you, stop screaming." She turned toward Sally Brown. "Please, please take the money back. Forget the reading, but let her ask the question. You can keep the money, and I promise I'll take her out of here if you'll just answer her question."

"Maybe," said Sally Brown. "What's the question?"

Samantha slipped a piece of paper from her pocket. "I wrote it down. I'll read it to you. My question is: 'Will I spend the rest of my life with Sam?'"

Sally Brown's face deepened to a darker shade of crimson. Katie was afraid the woman would have a stroke or heart attack. "If I answer this question, will you both leave and never come back?" the large lady asked.

"Yes, I promise." Katie held the money out to the psychic. "Take the money. Answer her one question, and we'll get out of here."

"Nothing free now," whispered Sally Brown and reached for the money. She shoved it into that invisible pocket in the muumuu and looked up at Katie. Tears glistened in her tiny eyes in that huge fleshy face. "Repeat the question."

"Will I spend the rest of my life with Sam?" Samantha read.

"Forget the man." Sally Brown's words were so soft she could barely be heard.

"That's not an answer to her question," Katie said quietly. "The answer to the question has to be yes or no."

"Yes. That's your answer. Yes! Now get out!"

"You know that woman's crazy, don't you?" Samantha asked Katie as they drove away from Summerville.

"I don't know. She almost made a believer out of me, but she's way off base on one thing. I've got a tape of my reading though I threw away my cassette player years ago. What did you do that set her off so?"

"Nothing. Absolutely nothing. She may have been mad because I tripped as I went in. She caught me and helped me sit down. Then she went nuts. Said she didn't want to do a reading for me. Said she'd give me free advice and kept repeating for me to forget Sam. I think she got scared I'd sue her about the doorsill being loose and just wanted to get rid of us." Samantha grinned. "But, Katie, she said Sam and I are going to be together. That means I'm going to win in the end. He'll be mine, and we'll live happily ever after!"

"But she kept telling you to get rid of him. Do you know why Sam and his wife divorced? Was he abusive? Why was she telling you to get rid of him?"

"She's just crazy. Do you have time for a short detour? There's a little shop I want to go to in Charleston while we're this close. I want to buy some insurance."

"Insurance? Why would you buy insurance here? You can buy it in Tanner."

"Not this kind."

"Do you want me to go by her house and get it?" Corley asked Sheriff Jolley.

"No, I'll do it. I just can't believe I didn't get that sample when I was there," Wade replied. "Do we have anything from forensics on the car yet?"

"Not the full report, sir, but the three slugs found in the Alfa Romeo came from the .38 we found beside the John Doe. I'll check on it. We don't have the autopsy report on him yet, but we both know the connection."

"Anything new from Charleston?" the sheriff asked, but his secretary broke in with a telephone call before Corley could respond.

"Sheriff Jolley, you have a call from Ms. Wray on line three."

Wade had barely said, "Hello" when Katie's words gushed out.

"I know you probably don't believe in this stuff, but my friend Sam said that Sally Brown has been called in on police cases before, just like on television. I wanted to let you know that we saw Sally Brown today, and she said the body's not Frankie, so he must not be dead."

"Slow down a minute. Where'd you see Sally Brown?"

"Sam and I went to her house in Summerville. I asked her about Frankie. She says he's not dead. Don't think I'm crazy. I don't usually believe in this psychic stuff myself but she really impressed me. I had to tell you what she said."

"I want to know more about that, and I need to see you anyway. What about that dinner I offered you last night? Have you ever been to Mama Clyde's Gullah House? It's just a little place right outside of town, but she specializes in authentic Gullah, and her seafood and chicken are the best around."

"You fed me the past two nights, but I really do want to tell you all about Sally Brown."

"Well, I'd like to know all the details." It didn't take long for Wade to talk Katie into going out to dinner with him. Corley laughed when Jolley hung up the phone.

"Is it details or hair you want, Sheriff Jolley?"

"I guess both. I can't believe I didn't get a hair sample

for her DNA comparison. Must be slipping. She says the psychic Sally Brown told her our John Doe isn't Barker, so she's sure he isn't dead."

"What's your gut feeling, Chief?"

Jolley ignored being called the wrong title this time. "It seems to me that it would be hard for anyone who owned a car like that Alfa Romeo to shoot someone in it and walk away, but Barker apparently gets what he wants from his father. He probably figures his dad will buy him another one. The body in Charleston makes me think Barker is the doer. If so, our John Doe truly is a John Doe. Anyway, it won't hurt to listen to what Katie has to say, and it will definitely make it easier to get those hair samples."

Corley made an obscene remark concerning hair and what else Jolley might want. He stood around a minute, waiting for the sheriff to respond, but when Jolley didn't say anything, Corley left.

On rare occasions, the painful thoughts that tortured Linda Pearson's nights invaded her conscious mind, and she had vague, disturbing memories while awake. This had been one of those days. The trouble began when Linda finally gave in to her mother's voice and got into the bathtub in the back of the house. She stood in the old tub wearing her underwear. She'd peeled off her pants and shirt but kept on her dingy cotton bra and panties.

Take off the rest of your clothes, Linda Louise. I just can't understand a grown girl like you not wanting to bathe more often.

"Mama, do I have to? I don't like to have all my clothes off. Daddy might come in."

Linda, you know your daddy had that stroke. He's not going to move out of that recliner. He can't walk well enough to come in here, and even if he did, he wouldn't know what he was seeing if he looked at you.

As Linda reached around her back to unsnap the brassiere, she thought she caught a glimpse of a man standing behind her. The shower scene in the movie *Psycho* flashed into her mind, but Linda feared something far more frightening to her than Anthony Perkins or Norman Bates. Grasping the loose cotton bra cups against her breasts, Linda turned. There was no one there. Not Norman Bates. Not her father.

Linda Louise, turn on the water.

"No," Linda said softly.

Turn on the water!

"No, I won't!" Linda screamed. She scrambled out of the tub, grabbed her dirty blouse and slacks and pulled them back on. When she left the house minutes later, she still wore the soiled shirt over her unhooked bra.

At the Downtown Diner, Courtney noticed that Miss Possum kept shaking her head back and forth as though denying something. Courtney was used to the woman's strange behavior but was surprised when Linda did something she'd never done before.

She left her waffle uneaten, got up, and shuffled away without even saying good-bye. Courtney thought she'd skipped out on the bill, but the money lay beside the untouched plate of food.

The clerk at the Shop & Save was equally puzzled when Linda Pearson stood in front of the beer case shaking her head back and forth, then went out of the store without her customary six-pack.

Bill Amick at Amick's Package Store over on Willow

Lane was even more shocked. Tennessee Linda hadn't been in his place in quite a while. Having gone to school with Linda, he remembered those wild days of her youth before she'd run off with that man she'd married. He knew she'd been back in town several years, but she hadn't shopped in his store half a dozen times since her return.

"Linda," Bill greeted her. "Long time no see. How's it going?"

"I need to buy a bottle," Linda answered and added in a lower tone, "Yes, Mama, I do need it. I have to have it, and today I'm going to get it no matter what you say."

"Same old brand?" Amick asked, reaching for a pint of Jack Daniel's and doing his best to ignore Linda's conversation with her dead mother.

"Yes, that's right, but let me have two of those, if you please."

Bill Amick rang up the purchase and accepted her money. "How have you been, Linda?" he asked as he handed her the bag and her change. "I heard about your losing your mom and your dad passing away so close to each other. That sure was tragic. I meant to send you a card or call you, but you know how it is."

"Don't worry about it, Bill. I surely do know how it is. I'm better some days than others." She turned away from him and said, "No, Mama. I'm not going to listen to you. I'm going to do what I gotta do." Linda walked out without waiting for Amick to say anything else.

At eight o'clock that Saturday night, Katie and Wade were at Mama Clyde's Gullah House ordering her special fried chicken dinner. Samantha was under the stars in Sam's outdoor Jacuzzi, and Tennessee Linda was into her second bottle of what had given her the nickname so many years ago.

Linda Louise, I don't know what's gotten into you. It's not even nine o'clock, and you know how I feel about you drinking liquor, even after nine.

"I know, Mama."

You should just pour the rest of that down the drain and go to sleep.

"No, Mama, maybe if I pour the rest of it down me, I can sleep, but not now. Sometimes you just gotta do what you gotta do."

I don't understand you, child.

"You never did, Mama. You never did."

What's that supposed to mean?

"It doesn't mean anything, Mama. Just let me drink enough so I won't think or dream. Tomorrow's another day. I'll get it back together then. Please just leave me alone tonight."

What about your poor old daddy sitting over there? You haven't even turned the television on for him.

"He's dead, Mama."

I know that, Linda Louise, but that doesn't mean you can't show him some consideration. You know he did everything he could to keep you from your troubles. What happened to you was not our fault. Your daddy and I did all we could.

"I know, Mama. I don't want to talk about Bert, okay?"

Just drink yourself into a stupor like you used to. I'm not even going to talk to you.

"Fine, Mama, fine."

Katie and Wade finished dinner before Wade confessed to

her that he needed fresh samples of her hair with roots for DNA comparison. She laughed and asked, "Do you plan to pull them out right here in the restaurant in front of God and everybody?"

"No, I thought I'd wait until we leave here." He held the chair for her and looked down at her feet. "Pretty sandals you're wearing," he said. Katie was glad she'd finally taken the time to polish her toenails a pearly pink.

Driving back to her apartment, Wade asked, "What exactly did Sally Brown say when you asked about Barker?"

"She said, 'No, the body you saw at the morgue isn't Frankie Barker.' That means he's alive, doesn't it?"

"Do you believe in this hoodoo stuff?" the sheriff questioned.

"I'm not sure. Do you?"

"Well, I think she told you the truth, but it doesn't necessarily mean Barker's alive. You asked about Frankie Barker. The man's name is really Fred or Frederick Barker, so there's no Frankie Barker whether he's our John Doe or not."

"Oh, damn!" Katie exclaimed, then added, "Excuse me. I know that wasn't a very teacherly thing to say, but I never thought about the Barker–John Doe business that way."

"I'm not one of your students. You can cuss around me."

"I try not to use profanity at any time, but you can count on the fact that my little ones never have and never will hear me say anything that's not professional. Not while they're my pupils, and I hope never when they're grown. I believe teachers should be role models, and . . ."

Sheriff Jolley's beeper went off, interrupting Katie. He pulled over and called in. "Sorry," he said to Katie when he'd completed the call. "I have to drop you off and go back to work."

"What's going on?"

"I'll tell you later. I did enjoy dinner though."

"I'd hoped you could stay and talk some more," Katie said. "Unless it would be as you say . . . inappropriate."

"Believe me, I'd rather be talking to you than doing what I'll be doing, but it can't be helped. I've got to go back to Charleston."

Once again, he checked Katie's apartment and made sure she had everything locked up before he left. Once again, he forgot the hair samples.

In her mind, Linda Pearson was many years younger as she lay scrunched up on the love seat. She'd run out of Jack Daniel's about the time she passed out, but her mind wasn't totally numbed. She remembered pulling into her and Bert's driveway after going to the beauty parlor. She'd wanted to have her hair cut, but Bert liked it long so she'd gotten a perm instead. The next-door neighbor was washing his car and had called out, "Nice curly do. Looks good."

Linda barely had the front door open when Bert snatched her in and snapped a pair of handcuffs on her wrists. She hated the cuffs and Bert knew it. That's why he put them on her anytime he was really mad. He grabbed Linda by her hair and pulled her to the bathroom. Quickly he produced another set of cuffs from his belt and used them to bind her already shackled hands to the showerhead. He snatched the shower massage loose and turned the cold water wide open, blasting her hair and face.

"How's that?" Bert's tone was as nasty as his expression.

"What do you think he'd say about your fine hairdo now?"

Linda struggled with the cuffs, trying to free her hands. She knew she couldn't release herself, but the urge to wipe the water from her face overpowered that knowledge. Bert continued to spray directly into her face intentionally. Linda gasped for breath. Could a person drown like this? Bert laughed. He dropped the massage hose and let it jerk around, spraying the tile. He reached out and began unbuttoning her drenched blouse.

"Did that cool you off or does my wife still think she's a hot little number? Maybe you need some more cooling off."

Without opening the remaining buttons, Bert ripped the blouse from Linda's body, threw it on the floor, then yanked off her bra and dropped it. Linda expected him to tear off her pants and rape her. She almost hoped he would. Frequently, when abuse led to sex, rape ended the scene, and he would leave her alone for a while afterwards. Instead, he turned off the water and left her still shackled in the shower stall.

Linda's drug of choice had always been alcohol, but she'd tried marijuana a few times as a teenager. Alteration of time was her main memory of those experiences. Now, in her nightmare, time altered as it had when she'd lived the scene in real life. It seemed that days, weeks, months, eons passed before Bert returned. In real life, Linda had known it had been a long time because her hair, slacks, and shoes had dried. Her arms and shoulders ached so horribly that she was almost glad to see him back, almost thought he might be going to end the episode.

"Well, well," Bert began, "has my little wife cooled off?"

Linda controlled her voice. If she showed anger or

begged, he would prolong the punishment. "Please let me go, Bert. Don't you want me to fix your dinner? I bought cornmeal and sour cream to fix that special cornbread you like so much."

"No, I've already eaten. You're not repentant enough."

Linda wanted to ask what she should repent, but she knew better than to say anything else.

"I thought you kept your hair long and straight for me, but now I know better. Not for your husband. Not for me. For other men. We can't have that, can we, Linda?" That's when Linda saw the scissors in his hand. "Do you want a wet cut or a dry cut?" He grabbed her head and locked it under his elbow. The pull of her arms from overhead was agonizing, but Linda didn't utter a word as Bert whacked her hair off as close to her scalp as possible.

"Now let's see how many men like your hair." He spit into her face. Linda hated that as much as she did the cuffs. It was worse when the cuffs kept her from wiping the saliva away.

"What's the matter? You don't like that? Let me wash it off for you!" Bert turned the water back on and sprayed it directly into her face, then lowered the nozzle.

When the biting-cold water sluiced over her breasts, the nipples stiffened. Bert reached out and brushed his hand roughly over them. "Look at that. Did Bert make that happen?" he asked.

Linda said nothing. She expected him to rape her there in the shower stall, but instead he unsnapped the cuffs holding her to the showerhead and shoved her into the bedroom with her hands still bound by the first set of cuffs. He only hit her a few times before the rape. In real life, he slept afterwards while she cried. Now, alone on the love seat, Linda's old friend Jack Daniel's finally erased the memory and mercifully granted her oblivion.

Teacher, teacher, little slut,
How I want to shut you up.
Always bossing me around,
But my gun can put you down.

Under his breath, Sheriff Jolley repeated the words written in red felt-tip marker on the creamy white wall over and over. He looked at Chief Legrand. "Hank, it's a nursery rhyme. Sing it to 'Twinkle, twinkle, little star.' It fits."

"So now we got a nut killing teachers and rewriting nursery rhymes. Didn't you say Katie told you her sister said he was a musician?"

"Claimed to be. Still doesn't make much sense. Why was the first victim a male if the perp's after teachers he classifies as sluts?"

Legrand looked past Jolley from the entry hall into the dainty floral-wallpapered living room crowded with forensics techs and photographers. "Do you want a closer look at the victim? You can go in if you want," he said.

"No, I can see enough from here. Same MO except the body wasn't moved to an alley, and he's gone all out to degrade her even more. What do you know about her?"

"Teacher named Patricia David. She was supposed to meet her boyfriend when he got off work a little after nine. She wasn't there to pick him up. He got mad and went off with some friends for a few beers. When his buddies dropped him off here, her car was out front, but she didn't answer the door. He thought she'd gone off with another man. Let himself in with his key, planning to wait and confront her. Instead, he found this." Henry waved his arm toward the murder scene.

"What about age? Forties?"

"No, mid-twenties. Twenty-six to be exact. What's interesting is that he cut off her fingers even though he left her in her own apartment, so the purpose wasn't to conceal her identity. I'm wondering if he'd planned to move the body and something interrupted him. Or did he just get so busy having fun with the markers that he changed his mind? Why get rid of fingerprints if you plan to leave the body in her own home displayed like this?"

Legrand took a pack of Marlboros from his pocket and opened the door. "I've got to step out and have a smoke."

"When you going to quit, Hank? You know those things will kill you."

"I lay off for a few weeks or so, but when I get called out to something like this, I wind up bumming them, so I started back carrying my own."

Standing on the small stoop at the front of the apartment, they both inhaled the salty Charleston air. It would have been a good scent on a bad night if the cigarette smoke weren't there.

"Hank, do you have a picture of this victim yet?"

"I'll get you a copy. The boyfriend gave us one. Signed 'Love always, Patty,' but I can tell you. She looked like Katie Wray. Younger, but basically, the same features. Almost exactly the same hair color. Even the style matches. We know she went to an educational supply store after work. I've got people tracking down what she did between then and when the boyfriend found her."

"What about him? Think he might have done it?"

"Not likely. Worked twelve hours. We'll check to see if he might have disappeared for a while, but my instinct says he's legitimately torn up about this. I sent him over to the ER with one of my men because he seemed to be in shock and was complaining of chest pains."

Chief Legrand carefully ground the cigarette out, rubbed the stub with his fingers, then put the butt in his pocket. "Don't want to add any evidence," he commented.

"The nursery rhyme and the fingers don't fit," Jolley said. "He wrote on the wall expecting it to be read, but like you said, the fingers weren't cut off to prevent fingerprints. The fingers may be souvenirs. The posing is new, isn't it? What position was your first teacher in? Was she posed too?"

"Nope, Shealy was just dumped."

"Damn it, Hank. No wonder the boyfriend's got chest pains. No face and her legs spread open like that with obscene graffiti all over her body. I didn't even know her, and it makes me sick. Can you imagine walking in and finding a woman you loved like that?"

"Know what surprised me, Wade? The boyfriend didn't cover her up. A lot of the time, when the victim's posed, if it's her husband or boyfriend who finds her, they cover up the body. He didn't touch a thing. Just backed out and called the authorities. Left her there naked and exposed like that with her face blown away."

"Maybe he watches *CSI* and *Forensics Files* and didn't want to destroy any evidence." Jolley paused. "I didn't know you'd had a posed victim before, Hank."

"Not many, but I read to keep up. You're right. At least he didn't mess up the evidence, if there is any."

"Now we've got two victims that were both schoolteachers and both looked like Katie Wray. I think I need to put surveillance on her."

"Couldn't hurt." Hank paused. "You interested in her, Wade?"

Jolley laughed self-consciously and then coughed. "Sometimes I think I could be, but we both know it would be a big mistake to even consider thinking about her until this case is closed."

"You lie, Wade Jolley. Just like you did when we were kids. Every time you lie, you cough or clear your throat first. You'd make a sorry poker player. I think maybe you're thinking about Katie Wray a lot, eh?"

"Maybe. Right now, I'm going to call my office and get someone over to her apartment to keep an eye on her. How much longer do you think you'll be here?"

"No telling. Those state guys are extremely thorough, and that medical examiner isn't known for rushing anything. He just got here right before you. I went ahead and called for state techs the minute I got the report. You know what we got, don't you, Wade? A serial killer who is obsessed with schoolteachers, and he's connected to your John Doe and to the woman you have your eye on. We've got a serial killer who's not wasting any time. Serial killers tend to start out with space between the murders. As time passes, the length of time between hits usually shortens. We've got two for sure, maybe three, in one week for starters. This is a spree. Get surveillance on Katie Wray."

SHOCKING SUNDAY

"OH, GOD, KATIE, you'll never believe what he did!" Glancing at the clock, Katie was surprised to see it was almost ten o'clock when she answered the telephone Sunday morning. When the phone had kept ringing and ringing, she'd rolled over and half consciously wondered why the machine wasn't taking the call. Then, as her mind had become fully alert, she'd remembered Sheriff Jolley's telephone call from Charleston in the middle of the night.

He'd asked her to disconnect her answering machine and take phone calls herself until he came by around midday. A little later, a deputy had shown up. He'd checked out Katie's apartment thoroughly, then advised her he'd be posted outside if she needed him.

When Katie finally answered the phone, she'd expected to hear Wade's voice, but the caller was Samantha. A distraught, sobbing Sam, gasping as though each breath would be her last.

"Calm down, Samantha," Katie consoled her. "I guess you're talking about Sam, right? What did he do?" She almost added "this time" to the question.

"We were together last night over at his house, but he insisted we come back to my apartment. He's never done that before. It was like he didn't want me at his place. After we went to bed, he got up about one o'clock this morning and said he had to go. He's never left in the middle of the night before. I've been by his house, and he's not there. I need you to go with me to find a willow tree."

"You need me to do what?"

"A weeping willow tree. Do you know where one is?" Samantha's sobs changed to whimpers and sniffles. "I drove down Willow Drive. Can you believe there's not a single weeping willow tree on that street?"

"Yes, I know that, and I also know where there's a willow tree, but I can't go anywhere until afternoon. The sheriff is coming by."

"Do you know what phase the moon is in?"

"What phase the moon is in?" Katie repeated after Samantha. She'd thought Sam wanted a tree branch for a lesson the next day. Now she didn't know what to believe.

"I'll come over about two o'clock." Sam ignored Katie's repetition of her question. "Will that be all right?"

"Why don't you make it four and we'll ride by his house again and see if he's back. Maybe he went out for milk or something."

Katie was glad Samantha had called and woke her up because Wade knocked on her door right before eleven. She offered him something to drink, and his acceptance seemed more than the usual gratitude for a simple cup of coffee. When she mentioned how tired he looked, he told her he'd been up all night and had just returned from Charleston.

"Why did you have to go back to Charleston?" Katie asked as she stirred cream and sugar into her coffee.

"Hank called me about another case."

"Another murder?"

"Yes, another teacher. The cases in Charleston are related, and probably tied in with my John Doe, who, by the way, still hasn't been identified."

"That's awful," Katie answered. "Are you hungry?"

"I hadn't thought about it, but I guess I am. Let's ride over to the diner and get something. We can talk there."

"I was offering to cook you brunch."

"Another time. I want your full attention while we talk. Besides, I can't stay long, and I'd rather you cook for me when we can spend some time together."

Katie wasn't really surprised to see Tennessee Linda sitting on her regular stool at the Downtown Diner counter when she and the sheriff entered. What did surprise her was that Wade went over to speak to Linda. Katie followed.

"Hello, Ms. Pearson," Jolley began in what Katie was beginning to think of as the sheriff's soothing tone.

"Why, hello, Sheriff Jolley, and hello, Teacher Girl," Linda replied. Katie nodded.

"Ms. Pearson," Wade said, "I just wanted to tell you anytime you want your yard cleaned up and all that kudzu removed, you just let me know. As a matter of fact, let me know if I can ever help you in any way."

"That's mighty kind, Sheriff Jolley, but I don't know of a thing I need."

"Well, you just remember to call on me anytime."

When Katie and Wade sat in a booth across the room, Katie said, "That was nice of you, Wade."

"That woman needs and deserves all the kindness in the world," he responded. "What do you want to eat?"

"Eggs and grits with cheese."

"Juice?"

"No, just coffee."

Wade placed the order and began telling Katie about the newest case in Charleston. Katie's eyes widened when he told her the victim was a teacher who matched her physical description. "If they match my description, they match Maggie's," Katie thought. "How on earth did my sister get mixed up with this man?" She shivered, though she wasn't cold. Where was Maggie? Was she a victim who hadn't been found yet?

"Did you notice the man sitting over there by the jukebox? He spent the night outside your apartment. You're his assignment for today. I'm going to have someone watching you until we have this thing solved."

"You're scaring me. Do you think the murderer's after me?" Wade was silent a full minute. The look in his eyes was haunted, and it was obvious he didn't want to answer her question. Finally, he spoke.

"I believe he's already killing you and Maggie by proxy. I've put out an all-points bulletin on Maggie. It seems he leaves the bodies where they will be found, which gives me encouragement that your sister is still alive because we haven't located her. On the other hand, how do we know how many others there might be that we don't know about because we haven't found them? We've concentrated on looking for Barker. Maybe we need to be searching landfills and wooded areas for concealed corpses."

Wade's words stunned Katie. Just as she opened her mouth to respond, a disturbance at the cash register distracted her and everyone else in the diner. A pretty little girl about three years old was screaming as though her heart would break. The man with her was attempting to open her clenched fist. The harder he tried to pry her fingers apart, the louder she yelled.

"It's the tip for the nice lady, Kelley," the man said, trying to console the child. "How many times have I told you not to take the money off the table? You have to do what Daddy tells you." The child shrieked even louder. Katie noticed that Tennessee Linda had slid off her stool and walked fairly briskly over to the cash register.

"Kelley!" The man's tone changed from cajoling to exasperated. Tennessee Linda reached the cash register and stood right beside the little girl. She held out a dollar bill.

"Let her have the money," Linda said softly.

The man turned toward the strange-looking lady with her pillowcase, weird makeup, and wild hair. "Excuse me," he said. "This is my child and it's my responsibility to teach her right from wrong. If I let her take tip money now, she'll wind up stealing when she's older."

Miraculously, the little girl stopped screaming and looked up, listening to the conversation. "Then let me trade her for the money," Linda answered. She knelt down and held out the dollar to the child. Her words were hardly more than a whisper. "Will you change my money for your money so Daddy can put it back on the table?"

Through her tears, the child smiled. She slowly opened her fingers. Her father snatched the money from the small hand. Linda gave a crisp dollar bill to her, and they both laughed. The man looked embarrassed. "Thanks, lady," he said. "It's my weekend to have her, and sometimes I don't know how to handle things. I want to be certain she learns right from wrong."

"Sure," Linda replied, "you're lucky to have such a sweet child."

"Yes, I am. Kelley, did you tell the nice lady thank you?"

"Thank you, pretty lady," the little girl said and smiled. She reached out and touched the tangled gray hair gently.

"Through the eyes of a child," Katie thought. "Maybe that's why I teach. Kids truly do see things from a different perspective."

"Put the money up," the man told the child. Kelley shook her head no. Tennessee Linda had turned and started to step away when the man said, "Let Daddy put it in your pocket."

Linda jerked as though she'd been struck by a bullet or a two-by-four. Her body lurched, then shook.

"No," she said quietly. Then louder. "No! No! No!" She bolted out of the diner. Through the plate glass beside their booth, Wade and Katie saw her run down the street.

"That was strange," Katie said.

"With everything that woman's been through, it's a wonder she isn't dead or crazy."

"Most folks do think she's nuts."

"Linda Pearson's not crazy. Maybe a little 'tetched' as my grandma would have called her," Wade said. "She's a whole lot eccentric, but all things considered, she's not bad. She's a survivor." Their food came and they began eating. "My grandma was quite a lady," Wade continued. "She died a few years back, but you would've liked her.

She used to say, 'There's losers, endurers, survivors, and winners.' Katie, I've already seen that you're a survivor. You've handled this past week well, and I think when I know you better, I'll find out you're a winner.'

Katie looked up into Wade's eyes. "Why, Sheriff Jolley, you'd better be careful. I might think that's an indication you want to get to know me better. That could be . . . inappropriate." She smiled at him, and though she didn't mean it to be, her expression was openly flirtatious.

Wade coughed. "Katie, I can't even think about anything except this case until it's solved." He turned and motioned to the waitress for more coffee.

Katie became serious. "Will there be someone with me at school, too? That could be awkward."

"I'd rather put you in an awkward position than a dead one."

"I hope you're exaggerating. You assure me I'll be safe, then you throw out lines like that."

"I told you what I think. I don't know when Barker will come after you, but I believe he will."

"Are you positive it's Barker now?"

"I believe it is, but if it's not him, I know it's a man."

"What makes you so sure? Couldn't it be a woman?"

"Not likely. The fact that the first two bodies were moved would indicate strength, and yes, I know there are some strong women. The positioning of Patricia David after he shot her also points to a man."

"Patricia David?"

"Last night's victim."

"There are plenty of women strong enough to move a body."

"Okay, I'll grant you that, but the MO is male, and I

FRAN RIZER

believe we're going to come up with semen on a lot of swabs that were taken. By the way, SLED has called in the FBI for a profile."

"I've read about that. They tell the person's age, job, kind of car, and everything, don't they?"

"Sometimes they do, and sometimes they're amazingly accurate about it."

The server removed their plates and refilled their cups. Katie looked around. Courtney wasn't working. "It's not really my business," Katie said, "but if you haven't been to bed yet, shouldn't you be drinking decaf?"

"No, I need the leaded version this morning. I doubt if I'll get to bed today. I shouldn't have even taken time out to eat, but I want to impress on you how serious you need to be about this. I'm sure you're on the killer's list. I've got someone watching you, but you've got to be careful and stay on the alert."

Katie noticed that her deputy walked to the register and paid for his breakfast as she and Wade stood up. He was out the door right in front of them. As they left the diner, Katie asked, "Why did you have me turn off the answering machine?"

"I'm glad you mentioned that. You can turn it back on. I noticed that your machine picks up on the third ring. Can you set it to ring more times before the machine kicks in?"

"It's new, but I'll read the instruction book to find out."

"Last night I had you turn it off so if he called you, he wouldn't become frustrated about getting a machine. I really don't want you to do anything that will make him mad enough to come after you right then. If he decides to talk to you, he needs to be able to reach you. A recording on the third ring could make him angry. That's the kind of

164

thing that might make him go straight over to where he's calling. I guess you could leave the machine on when you're not home and answer it quickly when you're there. Now that I think about it though, with you going to work Monday, it will be better if the machine is on so that if he calls, he can leave a message." Wade shook his head. "I can't even think straight right now."

Linda Pearson wandered aimlessly around town. She silently repeated the words over and over, words that echoed in her mind. Words that sizzled as painfully as South Carolina sidewalks burn bare feet in July. "Let Daddy put it in your pocket. Let Daddy put it in your pocket. Let Daddy put it in your pocket."

Through her confusion and pain, Linda found her way to the bookstore. She bought three crossword puzzle books and didn't notice the young auburn-haired man skulking among the display cases.

Linda Louise, you know you don't get three books in one day, and it's not even book day! What are you thinking of?

"Mama, just let me be. Please just let me be. You never believed me anyway. Just go away and leave me alone."

I don't know what's gotten into you lately. If I didn't know better, I'd think you were drinking Jack Daniel's all the time again instead of being a good girl and limiting yourself to beer.

"Maybe I was a good girl too often. Maybe I shouldn't have always been such a good girl and always done what I was told to do."

What on earth are you talking about? It's a wonder you weren't the death of me, child. What with all that drinking and carousing you did in school. Breaking your daddy's heart. Then running off with Bert. I know he didn't treat you good, but I think maybe you brought some of that on yourself, you know.

"Mama! How can you even say that? Nothing I could have said or done would have deserved what either of them did to me. Nothing. It took years for the shrinks to convince me of that, but you never believed me, and you never will. Leave me alone. Let me work the puzzles and stop thinking. If it takes three books to keep my mind off it, I'll buy three books. If it takes Jack Daniel's to let me sleep without having to live it all over again, I'll sleep with Jack Daniel's. Can't you see? I've gotta do what I've gotta do."

Linda Louise, you need to stop blaming everything on somebody else. You know your daddy and I tried our best to help you out of your trouble.

"Shut up!" Linda screamed. "Just shut the fuck up!"

Linda Louise, I didn't raise you to talk like that. I'm not going to say another word to you until you apologize!

"Good!"

Linda continued to walk. The day was gorgeous. Birds sang. Coastal Carolina weather at its best, but Linda saw nothing. Though she tried desperately to stop all thoughts, the words wouldn't go away: "Let Daddy put it in your pocket." Finally she found herself in front of the columned house where her troubles all started. She went in the gate, but turned away from the front porch steps. There was an old granite bench beside a huge oak tree around back. It faced the wooded area behind the house. Linda went to the bench, sat down, pulled a pen from her pillowcase, and began working a crossword puzzle in one of her new books.

Usually very skillful at crossword puzzles, Linda made repeated mistakes. She either couldn't think of a word at all, or she thought of the wrong word. Even as she read, she heard that sentence. Sometimes Linda worked puzzles for pleasure, and sometimes she used the crosswords to stop all thoughts except word meanings. Today it didn't matter. "Let Daddy put it in your pocket," echoed over and over in her mind.

Katie looked forward to Samantha coming over at four. She'd read the directions and changed her answering machine to pick up on the seventh ring. That should give her time to reach one of the phones no matter where she was in her tiny apartment. She'd also installed batteries in both of the landlines so the caller ID would work.

Wade had finally gotten the hair samples and assured her he would stay in touch. He'd looked tired and worried when he left, and the thought that crossed Katie's mind was unusual for her. She wished he could have stayed and let her hold him in her arms while he slept away all his weariness and worries. She shook her head as though that would chase away the unwelcome thoughts. She'd been hurt too much when she and Charles ended their marriage, and she'd seen Maggie involved with too many men who exemplified the expression "better left alone." Katie was once bitten, twice shy. The sheriff attracted her, but she wasn't really seeking a romantic involvement.

At five till four, Samantha bounced in like she'd never shed a tear in her life, much less sobbed her heart out that very morning.

"Ready to go, Katie? Can we take your car? Where's that weeping willow tree?"

"Slow down, Sam. Of course, we can take my rental."

"I'm sorry. It's not really so hot today. We can take the

Hyundai if you like. I shouldn't always want you to drive and use up your gas, especially when it's so expensive."

"Not so hot? It's way too scorching for me to ride to Beaufort with no air. I don't see how you survive it. Don't worry about taking my car. I want to drive. I hate to see the bill, but I love the rental. I was worried about you this morning. Can I assume you've heard from Sam and there was some reasonable explanation for last night."

"Oh, yes! He went home, and then he had a call from his brother. Their mom was having chest pains, and they took her to the emergency room, but she's all right. That's where he was."

"Did he give any reason why he left in the middle of the night?"

"Yes, and I didn't even have to ask him about it. He said he had some gas pains and didn't want to offend me. Katie, that man is so thoughtful. Wasn't it lucky that he'd gone home so his brother could reach him? I can't believe how lucky I am to have him in my life. This relationship is going to work. I just know it is."

"I guess so," Katie answered doubtfully. "Did you try his cell phone?"

"Oh, he only uses his cell phone for work."

As Katie drove into Beaufort where she knew of a weeping willow tree in a city park, Katie watched Samantha pull things from her handbag. "What are you doing?" Katie asked.

"Getting my stuff ready. Did you find out when we have a full moon?"

"No, Samantha, I didn't, but it's on calendars. You could have checked it yourself. Too busy riding by Sam's?"

"Don't be irritated with me, Katie. Someday you'll meet

someone who makes you feel like Sam makes me feel. I don't mean to impose on our friendship. It's just, you know, since Marc and I split, I guess you're my only real friend. Most of my old friends were couple friends. Now I have Sam, though." Samantha continued pulling things out of her purse and began wrapping masking tape around a matchbox.

"Sam, I'm not angry with you. There are things going on with this Frankie Barker business you don't know about and I'm worried about Maggie. My main concern with you is that I don't want you to get hurt."

"He won't hurt me. I told you, Katie. I love him."

"I know, and that scares me to death."

When Katie drove the car into the park, Sam was still wrapping the matchbox. "What's all this stuff, Sam?"

"It's the insurance I bought in Charleston. Magic spells to hold your man."

"WHAT?"

"That shop where we stopped in Charleston and you waited in the car for me. They sell spells."

"Magic spells? I think you're wasting your money with psychics and witches."

"The spells will work. I just know they will! For this one, you write what you want on parchment and seal it in a closed container. Then you bury it under a willow tree. It's best if it's under a full moon, but I can always do it again each time there's a full moon. I wrote that I want to be with Sam the rest of my life just like Sally Brown said I will." Samantha pulled a spoon from her purse. "This is one of my mother's silver spoons. It's best if you dig the hole with silver."

"Well, go do it and hope we don't get arrested," Katie

said as Samantha opened her car door.

Samantha bent over under the veil-like shelter of the weeping willow and quickly dug a small hole with the silver spoon. Katie decided that if anyone asked, she'd say Sam was under the tree looking for a lost contact lens. After Sam covered the tape-wrapped box with soil, she stood up and walked around the tree three times. Katie was afraid she'd start chanting, but Samantha walked silently.

Back at the car, Katie asked Sam, "Do you care where we eat? I'd like seafood."

"Any place is fine with me," Samantha said.

Katie mentally added, "Because she's not going to eat anything anyway."

"How about Steamer Willie's? We go right by there on the way back to Tanner."

"Fine. We can eat anywhere you want. I'm just so glad you knew where I could find a tree that wasn't in anybody's yard. I don't want to be caught trespassing."

"I think we could be doing something illegal digging in a public park, but how big a hole can you dig with a teaspoon? And you filled it back up anyway. I believe we were safe enough, but I have to be honest with you. I think you're wasting time and money on that foolishness."

"You have no idea how much I want to be with Sam forever."

The twisted tree branches around Steamer Willie's parking lot created an almost fairy-tale setting. The Spanish moss common to the area dipped so low that it actually brushed the antenna on the car when they pulled in. The interior was cool and inviting with shiny wooden tables, each centered with a sunken bucket for shells and other dining refuse. When Katie asked for a table out of the mainstream, the hostess seated them in a corner of the back room.

Katie ordered a frozen Margarita, and Samantha asked for ice water with lemon.

"Come on, Sam. Have something wonderful like a Margarita or a piña colada. If you've spent all your money buying spells, I'll treat."

"No, I really wouldn't enjoy it. Do you know how many calories are in those? Even a sip would gag me."

"Sam, I'm getting worried about you. When we first met, you'd have an occasional dessert or drink. As a matter of fact, when we first met, I thought you were absolutely the perfect size. Now you're too small. Do you eat at all? It seems you just slide your food around on your plate."

"You don't understand, Katie. Most men like tall, slim, long-legged women. I'm short. If I weigh even half an ounce too much, I'll look squatty."

"No way, Sam. You'd have to gain thirty pounds to even get near squatty."

"Look at yourself, Katie. You're tall. Do you know what I'd give to be as tall as you are? To be long-legged? To have hair like yours? Your hair is like mahogany. Mine is mouse brown unless I spend a fortune keeping it blond."

Katie laughed. "Well, I may be spending a few dollars on hair color myself soon. I found a gray one this week." She thought perhaps hair color to dye it red or blond might be a good idea. A way to change her from looking like the murder victims.

"You're kidding!"

"Nope!"

The server put their drinks on the table, and Katie took a long sip of the Margarita, licking salt off the rim of the glass as she drank.

"What'd you do?" Sam asked, referring to the gray hair.

"I pulled it out, of course."

"Aunt Sadie used to say that if you pull out one gray hair, two will grow back in its place."

"Oh, my, don't tell me that!" The server was back, pen and pad in hand, ready for them to order. Steamer Willie's was known for large servings with lots of sides. The average platter came full of entrée plus coleslaw, corn on the cob, home-fried potatoes, and fresh green beans as well as bread. Katie looked at the menu. "I think I'm going to pass on a platter and create my own combination off the appetizer list," she said. "I'll have spicy steamed shrimp, Oysters Rockefeller, and a side of stone crab claws."

The waitress wrote it all on her order pad, then turned to Samantha. "I'll just have the small shrimp cocktail," Sam said.

"Don't you want anything else?" asked Katie. "I told you it's my treat."

"No, that's what I want. Please don't bug me about it."

"Okay. Didn't mean to get into your business." Katie nodded dismissal toward the server, then continued, "I'd just like to see you eat more. You're skin and bone."

"No, I'm not, Katie. I'm fat. Just look at me!"

Samantha held up her bony right arm. "Look at that flab, Katie. Sometimes when I look in the mirror, I just feel sick about it."

"Have you thought about seeing a doctor, Sam?"

"Do you know one who will give me diet pills?" Sam responded in total sincerity.

Katie laughed. "It's not funny, Sam, and I'm not laughing at you. I'd just rather laugh than cry. Let's change the subject. Are you all ready for tomorrow?"

"Oh, sure. Are you?"

"Technically, I'm ready, but for the first time ever, I just don't want to go back. It's all this business I told you about."

"Yeah, that guy. Do they know yet if he's the one who was killed?"

"Not really." Katie took a long, salty draw from her Margarita and glanced around the room. "Oh, damn," she said softly. "Sam, you're going to have to drive home."

"Why? Do you plan to drink enough of those to get high?"

"No, but the man sitting over by the window is with the sheriff's department. I don't want to drive after he sees me drinking tequila."

"How do you know he's with the sheriff's department?"

"I know he is because the sheriff pointed him out to me this morning," Katie answered, thinking, "and he's probably wondering what the hell we buried under that willow tree."

Having eaten at the diner, Katie didn't expect to be really hungry, but when her food came, it all looked delicious. She ate every morsel. Sam took the shrimp off the fancy stemmed dish they came in and slid them around on the salad plate under the dish. She may have eaten two bites, but Katie wasn't even sure about that. Knowing Sam ate only once a day, Katie asked, "Have you already eaten today, Samantha?"

"No. I'm not really hungry. Why don't you eat these?"

Katie tried to play it off lightly. "Oh, so you want me to

be a tall, fat woman? I believe I've had enough."

Against Samantha's protests, Katie paid the entire bill. As they drove from Beaufort toward Tanner, Katie asked, "What other spells did you buy in Charleston, Sam?"

"I bought the one we did today, and I bought something called bottling. You take a piece of parchment and a new red ink pen. Write a name on the parchment seven times. Roll the paper toward yourself and then put it in a small container. I used an aspirin bottle I'd washed out. Mix vinegar and salt together and pour over the parchment until the jar is full. Seal it shut. Each day you shake the bottle as many times as you can. While you shake it, you say what it is you want the person to do. I bottled Sam. I shake the container and tell him to love me. If I find out for sure he's seeing another woman, I'll put her in a bottle and shake it. Then I'll tell her that Sam doesn't like her and she should leave him alone."

They turned off Highway 21 and headed toward Tanner.

"It really works, Katie. The lady promised me it really works."

"What is it, Sam? Is it black magic? Is it root or voodoo? What are you playing with here, Samantha? If you really believe it works, then you're fooling around with something you shouldn't take lightly," Katie cautioned.

"Lightly? I'm not taking it lightly, Katie. I want it to work. You don't know how bad I want the spells to work." Sam's reply had started adamantly, but she ended the statement in a pathetic, sad tone.

"You told me in the restaurant that your aunt told you if you pull out one gray hair, two will grow back. My mother was full of wisdom too. Now I'm going to share two of her sayings with you, Sam. First, she said if a relationship doesn't come easy and comfortable, it's not meant to be. I think you're working too hard for this."

"No, it's good, I tell you. When we're together, it's perfect! If we could just get married or live together, I wouldn't have all these doubts and problems. I'm fine when we're together. I only have fears when we're apart."

"Samantha, even if you marry him, you won't be together every minute of every day. I don't want to make you mad, but I'm not sure now if it's this Sam you want so desperately or if it's just a relationship you want."

"What difference does it make? Sally Brown says we'll be together for life. I'm just taking out a little insurance to make sure she's right. What was the other piece of advice your mother told you?"

"The other one is Maggie's favorite. She swears Mom told her, 'Don't ever put all your eggs in one bastard.' "

CHAPTER 11

LINDA PEARSON worked all the puzzles in her books before she walked over to the Piggly Wiggly. She bought two six-packs of beer and two packs of cigarettes. Her eyes were red from crying, and as Linda left the register, the clerk heard her mumble, "Let Daddy put it in your pocket."

She missed one turn on the way back to the house and had to walk several blocks out of her way. She came up on the back of the property off Elm Street instead of the front on Oak Street. After searching for an opening in the fence, she finally got into the woods behind her house. It was hard to find the house through the trees, but eventually she did. When she reached the bench in the backyard, she sat down by the oak tree. She popped the top off her first beer and slugged it down like she had the Jack Daniel's in those long-ago drinking games she'd played as a teenager.

Linda Louise, this is ridiculous. You don't need twelve beers, and you shouldn't be out here drinking in the yard.

"I told you not to talk to me."

I'm your mother. I'll talk to you anytime I want!

"If Amick's was open, I'd go buy me a fifth of Jack. What do you think of that, Mommie Dearest?"

Don't you talk to me like that. I took care of you my whole life. Don't you call me names! I never mistreated you like that woman in that old movie. Even when your trouble came, your daddy and I did our best to help you.

"But you never believed me. You didn't believe me ever! Just leave me alone a while. The beer will help. The thoughts will go away, and I'll be okay." Linda tossed the beer can across the yard, popped the top on another, and slugged down the second as rapidly as she had the first. That first six-pack was gone in no time at all. Before she opened the first beer of the second pack, Linda lit another cigarette. She sat still, smoking in silence. The alcohol wasn't working very well. She still heard those words: "Let Daddy put it in your pocket."

Somehow it seemed even worse when the memories came while she was awake, when she knew they were coming. She'd been fighting them off since she left the Downtown Diner that morning. She was an adult, over sixty years old, viewing what happened to a tiny little girl. Yet she felt, again, everything that happened to that three-year-old child.

The man was tall and handsome, and he carried her into the old-fashioned bathroom and stood her on the floor. He leaned across the claw-footed tub and turned on the water, checking carefully to be sure it wasn't too hot or too cold. He plugged the stopper into the drain, then turned his attention to the child.

Gently, the man untied the ribbon sash on the back of the little girl's dress. He carefully unbuttoned it. He talked to the child the entire time.

"Now let Daddy get this dress off so we can take our nice, warm bath," he said as he slipped the garment over her head. "Now sit down, Lindy Lou, so Daddy can take off your shoes."

The child obediently sat on the tile floor and stuck each foot up to him. He unsnapped the patent leather Mary Janes, took them off, then tugged off the frilly lace socks. "Stand up now so Daddy can take off your pretty panties." The little girl did as she was told. He pulled the ruffled panties down. Linda lifted one foot, then the other, so Daddy could remove that last item of clothing.

"Look at Lindy Lou, all pretty and pink," Daddy said. "Wonder if she's ticklish?" He tickled her under her arms and Linda giggled helplessly. Daddy's hands moved down the child's body. He slipped his left hand under her fanny, lifting her up on his arm. He cupped his right hand between her legs and held it still for a moment. "Wonder if Daddy can find Lindy Lou's special tickle tonight?" he asked. The child squirmed as the man's fingers began to probe between her legs. "Is this Lindy Lou's tickle?" he asked and wiggled one of his fingers. He moved the finger forward and asked again, "Or is this Lindy Lou's tickle?" He wiggled the finger again. Linda squirmed again. Then the man lifted the child into the bathtub.

He didn't use a washcloth. He rubbed soap between his hands until they were covered with bubbles, then he rubbed the lather all over her small body. Frequently he tickled her and she giggled. He splashed water over her to rinse the soap away. She looked like a golden-haired cherub, all beautiful, wet, and glistening.

"Now Daddy has to wash Lindy Lou's pocket," he said. The small child pulled back slightly. The man ignored her action and used his left hand to stand her up. With his right hand, he reached between her legs and inserted his finger into her tiny vagina. The child rose up on her tip toes attempting to move away, but her daddy held her still.

"Just a minute, Lindy Lou. If we don't get you all nice and clean, Mommy won't let me bathe you again. Be still while Daddy washes your pocket."

The grown Linda Pearson shook her head violently. She grabbed her pillow case with the rest of her beer and cigarettes and stomped into the house.

"You bastard!" she shouted at the empty recliner. "You goddamned bastard! I was just a baby, just a baby!" She sat at the table and drank the rest of the beer knowing it would make her sleepy and knowing that the sleep might be filled with dreams. Her fears came true.

Linda lay on the love seat in a tight fetal position. Once again she could see herself as a child, but in her dream state, she was able not only to see herself, but also to feel what the child experienced. She was six years old, and Mommy had gone to spend a few days with her aunt, who was having a baby. Mommy had left Linda with Daddy.

By now, Linda was accustomed to Daddy having to play with her tickle and wash her pocket when he bathed her. Sometimes she tried to tell him no, but Daddy always said that if he didn't bathe her right, Mommy would make him leave. She didn't understand because Mommy never paid much attention to washing her tickle or her pocket. In fact, Mommy didn't seem to even know what she was talking about when she'd dared ask her something about her pocket one time. When she told Daddy, he told her not to talk to Mommy about it again.

After Daddy finished bathing her, he wrapped her in a big fuzzy towel and carried her out of the bathroom into her bedroom. Instead of putting her nightgown on, he lay the child on her bed, turned around, and shut the door.

"See, Lindy Lou, Daddy has a big tickle," he said and slid down his pajama bottoms. Linda couldn't stop staring at the thing in front of Daddy. It stuck straight out and looked enormous to the little girl. He stepped closer to the bed. "Do you want to touch Daddy's tickle?" he asked.

"No," Linda whispered, afraid, but not quite sure why she was scared. Daddy's touching was uncomfortable physically and emotionally as well as frightening. Linda was too young to distinguish her feelings and would not have had words to describe them. She only knew that Daddy got a strange look on his face sometimes during her bath. She didn't like it when he looked like that.

"Yes, touch Daddy's tickle. It won't hurt you, Lindy Lou. Daddy touches Lindy's tickle and makes it feel good. Touch Daddy's tickle so it will feel good too." He took her hand and guided it onto himself. It felt different from anything Linda had ever touched before. Daddy began to tremble. "Let Daddy put it in your pocket," he moaned. Then he pushed Linda down on her back, spread her legs with his hand, and thrust his hard penis directly into his six-year-old daughter.

The child in the dream screamed in agony, and the woman on the love seat screamed now, and in the grown Linda Pearson's mind, blood spread over the bed, onto the floor, and saturated the walls like it did beside the elevator in the Overlook Hotel in that old movie, *The Shining*.

Linda screamed, but there was no one to help her, just as there had been no one there to save that innocent child.

> *Patty cake, patty cake,*
> *Mr. Law Man,*
> *You'll never catch me*
> *As fast as I am.*

Shug sang the rhyme over and over, ending it each time with his loud, maniacal laughter. The first teacher he'd ever "known" had loved for him to make up his rhymes when he was over at her place or in the supply closet after school. Of course, she'd called them poems.

It was a damn good thing he'd been naked when he finished off Miss Patty. A shower at her place after he'd put her back on the couch, wiped her off, and written his messages had enabled him to return to the hotel room all clean.

Screw Charleston. Shug was ready to move on. He considered going on up to Myrtle Beach, but that was probably where Susan and his father would tell the cops he'd go. They both knew how much he loved the ocean, and that particular stretch of South Carolina coast between Garden City and Myrtle Beach was his favorite.

Shug inhaled and almost retched with the stink of the room. Foul odor seeped from his bass case. He wished he'd thought to put his souvenirs in little jars of alcohol. Maybe they'd make a nice gift for Maggie. Screw Charleston. The killer loaded his belongings into the Ford and put his gun and prepaid cell phone on the seat beside him. He headed back down Highway 17—toward Tanner.

Only twenty miles out of Charleston, Shug changed his mind. He had unfinished business in Myrtle Beach. Might as well go there first, before taking gifts back to Tanner. He did a U-turn and headed in the opposite direction.

MONDAY
MADNESS

CHAPTER 12

CORLEY CHARGED into the sheriff's office so excited that he was almost shouting. "Chief, did you have your radio on? Did you hear the request?"

Jolley winced at the name "Chief," but ignored it. "Hear what?" he asked.

"I was listening to 102.7 on the way in. The special requests show. The DJ played one for a teacher from Frankie. The song was that old seventies rock tune 'Maggie May' by Rod Stewart. Sheriff Jolley, it had to be Barker. That's way too much to be a coincidence, don't you think?"

The sheriff looked up from the papers he'd been reading. "What'd the caller say and do they have him recorded?"

"I'm going to call the station now. I think most calls on that station are delayed, so they should have it recorded."

"Make it fast. Henry Legrand called. The feds are in Charleston now, and we've been invited to sit in on the preliminary profiling. There are several jurisdictions involved, and they'll all be represented. Special Agent John Gross is there. They're starting at ten this morning, so we need to be out of here in about fifteen minutes."

Corley's eyes lit up at Gross's name. Almost everyone in law enforcement had heard of him. He was one of the top profilers. "I'm going?" Corley asked.

"*We're* going."

The sheriff had expected a lot of people to be at the meeting, but he still wasn't prepared for the extra chairs around the giant table in Charleston PD's largest conference room. Hank met him and Corley, then gestured toward the two remaining seats. The sheriff glanced at his watch. 9:45 A.M. Apparently, everyone was as eager to hear this guy as he was.

Jolley recognized several of the officers, both local and state, but he could've ID'ed Gross if the room had been filled with strangers. Well over six feet tall, he was dark-skinned and wore an expensive suit of an even deeper hue. He was the total professional. If Wade had answered a knock at his door and seen this man, his first thought would've been "FBI." Like several African-Americans Jolley knew, the man's age was indeterminable. His skin was unlined, even around his remarkable obsidian eyes, but his short gray hair and the respect he'd earned in his field belied his youthful appearance.

"Good morning," Chief Legrand said. "Everyone's here now and since we're all eager to begin, let's get started. This is Special Agent John Gross. We've all heard of him, and I feel we're lucky that he's been sent to help us. It's all yours, Agent Gross," Hank said and nodded toward him.

"First," Gross remained standing as he shuffled through several folders on the table, "I've examined your reports, and while there are things I want to see for myself, I'm prepared to share some preliminary observations. We have a serial killer who is either killing at a rapid speed from the onset or has killed secretly before and has accelerated frequency now that he's decided to allow the crimes to become public. In case that's what has happened, we're checking for any missing teachers in this or surrounding states for the past two years.

"Three murders in a week is a killing spree. You'll have to stop him because spree killers don't stop themselves." Gross paused, obviously for dramatic effect, and it worked. Every person in the room moved slightly forward in their chairs.

"What we're looking for is similarity of victims. The first is an unknown male. Second and third are both female teachers who shared striking physical similarities. I've viewed these three bodies and examined the postmortem reports. Even though there are no faces, I'm prepared to state that aside from gender, the three of them probably looked alike. The John Doe victim was slender and approximately the same height and weight as the females. Hair color was also a similar shade, and length of hair was comparable. Based on this, we can say our perpetrator is seeking a certain type of victim.

"The second similarity we see is the MO. All three victims were shot in the back of the head multiple times. Hands were mutilated on each of them. Postmortems indicate the mutilations were the same. The first two bodies were moved after death. The third was found at the scene of the crime. The third event also provided us with the murderer's first attempt to communicate. It's possible the rhyme was put on the wall for the victim, but in all probability, it was written for us, the law enforcement agencies involved in this case. The communication is in the form of a nursery rhyme which ties in with his preference for teachers." Gross took a sip of water.

"Ladies," the agent said, nodding in turn toward each of the two females in the room, "and gentlemen." His eyes scanned the room. "I refer to our killer as 'he' because I have no doubt that we are dealing with a man and that the same man killed the John Doe in Tanner and both of the teachers in Charleston." Gross paused and looked around the room slowly and solemnly.

"Sir," Corley began before a stern look from Jolley silenced him.

Gross turned his gaze toward Corley. "Officer, I appreciate your eagerness, but I'll give you the opportunity for questions at the conclusion of my summary." He looked back at the group and continued, "I was called in to profile your perpetrator, and I say 'your' because right now he's killed in two jurisdictions and the capital city of this state is also represented here because the prime suspect makes his usual residence in Columbia. Your state agency, SLED, is present because they were correctly called in from the beginning as we know it.

"Chief Legrand," he nodded at Henry, "has asked for federal assistance and based on my findings, I'm recommending to each of you that every jurisdiction involved cooperate fully with each other.

"The posing of Patricia David's body clearly shows escalation in the UNSUB's anger. As I profile this killer, he's just beginning. He profiles as a paradox. The method of death is consistent with executions. The elimination of faces shows a desire to disassociate himself from his victims. This generally indicates the perpetrator knew the victim prior to the crime, and, in agreement with this, I'm convinced these are not random victims.

"Removal of fingertips shows a desire for anonymity of victims, yet the third victim was left in her apartment with a message on the wall. Thirty years ago, I would have profiled this killer as a 'Ted Bundy' type. Young, physically attractive, educated, able to converse with and gain the confidence of whomever he encounters. I would have told you that he lives alone, moves frequently, and probably drives an old Volkswagen Beetle." Once again, the man paused for dramatic effect.

"Most of that is still true; however, there aren't too many old VWs still on the road, so we'll retract that, and there's an element in this case that changes other parts of the profile.

"When Blair County Sheriff's Department investigated the John Doe body, there was a weapon nearby that led to a woman who'd spent the summer with a man named Fred Barker. She'd put this man out just the day before. It appeared probable from the beginning that Barker is either the killer or the John Doe first victim. Barker is missing.

"Since then, Barker's car has been discovered with evidence indicating the first murder took place in it with the victim sitting in the passenger side. Far from a ragged old VW, this car is an almost new Alfa Romeo. Forensics has failed to positively identify the victim. Speculation remains that he is either Barker or was murdered by

Barker." He stopped and surveyed the room slowly.

"In the past, Barker has moved out, gone home for a while, then sought another teacher. What was different this time? What triggered Barker to go on a killing spree?" Another dramatic pause and a sip of water.

"Rejection! Pure and simple. The curse of man since Adam. This woman rejected him before he was ready to move on. She's now missing, and her sister is frantic. The sister bears a striking resemblance to the woman who rejected our UNSUB. He's teaching her a lesson, a hard lesson. Which one of you is Sheriff Jolley?"

Wade nodded. Gross looked at him eye to eye. "I understand you've put a guard on that woman. Is there anything new?"

"Yes, sir, there is. Just this morning someone called in a request to the oldies rock station and dedicated the Rod Stewart song 'Maggie May' to a teacher named Maggie. The woman Barker spent the summer with is named Maggie. We have her sister under surveillance. The station uses a delay system, so they had a recording of the request. We'll be playing a copy of it for Ms. Katie Wray when we return to Tanner. Of course, we're hoping she can identify the voice, but she only heard Barker's voice in the background when she spoke with her sister by telephone. We'll also have local authorities play the recording for Barker's wife in Columbia."

"Sheriff Jolley, I suggest that when a man wants to catch a shark, he chums the water before baiting. You have bait available. This case calls for proactive techniques. I'm not suggesting you just throw Katie Wray into the chum unprotected, but unless you can lure him in, this man will kill and kill over and over again. The mental illness also makes predictability impossible. There's no telling what kind of rampage might be brewing inside him."

The FBI agent closed his eyes and thrust his shoulders back. He began to snap his fingers and pat his foot. When the rhythm was established, in an amazingly Rod Stewart sounding voice, he belted out:

Wake up, Maggie, I think I got something to say to you.
It's late September and I really should be back at school.
I know I keep you amused, but I feel I'm being used.
Aw, Maggie, I couldn't have tried anymore.
You led me away from home just to save you from being
    alone.
You stole my heart and that's what really hurts
The morning sun when it's in your face really shows
    your age.

Gross stopped abruptly and cleared his throat. "I believe the song ends like this:

Oh, Maggie, I wish I'd never seen your face
You made a first-class fool outta me
You stole my heart, but I love you anyway
Maggie, I wish I'd never seen your face.

The officers applauded, and Agent Gross laughed. "My apologies for the singing, ladies and gentlemen, but listen to the words. It really fits Barker's situation. We may not need a plan to use Ms. Wray for bait. He may already be planning to hit her next.

"I'm also suggesting that Chief Legrand have Barker's wife and father interviewed again. We need any information we can obtain on other teachers Barker's romanced. That's about all I can tell you now. There'll be more as I get deeper into these cases. I believe I've covered everything, but if anyone has a question, the floor is open."

Most of the questions were repetitious. One of the officers hadn't seen or heard the "Teacher, Teacher" rhyme and wanted details. Another questioned the postmortem reports. Wade had a problem with Gross having the John Doe autopsy results before he did on his own case, but said nothing. No point in riling the feds, plus, personally, he felt the man was right on target except for wanting to use Katie as bait. It would have suited Wade to ship her off to parts unknown for safekeeping until Barker was locked away.

When the session ended, Gross looked at Corley and asked, "Sir, didn't you have a question earlier?"

"You've already answered it," Corley responded.

Hank told Wade he was sending out to a deli for lunch and invited him and Corley to stay.

"No," Jolley answered, "we need to get on back." Hank walked outside with Wade while Corley went for the car.

"I don't blame you," Chief Legrand said. "I think I'd put my best man on Katie, or are you planning to guard her yourself."

"I want to, Hank. Believe me, I'd like to do that, but unless I know he's coming for her, I can't very well bump myself down to surveillance. This is our biggest case right now, but there are other situations in Tanner that need my attention also."

"How about Corley? He's one of your top men, isn't he?"

"Yes, he's better trained and more experienced than most

of my men. He's had an attitude about Katie from the get-go, but I'll make decisions about that after I get back and listen to the tape. That might tell us for certain if it's Barker we're after."

"Gross seems sure."

"Yes, but I still want to hear what Katie says. That'll be proof to me."

"Hey, Wade, we go back too far. You just want to get back and make sure she's okay, right?"

"Yeah, you're right." Corley pulled up in the cruiser. "Here's the car," the sheriff commented, then added, "I'll be in touch."

On Highway 17, headed back to Tanner, the sheriff told Corley he was considering giving him a shift guarding Katie. Corley seemed pleased.

"I'm surprised," Jolley added. "I thought you might consider that beneath your education and experience."

"Chief, I mean Sheriff, it's the opportunity of a lifetime. I hope the bastard comes when I'm with her. I'll get him." They rode silently about ten miles. The sheriff was hoping exactly the opposite. He wanted to collar the killer without his ever getting near Katie Wray.

Linda Pearson spent the morning sleeping. Totally dream-free for a change, she slept long and hard. There were no daddies, husbands, or mamas in her mind.

When she woke, she went to the kitchen, removed the ATM card from beneath the canister, and headed through the parlor. She turned back, returned to the kitchen, and wet a kitchen cloth under the ancient tap. Linda opened the pantry door. A small mirror hung on the back of the door. Peering into the mirror, Linda scrubbed her face.

She reached to the rear of the pantry and pulled out a tarnished, silver-handled hairbrush. Leaning forward, she brushed her thick hair vigorously, shook it, and looked in the mirror without noticing she'd forgotten her makeup.

Moving her head back and forth in a negative motion, Linda closed the pantry. She picked up the pillowcase from the kitchen counter and went out the back door. She glanced at the stone bench, saw a crossword puzzle book lying on it, picked it up, and dropped it into the pillowcase. No memory of what had consumed her mind when she left the book there invaded her consciousness. Linda was humming as she walked around the house and out the front gate.

She walked briskly into the drugstore and bought shampoo, conditioner, and cigarettes. At the Downtown Diner, Linda Pearson ate every bit of her waffle and jelly.

"Coatney," she said to the waitress, "you know the only way to survive in this world is to do what you gotta do." Courtney Williams stood poised behind the counter with a counter cloth in one hand and an order book in the other. It had been a long while since she'd seen Miss Possum look so good. Her hair was less tangled, and her blue eyes were clear and shining.

"What you gotta do, Miss Possum?" Courtney asked.

"I gotta have me some dessert today." Linda ordered a piece of chocolate cream pie and left not a crumb on the plate. She walked out with a perkiness in her step that made Courtney Williams feel good the rest of the day.

When Linda opened the front gate, she actually saw the house for the first time in months. She wondered if the man at the bank would authorize repairs and paint. She walked across the porch to the broken railing and tried to pull some of the kudzu out from between the posts. It wouldn't budge, and tendrils had snaked across the floorboards and woven themselves through holes in the wood.

She thought there might be an ax in the garage out back, but the last time Linda had tried to get in to see Daddy's old car in there, the whole building had looked like a kudzu-covered hump. Though she'd known where the doors were, she'd been unable to get to them through the cursed vine.

Her mind flashed to the kitchen pantry. The only food in there was a few canned goods bought before Daddy died, and Linda kept her personal things on one shelf, but some small tools were piled on the floor at the back.

Linda found a hatchet at the bottom of the heap. Hours later, most of the kudzu was off the railing and the porch.

Sweat drenched Linda from head to toe, and her whole body already ached, but it was a good feeling. She went around back, actually considering tackling the kudzu on the garage, but reality set in. The garage would be a tremendous task. Better to start it early one morning. She glanced at the stone bench, and a momentary thought brought a glimpse of the scene she'd remembered sitting there. "Let Daddy put it in your pocket." The words whispered softly in her head. Linda dropped the hatchet in front of the garage and ran back to the front door of the house. Inside, she said adamantly to the empty recliner, "You will not ruin my good day!"

In the kitchen, Linda set an old beige Tupperware pitcher by the sink to pour water over her hair. She had the shampoo opened before she stopped and said aloud, "Sometimes you gotta do what you gotta do." She walked purposefully to the bathroom in the back of the house.

Linda Pearson filled the old claw-footed tub with water, stripped down, and climbed in. She had no rituals like Katie Wray. There was no music. No glass of wine. No bath oil beads, and she didn't slide down under the water in pleasure. Showers and tubs would never be places of comfort to Linda Pearson. There was a job to be done, and since sometimes "you gotta do what you gotta do," Linda did it.

She scrubbed every inch of her body, even between her toes. She shampooed her hair three times, then left the conditioner on a full ten minutes before rinsing it out with clean water.

By the time Katie and Samantha said, "Good-bye, see you tomorrow," to each of the students, Linda Pearson was wearing clean clothes and sitting on the front step letting that long, lustrous, gray-streaked mane dry in the sun.

Samantha stood in Katie's classroom before Katie returned from seeing her students onto their buses.

"How'd it go?" the impeccably dressed Katie Wray asked Sam when she saw her there waiting.

"Fine. Looks like a good group this year. How do yours look?"

"Since almost three-fourths of them were in your class last year, they're well prepared. I should have a good year." Katie began packing things into her briefcase. "You know, Sam, you really are an excellent first-grade teacher. I can see your influence and teaching in students you taught the year before from their very first day in second grade."

"Thanks, Katie. Listen, before we go to the meeting, do you know how to cook that stuff with shrimp and sausage and corn all in one pot?"

"Beaufort stew?"

"He called it something else."

"Same difference. Sure, I know how to cook it. Charles loved that stew."

"Sam's birthday's in a couple of weeks and he wants me to cook that for him. He's out of town for a few days. If I buy everything, can you come over tonight and show me how to do it?"

"There's nothing to it. I can write it down for you."

"No, I want it to be perfect. Sam's out of town. I'll be home alone. Please come. It'll be fun to practice cooking with you there."

"Okay." Katie picked up her purse and briefcase. Samantha grabbed her canvas tote bag, and they went into the corridor. A heavyset man who had been leaning against the wall followed them down the hall.

"Who's the man behind us?" Sam asked. "Do we have a new male teacher?"

"No," Katie answered. "He's one of Sheriff Jolley's men. Did you read about the schoolteachers killed in Charleston?"

"Yes, I saw it on the news. It scared the dickens out of me. When I first looked up at the television screen, I thought it was a picture of you!"

"Well, the sheriff thinks the Frankie I told you about is involved in those murders in Charleston and the dead man they found here last week. That guy's watching me like the deputy Sunday in case Frankie tries to contact me."

"Geez!" Samantha exclaimed, then immediately went

back to thinking of Sam's upcoming birthday dinner. "Can you make me a list? I'll pick up the ingredients on the way home. What time will you be over?"

"The earlier, the better. I want to get a good night's rest."

"Since we're cooking after you get there, how about five or five-thirty?"

"Perfect!"

When they reached the library doors, Katie saw Wade. He grinned at her, and Katie hoped he'd come to tell her the case was solved.

"I need to talk to you," he said, and she could tell from his tone that this wasn't good news."

"I'm supposed to go to a faculty meeting."

"It's important."

Katie turned to Sam. "Get shrimp, smoked sausage, corn on the cob, an onion, couple of potatoes if you want 'em. No, forget the potatoes. You won't eat starches anyway."

"But Sam eats potatoes, and I want it to be just like I'll do it for his birthday."

"Okay, get the potatoes. I eat potatoes. And buy a can of Old Bay Crab Seasoning. You'll need lemons and cocktail sauce, too—the kind with horseradish in it. Tell the principal I'm with the sheriff."

Wade smiled as Samantha turned away and said, "Frogmore stew?"

"That's it!" Samantha almost shouted as she turned back toward Katie and Jolley. "That's what Sam called it. Do you know how to make it?" she asked the sheriff.

"Sure do. Grew up on Frogmore stew."

"Is it the same as Beaufort stew? Katie knows how to make Beaufort stew, but Sam wants Frogmore. If you can, come over with Katie at five-thirty. You can show us the difference between Beaufort stew and Frogmore stew."

"I might just do that," the sheriff answered. He escorted Katie out to his car and opened the door for her. "This won't take long," he said. "Then you can go back to your meeting."

Katie laughed. "I don't want to go back to the meeting. I'm going home."

"Thought you were going to teach your little friend how to make Beaufort stew."

"But she wants to make Frogmore stew," Katie teased.

"It's the same thing."

"I know that and you know that, but I don't think Samantha believes it."

The deputy got in his patrol car and watched them. Wade nodded toward him. "Has he gotten in your way?"

"Not really, and the kids didn't seem to even notice him."

"Good, because there's going to be someone with you until this is over. I've just come back from Charleston. The FBI profiler thinks our John Doe is another of Barker's victims, not Barker." He opened the console and took out a CD.

"Katie, when I was at your house, you were listening to '70s rock. When your radio's on, what station do you listen to?"

"102.7."

"Did you listen to them this morning on your way to work?"

"No, I get tired of the DJ's silliness. I played a CD. Why?"

"A man called in a dedication about the time you

would've been on the way to work. This is a recording of it. They do delayed calls, so we were able to get a copy. I want you to listen to it."

"Play it."

Wade slid the CD into the player.

"Here's our next caller. Go ahead. You're on the air. What's it gonna be and who's it for?"

"How about an old Rod Stewart for a pretty teacher? We sure didn't have teachers like Maggie when I was in school."

Katie gasped, and Jolley hit "pause."

"That's Frankie," Katie whispered. "That's his voice. I've heard him talking to Maggie when she was on the phone with me, and Maggie told me he used to say that all the time. She'd tell him that line is older than public education, but he'd just laugh. She said he loved my old Rod Stewart recordings. The song's gonna be 'Maggie May,' isn't it?"

"Yes, Katie. That's what he requested. Do you want to hear the rest of it?"

"Why not? Frankie used to sing 'Maggie May' to my sister. Rod Stewart definitely sings it better than he did when I heard him singing to her while she tried to talk to me on the phone. He couldn't stand not being the center of attention. He was even jealous of her talking to me. So—Frankie's alive. Then who'd he shoot in his . . ." Her lip quivered. ". . . his, his car?" She managed to finish the question before her face crumpled.

Wade sat, unsure of what to do while Katie cried. Lord knows the woman had reason to cry. She was probably scared to death both for herself and her sister. In any other situation, he'd have patted her shoulder or done something, but he didn't quite think the sheriff of Blair County should be hugging or patting a teacher in the school parking lot, especially with a deputy watching.

He did, however, hand her a tissue. Katie wiped her eyes and tried to smile. "I'm sorry," she managed to say.

"It's okay. I can imagine you're experiencing all kinds of emotions right now." He reached over and patted her hand, then thought, "Too little is worse than nothing at all," and pulled his hand back.

"Does he say anything else?"

"Yes."

"Then play the rest." She sat back, stony-faced.

"If it's for someone named Maggie, I guess you want to hear 'Maggie May,' " said the DJ.

"You got it! Play 'Maggie May' for Maggie the teacher, and, Maggie, I just want you to know you can't save face, so don't even try."

Sheriff Jolley and Katie sat silently in the car while Rod Stewart accused Maggie May of leading him away from his home, stealing his soul, and hurting him. When Stewart finished with, "Maggie, I wish I'd never seen your face. I'll get on back home one of these days," Wade asked Katie, "You're positive that's Barker?"

"No doubt at all. I recognize the voice and the words. 'You can't save face' is from the song but it's a threat, too. Look what he's done to the faces of his victims."

"Yes, I'm afraid it is, but I'm going to have someone watching you every minute."

Even with red-rimmed eyes and tear-streaked makeup, Katie's grin was flirtatious. "*Every* minute?"

"Well, you'll be protected every minute. Corley and I are going to pull shifts, too."

"You? You're the sheriff. Why would . . . oh, you really think he's coming after me, don't you?"

"I'm afraid so."

"Why don't you pull the early shift and eat Beaufort stew with Sam and me? I'm sure there'll be enough, or do all of my bodyguards have to stay in the hall and car like the deputy does?"

"Actually, I can show you two ladies a thing or two about making Frogmore stew. You'll be surprised what a good cook I am."

"That'll thrill Samantha. She's learning to cook for this guy she's dating. She'll appreciate a male's opinion."

"Why don't I just pick you up at five?" Katie nodded consent, and Wade added, "Before you get in your car and leave, let me tell the deputy I'll relieve him at five."

"I'll head on home and be ready when you get there. Will you really do the cooking?"

"Sure!" The sheriff grinned, "It will be my first time ever to prepare dinner for two pretty teachers."

Katie and Samantha sat on stools in Sam's kitchen and watched Wade cook for them. The sheriff kept up a running monologue of instructions, jokes, and off-the-wall commentary. Katie laughed and Samantha giggled, "You should be on *Chopped* on the television cooking channel."

When Jolley went out to his car for a few minutes, Sam whispered, "You oughta go after him, Katie. He's cute." Katie admitted to Sam and to herself that Wade Jolley was indeed attractive with his sandy brown hair in his face and Sam's apron over his jeans. He was also entertaining and extremely charming.

Katie felt a pang of jealousy wondering, "Is that extra flair for me, or is it for Samantha's benefit? Is he especially attracted to tiny, young blondes?"

As Wade announced dinner was ready, someone beat on the door. Not a knock. It was pounding. The playful Wade reverted to Sheriff Jolley.

"Let me get it," he said as he walked briskly around the two of them toward the front door. Katie was hoping it was Samantha's friend Sam. She really wanted to get a look at "Mr. Wonderful."

"Who is it?" Jolley demanded in his sheriff's voice. Katie could picture him pulling a gun.

"Samantha?" The voice from outside was female. "Is this Samantha Branham's apartment?"

"Who is it?" the sheriff repeated.

"Aimee Martin from school."

"Oh," said Samantha, "let her in."

The minute Wade unlocked the door, Aimee charged through it. She looked different from the Miss Martin they saw at school. Her skirt was a little tighter; her blouse, a little more revealing; and her heels, a little higher. "Oh, Katie," she gasped, "I didn't know you were here. I walked here from Kenny B's. I don't have my car, and I just remembered that Sam lives near. Can one of you give me a ride home?"

"We're just about to eat," Samantha answered. "Have you had dinner? Wade's cooked Frogmore stew. Oh, I guess I should do introductions." She looked at the sheriff, "Do I introduce you as Sheriff Jolley or Wade?"

"Oh," Aimee interrupted, "when you came to the school to see Katie, I thought it was business."

"It was," replied Wade, "but this stew is going to be pure pleasure. Add another plate, ladies. Dinner is ready."

Everyone except Sam ate several servings. Samantha pulled her usual trick of moving bits of food around on her plate but eating very little. Four people loading one dishwasher was crowded, but fun. Katie felt more relaxed than she had in a week. For a few minutes, there were no thoughts of Maggie.

"You can come cook anytime," Samantha exclaimed to Wade.

"Your chef would be most happy to cook for you lovely ladies again." Wade replied enthusiastically, then added matter-of-factly, "especially since I live right around the corner."

When the kitchen was clean, Sam served coffee in the living room. "Is your car broken down somewhere?" Wade asked Aimee. "Do we need to check on it?"

"No, my car's back at my apartment. My friend Suzanne, maybe I should say ex-friend after tonight, called this afternoon and demanded I go to Kenny B's for happy hour with her. I agreed to meet her, but she insisted on picking me up. Said she had her eye on a guy she met there last week and wanted to come in with someone so it wouldn't look like she was stalking him."

"What happened?" asked Katie.

"We walked in. You know how Kenny B's is during happy hour. The place was packed. Some folks call Kenny B's upscale. I think of them as the plastic people with every hair and drop of makeup perfectly placed. It's not my kind of crowd anyway, and the minute we walked in, Suzanne spotted this guy at the bar and zoomed in on him. The next thing I knew, she came and told me she was following him over to his house so he could show her his hot tub. Said it was out under the stars."

Samantha had been idly running her finger around the rim of her coffee cup. She looked up with a surprised expression.

"What's his name?" Sam asked.

"She didn't even say. Suzanne says he's some big dog advertising executive. Got an old Jag he drives. You know the type, Mr. Sm-oo-oo-th."

Samantha jumped up and ran to the bathroom. Katie followed her and heard the click of the lock.

"Sam? Sam?" There was no answer, but Katie could hear the sound of retching. "How can anyone who never eats anything be in there throwing up?" she thought.

The sheriff and Aimee crowded in behind Katie. "Is she okay?" Wade questioned.

"What's wrong with Samantha?" asked Aimee.

"I think your friend Suzanne just followed Sam's boyfriend home," whispered Katie, then turned toward the door and spoke more loudly, "Come on out, Samantha. It could be a mistake. Come on out."

"I'll be out in a little while," Samantha gasped.

Wade stepped closer to the door. "Okay," he said, "we'll drink our coffee and when you feel like it, come on out and we'll talk about it." Katie was again impressed with the calming quality of the sheriff's voice.

When Sam finally came back into the living room, she was pale and shaking. "Let me get you a fresh cup of coffee," Katie offered.

"No, I don't drink it without cream."

"There's cream for it

"Cream's fattening."

Jolley looked at Sam, then back at Katie. "Samantha, it's none of my business, but you don't have to worry about anything being fattening."

"I just need to lose a few more pounds, but I don't want to talk about that. Aimee, what did this guy Suzanne followed home look like?"

"I really didn't see. It's so dark and crowded in Kenny B's, and they were at the bar. I never went over there. When Suzanne came back to tell me they were leaving, he wasn't with her. I can't believe she left me stranded at Kenny B's."

"What color is the Jaguar?"

"I don't know. I didn't see it. Listen, can one of you take me home?"

"If Katie and Wade are ready to call it a night, I'll take you home," Sam offered. "I want to go for a ride anyway."

"Samantha," Katie interrupted, "let us take Aimee home. We'll drop her off. You don't need to go check Sam's house."

"He said he was gonna be out of town."

"Maybe it's a misunderstanding," said Aimee. "Maybe your friend lent his car and hot tub to a buddy while he's on his trip. I really hate I upset you so much."

"You didn't upset me. He's upsetting me if he's lying to me."

Sheriff Jolley said nothing. To Katie, he looked a little awkward, even embarrassed. She turned to him.

"What should we do?" she asked.

"Don't ask me. I'm not good with these relationship things. She's not going there to fight or shoot him, is she?"

"No," Sam said emphatically. "I'm not even going to stop. I just want to see if his car is there." She turned back to Aimee. "What kind of car does this Suzanne drive?"

"A blue Honda."

"Okay, let's go."

When Samantha and Aimee drove away, Wade suggested frozen yogurt to Katie and she agreed.

"I really should have the sugar-free," she said as they entered the store.

"Not you, too!"

"That's what I should have after all the stew I ate, but I think the chocolate macadamia's what I want."

They sat at a small table and between licks, Wade asked, "Does your friend ever eat? I noticed she just played with her food."

"She's been weight-conscious since I met her, but it's really gotten worse since she split with her husband. I'm afraid she's going to become anorexic."

"You're too close to the forest to see the trees. Take a good look at her. She's not going to *become* anorexic. She *is* anorexic."

"She still thinks she's fat."

When they left TCBY, Katie asked Wade to drive back by Sam's apartment. Her car was in the drive, but nothing happened when Katie ran up and rang the doorbell. Katie called on her cell phone, but no one answered. Wade became concerned. "Do you think she's suicidal?"

"No, she unplugs the landline, switches her cell off, and sleeps when she's upset with him." Katie paused. "I've been thinking that maybe I should go on television and appeal to Maggie to come home if she can or for whoever has her to let her go. You haven't found her body. Maybe she's still alive. What do you think?"

"Under other circumstances, I'd encourage you to do that, but considering that you look like the women who've been killed, I don't want you calling attention to yourself."

He pulled to the curb, parked, opened the car door for her, and escorted Katie to her entrance where Deputy Corley waited. "I'm going home," Wade said. "I'll talk to you tomorrow. Corley will be here all night. If anything frightens you, just call him."

Katie went to sleep confused. Her mind bounced between feeling like Maggie was okay wherever she was and fear that she'd been kidnapped or killed. The sheriff puzzled her, too. She'd thought he was her guard for the night. In fact, she'd been hoping he would stay.

TERRIBLE
TUESDAY

CHAPTER 13

KATIE HARDLY EXPECTED to see Samantha at work Tuesday morning, but she was entering the building as Katie pulled into the parking lot. Seeing the rented car, Samantha stopped and waited for her. She didn't mention the patrol car or the deputy following Katie. "I'm sorry about last night," Sam began and held the door open for Katie.

"I'm sorry," Katie answered. "I'm sorry you're getting hurt."

"It was all a misunderstanding."

"How do you know? What happened? We went back by your place and you didn't answer the telephone or the door." They headed toward the office to sign in.

"Sam came over about midnight."

"He what?"

"He came over at midnight and beat on the door until I just had to let him in. He's sorry about his mistake."

"What mistake? Lying to you?"

"No, his mistake in not realizing he could have called me when the trip cancelled and I wouldn't have felt last-minute. He didn't mean to lie. He'd planned to go out of town and when that changed, he was afraid I'd think he figured he could just call me anytime. He went to Kenny B's for one drink, and this girl kept asking him about his hot tub. He thought she was interested in buying one, so he offered to show it to her. He didn't even remember her name. It was just a big misunderstanding."

Both teachers signed in, checked their mailboxes, and headed toward their classrooms. Sam followed Katie and kept talking as Katie took the chairs down from the children's desks.

"How did he know you knew about Suzanne?" Katie asked.

"He didn't when he came over. He just missed me so much he couldn't stand it, so he came by hoping I'd still be up. I was so mad that when I did let him in, I really lit into him. I'm so embarrassed about all the ugly things I said."

"So, he just let this woman come look at the hot tub, then she went on her way? What did you see when you went by?"

"A blue Honda was parked in the drive behind the Jag, but I didn't go around the house. If I had, I would have seen that he was just showing her the hot tub. Nothing happened. I've just got to learn to trust."

"That was early last night. What was he doing from then until midnight?"

"Oh, Katie, you're so suspicious! I didn't ask, and I'm

not going to ask. He loves me. That's all I know and all I care about."

"I don't mean to upset you, I really don't, but . . . "

"Then don't! I've got to go take my chairs down." Samantha didn't stomp away, but she walked out as though she wanted to.

Katie saw Sam again midday on the primary recess ground. At first, Samantha seemed to be avoiding her. Then she came over. "I'm sorry about this morning," Sam said. "It's gonna be okay, Katie. I know it is. Guess what we're doing after school today? He's seen this old house that would be a perfect place to restore, and he wants to take me to look at it."

"Sounds like fun." Katie tried hard not to sound sarcastic or sympathetic which were both good words to describe how she felt about Samantha's Mr. Wonderful, considering the way things were going. "When did he invite you to go look at the house?"

"This morning before he left."

"He spent the night?"

"Don't be judgmental, Katie. I'm grown."

"When have you ever known me to be judgmental? Besides, even if I felt judgmental, I wouldn't be with you."

Samantha grinned. "I know, Katie. You've never been critical of me except when you try to make me eat. I'm just so excited. You know the house he lives in is where he lived when he was married. I think he's looking at houses because he doesn't want to start something new where he was with his wife. Don't you think that might be why he wants to show me the house? Maybe he's getting ready for commitment."

"Maybe. Just take it easy, Sam. Give it time. Get to

know this man really well." Katie's mother's taste in music had been old rock and old country, so she'd grown up with Ernest Tubb and Conway Twitty echoing in the hall outside the kitchen. "So he didn't call and let you know his plans had changed and he wasn't out of town because he didn't want you to think he thought he could just call you at the last minute?" Katie thought. "Then he showed Suzanne his hot tub because she might want to buy one. And, after the sales pitch, he showed up at your house at midnight and slept with you. I wonder if Mr. Wonderful was singing George Jones's 'I Always Get Lucky with You' when he arrived?"

"Oh, Katie, you're so cynical and jaded," Sam said as though she could hear her friend's thoughts. "Be happy for me."

The bell rang and the children began lining up. Samantha didn't hear Katie's mumbled, "I'm trying. I swear I'm trying!" as they led their students inside.

Chief Henry Legrand called Sheriff Jolley from Charleston near lunchtime. "Wade, we've got something else going. Gross and I talked to Barker's father in Florida. We got the name of another teacher he paid off after Fred spent time with her and stole from her. Name's Janice Woods. She lives in Myrtle Beach. When the Myrtle Beach authorities tried to contact her, they thought she'd already gone to work. Talked with neighbors. No one saw her leave this morning. Checked with the school where she teaches. She didn't show up or call in today."

"What's her work pattern? Would this be unusual for her?"

"Very unusual. She's always dependable and reliable.

She worked yesterday, and they haven't found anyone who's seen her since she left the school. Her apartment is clean and neat. Bed's made. A coffee cup and cereal bowl in the kitchen sink are the only signs anyone even lives there. Can't tell if they're from yesterday or this morning because they've been rinsed out. Even though an adult's not legally considered missing this soon, Myrtle Beach is issuing an APB on her right now, and you know we've already got one out on Fred Barker. Do you still have someone watching Katie Wray?"

"Yes, Corley was there most of the night, and I sent someone else to relieve him early this morning. I want Corley to get some sleep and go back tonight. I think if Barker tries to go after Katie, it will be after dark."

"Could be. Wade, I've got real bad vibes about this whole thing. We just got a picture of Janice Woods off the computer. Would you like to describe her or do you want me to?"

"Dark, shoulder-length brown hair and beautiful dark eyes?"

"Yes, and the features are similar. She looks like Katie and the other two."

"Hank, if Barker is killing these teachers, who's my John Doe? There has to be a connection."

"I agree they're tied together, but I don't know exactly how. I just wanted to let you know about the Myrtle Beach case. I'll keep you posted, and I'll ask Gross if he has any further thoughts on the John Doe."

When Jolley disconnected from the call with Legrand, he told his secretary to order a computer cross reference on anyone reported missing in South Carolina during the past week. They'd done this earlier, but Hank's comment that they were issuing a missing person bulletin on Woods before the usual time lapse made Wade wonder if he'd checked too soon. Perhaps John Doe had been missing but it hadn't been officially reported when the computer checks were run. They were specifically looking for any missing person who matched the John Doe's physical description.

The sheriff half expected the next call to be Henry again, but he recognized the young female voice immediately.

"Sheriff Jolley?"

"Yes, Mrs. Barker. This is Sheriff Jolley. How are you?"

"I'm okay, but you said I could call you, and I want to know what's going on."

"What exactly do you mean, Mrs. Barker? Have you heard from your husband?"

"No, but they just showed Fred's picture on television and said that he's a person of interest, wanted for questioning about a murder."

"I didn't know that was on the news yet, but the Charleston police want to talk to Fred about a teacher. You remember the one your father-in-law paid for the jewelry? The teacher Fred stayed with in Charleston was found murdered. That's why they want to talk to him. Have you heard from him at all?"

"Nothing since he called last week from that teacher's house and said he was coming home. Do you think she did something to Fred?"

"No, I think we'll find him."

"Do you want Fred to call you if I hear from him?"

"Yes, but if he's in a bad mood, don't try to force him to do anything. In fact, I'm going to call the sheriff in your area and see if they have someone watching your house in case Fred comes home."

"I'm not scared of Fred. He loves me."

"I know, but I'd rather not take any chances."

"Fred won't hurt me or the babies."

"You just be careful, Mrs. Barker."

"I'll call you if I hear from Fred."

"Yes, and please be careful," Jolley repeated.

"I will," she said, then almost whispered, "good-bye."

The sheriff thought Barker's wife had sounded more mature on the telephone than when he'd talked with her in person, but he doubted seriously whether she had any understanding of the man she'd married.

Twice during the morning, Linda Pearson heard Daddy walking around in the back of the house. "Stop it!" she told him, "Go back to your chair where you belong!"

Linda Louise, what are you fussing about now? Why are you so irritable all the time?

"Mama, maybe I'm aggravated because you two won't leave me alone. Daddy knows he's supposed to stay in his chair. He knows he can't walk or talk anymore, so why is he up rambling around?"

I would think you'd have a little compassion for your poor father after all he's been through. You weren't here the whole time when he had the first stroke. He didn't know where he was sometimes. Why, I've seen your daddy cry.

"My daddy should have cried lots of times long before he had those strokes."

Linda Louise, I'm just not going to listen to that. You know your daddy and I did everything we could to help you out when you had your trouble.

"Maybe you did, Mama. Maybe you did, but why didn't"

you help me before then? Why didn't you help me when I was a little girl and tried to talk to you about it?"

Linda Louise, I couldn't believe all those lies you made up when you were little. Then, when you got older and started drinking, Lord knows what you'd say.

"We had money, Mama. Why wouldn't Daddy send me to college? My grades were good enough. I wanted to be a teacher, but Daddy wouldn't let me go."

We've talked about that before. Daddy just couldn't let his pretty little Lindy Lou go off to college away from her Mommy and Daddy.

"But I did. I did go off away from both of you."

Well, you got yourself pregnant and ran off with Bert. We couldn't do a thing to stop you. It broke Daddy's heart. It just broke his heart to have his little Lindy Lou run off like that. We thought at least we'd have a grandchild to love. Then you must have lost the baby because we never got to be grandparents.

"I wasn't pregnant, Mama. I was never pregnant."

If you weren't pregnant, why'd you run off?

"To get away, Mama. I ran off to get away."

I don't see why you've always wanted to blame everything on us. Your daddy and I did the best we could with you. Linda Louise, you know your trouble just about killed both of us, but we did everything we could.

"Mama, it was just too late." Linda sat down on the love seat. "It was too little, too late, but I don't want to talk about it. I want Daddy to stay in his chair where he belongs."

Linda Louise, he's in his chair. The poor man can't get out of that chair.

"But I hear him, Mama. I hear him walking around. He's just trying to trick me into thinking he can't move. Then when I don't expect it, he'll grab me."

Don't be ridiculous. Your daddy would never grab you for anything except to hug and love you. You were your daddy's darling. It just broke his heart when you ran off with Bert. That's why we didn't let you come home at first. We thought you needed to learn your lesson, but when we found out what happened and you had your trouble, we stood by you. Hired that lawyer even if it didn't help. It's time for you to stand by us.

"Yes, Mama. I'm doing that. I'm staying here in Tanner and taking care of you and Daddy just like I promised. You don't think it's rats I hear in this house, do you?"

Rats! The Pearsons have never had rats in our house!

"If it's not rats, it's Daddy. He's walking around trying to fool us."

Don't be ridiculous, Linda Louise. I'm telling you your daddy can't walk or talk anymore.

"Mighty convenient, wasn't it? After all those counselors and shrinks convinced me that I could have closure if I just confronted him, I finally come home with the courage to tell him what I think and to talk about what all happened, and Daddy can't talk anymore. Mama, I'm going to the diner to eat. Daddy better be sitting in his chair when I get back."

Linda took her ATM card and pillowcase and left the house. She paused on the front porch and thought something about the railing looked different, but she couldn't quite figure out what had changed.

Shit! Shug was pissed. Not just at all the teachers he'd known in the past, but at himself. What had made him haul Janice's body back to Tanner? He should have dumped the bitch somewhere in Myrtle Beach. He'd hidden her in the trunk of the Ford, but he knew it wouldn't take long for it to start stinking even worse than what was already coming from the bass case back there. Told over and over how smart he was as a child, the killer felt dumb.

Stupid! Idiot! Dimwit!

He hadn't thought out anything. He'd had a strong desire to return to Tanner, but he'd made no plans of where to go when he got there. Even the clerk at a no-tell motel might report him if he tried to register. His picture was all over TV. His money was almost gone, and he was scared to try to draw any from the ATM. They had cameras at those machines.

His picture on the news was a photo that Susan must have supplied to them, so they'd spoken with her. Sure, they were calling him a "person of interest." Like they only wanted to talk to him. Screw that. They'd tied the deaths together, and they all linked up to him. Except Patty.

He'd never known her before he met her at that educational supply store. He smiled at memories of the afternoon in her apartment. The grin widened as he thought of the words he'd scrawled on her body after positioning the faceless corpse on the couch.

The problem now was finding a good place to get rid of Janice's body. A safe place to dump the bitch.

Shug laughed long and loud. The church. He laughed again. The old burned-out church on Rutledge Road. The place where the killing had started. They wouldn't expect him to dump a body in the same place he'd removed one from before.

But first, gasoline. The register showed almost empty, and the last thing he needed was to run out of fuel and have one of those Department of Transportation good Samaritans stop to help. Recognize him. Smell the stink from the trunk of the car. Make him open his souvenirs.

He swerved off the road to a small mom-and-pop type store with two gas pumps in front. Shug nearly made a big mistake. He'd pulled his debit card from his pocket and almost slid it in the slot on the gas pump before he remembered that he should not use any kind of debit or credit card anymore. That would be a direct signal to the cops where he was, and he didn't want anyone, much less that sheriff he'd seen on television, to know he was back in Tanner.

Inside the small service station, the smell of boiling peanuts mixed with the vinegary scent of the open jar of pickled boiled eggs on the counter. The killer walked over to the cooker and peered down at the nuts tumbling in the hot water. He knew—had known since he was a child— that peanuts aren't really nuts, but he'd grown up calling them nuts and loving everything made with them.

The killer went to the john. Hidden behind the door of the one stall, he counted his money. He had more than he'd thought. He decided to buy supplies in case he wound up having to hide out somewhere. He bought a loaf of bread, a big jar of peanut butter, a couple of bananas, and two large bags of boiled peanuts.

Back on the road, headed for the church ruins, the killer spit peanut shells out the open window as he drove.

Damn!

Where had he left his mind? He rolled up the window and began tossing the shells onto the floor on the passenger side. He sure as hell didn't need to be stopped for littering.

The sheriff had no luck with missing persons in South Carolina, but as soon as he added North Carolina and Georgia to the search, he could have kicked himself for not doing it earlier. The clerk called him less than five minutes later. Reported missing from Charlotte, North Carolina: male Caucasian; twenty-four years old; five feet, eight inches tall; approximately one hundred and thirty-five to one hundred and forty pounds; brown eyes and shoulder-length brown hair. His name was Carlton Johnson, and he was a known cross-dresser.

"Bingo!" Wade exclaimed when he looked at the photo on the computer screen.

"See what else Charlotte can send us," he said to the clerk. "Do they have X-rays or anything that might help us match our John Doe to Carlton Johnson legally? I think we've got a match, but we need to make it official. I'm going by the elementary school and talk to Katie Wray if she hasn't left yet.

Katie wasn't at all surprised to see Wade Jolley standing by her car in the almost empty parking lot when she and her assigned deputy came out of the school. "He's definitely better-looking in jeans," she thought, "but the uniform's not bad either."

She nodded toward him, and he invited her into his car. The deputy took a seat in his own car.

"What's happening?" Katie asked.

"Lots. Barker lived with a teacher in Myrtle Beach for a while. She's missing. We've also got a cross-dresser from Charlotte, North Carolina, who disappeared last week. His physical description is close to our John Doe. Katie, did you realize you and Barker are just about the same size?"

"Yes. Maggie said he was her size, and she and I could pass for twins. I'm older, but we can still share clothes."

"My John Doe has no face. You and the photo of the missing person from Charlotte look alike. I'm wondering if John Doe was found unclothed because he was wearing women's clothes when he and Barker made contact."

"Don't ask me. I'm the one who thought those guys in the band were all women." Katie said it seriously, but there was a grin in her eye.

Wade patted her hand. "A little innocence is nice in a woman."

"You're calling me naïve?"

"I'm not insulting you. I meant it as a compliment."

"I'm not sure whether it's a compliment or not, but I'll accept it as one. Lately, I've been feeling more idiotic than naïve. I can't believe all that's happened since I've been home. I'm worried sick the next body found will be Maggie, and I feel guilty. If I hadn't gone west, Maggie couldn't have let him stay with her."

"Everybody's vulnerable at times. She happened to meet an experienced con man on what you said would have been the anniversary of her first divorce. She was taken in." Wade forced himself to smile. "Let's hope there's not another body and your sister shows up safe and sound."

"She said they had some really good times. He was kind. He was gentle. He listened to what she said, and he understood how she felt. Even when she told him he'd have to leave at the end of the summer, she said he seemed to understand and accept it."

"The FBI agent thinks Barker took that as rejection."

"Maggie said Frankie never acted like it bothered him.

He always seemed up." She thought for a moment, then added, "Except one time. She said they went to this really pretty park on a mountain, up near Greenville."

"Paris Mountain?"

"That's it. The one with the buildings and bridge made out of rock. Frankie kept telling Maggie how pretty the park was, so one day they took a picnic and drove all the way to Greenville. They sat at a wooden table and talked about how nice it would be up there in the fall when the leaves turn. He said they wouldn't be together in the fall."

"That makes sense. Your sister had told him it was over at the end of the summer."

"But he cried. Tears came to his eyes. He was always so upbeat. Everything was always fun with him, so she was really surprised. He cried and she held him in her arms. Maggie was impressed with his sensitivity about good-byes. They just held each other and cried."

Katie added, "I might as well tell you, from what Maggie said, it's easier for me to believe the body you found is Frankie than to believe Frankie hurt anyone. Maggie described a sense of gentleness about him."

"I fear that was part of the con he pulls on women."

"Then maybe Maggie and I are both naïve. I trusted him because she did."

"Back up, Katie. Don't let yourself feel sorry for him. It appears he's killed at least three people, possibly four."

"It's just hard to believe," Katie answered. "Hard to believe," she thought, "someone who's been in your bed, even though not with you, is out killing people, out blowing people's faces away and chopping their fingers off."

"I know, but until it's proved otherwise, I want you

to believe that Frankie or Fred Barker is extremely dangerous. That's why we have you under surveillance. Yes, we want to catch him, but it's also to protect you."

"He's after Maggie, not me."

"What?" Wayne exploded. "You sound just like his wife. The man's mentally ill and out for revenge. He *will* hurt you if he gets the chance!" The sheriff looked as angry as he sounded. "Besides, we don't know if Maggie's even alive."

Katie's heart dropped to her stomach. Just a few minutes ago, he'd told her Maggie might be alive. She didn't even want to consider the possibility that the maniac had already done something to Maggie and was now confusing the two sisters.

"What did you want to tell me or ask me?" Katie's lips trembled. "I'm really tired, and I'd like to end this conversation and go home."

"I guess I came to tell you there's another teacher missing in Myrtle Beach before you see it on the news."

"I don't watch the news. I still don't have a TV."

Wade looked up at her with just the hint of a smile. "Oh, for a moment, I'd forgotten your sister's summer romance made sure you don't watch the news or microwave your dinner. Wasn't that the same fellow who's so nice and gentle?"

"You're the sheriff. You're supposed to be professional with me, not sarcastic." Katie spat the words.

"I am being professional. I'm worried about your safety. You live in my jurisdiction."

"Then let me go on home. If you want to worry about me, come over to my place and worry."

"Do you mean that?"

Katie looked at Wade, and it was impossible for the sheriff to read her. "Yes," she said softly. "Can I go now?"

"Go head then." The sheriff reached over and opened the door for her. "Look, I know you haven't had time to fill out insurance forms on your losses and we've done nothing about sending a list to Barker's dad. I've got two televisions at my house. Let me bring you one to use for now. Watch the news. This case is snow-balling."

"Yes, the big shot sheriff will lend the poor schoolteacher his extra TV. I don't think so. I have some money in savings. I'll pick one up tomorrow."

"I've made you mad, haven't I?"

"How would you feel?"

"I'd be angry and hurt and confused. But I'd let the sheriff lend me the television."

"Okay. Bring it by whenever you want, but call first."

"Are you expecting company? Would I be interrupting something?" Katie heard an unexpected edge in his voice.

"You sound like your deputy now."

"What? Has Corley been rude to you?"

"So you admit you're being rude to me."

"I never understood women and I never will. I'll bring the TV over later. I'll bring something to eat, too. You just go home and rest." Wade got out of the car and walked around to her side. He followed her to the rental as he added, "And I'll call before I come."

They were both standing outside the door on the driver's side when Katie noticed the gift-wrapped package on the front seat. It was small and flat, not quite six inches square. Wrapped in silver foil, it was topped with a big pink bow.

"What's that?" Wade asked.

"I don't know," Katie answered as she reached for it.

Wade yanked her away from the car so suddenly that Katie first thought he'd hit her. He must have waved or called the deputy over because before she knew what was happening, Wade was shoving her back into his car and the deputy was beside them. The sheriff slammed the door behind her.

"Move her down the street now!" the sheriff instructed. The deputy jumped in and drove Jolley's car out of the parking lot. He stopped about a block away with the police radio on. In a few minutes, Jolley's voice came through. "You can come back now. It's two CDs. The package is okay."

The deputy pulled Wade's cruiser back into the school parking lot. Jolley stood beside Katie's car. He was holding the open box with gloved hands. He walked over and showed the package to Katie. The CDs were *Rod Stewart's Greatest Hits* and *Janis Joplin's Greatest Hits*. He thrust a piece of paper in front of her. "Is this Barker's handwriting?"

"How would I know?" Katie answered, immediately regretting the whine in her tone. "I heard his voice on the phone, never saw him or his writing."

The note read, "From me to you, Stewart's second track, Joplin's seventh." Scrawled across the bottom was, "Love ya, Frankie!"

"How the hell did we let him get so close he could put a package in her car right here in the school yard?" Jolley demanded.

"I was watching her, not the car," the deputy defended himself.

"I know that. I'm putting this in an evidence bag in your

vehicle. I want the package and her car printed. I'll take Ms. Wray home. Get a tow for her car and have forensics check it out. I'll be on the radio. Let me know what shows."

"Yes, sir."

"Sorry, Katie, it looks like now you don't have a car or a TV." Wayne slid under the steering wheel of his cruiser.

"Do you have a spare vehicle you can lend me?" Katie smiled as she asked the question.

"I'll just drive you whenever you need to go somewhere."

"Is that a promise?" Katie smiled again.

"It could be a threat." Wade grinned.

"Is that package a threat?" Katie wasn't smiling anymore. "What's the second track on the Stewart CD? 'Maggie May'? What about the Joplin?"

"The Stewart track's 'Maggie May.' Joplin's is 'Get it While You Can.' I'm not familiar with that. Are you?"

"Of course I am. You may like all kinds of music, but you're obviously not a Janis Joplin fan. I have the same CD at the house. I'll play it for you when we get there, but it doesn't make sense. Frankie hated for Maggie to play Janis Joplin. He told her it brought back sad memories."

"The Myrtle Beach teacher's name is Janice Woods. Maybe he connected Janis to Janice."

Katie expected to go directly to her apartment, but Wade drove instead to one of the newer Tanner residential areas just beyond Samantha's apartment complex. He pulled up in front of a neat beige brick house with brown shutters, parked, and said, "Come on in."

"What are we doing?"

"Getting the television. And I think we'll raid the refrigerator and find something to eat tonight."

"Is this your house?"

"My house. You don't think I'm out stealing TVs and robbing refrigerators, do you? After all, I am the sheriff."

"Not really. Where's your wife?"

"What wife?"

"The mother of the kids that go with the swing set in the yard."

"The swing set is for my six-year-old niece who comes over sometime. There hasn't been a wife for about ten years. She didn't like the hours I work."

As they entered the front door, Wade gently pushed Katie against the wall and said, "Wait here." She noticed a beautifully framed picture of a familiar-looking little girl on a table in the entry area. She was trying to place how she knew the child when Wade returned. "Just wanted to check out the house. Can't be too careful, though I don't know how or why he'd expect you to be here."

The floor plan was very open. From the great room, Katie could see the kitchen. "Just look," she said, looking around the immaculately neat rooms, "not a dish in the sink. I'll bet your bed's made, too. You lied to me."

"Cleaning service one day a week. I knew it would be tidy before I brought you in. The maid came today."

Katie followed him into the kitchen. Wade stood with the door to the refrigerator wide open. He peered inside with great interest. "Actually, this might be a good place to hide you," he said from behind the door.

"Where?" Katie laughed. "In your refrigerator?"

"No, in my house. Why don't we stay here for a while? I'll cook you dinner. We can watch television or if you want a movie, there's a whole collection of DVDs."

"I thought you wanted to hear the Joplin song."

"I do. I'll check it out on YouTube."

"What are you looking for in the fridge?"

"Actually, I'm just standing here cooling off. It's been a long time since I've brought a beautiful woman to my house. I'm reminding myself that this is business."

Katie walked over and stood peeking at him over the refrigerator door. "Is it all business?" she asked with a smile.

"It has to be. I can't let myself be distracted; I need to protect you."

"So it would be inappropriate if I leaned over the door and kissed you?"

"Totally and completely inappropriate. Damn it!"

"Then I'll just ask you to hurry and pick out what's for dinner. I didn't have any lunch. If you're going to feed me, feed me soon."

Wade pulled two individually wrapped packages from the freezer compartment. "Steaks. Potatoes. I've probably got something for salad, and if I dig around, I'll find some of my mother's homemade sourdough bread."

"And you say you don't entertain often?"

Jolley closed the refrigerator and looked at her seriously. "I really wish this were as simple as bringing you home and cooking dinner for you."

"I do, too, and I wish Maggie were here, too."

"Actually, I wish I'd met you last year. Maybe you'd have been so busy with me that you wouldn't have left for the summer."

"That's a possibility."

"This conversation's getting too serious," Katie thought.

She said, "May I turn on the TV? It's time for the news."

"Sure. I'll pop these steaks into the microwave to defrost. We'll be eating before you know it."

Wade busied himself in the kitchen. Katie turned on the news and sat on the sofa. Wade closed the microwave door and joined her. The first item was the search for Fred Barker. Katie recognized the picture of Frankie his wife had given Jolley. Information concerning Barker was to be called in to SLED, the Charleston Police Department, the Columbia Police Department, Richland County Sheriff's Department, or Blair County Sheriff's Department.

"It could still be someone framing him," Katie commented.

"It's not, Katie. Face it. He's guilty."

"I know. I guess I'm just wishing. My mom used to tell me if I didn't be careful, I'd wish my life away."

"My grandmother was the one who always had a quotation or a wise saying about anything and everything," Wade commented as he returned to the kitchen.

When they finished eating, Katie cleaned up while Wade was busy with the radio and telephone. "Wonder why nobody's snagged him?" she thought. "He's even neat in the kitchen. I'll bet that maid never finds a mess here."

"You didn't have to do that," Wade told her when he came back into the kitchen. "I have to take care of some official business. Corley's coming over. I want you to stay here. Unless Barker followed us, this could be a good safe place for you."

Katie hesitated. "How long do you want me to stay? 'Til you come back?"

"Overnight at least. Barker's fingerprints are all over

your car and that package, but I guess we knew he's the only one who would have chosen those particular CDs."

"I don't have things for overnight or for school tomorrow," Katie protested, but only halfheartedly.

"I really don't want you working until we find Barker."

"I can't miss school. Especially not right now during the first week."

Wade put his hands on her shoulders and turned her to face him. "Katie, Barker shoots people. I hope to hell he never gets near you, but do you really want to lead him into an elementary school?"

Katie's face drained to a pasty white. "Oh, God, no! I never thought of that!"

"If I could, I'd stay right by your side until this is over. I can't, but I have to do what I think will keep you safe. Please stay here. Rummage through my room and find yourself something comfortable to wear. Choose any bedroom you want and sleep here tonight. When I bought this house, I thought it was a crazy floor plan. There's no real back door. What we call the back door is off from the kitchen on the side of the house. Deputies can watch both entrances from the front."

"Why do you always guard me inside and others are always outside?"

"Would you feel more comfortable with Corley inside?"

"No."

"I really don't think Barker will come while you're here, but I'm going to give you a two-way transmitter. You can call Corley in if you get frightened."

"Why do you have to go?"

"They've found the teacher from Myrtle Beach. She's here in Tanner."

"Is she okay?"

"No, she's not. She's . . . " A knock on the door interrupted him. Corley reporting. He handed Katie a transmitter and showed her how to use it. The sheriff and deputy walked out without the sheriff finishing his statement about the teacher from Myrtle Beach, but Katie didn't have to hear the word to know her condition. The teacher was dead.

WICKED WEDNESDAY

CHAPTER 14

MURDER STALKED TANNER during the wee hours of Wednesday morning, but law enforcement officials were busy with what remained of Janice Woods. Charleston Police Chief Henry Legrand and FBI Agent Gross had arrived about midnight and were now drinking coffee with Jolley in his office.

"Damn it, Wade!" Hank said, "Nobody's blaming you for not putting a guard on Katie's car."

"But I should have, and I'm not so sure about hiding her out at my house. This jerk seems to stay one step ahead of me."

"I think it's a good move," Hank said. "Putting her at your house. In Charleston, I'd have put her up in a hotel, but your home is better."

"I'm not so sure about that," commented Gross.

"Why?" asked Henry, "you want to use her as bait?"

"We don't work that way down here," Wade answered tersely and glared at Gross.

Legrand laughed, though it was strained. "Not with Katie Wray, we don't. Eh, Wade?"

"That's got nothing to do with it. I wouldn't want to use any woman as bait for Barker."

Gross looked up. "I don't know about that. I predicted escalation, and you have to admit the posing of the David woman was a step up from Shealy, and dismemberment of Woods is even more escalation from posing David."

"What would you call the business of the package on Katie's front seat and the location of the body?" asked Legrand.

"Focus. He's zeroing in on his main target, and whether you like it or not," he stopped for one of his dramatic pauses and looked at Sheriff Jolley, "his main target appears to be the woman who rejected him, Maggie, but I believe he thinks Katie is Maggie. That's encouraging. If he's killed Maggie, he'd know Katie isn't her."

"Not necessarily," Hank said. "Don't forget this guy is crazy."

"I won't argue with that," answered Wade, "but I don't want to use Katie as bait. This man is crazy like a fox. Diagnosed or not, I think he's got a first-class streak of mean as well as crazy."

"Probably," responded the FBI agent. "Why didn't your people discover the body immediately?"

"You're in the South," Hank laughed. "We move slow."

"Actually, I instructed them to dust the package and Katie's car for prints after we found the CDs," Wade said.

"The vehicle was only downtown a couple of hours before it was detailed. When the technician opened the trunk, he saw and smelled the bass guitar case. Being a homegrown musician himself, he opened the case to look at the instrument. You know what he found inside."

"Yes, we had a look at it, " Henry responded. "Wonder where her head and legs are and why he changed MOs so much this time? When do you expect the state to get back to you with forensic reports?"

"Maybe later today, except for toxicology, and nobody thinks Barker poisons these women. This case has been assigned top priority. I keep wondering where he's left the rest of the body. He meant for Katie to find the instrument case. She said Maggie'd never looked in it. I can't help but wonder when he thought Katie would look in the trunk."

Hank smiled at the sheriff. "She's a nice lady. I don't even like to think about her seeing what was in that case, but get real, Wade, sooner or later, the odor would have drawn her to the back of her car."

Jolley grinned. "The first day I met her, I took her to look at John Doe's corpse. Didn't plan to let her look at the head, but she wanted to see if it might help her with identification. She handled it very well. Surprised the hell out of me."

"When do I get to meet Ms. Wray?" asked Gross. "I'd really like to interview her. I think she could give me more insight into Barker."

"If you two are staying in town, later this morning will be fine. She won't be working today," Wade said.

"Good. Will you bring her in?"

"No, I'd rather she stay exactly where she is for a while. Henry, why don't you bring Agent Gross over to the house at about eleven?"

"Sure, unless something else breaks on this case between now and then."

"As in another body?"

"Or as in the rest of the one we've only got parts of right now."

The sun was already shining through the pink, ruffled curtains at the windows when Katie awoke. The stuffed animals perched on the white wicker rocking chair in the corner were not something the tailored Katie Wray would have used for decoration. She'd assumed this room was for his niece. Any little girl would love the white wicker and pink frills.

Katie had found a pair of PJs in Jolley's chest of drawers. He wasn't any taller than she was, but he was broader. She'd tied a little knot in the waistband of the bottoms to hold them up. The shoulders of the pajama top fell down to her elbows. If he insisted she stay here, someone would have to get her some clothes. Suits and low heels were her norm for work, but away from the job, Katie liked casual.

There were no sounds in the house, so she peeked out through the frilly curtains. Wade's car wasn't there, but Corley was still outside. Just to be on the safe side, she picked up the two-way transmitter.

"Deputy Corley, this is Katie Wray. Is Sheriff Jolley with you?"

Corley's voice was crisp and efficient. "No, ma'am. He hasn't been back all night. I can radio him if you like."

"No, just curious. Are you staying here? When do you change shifts?"

"Normally, I'd be gone by now, but the sheriff told me to

wait for him, so I'll be here until he comes back. Do you need anything?"

"No. Do I say, 'over and out,' or anything like that?"

"It's not necessary. Just let me know if you want something."

As soon as Katie had a pot of coffee started, she called Samantha on the telephone. "I called the sub-center last night," Katie tried to tell her, but Sam was too excited to listen.

"Katie, it's the perfect house! It's just made for raising a family. I know, I just know he's ready for commitment. Let me tell you about it. It's got this big porch that wraps all around the . . . "

"Sam, don't you have to go to work?" Katie interrupted.

"Yeah, I'll tell you about it at work."

"No, I'm not going in. That's what I called about."

"Are you sick?"

"No, I'm not sick."

"Katie Wray! I can't believe you're staying off work if you're not sick!"

"It's this Frankie thing. I called the sub-center last night and called the principal too, but I want you to just look in my room and make sure everything's okay for the substitute. My lesson plans are on my desk."

"As always!" Samantha interjected. Once or twice, Sam had been absent and Katie had hurriedly written plans for her because Samantha hadn't left them on her desk as she was supposed to.

"Katie?" Sam's voice was more serious than usual. "I saw a picture of another woman who's missing. Not from Charleston, from Myrtle Beach. She looks like you, Katie, and they're showing a picture of a man named Fred Barker who's wanted for questioning. Is that the guy your sister spent the summer with?"

"Yes, Sam. That's the man we call Frankie."

"Gee whiz, Katie! He looks too hot to be a killer."

"I told you how good-looking he is, Sam. I hope they're wrong and someone's framing him, but Sheriff Jolley thinks he's guilty."

"My caller ID says 'Wade Jolley.' Are you at his office?"

"No, I'm at his house."

"At his house? What's it like? I've never been in a sheriff's house before. Can I call you there?"

"I don't know, Sam. I may go back to my place today. I'll call you after school, and you can tell me all about the house you and Sam saw yesterday."

"I can call you there. The number's right here on my caller ID."

"Hey, Samantha, don't tell anyone why I'm not at work or where I am, okay?"

"Sure. You're not going to believe this house. I've got to take you over and show it to you. Sam called it a 'fixer-upper,' and he was asking me what kind of wallpaper I like and everything. I just know what he's thinking!"

"Go to work, Samantha. I'll talk to you later."

By the time Jolley came home, Katie was dressed, had finished half the pot of coffee, and had the television on long enough that she'd seen the public service announcements seeking information on both the schoolteacher named Janice Woods and on Fred Barker, who remained "Frankie" in her mind.

Wade stopped on his way in and used Corley's transmitter to announce to Katie that he was back.

"Hey, how'd you sleep?" he asked when he came

through the door.

"Fine. I felt like a little girl."

"You must have slept in Jennie's room. The pink and white one with ruffles and stuffed animals?"

"Sure did. Your niece must come often for you to keep a room like that for her."

"Not as often as I'd like, but I usually bring her over when I take time off. I wish I could have her more. She lives with my mother, and Mom's health is not the best in the world, especially to take care of a six-year-old." He pulled out his wallet, flipped it open to a photograph of a pretty child, and held it out to Katie. It was the little girl in the picture on the table in the foyer, but this was a more recent shot. Katie recognized the studio stamp and date from school pictures at Tanner Elementary the previous year. She recognized the child then.

"That's Jennifer Hatten." Katie exclaimed. "She's in my class this year."

"That's my Jennie. I haven't talked to her much the past couple of weeks. She hasn't even told me who her teacher is this year. She's my sister's girl."

"Your sister lives with your mom?"

"My sister and her husband were killed in a car wreck two years ago when Jennie was four." Wade closed the wallet and put it back into his pocket. "I'll probably wind up adopting her or at least raising her. She lives with my mother right now, but Mom's getting up in age." He paused. "I'm glad you're going to teach her." He looked into Katie's half-empty cup. "Is the coffee fresh?"

"I've drunk most of it, but there should be a cup left."

"Did you eat?"

"I'm not a breakfast person."

"You're a teacher. You know breakfast is brain food. There's all kinds of stuff to eat in there. Just fix what you want anytime."

"I found your pajamas and your coffee. I don't think I'm too shy to look for food when I'm hungry."

"Which pajamas?"

"The red-and-white plaid ones."

"Oh, Lord, those are some my mother gave me for Christmas one year. How about I cook us breakfast?"

"You've been up all night. Something happened that you haven't told me about, and you want to cook breakfast? Why don't you just eat some cereal or something and talk to me. What's going on?"

"Pop Tarts."

"What?"

"Pop Tarts. That's what I eat when I don't cook. Not cereal. S'Mores Pop Tarts. Remember that so you can have some over at your place in case I ever spend the night there." As he talked, Wade opened the pantry, pulled out a box of Pop Tarts, and dropped two into the toaster.

"So you think you might be spending the night at my house?"

"Could be. Maybe you'll invite me when this case is cleared up."

"How about tonight?" Katie teased.

"Not tonight. I can't let you go home yet. Besides, until the case is cleared, it would be . . . "

"Inappropriate!" Katie finished for him.

Wade sat on a stool at the counter and started eating his Pop Tarts. "Tell me what's happening," Katie said.

"Special Agent Gross with the FBI is coming over to talk to you in about an hour, Wade began. "Don't worry.

Hank's with him, and the two of us will be right here with you. He's going to ask you about Barker, hoping you can add something to help him with his profiling so he can second-guess the guy and we can catch him." He drained his coffee cup and poured it full of milk. "Will you think I'm piggish if I eat another Pop Tart? Aren't you hungry? My dinner from last night's been gone for hours. You're not like your little blond friend, are you? I don't date women who don't like to eat."

"Date? Who said anything about a date? We were talking about the FBI agent coming over to talk to me." Katie's words were spoken seriously, but her expression was pure flirt, and she knew it.

"You're right. I guess I'm dodging telling you why I had to leave last night. I'd rather sit here and kid with you than tell you what I have to say."

"Then you're just kidding about a date? Even when it's no longer 'inappropriate'?"

"No, and you know I'm not kidding. I want to take you out for the finest evening of your life, but right now, I need to remember that I'm the sheriff with the biggest case this county's ever had. Janice Woods, the teacher from Myrtle Beach, was found last night."

"She's dead?" Katie asked just to confirm what she already knew in her heart.

"Yes, she's dead."

"Where did they find her?"

"They found her in the trunk of your rental car, Katie."

"What?"

"We towed your car from the school parking lot. Frankie's fingerprints were all over it. Now you've got me calling him Frankie. Barker's prints were all over the car and the package. When they opened the trunk of your car, they found an instrument case."

"Bass guitar?"

"Yep, and the body was inside the case."

"You can't fit a body in a guitar case!" Katie gasped. "Unless . . . unless . . ."

"That's what he did, and it still didn't all fit. We don't know where the other parts are, but the hands were among the pieces in the case, so we've got fingerprints. Identity is already confirmed. Janice Woods was thirty-five, taught first grade. Lived alone except for her poodle and a few weeks when Barker had her convinced he was in love with her. I wanted to tell you before it hits the news."

"They've been showing her picture as missing on television. She looks like me."

"Yes, she did."

"He didn't really like Maggie for herself. He picked her because she looks like the type he always goes after, didn't he?"

"Who knows, Katie?" Wade looked at her with concern. "Are you okay?"

Katie nodded, and Jolley added, "I'm going to get a shower and change before Hank and Gross get here."

Corley announced on the two-way transmitter that Chief Legrand and Agent Gross had arrived before Wade finished his shower. Henry hugged Katie hello. Gross looked surprised but said nothing. "We know each other," the police chief explained. "Besides, I keep telling you things are different in the South."

Gross laughed. "I know. I know. You keep forgetting I'm from the South, too."

"Would you gentlemen like coffee? I just made fresh,"

Katie offered. "The sheriff is in the shower. He should be out shortly." She assumed the hostess role, knowing that she'd be more comfortable, as if she were on her own turf.

Both men accepted coffee. When Wade came into the kitchen, he offered them Pop Tarts. They refused, explaining they'd stopped at the Downtown Diner on the way over. Katie was very aware that she was wearing the suit she'd had on all the previous day. She felt wrinkled and tired though she'd slept well. Gross removed a digital recorder from his briefcase, put it on the table between them, and asked, "Is it okay if I record our conversation?"

Katie nodded her consent, and the agent turned on the recorder. Katie felt an overwhelming dismay.

Henry sensed her discomfort. He said, "You and Agent Gross have something in common, Katie. He's a big fan of old rock."

"Really?" she said, but she thought, "Why are we sitting here talking about music when my sister slept with a murderer in my bed all summer? A killer who chopped up a woman and put her in the trunk of my car. And where is Maggie? Is she chopped up and hidden somewhere, too?" Tears filled her eyes.

"Did your sister and Barker listen to this music together?" Gross began.

"Sometimes. She said they listened to music a lot in the car, but the one he really got into was 'Maggie May.' He liked Rod Stewart and even learned all the words to 'Maggie May' so he could sing it to her. He told her he'd never heard the song before until she played it for him. And you know that Barker would never lie." She finished with a solemn expression. Henry laughed. Gross looked confused.

"She's teasing you," Wade commented.

"Teasing?" Gross grumbled and looked hard at Katie. "You're able to joke around when things are as serious as they are? We saw a body in the trunk of your car last night, and your sister still hasn't turned up."

"Not my car," Katie said. "A rental car. My Fusion's missing."

"You seem to take all of this very lightly," Gross said.

"Look, Agent Gross," Katie replied, "this whole thing started when my sister didn't meet me at the airport Sunday a week ago. Apparently Barker's doing horrible things to women. I'm holding on to a thread of hope that my sister is safe somewhere because I'll go crazy if I think of her as one of that man's victims. I can tease and answer you or I can sit here and cry and not be able to tell you a thing."

"Then tease me, Ms. Wray. Tease me. My work is far too serious all the time, so if it helps you to tease, do it. Let's just talk, okay?"

"All right, but I really don't know how much more I can help you. I talked to my sister briefly almost every day, and I could hear Frankie in the background. He was like a small child who wanted all of her attention. The only time he wasn't constantly interrupting was on weekends when he was gone."

"I see. You just told me something important even if you think it's not a big thing. I know you never met Barker or actually talked to him yourself, but I'm going to ask you all kinds of questions. I want to know this man inside out. I want to know everything your sister ever told you about him."

"You'd probably learn more by speaking to his wife."

"I've talked to Barker's wife, and I've had a long conversation with his father. By the way, Barker's father says he's going to send you money to pay for the things his son stole from you. I got the idea he wished he could just pay for everything, including the deaths — make it all go away. He seems torn between feeling guilty for what his son has done and being tired of cleaning up after him."

"Maybe he should have spent the money on some therapy for Frankie."

"His father said he's been in treatment several places. Young Fred spent a lot of his high school years institutionalized after his mother committed suicide. But I didn't come here to tell you what I know about Barker. I want to know what you know. I even want to hear about anything said to or about Barker that you don't think has any significance. Coupled with what others have told me, the tiniest bit of information could tie in. I want to find this man before he kills again."

"Yes, sir," Katie said and Gross grinned.

"The 'sir' isn't necessary. I'm not trying to intimidate you. These two officers call you Katie. May I call you Katie?"

"Certainly."

"Chief Legrand and Sheriff Jolley call me Agent Gross, but, Katie, you call me John, okay?"

"All right, John."

"Some of the questions I ask will be highly personal about your sister. Remember that this is only for the investigation. It's not personal. Sometimes it's easier to answer those questions with a stranger than with friends. Would you prefer for Chief Legrand and Sheriff Jolley to leave the room?"

"No," Katie said as she poured herself another cup of coffee. "If they leave the room, you'll just let them listen to the recording later. In fact, I doubt that you can ask me anything more personal than what I've already said in my statements to them."

"Katie." Gross used one of his long pauses. "I have to warn you. I've already read your statements. I'll be asking more-pointed questions. They were seeking certain information of one kind. I'm trying to know this man even better than your sister does. Since she's not available, I have to get the information secondhand through you. I want to know how he feels, what he thinks. I want to know what he likes and dislikes. I want to know him, as I said, inside out."

"Go ahead." Katie finished her coffee and looked longingly at the carafe, but she decided she'd had enough caffeine.

The agent's questions began as repetitions of the questions Katie had already answered. Once again, he wanted to hear all about how Maggie said she'd met Frankie. Katie found herself going into great detail about how Maggie had been depressed and couldn't sleep. She'd gone to the all- night drugstore, the one with a large book section in the back. The man had seemed nice. They'd gone back to the apartment to talk.

"Are you and your sister a lot alike?" Gross questioned.

"We look alike."

"I mean do you have the same lifestyles. I don't see you as someone who'd pick up a man and take him home with you. I'm wondering what would make her do that."

"I've never done it, and I don't think it's something my sister does on a regular basis either. She was vulnerable.

Her mind was on her first husband. It was the anniversary of their divorce. I can see how it happened. I've always been more cautious than my sister, but I confess it was a dumb thing even for Maggie to do. When I scolded her, she told me he was the kindest man she'd ever met and that he treated her like a lady. At the beginning, she told me several times that he was 'almost too good to be true.' "

"When did Maggie say they became intimate? The first night?"

"No, they talked all night. Their first intimacy was when he came back on Sunday."

"Was he ever forceful?"

"I'm not sure I know what you mean. He certainly wouldn't have been hitting her or anything like that. Maggie would have told me. She'd have run him off, too."

"Did he ever make her do anything she didn't want to do? If he did, would she have told you?"

"No, she described him as gentle. The only time she ever told me he'd shown anger was when they watched a documentary about female teachers molesting underage students. When they showed the piece about the woman whose lawyer said she was too pretty to go to jail, and one of the reporters added that they didn't have teachers like that when he was in school. Maggie said Frankie went on a tirade about that."

"Katie, the next question is a personal one. Did Maggie talk to you about sex?"

"Of course."

"Did she ever tell you about doing anything kinky with Barker?"

"Why do you ask that?"

"The posing of the second body in Charleston has sexual

connotations. I want to know about Barker's sexual preferences."

"Posing?" Katie asked and looked at Wade.

"Posing means the killer arranged the body like he was setting it up to expose her," said Hank.

"How did he display her?" Katie sounded sincerely confused. None of the men replied.

"Answer me, damn it!" she demanded, but the men still didn't respond to her question. "You're agents of the law and I'm a grown woman. I'm not a child. He cut up the last one. What did he do to the one before?"

"Katie, it's not going to help you to know those details," Wade began in what Katie thought of as his "soothing" voice.

"Don't baby me," Katie snapped. "Just tell me!"

"He left a rhyme on the wall in red felt-tip pen. He blew her face off like the John Doe. He had sex with her in every way imaginable." Wade spoke like a robot, just a mechanical recitation of facts.

"Why is that called posing?"

"That wasn't the actual posing," Henry took over for Wade. "The posing refers to the position of the body when she was found. He had taken the middle cushion off the couch and propped her body into the space he created. He placed her arms and legs in the classic spread-eagle position."

The professional Katherine Wray voice took over. "I've read about posing then. I just didn't remember that's what it's called. Didn't the Boston Strangler do that?"

"How do you know about the Boston Strangler?" Wade asked.

"I've read about him and the Zodiac Killer, Son of Sam,

and lots of others, but we're talking about posing. Didn't the Boston Strangler leave those women in lewd poses?"

"Yes," Special Agent Gross replied. "It's not really uncommon in certain types of cases, and you're right, the Boston Strangler was a poser."

"I've read about it in true crime books." Katie frowned. "What else did Frankie do to her?"

"He wrote on her as well as on the wall," Gross continued. "He used felt-tip pens and wrote all over her body. Graffiti kinds of things. Arrows pointing to her genitals and comments about what he'd done to her. That's why I want to know if Barker was into kinky sex with your sister."

Again, Katie let her professional Ms. Wray voice take over. "That depends on what you think is kinky. She said Frankie was good in bed."

"Did he ever do anything sexually bizarre?"

"Bizarre? Give me an example. I'm not sure I know the difference between bizarre and kinky." Once again, the voice was almost clinical in its professionalism.

Gross leaned back and sighed. "An example? Let's see." Jolley thought the following pause was for effect. Katie assumed the agent was actually thinking. "Ted Bundy's girlfriend said he was very straight with her sexually, but one night she woke up and he was under the covers with a flashlight examining her. That's not exactly kinky, but it is somewhat bizarre. I'm just asking if Barker ever did anything unusual that your sister thought was strange enough to tell you about."

"I remember that. I read it in Ann Rule's book about Ted Bundy. No, Maggie never mentioned anything bizarre or kinky."

"Did he ever talk about his family?"

Katie bristled. "She had no idea he was married! He told her he'd never been married. Didn't even claim to be separated or divorced. Maggie didn't know he had a wife and children."

"I don't mean the wife and children. It's clear in your other statements that neither you nor Maggie knew he was married. The family I'm asking about is his parents. Did he ever talk about his mother or father?"

"No. Not that Maggie mentioned." She looked over at Wade. "You didn't tell me about a rhyme on the wall. Was it the 'Teacher, Teacher' one?"

Jolley's surprise showed. "You know that 'Teacher, Teacher' rhyme?"

"He used to say it to Maggie all the time. She told me, and I've heard him chant it to her while she talked to me on the telephone." Katie recited the poem in a childish rhythm:

> *Teacher, Teacher, little girl,*
> *You sure give my heart a whirl.*
> *Teacher, Teacher, oh, so sweet,*
> *I love you from head to feet!*

The three men breathed a sigh in unison.

"What is it?" Katie asked. "Is that what he wrote on her wall?"

"No, it's not," answered Legrand, and he quoted the version written on the wall at Patricia David's apartment. Wade had seen Katie in tears before, but this was the first time Legrand or Gross saw her cry.

After an hour and half of questions, Gross had

established very few facts that weren't already recorded in Katie's previous statements of what Maggie told her. Frankie was a good driver and didn't show signs of road rage. He was fond of pizza and movies. He never opened his bass case, but he did sing to her sometimes. He especially liked live music and dancing. He sang "Maggie May" to Maggie frequently. Katie told Gross about the afternoon at Paris Mountain and how Frankie Barker cried like a little boy in Maggie's arms.

Gross shook his head slightly. "I'm going to sort through all this and see what I come up with. Basically, nothing we've said here changes anything I've already stated. The man has a mental condition. In the past, he's taken up with teachers and left when he became bored, changed his mind, or whatever. This time, your sister put him out. I think we're dealing with one helluva reaction to rejection, and I know he'll come after you unless we catch him first. He either thinks you're Maggie or has transferred his feelings to you if Maggie's dead." He looked at Sheriff Jolley. "I'll want to talk to you later. I still believe we need to lure him in."

"I'm sorry," Wade said to Katie as Gross and Hank left.

"For what?"

"For having to ask you to do that and for you hearing those details. I'm going to have to be out for a while. Corley's gone home and Alcott is outside. I know you want some clothes besides that suit you're wearing and my red-and-white pajamas, but in case Barker's watching your apartment, I don't want anyone going in to get your things and giving him the opportunity to follow them back here. If you'll make a list, I'll send a female deputy over. She can do some shopping for you. Pick up a toothbrush, whatever women need, and a couple of outfits."

"I feel I should say that's not necessary, but a pair of jeans would be nice. How long do you plan to keep me here?"

"Katie, right now I don't know. Just bear with me a day or so. I think this is the safest place for you right now."

"Can I make a long distance call on your phone? I'll charge it to my number."

"I don't mind a long distance call. There's no extra charge unless you're calling Japan or somewhere like that, but I don't want anyone to know where you are."

Katie laughed. "If who I want to call is legit, she might already know where I am."

"Who do you want to call?"

"Sally Brown, the psychic in Summerville. Don't laugh. I don't really believe in psychics, but I want to ask her something."

Wade smiled. "I've thought about calling her in on a case before. She's worked with some other agencies. What I'd rather you do is make a list for your shopping trip; then write out what you want to ask her."

CHAPTER 15

WHEN A DEPUTY used the transmitter to inform Katie that a female officer was coming in to talk to her, she expected a stranger. Deputy Haynes was a surprise. Katie had gone to school with her.

Whatever Vanessa Haynes thought, she kept to herself. She took Katie's list and skimmed over it, asked a few detailed questions, then left, promising to be back within an hour or so.

While she was gone, Katie called Sam, but Samantha was so full of enthusiasm about Mr. Wonderful taking her to see the house that Katie really didn't say anything. She let Sam describe each room and what colors she planned to use and even how she planned to decorate the nursery. Katie was glad when the deputy announced on the two-way radio that Officer Haynes was back.

True to her word, the officer returned with everything on Katie's list plus a few additions she'd thought of herself.

"Ms. Wray," Haynes said as she handed Katie two bags full of purchases. "I was one of the deputies at your house after you left the day we fingerprinted over there. When we looked through your apartment that day, I noticed you'd had lots of bath oil beads and stuff like that. Knowing Sheriff Jolley is a bachelor these days, I added some of those things to your list.

"Thank you. I guess my being here looks strange to you."

"Not at all. It's common police procedure to hide people out sometimes. We don't have an official safe house. In this size town, Sheriff Jolley's house makes more sense than the motel. If you need anything else, just tell the sheriff to let me know."

Katie was pleased with the deputy's shopping and glad Wade had thought to send a female. Haynes had added Katie's favorite perfume as well as bath oil and the same brand of soap Katie used at home. "Quite an observant officer," Katie told herself. "I really should tell Wade how much she noticed the day she worked the theft at my apartment. No point in keeping all this unopened. I might as well get a bath and change."

When Wade came in, Katie was curled up on the couch in jeans and a pink tee, painting her toenails with polish Vanessa Haynes had also added to the list.

"You look more comfortable," the sheriff greeted her.

"Deputy Haynes brought a lot more than I had on the list. You may be shocked at the receipt. I was surprised that she knew all my favorites after only one trip to my apartment." Wade grinned.

"You added to my list, didn't you?" she asked.

"She called and asked about bath oil, and I suggested a few more things while we were talking. Did you see the mid-afternoon news?" Jolley said.

"No, I was bathing and changing."

"Nothing you don't already know. They've tied the three teacher murders together and given a brief bio on each of them."

"My name's not on the news, is it?"

"No. It won't be unless someone leaks the theft report or names the renter of the car. We didn't release the details of where the body parts were found. Reporters have been told that information is not available because it could jeopardize the case."

"Or until Barker comes after me," Katie added and shuddered.

"I think he would already have come if he knows where you are, and I genuinely feel you're safer here than anywhere else. Did you make your list for Sally Brown?"

"I want to talk to her myself."

"Let me place the call. I don't want you talking to anyone who might learn where you are through caller ID, and I don't want you sticking so much as your nose out the door."

"You know I only have three days for personal leave a year. I'm taking one today. I can't just stay off forever."

"Have a little faith. We hope to nail him soon. Have you looked out the window lately?" Katie shook her head no.

"The state has issued us some people and vehicles," Wade said. "Sometimes the car outside now may be SLED instead of local. SLED's also got people watching your apartment and the school. Gross thinks what Barker did with your car was a calling card. If he's right, we should have Barker soon. Don't discredit the public either. All those news bulletins showing his picture may lead to a call that places him where we can just go pick him up."

"You're optimistic."

"I hope I'm being realistic, not optimistic. Right now, we've got elementary schools in this state planning memorial services for teachers of little children. I don't want that happening anywhere else, and I sure as hell don't want it happening in my town."

He paused, then smiled as he changed the subject. "I can't believe Jennie's in your class this year. That's a real coincidence."

"Not really. There are only two second-grade classes at the school."

"I'm glad even if the odds were fifty-fifty."

Sheriff Jolley didn't need to make a decision about letting Katie talk to Sally Brown. He let Katie listen in on the bedroom extension, and when he called and identified himself, Sally Brown's tinkly little voice replied, "I've been expecting your call. You want to know about the teacher murders." Katie could picture the big lady sitting in her little house in Summerville. She wondered what color muumuu she was wearing today.

"Yes, Ms. Brown. That is what I want to talk to you about."

"I will tell you that you will catch the murderer, but someone else will die before that happens. Someone you feel close to. If you want to know more, I will come to Tanner tomorrow and speak with you in person. I have worked for the authorities before. I don't charge the law my regular fees, but I'm accustomed to being paid a stipend for my travel and services."

"That's no problem. I'm willing to pay a stipend and your expenses. We're primarily interested in places. We want to locate the man we believe is responsible and find remaining parts of a body as well as any corpses we don't know about."

"It will help if you have a photograph and something that belonged to each of them. Shall I report to the sheriff's office?"

"Yes. What time should we expect you?"

"Would ten in the morning be all right?"

"We'll be waiting for you."

"Good-bye, Sheriff Jolley. Good-bye, Ms. Wray. Tell your little blond friend hello." The dial tone replaced the tiny voice.

Katie walked out of the bedroom. "Wade, she knew I was on the line."

"She sure did. I'm a doubter, but we don't lose much by consulting her. I'll see if Henry and Gross want to sit in. Katie, your little blond friend must be Samantha."

"Of course. I told you Sam and I went to Summerville to see Sally Brown."

"Are you sure the man she told Samantha to stay away from isn't Frankie?"

"No, Samantha asked about her Mr. Wonderful, Sam Campbell. Sally Brown kept telling Samantha to stay away from him. She told her to forget him. Come on, Wade, everyone except Sam sees that the man's a liar. I'm not criticizing him for seeing other people. That's their agreement. They're not in a committed relationship, but he lies to her all the time."

Katie described Sally Brown to the sheriff. "Wait until you see her, Wade. Just wait!" Katie's voice bubbled. "I want to be there, too!" Wade shook his head no. Though she knew it sounded like she was whining or nagging, Katie persisted until Wade said, "I'm answering you as the sheriff, absolutely not.

Daddy had finally stopped walking around in the back of the house, but not before Linda became so aggravated that she bought three six-packs for the night.

Now, Linda Louise, her mother nagged, *you know you don't need any beer, certainly not that much.*

"Just be glad I didn't think about it until after the sun went down or I'd have gone to Amick's and got something good for tonight." Actually, the old law that liquor stores had to close at sundown had been changed for years. Liquor stores stayed open until seven at night, but most South Carolinians still associated sundown with closing time. During the brown-bagging days of Linda's youth, the legal hours for red-dot stores, as they were called because of the large red circles that identified stores that sold alcoholic beverages, were from sunup to sundown.

Look at your daddy over there in that chair all helpless like that. You should just get on your knees and thank the Lord you've got your health. You should be praying that strokes don't turn out to be hereditary. That's what you should be doing instead of drinking, Linda Louise.

"Tell you what, Mama. If he'll stay in the chair and not be walking around in the back, and you'll stop telling me what to do, I'll save some of this beer for tomorrow."

Linda sat down at the table and looked across at the recliner. "Okay, Daddy? Will you just sit still and not be up tonight?"

Linda Louise, you know your daddy can't talk anymore.

"Yes, ma'am, but it's only polite to talk to him anyway. I'm going to leave the TV on for him. I might even watch it with him while I have my beer."

Linda popped her first top for the night and drained the can in one long gulp. She lit a cigarette and began the methodical consumption of three six-packs and two packs of cigarettes. She didn't make it over to the love seat. Her head fell onto the table, and she slept there with the television playing to the empty recliner.

"No," Linda whimpered in her sleep. "No, Bert, I didn't go off today. I stayed home and cleaned house. Haven't been out."

"Don't lie to me!" the big man yelled as he snatched her up by her collar. He stood there holding her with her toes barely touching the floor. "If you haven't been out today, why isn't my supper done? I'm home and it's not ready!"

"You came home early, Bert." Linda responded though she knew it was better not to answer him when he was angry.

"I'm the man of the house. I'll come home anytime I want to, and my dinner better be ready when I get here."

"It won't take long, Bert. The roast and green beans are almost done. All I have to do is put the cornbread in the oven. It's that cornmeal mush kind with corn and sour cream that you like."

"But it's not done yet. It's not done because my wife's been out somewhere today instead of home taking care of the house I provide. It's not done because my wife started too late to cook the groceries I provide. I think now I'll have to provide my wife with a lesson so next time my supper will be ready when I get home."

"No, Bert, no!"

"A little cooling off is what you need. Hot-to-trot is what my mother called women like you. I'm going to cool off my little hot-to-trot wife."

"No, Bert, please, no," Linda begged, but she knew it wouldn't do any good. It never did. He dragged her into the bathroom and shoved her into the shower stall. A pair of cuffs hung from the showerhead. He didn't even bother to move them anymore, and Linda was afraid to touch them herself, even when he wasn't home. He yanked her arms above her head and snapped the handcuffs on.

As always in recent months, he tore her clothes off except for bra and panties. He pulled out his pocketknife, flipped it open, and held it in front of her face. "A few scars on that pretty face will keep you home," he snarled. "Just a few slices and I'll bet my wife will be ready for me when I get home." He'd never actually cut her, but even the dreaming Linda knew the day was coming.

In real time, Linda Pearson slipped from the chair and slid onto the floor. Her arms snaked up over her head and her wrists crossed as though they were bound. Her body writhed as the old scene replayed in her mind.

Bert didn't cut her. He reached out with the knife and slipped it under the crisscross of her bra between her breasts. The metal was cold against her skin. The blade popped forward slicing the fabric. Then he slid the knife under the sheer fabric over first one hip and then the other. Her panties fell to the floor of the shower stall. Linda stood totally naked as he turned on the cold water and began sluicing the water over her body. "Just cooling off my little wife. Just cooling off my hot-to-trot wife. Dance for me, Linda. Dance like you used to dance when I first saw you."

"No, Bert, no," the woman on the floor whimpered as the woman in her mind bounced from toe to toe in a fruitless effort to avoid the biting coldness of the water needling over her body.

"That's right, Linda. Dance for me. Have you had enough? Do I need to leave you here for three days like the last time or does my little wife want to come on back and finish cooking for me?"

The tears pouring down Linda's face were lost in the water drenching her from the shower. She tried to nod her head yes. Surprisingly Bert cut off the water, unsnapped the cuffs, and threw her a towel.

"Get yourself dressed and cook my supper!"

In the kitchen, Bert stood over Linda as she pulled the roast from the oven and set the Pyrex baking dish on a wire rack. He taunted her about her stupidity as she mixed the cornmeal, eggs, sour cream, milk, butter, and corn in a bowl. "How long does it have to cook?" he asked as she poured the mixture into the big cast-iron frying pan.

"Twenty minutes," Linda mumbled.

"Speak up, bitch! I asked you how long it cooks."

"Twenty minutes!" Linda screamed back.

Bert grabbed Linda's hair and yanked it as he spit into her face and slammed his right fist into the side of her head. Sometimes he pulled out pieces of her hair. This time he just gripped it tight.

"Don't you ever yell at me! You're going back to the shower, and it won't be three days this time. It'll be for a week or until you learn your lesson. I don't care how much you cry about cramps in your muscles, and I don't care what a mess you make of yourself. Maybe I've been trying to cool you off when what you need is warming up. Look at you! You're a wreck!" He released the handcuffs from his belt with his right hand while holding her hair with his left. "I'm turning the hot water on you this time!" he threatened as he let her hair go and grabbed her wrists.

Then Bert did something he'd never done before in his life. He dropped the handcuffs. When he bent forward to retrieve them, Linda snatched up the black cast-iron frying pan of cornbread batter and did something she'd never done before. She struck back. For the first time ever, she hit him. She hit Bert just as he straightened up. The skillet smashed into his upturned face and crushed his nose. Blood flew everywhere as the batter dripped onto his face and shoulders.

"I'll kill you for that," Bert said.

He didn't scream. He didn't yell. He wasn't shrieking. He said it calmly, and Linda knew he meant it. In that split moment, she also knew he'd make her suffer the tortures of the damned first. Death would be a merciful release from all the things Bert could think of doing. With both hands grasping the handle, Linda lifted the heavy pan back over her head and slammed it forward.

The cast iron hit Bert's head with every ounce of force Linda could summon, but he still moved. She pounded him again and again and again. When he finally crumpled on the floor, Linda collapsed beside him. She slammed the skillet into his head until there was nothing but mush where his skull had been. She looked at the mess on the floor—cornbread batter and bits of skull mixed with human brains and tissue. She laughed hysterically and said two words before she collapsed into gut-wrenching sobs. What Linda said in real life back then were the same two words she dreamed now: "Cornmeal mush."

Lying on the floor, Linda Pearson cried in her sleep just as she had sobbed while sitting on the floor beside Bert so many years ago. After a while, her tears stopped. Her arms moved from above her head and she turned onto her side. She curled into a tight fetal position on the floor and slept soundly the rest of the night. She heard no noise from the back of the house.

Fuck! The ride out to the old church ruins had been a waste of gasoline and time. Yellow crime scene tape circled the trees around where he'd left the sports car parked. That told Shug the church ruins wouldn't be such a good place to hide Janice's body. So long as the space was marked, law officers or those CSI guys might return to the site at any time, including while he unloaded her.

Shug had opened the peanut butter jar before he realized that he didn't have a spoon. He pulled his switchblade from his pocket and used it to dip and spread the peanut butter as well as to slice the banana. He carefully licked the blade clean, closed it, and shoved the knife back into his pocket. He took the first bite of sandwich before he began cursing himself.

The church ruins weren't a good spot to dump Janice because someone might come at any minute, so why in hell was he sitting there eating an Elvis sandwich? Shug shook violently, then laughed out loud. He'd best get control of his mind. He wasn't thinking straight, and that could send him straight to the electric chair. Not really. South Carolina's "Old Sparky" had been retired and replaced by lethal injection, but that had no more appeal to him than electrocution. He'd always been smart. Good-looking and smart. That's what his seventh grade teacher had told him. Now, he needed to use his brains for more than making up rhymes.

Shug started the car and threw it into reverse. Screw this place. He sped away from the church ruins in search of somewhere to put the remains hidden in the trunk of the car.

THURSDAY THRILL

CHAPTER 16

KATIE HEARD a familiar voice crying—Samantha sobbing through the sheriff's answering machine in the other room. "This is getting to be ridiculous," Katie thought, but she quickly jumped out of bed and ran to the telephone. She hadn't told Wade that Sam knew how to reach her, and the last thing she wanted was a long tearful message from Samantha recorded on his machine.

"I'll have to try to erase the message off the machine and delete her number from the caller ID," she thought. "No, that's lying. I told Wade how Samantha's Mr. Wonderful tells lies. Now I'm thinking about hiding the truth from him. I'll just explain it to him." She sighed.

"Hello, Sam, what's wrong?" Katie looked at the clock. It was almost nine. "Even earlier than the last time she woke me from a sound sleep," Katie thought. "Why aren't you working?" she asked Sam. "What's the matter?"

"I told them I was sick to my stomach. I am, Katie. I've been throwing up ever since I got to work and Aimee told me."

"Told you what?"

"Her friend Suzanne . . . " Sam's words were smothered by her sobs as she struggled to catch her breath.

"Calm down, Samantha. Take a few deep breaths and tell me what Aimee said to you."

"The house." Once again Katie could barely distinguish what Sam was saying. Finally, Samantha spoke more clearly. "He took Suzanne to see the house. He asked her about colors and wallpaper, too. Sam took Suzanne to the same house he showed me." She sobbed uncontrollably. "I can't stand it, Katie. I thought it was going to work. I really thought he cared about me."

"Now, Samantha, you told me he said he wasn't ready for commitment," Katie tried to reason while her mind shouted, "Son of a bitch!"

"But, Katie, he swore to me that he wasn't interested in her and she just went to look at his hot tub. He's lying to me. If he wants her, why did he come over to my house and spend the night?"

Katie didn't have the heart to tell Samantha what she thought, so she said, "I don't know Sam, but I agree with you. He's been lying to you." Those were the words she spoke, but she thought, "Yeah, Suzanne played hard to get, so Mr. Wonderful went where he knew he'd be welcome, and you let him in and gave him what he came for, Samantha."

"You think I'm worth more than that, don't you, Katie?

Don't you think I deserve better?"

"Samantha, I know you deserve better than Marc or Sam. There's somebody out there who will treat you better than either one of them has. Where are you?"

"At my apartment. I just came home. I can't stand any more. I feel so sick . . . Oh! Katie, a man called here this morning and asked where you are."

"What? Did he tell you who he is?"

"No, he just asked wasn't I your friend and if I knew whether you'd be at work today or where you are. I told him no, since you told me not to tell anybody."

"What did he sound like?"

"I don't know. He just sounded like a man."

"The sheriff may want to talk to you about it."

"Okay. What should I do, Katie?"

"Wait for Wade to call you. I'll tell him about the man."

"No, I mean what should I do about Sam."

"I can't tell you what to do, Samantha. All I can tell you is that I'm your friend, and I'll be here for you no matter what you decide." In her mind, she said, "Dump him! Dump him!"

"I'm gonna be sick again. I'll call you back!" Sam slammed down the receiver, and Katie sat listening to the dial tone trying to remember if Maggie would ever have spoken to Frankie about Samantha. "She and I didn't see each other all summer, and I don't think we even talked on the telephone, but Frankie and Maggie spent so much time together. Would she have mentioned Samantha? Who else besides Frankie would be looking for me?"

Katie thought about asking the deputy outside to radio Wade to call her but decided to bathe and dress first. Sally Brown was due in the sheriff's office at ten, and Wade had promised he'd consider letting Katie talk to her. She didn't know if he'd bring the psychic to the house or let her talk on the telephone. Katie had written out three questions for Sally Brown and given them to Wade, but she really wanted to talk to the psychic.

"Dream on," Katie told herself. "Wade's not going to let me talk to anybody. I may as well just get busy and not even think about it." Katie started a pot of coffee and pulled a package labeled "pork chops" from the freezer to thaw for dinner. The least she could do was cook.

Sally Brown arrived at the Blair County Sheriff's Department in full glory at five minutes before ten. The sheriff had told Gross and Legrand that this was a real long shot, but neither of them had laughed at him or seemed especially skeptical. They had a "What have we got to lose?" attitude. Having been told by Katie to expect a large lady, the sheriff added chairs to his office and left the double-seater couch vacant. Not one of them, however, was prepared for Sally Brown.

The woman walked right through the reception area straight into the sheriff's office without bothering to be announced by the clerk. The man who followed her was as slim as she was large. Today, Ms. Brown was wearing a black and silver garment which none of the men could identify by name. To Wade, it looked like a tent. Her blond hair was piled on top of her head in masses of ringlet curls, and she wore silver eye shadow as well as silver nail polish both on her fingernails and on her toenails. The lady was once again barefooted.

"Gentlemen," she announced, "I have come to help you." Though Katie had given Wade a vivid description of the psychic and he had spoken to her on the telephone, the sheriff was still surprised by the delicate little voice that came from this gargantuan lady. Just unbelievable.

"This is my husband, Harold. He has driven me here, and since my work sometimes makes him nervous, we would prefer that he be given somewhere else to wait while I talk with you." Harold said not a word, but he nodded his head up and down. The head bobbing up and down on the spindly neck reminded Wade of a turkey, and he had to suppress the smile this image summoned.

"Perhaps Harold would like to wait outside the office in the lobby area. You came through it on your way in."

"Certainly. Harold, go sit." Harold backed out the door bobbing his head up and down even more vigorously. Sally Brown looked around and sat on the double-seater. She filled it completely.

"Did you get the items I requested?" she asked.

"I have three pictures for you. Fred Barker, Janice Woods, and Carlton Johnson. I prefer not to tell you who is who or why I've chosen those three pictures. I also have part of a garment that belonged to Janice Woods. We haven't had time to obtain items belonging to the other two."

"You don't have to tell me anything. I'll just want to hold the photos and the garment for a while. Then I'll tell you what I can."

Immaculately dressed as always, the trim, fit John Gross said in his professional voice, "We have certain questions to ask you, Ms. Brown."

Sally Brown turned toward him. "First, it's Mrs. Brown. I just told you that Harold is my husband. Second, I don't answer questions unless I'm paid by the question. For one hundred dollars, I will tell you whatever I know about these three people. Believe me, I am giving you the deal of a lifetime. If you wish to ask specific questions, it will cost seventy-five dollars for each one. The one hundred dollars you may pay me as I leave, or the sheriff can even mail me a check. If you wish to ask questions, the money must cross my palm before I answer. Are we clear?"

Legrand grinned and said, "This is the South," to Gross.

"He's from the South," Sally Brown said to Hank.

"Let's go for the hundred-dollar reading first. If we decide we want questions, they can come later," Sheriff Jolley instructed and set the three photographs on his desk. He also handed a piece of fabric across the desk toward the psychic.

"Put the cloth beside the pictures," Mrs. Brown said, and Wade thought how accurately Katie had described the woman's voice as "tinkly."

"I will need quiet." She picked up the photograph of Carlton Johnson first and laid one hand under the picture; the other, over it. She closed her eyes. The men in the room sat still and silent while the psychic held the photo. Jolley was reminded of the FBI agent's habit of long, dramatic pauses. Gross looked bored. Hank seemed keenly interested. Wade wondered what Katie was doing.

"Dead. I don't need to tell you where to seek his body. You have the corpse. His death was violent and sexually related. That is all." She laid the photograph back on the desk but turned it facedown before picking up the picture of Janice Woods.

She held this photo totally enclosed in her hands as she had Johnson's, but her face contorted even before she closed her eyes. "It's too painful." The tiny voice whispered from the large body. "Too painful. She trusted him. He'd left her once, and when he came back, she really believed he'd changed his mind. She trusted him a second time." She placed the small rectangular piece of paper back on the desk, but this one she put faceup. "Later," she said softly.

"Why do you not have pictures of the Shealy woman or Patty David?" the tinkly voice inquired. "He ambushed Mary Ellen Shealy. She'd learned her lesson from him the first time around, but he got to her. She didn't have a chance. He struck so fast she didn't know what happened. He followed Patty David from a store to her place. Told her he was interviewing teachers for a magazine article. She let him in, but he refused to leave. He stayed all afternoon."

Mrs. Brown didn't pick up the picture of Barker. She laid both hands over it and covered it completely on the desk, then closed her eyes again. "He's hurt. He's troubled. He feels pain, but he inflicts more pain than he feels. He's acting out revenge, but he also wants attention. He's always wanted to be noticed. His poems are for attention, and there was a rhyme for every teacher. Even as a child, he always wanted the teacher's attention. He became angry when she called on anyone but him. Yes, you will locate him, but you will be too late. He's near." Her words cut through Wade Jolley like a machete.

Slowly the fat hands inched toward the cloth. The silver polished fingertips barely touched the edge of it. She opened her eyes and stared at the cloth. "Janice Woods was wearing this when she met him the first time. It was no coincidence that she had it on again the last time they met. He convinced her he wanted to start over. She trusted him. She thought he wouldn't hurt her physically. He proved her wrong." She paused, and when she spoke again, her voice was at least an octave lower. "What you seek is in water." Her head bent forward and she sat motionless for several minutes. When she looked up, she smiled.

"Gentlemen," the voice was like a crystal bell now, "I have given you far more than a hundred dollars' worth. The rest of this is free." She looked directly at Jolley. "Sheriff, tell the teachers I meant everything I said in Summerville. Remind the blonde that she must forget the man now. Tell the tall one that she has seen her child." The huge woman placed each hand solidly against the arms of the double seat she was in and began pushing down to balance herself to stand. Wade rose from behind his desk and walked around to her, offering his hand to help her rise. "Thank you, but I can do it."

"Where is the water?" asked Gross.

"That would cost you seventy-five dollars, but I won't take that money because I don't know exactly yet. When that answer comes to me, I will telephone. It won't cost you more money because I will offer the information and not count it as a question. I'm tired now. The photographs brought me pain. Will one of you please call Harold inside this office? I'm ready for him to drive me home." Chief Legrand stepped out. Sally Brown looked up at Jolley. "Sheriff, you may mail my check. One hundred will cover the stipend and expenses."

"Actually, I'm prepared to pay you before you leave, Mrs. Brown. Thank you for driving all the way from Summerville."

Hank and Harold came into the office. Harold knew

exactly what to do. He stood in front of the psychic with his feet planted apart and held his arms out to her. She lifted her hands, and that small man pulled the tremendous woman to her feet.

"I'll walk out with you and see that you receive your pay," Wade said. "If you learn more, do call me. If there's an additional charge after you call, you know I'll treat you right."

"Thank you, Sheriff. You are a gentleman."

Katie called Samantha's apartment repeatedly, but there was no answer. When Wade's telephone rang, Katie thought Sam was returning the call to the number on her caller ID and snatched it up immediately before Wade's caller ID registered the incoming number.

"Sam?" she asked.

"No, this is Wade. Should I be jealous?"

"No, you know Sam is Samantha."

"I know that. I cooked over at her place, remember? Frogmore stew. How does she know where you are?"

"She really needs to talk to me, Wade, and some man called her this morning wanting to know where I am and why I'm not at school. I think it may have been Frankie. Now she's not answering her phone. I'm worried."

"What? Why didn't you contact me? You think Barker called Sam looking for you, and you didn't let me know!"

Katie had seen the sheriff upset before, but this was the angriest she'd ever heard him.

"I knew you were busy with Sally Brown coming and with Hank and Gross there. I didn't think it mattered if I waited until I heard from you. Sam didn't tell him anything."

"How did Samantha know how to reach you?" He still sounded angry.

"I called her yesterday. She got your number off her caller ID." Katie waited, but all she heard was a long sigh.

"Wade? Are you mad at me?" knowing she sounded like a little girl and hating it.

"Yes, I am, but I'll get over it. Katie, you've got to remember that I'm the sheriff. I'm in charge of this investigation. Even if I didn't care about you at all, I'd need to know anything that happens concerning you or Barker. When I tell you not to talk to anyone, it's not Wade Jolley speaking. It's Sheriff Jolley."

Katie answered, "Yes, Sheriff Jolley," but all she'd really heard was, "Even if I didn't care about you at all." She felt as confused and miserable as Samantha. Her first concern had to be about her sister. Where was Maggie? Would they find her in the trunk of a car or in an alley? With that on her mind, how could she get even a little excited at the thought the sheriff saw her as more than a potential victim?

"Are you calling me Sheriff Jolley instead of Wade being sarcastic or because now you're mad?" he asked.

"No, just to reassure you I'll remember that what you tell me is because you're the sheriff and you have to catch Frankie before he hurts someone else."

"Katie, Barker's doing more than hurting people!"

"I know." Time to change the subject. "What did Sally Brown say?"

"Don't change the subject. Barker is not the gentle soul your sister played house with all summer. He's killing. He's degrading. He's butchering teachers. You have to accept what he is." Wade stopped. When he spoke again, he was calmer. "Now, tell me about Samantha. Is she at work now?"

"No, she went home sick."

"I'll go by there. I've seen your psychic. The lady may actually be gifted. Very cryptic answers and nothing really specific, but I've got a feeling she could wind up being a worthwhile investment. Gross and Hank say that she didn't tell us anything she couldn't have based on what's already been in the newspapers and on television, but I think she may have made a believer out of me. Now a question for you. On the paper you gave me, you wrote three questions. Did you know she charges seventy-five dollars for a question?"

"If she said that, she was giving you a discount."

"Well, she answered your three questions for free, but the interesting part is that I didn't give her the questions."

"What did she say?"

"You wrote, 'Has anything changed?' She said, 'I meant everything I said.' You wrote, 'What should Sam do?' She said, 'Forget the man now,' and, Katie, she said 'now' in bold print, all caps. Your third question puzzled me when you gave me the paper. It might be personal, but why did you ask that question?"

"It is personal, but I'll tell you. When she did the reading at her house, she told me that I'll have a child within two years. It made me doubt her because one of the problems with Charles and me was that I've been told I can't have children. I wanted to adopt, and he was against it. In Summerville, Sally Brown told me I'll have a child within two years. It made me discredit everything she said, but she warned me about Frankie, so that part sounded true. That's why I wrote, 'Will I adopt a child?' Did she answer that too?"

"I'm going to quote her word for word. 'Tell the tall one that she has seen her child.' You haven't been dreaming about babies, have you?"

"Not that I remember. Did she say anything useful to the case?"

"She seems on target, but she hasn't told us where to look. She says what we haven't found of Janice Woods is in water. That doesn't tell us anything really, but she did say she'll call when she knows more. I'm sitting there thinking she's scamming us out of a hundred bucks and then she whammies me by answering three questions that are on a folded piece of paper in my pocket."

"If I'd known about the phone call to Sam, I'd have written a question about that. Maybe we'd have gotten another free answer."

"Listen, I'm going by Samantha's apartment. That black Hyundai's hers, right?"

"Yes, that's her car."

"I'll call you when I know something. If you hear from her, tell the deputy outside to radio me."

The phone rang immediately after the sheriff disconnected, and Katie answered it expecting it to be Wade to add something to his Sally Brown report.

Samantha said, "Katie?"

"Sam, where are you?"

"I'm shopping. Guess what? I'm a size two!"

"Are you okay? The sheriff is headed to your apartment to check on you."

"I'm fine. I've made some decisions. Sam and I are supposed to go to a party tomorrow night. I'm buying myself this gorgeous, knock 'em dead outfit to wear, a gorgeous, knock 'em dead size two outfit to wear to the party!"

"What about Suzanne?"

"She can have him. I've decided you're right. There's somebody better waiting to find me, and I won't meet him if I'm sitting home crying over Sam. After the party, I'm telling him it's over. I'm not seeing him anymore, and he can cook his own damned Frogmore stew for his birthday."

"You go, girl! I've gotta let Wade know you're okay. He's gonna want to talk to you about that telephone call this morning. Call me back when you get home."

Tennessee Linda was having a Tennessee day. All she could think about was Jack Daniel's. Her mother had been silent since yesterday, but Daddy had walked around all morning. She could hear him in the rear of the house. She almost went back there to search for him, but suddenly she was overwhelmed with fear that if she went to look, she might actually see him and even worse, he might grab her. That thought terrified Linda.

In addition to the sounds of Daddy walking around when he most assuredly was supposed to be unable to walk or talk, Linda had vague, conscious memories of dreaming about Bert's death. She hated that nightmare worst of all. Her stomach growled with hunger, and she took the ATM card and left the house. Linda knew her first stop would be the money machine, as she called it. She didn't know if the second would be the Downtown Diner, Amick's, or the Shop & Save. What she did know was that she had to get out of the house for a while.

The minute Linda walked through the diner door,

Courtney Williams knew Miss Possum was having a bad day. Her hair fell down her back in a messy tangle, and her eyes looked glazed. She stood and pushed on the door so long that Courtney thought she'd have to go around the counter and open it for her before Miss Possum finally remembered or read the "pull" sign. She climbed up on her stool and barely nodded when Courtney asked her if she'd have her usual, and she got up to leave before she'd eaten even half of her waffle. As she left, Sheriff Jolley came in.

"Hello, Ms. Pearson. How are you today?" the nice young sheriff asked.

"He keeps walking," she mumbled.

"I beg your pardon?" Jolley asked.

"Oh, nothing. I just keep hearing Daddy walking around in the back of the house."

"Yes, sometimes memories just won't leave us alone. I noticed when I went by that you let someone work on that kudzu for you. It looks much better."

The blank eyes took on a bright sparkle. "I did it myself!" she exclaimed with pride.

"You did it! That's hard work for a lady. Next time, give me a call," Wade said. Then, realizing how much pride he'd heard in her voice and how what he'd said might have sounded to her, he added, "I'll be glad to help you with it."

"I might just do that, Sheriff."

"It's hot outside. I'm just getting an iced tea to go. Could I give you a lift, Ms. Pearson?"

"Why, no thank you. A lady needs to get some exercise, but I thank you kindly for the offer."

There seemed to be a bit more pep in her walk as she

went on her way, and she was actually holding the pillowcase high enough that it didn't drag the sidewalk.

Wade silently wished he could do more for Linda Pearson than just exchange a few pleasantries with her, but he definitely didn't want to do what many of the townspeople thought he should do. Her father had left enough money to support her, and she harmed no one. "The woman's already spent too much time locked up," the sheriff said softly to himself.

FREAKY FRIDAY

CHAPTER 17

SUNRISE ON FRIDAY MORNING was a welcome relief to Linda Pearson. It meant that another day had begun and she could remedy her mistake from the day before. Years ago she'd had a favorite teacher who used to say, "It's no sin to make a mistake so long as you fix it." It wasn't exactly grammatically perfect, but Linda thought that saying held a lot of truth. Today there would be no beer from the Shop & Save. Instead, there would be a trip to Amick's, and it wouldn't be for a pint or even two pints. It might even be a very early trip.

The beer had done nothing for Linda the night before. By the time she'd finished the three six-packs she'd bought, it was after midnight, and the Shop & Save was closed. Linda had tossed restlessly on the love seat, hoping sleep would come. She'd listened intently for the sound of

Daddy walking, and occasionally she'd heard his steps, but he'd been silent most of the night. The beer hadn't put her to sleep, but it had filled her bladder and repeatedly through the night she'd had to go to the small half bath off the kitchen. It was just a toilet and small lavatory. Mama always said they'd put it in for the kitchen help when inside plumbing had been added to the house and every time Linda used it, Mama nagged.

Linda Louise, why do you insist on using the maid's toilet? Go back to the big bathroom.

"I don't need a full bathroom just to pee, Mama. I'm not taking a bath, and I'm not going back there with Daddy walking around."

Your daddy isn't walking. You know he can't walk or talk anymore. He hasn't taken a step since his first stroke.

"You're both dead, too, Mama, but that doesn't keep you from talking and him from walking."

Linda got the ATM card from the kitchen, picked up her pillowcase, and went out on the front porch. She had sat on the stoop in the dark. She was sitting there waiting for sunrise. Then she saw Bert's ghost. When she first saw him dash across the side of the yard toward the back, she thought it was Daddy, but he had hair, and Daddy had been bald as a doorknob when he died. Seeing Bert's ghost frightened Linda so much she'd wet her pants. She was too scared of Daddy to go back inside the house right then and too scared of Bert's ghost to go around back. Linda just sat where she was. The sogginess felt bad, but she'd reasoned that Daddy would be still when morning came, and ghosts don't roam in daylight.

Wade Jolley spent a restless night, too. After talking with

Samantha, he'd been convinced the call about Katie had been Barker. He assigned a deputy to tail Samantha just to be on the safe side. After all, she was a teacher. She didn't look like Katie, but with Barker, anything was possible. He'd altered his MO with Patricia David and changed it completely when he murdered Janice Woods. Blair County's sheriff's department wasn't very large. At the rate things were going, even with SLED's assistance, Wade would soon have all his deputies assigned to protective surveillance. Corley had grown disillusioned that Barker would come after Katie with Wade hiding her and expressed a desire for a more active assignment.

What more active assignment was there for him? Until someone spotted Barker, they had nothing to do but check out leads called in from the news spots and wait on reports. Nothing was giving them anything really new.

John Doe had been positively identified as the missing Carlton Johnson from Charlotte, North Carolina, but that didn't give them any clues where Barker might be now. His home was being watched, but Barker hadn't been seen near his wife or children. Susan Barker had assured authorities she would notify them if she heard from him, and, for some reason, Wade believed her. He considered having a few local ponds and a lake dragged, but that seemed a bit extreme based just on Sally Brown's telling them they'd find the rest of Janice Woods in water. Hell, Tanner was a coastal town. Water could mean the Atlantic Ocean.

Word had gotten out that the Blair County Sheriff's Department had called in a psychic. A SLED agent had asked why they hadn't been invited to the "séance." As Wade tried to form a reasonable answer, the man had laughed. Reports were coming in from interviews with friends and family of the deceased individuals. No doubt at all in Jolley's mind that Frankie Barker had murdered every one of them. No doubt that Barker was seeking Katie. Gross kept telling him to lure Barker in with Katie. The sheriff couldn't do that. He didn't think he would do it even if the woman in question had not been Katie, but he knew he couldn't use Katie Wray as bait.

As all of this rolled around in the sheriff's thoughts, he was painfully aware that Katie lay in a bed just on the other side of his bedroom wall. By the time he finally got to sleep, Linda Pearson was smiling at the sun peeking over the horizon, and a restless Katie was tiptoeing into the sheriff's kitchen to make coffee. She'd totally given up on sleep for the night, and she wondered how Wade would react when she told him she'd have no choice but to go to work Monday. This Friday was the last of her three days of personal leave.

"Wade's got a guard on Samantha now, too," Katie thought. "Like Sam doesn't have enough trouble in her life without a psycho Maggie picked up last summer calling her and maybe even looking to kill her. How'd Frankie find Samantha's number? How'd he even know who she was? But most important, where is Maggie?"

The coffee smelled good. "At least I make decent coffee," Katie thought. "Wade ate the pork chops, but I'll bet he thinks I can't cook. I haven't burned anything in years, so why'd I scorch the pork chops? And I was so scared the potato salad would wind up being mashed potatoes with eggs and pickles, I didn't boil the potatoes long enough. They tasted like little rocks. He's a better cook than I am, but I'm a better cook than last night's dinner made me out to be."

Katie thought of her usual cure for the miseries. She picked up her coffee cup and headed for a long, hot, soaking bath. She was totally immersed except for her nose when she heard knocking on the door.

Lifting her head from the water, she heard Wade. "Katie, Samantha's on the phone. She says she's okay, but she has to talk to you. She's crying. Can you talk to her? Open the door a crack and I'll hand you the cordless."

"What's wrong with me, Katie?" Samantha sobbed. "Why doesn't Sam love me?"

Katie didn't even bother to try to answer that. "What time is it, Samantha? Are you going to work?"

The change of subject softened Sam's sobs to sniffles. "It's early. There's plenty of time, but I haven't decided. I may call in sick, but I don't have my lesson plans on my desk. Are you going in?"

"No, Sam. I'm not going today."

"You're not even going by? I thought maybe you could write some plans and put them in my room for me."

"Sorry, Samantha. I'm not going at all."

"Did you know your boyfriend put a guard outside my apartment?"

"He's not my boyfriend."

"He treats you better than anybody treats me."

"The sheriff assigned someone to guard you, Samantha, same as me."

"But he's letting you stay at his house."

"Okay, Sam, he's treating me better than you. Do you want me to ask him if you can come over here to be guarded? It would probably save the county some money."

"If I do that, can you look at this new outfit and tell me how it looks on me?"

"Samantha, if you come over here, he probably won't let you go anywhere tonight. He may not let you go anyway."

"Oh, no! I'm going to the party. I'm wearing this outfit, and then I'm telling Sam that I'm not seeing him anymore."

"Samantha? Let's talk about it later, okay? I'm taking a bath right now."

"You're in the tub with the phone? Isn't that dangerous?"

"Well, actually, I got out of the tub to talk to you, but I really want to get dressed and talk to the sheriff. I think you woke him up.

"Are you two sleeping together?"

"No, Sam, I've got my room and he has his own."

"If I stay home today, will you talk to me later?"

"What about your lesson plans?"

"What are you going to do about yours?"

"Didn't you see in my plan book? I put mine on my desk for the whole week before I left last Friday."

"I'm going to start being more like you, Katie. Just as soon as I get myself over this Sam thing. I'm going to be a good teacher. You just watch me!"

"You already are a good teacher, Samantha. You just need to be more organized."

"I'm going to call the sub-center and then write my plans and take them over to the school. I'll call you when I get back. Bye."

"I'm sure you will," Katie thought. "You'll call and tell me you love Sam and you hate Sam. You'll spend all your money to impress him at this party. You'll tell me you're not seeing him anymore, then cry because he doesn't love you." Katie dried off, dressed, and went out to face the day and the sheriff.

"What's wrong?" Wade asked when she entered the kitchen. He was sitting at the counter eating Pop Tarts.

"She's got man problems with that Sam she's been dating." Katie poured herself a cup of coffee. "She doesn't have to stay out of sight like me, does she? She's got a really important date tonight."

"Not really. I do plan to keep someone watching her, but it's because I think Barker may attempt to reach you through her. Samantha doesn't fit the looks he seems to prefer. The reason I don't want you out and about is because I hope he doesn't know where you are. If he's watching Samantha, he already knows where she is. He'd just follow her to where we tried to conceal her, so hiding her doesn't make much sense."

"None of it makes sense to me."

"Serial killers never make sense. That's one reason they're hard to catch."

"Maybe Sally Brown will call you back today and tell you where Frankie is or where the rest of the body parts are or what's going to happen next."

"Maybe she'll call back and tell us if your baby will look like me," Wade teased.

"I told you I can't have babies," Katie answered solemnly. "I never smile about that," she added sadly.

"I apologize. Sometimes I'm not very thoughtful."

"Yes, you are. You're one of the most thoughtful men I've ever known."

Samantha did call Katie back, but it was after Wade left, and Katie let her talk as long as she wanted. She told Katie all about her wonderful new silk outfit, repeatedly referring to it as her size two. Katie tried to ask her if she'd eaten anything lately, but Samantha couldn't get beyond the fact she fit into a size two. Finally, she told Katie she had to get off the telephone so she could wax her legs, polish her nails, pluck her eyebrows, and give herself a facial.

Katie laughed, "I hope this is a great party. It's going to take you all day to get ready for it."

"I just want Sam to see what he's losing."

Katie rummaged the freezer again and selected a pot roast. It would be hard to ruin that. She found fresh potatoes in the pantry. There were even carrots and celery in the crisper. She watched television, but the constant APB reports on the news agitated her.

Every time Frankie's picture appeared, they showed photographs of his victims. It was like looking into a mirror over and over and knowing the image staring back at her was dead. Thank God Maggie wasn't among the photos. But where was she? And what if he changed and targeted all teachers, starting with Samantha?

Katie called her friend. "Have you done all those great things to yourself yet?" she asked Sam.

"I don't have time to talk, Katie. I'm too busy. I called and got an appointment to have my hair lightened a little more. They're going to work me in. I gotta go. I'll call you tomorrow."

"Sam, I'm worried about you. I . . ."

"No time, Katie. I gotta go. Talk to you tomorrow."

Jolley had one piece of news for Katie when he returned. There'd been a phone call late last night from Ann, the Platinum Posse lead singer. Barker was in the club where they were playing. By the time Hank's men arrived, Frankie/Fred was gone. Wade didn't tell Katie about Barker asking the musicians to play "Maggie May." Of course, Nan had told him Platinum Posse didn't play any of that old stuff. Barker had laughed and replied, "Some old stuff is really good."

Before he left, Wade told Katie, "If you're getting bored all locked up here, why don't you watch a video? I told you there's a whole cabinet full, and there's a stack of books beside my bed. I've got the newest Dean Koontz and Stephen King in there."

Katie answered, "I'm too nervous now to concentrate on reading. I'm more likely to watch TV. Will you be home for dinner?"

Wade laughed. "You sound like a wife."

"Not me," she laughed back at him. "I don't want the name without the game." As she locked the door, she wondered how they could laugh at anything, then realized laughter was a defense against falling apart—completely totally apart.

The sheriff didn't come back until dinnertime. They sat down to a perfectly cooked beef roast just about the time Linda Pearson sat down with a fifth of Jack Daniel's and a carton of generic cigarettes. Not that she planned to drink and smoke it all in one night, but she didn't intend to run out before the stupor released her from the mental pains.

Mama had talked and talked and talked at her all day. Daddy had silently demanded television one minute and walked around in back the next. The memory of Bert's ghost made her nauseous. She'd never seen his ghost before. He haunted her dreams regularly, but Linda's last sight of Bert while she was awake had been when she'd glanced back at the cornmeal mush as she walked from the kitchen to another room to call 911 years ago. She had no intention of risking a Bert ghost getting hold of her without ample antifreeze in her system.

Before Linda finished her first Donald Duck glass of Jack Daniel's, Wade was called back to work. Katie finished her dinner alone, then changed clothes, and curled up on the couch to watch TV.

SATURDAY'S SORROW

CHAPTER 18

"KATIE, WHO'S SAMANTHA'S next of kin?" the sheriff shouted as he burst through the door a little after midnight. Across town, Linda Pearson was passed out in a liquor-induced stupor.

"Next of kin? She's dead? Sam's dead?" Katie had fought so hard for days to stay controlled. Now she fell totally apart. "He got her, didn't he? Frankie got her."

"No, Barker has nothing to do with it. There's been an accident. Who's Samantha Branham's next of kin?"

"She has no next of kin, Wade. I'm all she has. She's an only child. Her parents are dead, and the aunt who raised her died a year or so ago. Where is she?"

"Who's her husband?" Jolley asked again.

"They're getting divorced." Katie grabbed her purse and pulled on her shoes. She loosened her jeans and stuffed in the blue denim shirt she wore. Any other time, Wade would have been eager to see the brief flash of midriff she exposed, but he didn't even notice it now.

"If the divorce isn't final, he's still her next of kin. Who is he? How's he listed?"

"Marc with a 'c.' Marc Branham. He's a lawyer. His office is in Beaufort, but he lives on Jacob's Island. Take me to Samantha, Wade."

"Come on. That's why I came home instead of calling. I've already been to the hospital. I went there the minute the deputy following her called in. Samantha's not going to know you're there, but I knew you'd want to go."

"I'll know I'm there. Let's go."

Jolley pulled up in front of the emergency entrance and gave Katie directions to the ICU. He could tell she'd have no patience with waiting for him to park and walk her in. The minute she dashed away from the car, the sheriff realized he'd just turned her loose without protection. Wade drove away from the emergency entrance, curbed the Taurus, and ran in behind her. He barely missed the elevator as the door closed behind her.

Katie had been in an Intensive Care Unit just before her mother died, but she'd never seen anything like Samantha looked lying there. A nurse had led Katie back to where Sam was curtained off. The person on the gurney didn't look like Samantha. Her head was stabilized by a cage-looking metal device Katie had never seen before, not even on television. There were machines all around her, and each one of them had a tube leading into little Samantha.

Tears streamed down Katie's face. There was a sheet pulled up waist-high, but from there up to the tracheotomy, Samantha was covered with a piece of fabric that hardly looked bigger than a washcloth. It covered her chest totally, then lay out flat on the bed several inches on each side of poor Sam's tiny rib cage, which rose and fell rhythmically with the artificial breath of the ventilator. Samantha's skeletal arms lay on the cloth by her sides.

Katie was so focused on her friend that, at first, she didn't notice the man standing on the other side of the bed facing her. When she saw him, she asked, "Are you the doctor?"

"No, I'm Sam Campbell. You must be Katie. I'm sorry I didn't introduce myself. I think I'm in shock. I just can't believe this happened."

"Shock?" Katie thought. "He doesn't even seem upset. He's as calm and cool as a smooth-talking bastard ever is." The words stayed in her mind and she said nothing.

"It was just a minor bump," Campbell continued. "She had asked me to pull over, so she could tell me something. I told her we'd talk back at her place, but she insisted I stop. We went over just a tiny little ditch. It wasn't even a ravine. There's not a scratch on the car."

Sam rattled on, digging his grave deeper in Katie's mind. "I thought she'd fainted. I didn't even realize she must have hit her head. I was going to take her back to the house and get a cool cloth to revive her, but before I had time for anything, a patrol car drove up beside me. The officer called for an ambulance and started CPR. They've put all these machines on her, but she won't wake up."

Katie hadn't heard most of what "Mr. Wonderful" said, but one statement had jumped out at her.

"You took time to check your car for scratches?" she asked in disbelief.

"I did that while the paramedics brought her in. I really thought she'd only fainted. I just can't believe Samantha's hurt as bad as they say she is. It was hardly a bump."

The two of them stood on opposite sides of the childlike body lying there. Katie stroked Samantha's forehead. It felt like skin stretched over a Halloween skull. She noticed the lighter shade of blond, but the hair looked damp and wispy fanned out on the sheet. Samantha didn't have any bruises or blood showing at all. It was hard to believe she'd been hit hard enough to cause this without even bruising or cutting her head.

"I can't believe she's hurt as bad as they say," Sam Campbell repeated.

"Are you crazy? She's breathing with a machine, and there are all kinds of other things hooked to her. They've called for her next of kin!"

"Katie?" the masculine voice behind her was vaguely familiar. She turned. The man standing there had obviously dressed in a hurry. His shirt was buttoned wrong, and he had on bedroom slippers.

"Marc?"

"Oh, my God, Katie! I came as soon as they called. They're telling me Samantha's not going to make it." Katie stepped toward Marc and put her arms around him before she saw the petite blonde standing behind him.

"Get her out of here!" Katie screamed. "Get her the hell out of here!"

Two nurses ran in, and the blonde backed out, eyes wide with shock. One attendant put her arm around Katie's shoulders as she collapsed in tears again.

"Come out into the waiting area for a while," the nurse comforted softly.

"No, please let me stay. I'll be quiet," Katie sobbed. "I promise I'll be quiet." The nurse patted her back gently.

The other attendant bustled around checking tubes and machines. She said, "There's only supposed to be one person in here for ten minutes every two hours, but under the circumstances, you can stay. You'll have to be quiet though, so you don't disturb the other patients."

Katie stepped closer to the frail body. "Samantha, I'm sorry. I didn't mean to scream," she whispered.

"She doesn't hear you," the woman said in a professional tone that Katie herself sometimes used under different circumstances. The nurse looked up and started to say something to the sheriff when he came in, but apparently his uniform stopped her. Both nurses left, and Wade stood with his arm around Katie. Marc stared at his wife in horror. Sam Campbell had backed into a corner and mumbled to himself that it wasn't possible for Samantha to be so injured.

A doctor dressed in green surgical scrubs walked in. He didn't even look at Samantha. He peered around the group and asked, "Who's the next of kin?"

"I am," replied Marc.

"I'd like to talk with you outside, please."

"Do you want me to go with you?" Katie asked in her professional Ms. Wray voice.

"No, you stay here with her. My God, I can't believe that's Samantha. How long has she been like this, Katie? She's barely a skeleton." He reached out and gently touched Samantha's exposed bony arm before following the doctor out.

"I swear to God I wasn't speeding," Mr. Wonderful began again, louder now, as he turned toward the sheriff.

"I didn't even know she was hurt. She wanted to talk. She told me to pull over. I thought she'd fainted."

Wade looked at the man, and Katie saw disgust on the sheriff's face. "I think," he said, "you need to either hush or go out to the waiting room."

Katie stood by Samantha and silently prayed for her. "Oh, Lord, let this all be a mistake. Take it back. Make Sam wake up and be okay." She prayed, and she thought, "Funny how you can go for years without praying very often, but when you need to do it, you remember how." Katie prayed, but when Marc came back, she knew from the look on his face that it was as bad as it looked. His face was drained of color except around his eyes which were red.

"Samantha's dead, Katie. She was probably legally dead when the deputy started CPR at the roadside. They've done all they can, but she'll lie here just like she is until the machines are disconnected. There's no hope at all. They left this stuff hooked up after they knew she won't come back. They wanted to give her family a chance to see her. They didn't know Samantha doesn't have any family." His voice cracked. "She doesn't have anybody but you and me." He paused. His expression was anguished. "I signed for them to cut it all off." His shoulders heaved and he sobbed. "I told them to use whatever organs they could, but . . ."

"That's good, Marc. She'd want to be an organ donor."

"She can't. The doctor said it would be like trying to transplant organs from a prisoner in a concentration camp. Her organs are starved. They're not healthy enough to transplant. They won't even take her corneas."

The doctor pushed the draperies aside and stepped into

Samantha's area. "She knows nothing, but if you want to say good-byes, you may." The men shook their heads no, but Katie leaned over the pathetic body and stroked the skeletal forehead. Sam had become even thinner during the three days since Katie had last seen her.

"Rest easy, Samantha," Katie whispered. "Go to your mom and dad and your aunt and rest easy. I love you." The tears streamed down her face, falling onto the cloth covering Sam's chest. "I'm going to miss you so much."

"You may all step outside now," said the doctor.

"Do I have to?" Katie asked. She'd seen movies where the medics turned off machines and people didn't die right away.

"I can't leave her in here to die all alone." Katie's mind raced. "What if they're wrong? What if she knows what's going on?"

"No, you don't have to leave if you don't want to go out. This is very difficult for some people," the doctor replied.

Mr. Wonderful and Marc were backing toward the curtain leading to the hall. Wade stayed by Katie, who stood close to the bed. She was stroking Samantha's hand when the machines stopped. Katie expected her friend to take at least a few ragged breaths. There were none. The room was totally quiet, and the childlike chest moved not at all. No buzzers sounded. No lights flashed. No one came running in to resuscitate Samantha. Her death was silent.

The doctor checked Samantha's pulse and listened to her chest through his stethoscope. He glanced at the straight lines racing across the monitor screens. "It's over," he said. Katie stood by the body a few more minutes, then allowed Wade to lead her out after one more touch on

Samantha's hollow cheek. As they went through the corridor, the doctor was talking to Marc and Sam. Marc's little blond mouse had her arms wrapped around him. Mr. Wonderful was still mumbling, "I really thought she'd just fainted."

Katie glared at Sam Campbell, then asked the sheriff, "Aren't you going to arrest him?"

"For what? The deputy said Campbell pulled off the road at a place anyone would think was okay. There was no car accident. He pulled off the road and Samantha's neck apparently snapped. Look how frail she was. I'm sure her bones were fragile and brittle from malnutrition. That Jag's so old it doesn't have headrests. I'll have to request an autopsy, and there'll be a coroner's inquest, but the man didn't kill her. It was an accident. He'd had seat belts added to the car when South Carolina made them a law. There's no legislation requiring headrests. He'll walk away and forget it ever happened. He'll be in Kenny B's picking up someone new next week."

Katie's response was low and muffled.

"What did you say?" Wade asked her.

"I said he killed her. That bastard killed her as surely as if he'd shot her with a gun."

In the car, Katie turned her tearstained face to Wade. "I want to go home. Please take me to my apartment."

"No, Katie, I can't."

The sheriff skillfully drove the Taurus through the dark streets back to his own house.

"I've been out now. You've got people watching my apartment. Take me home," Katie begged. "Please take me home."

"No, Katie, I can't. I was at your apartment when I got

the call about Samantha."

"If it was an accident, why'd they call you?"

"One of my deputies was following them. He's who performed CPR and called an ambulance. He called me because he knows how involved I am in this whole case."

"Why were you at my apartment, and if you were there, why can't I go there?"

"We'll talk about it later."

"No! Tell me now!" Katie's voice was loud and angry, but Wade could hear the tears ready to begin again.

"You don't want to know, Katie. Trust me on this. Deal with tonight now. Deal with your apartment tomorrow."

"What's wrong at my apartment? Is Frankie there?"

They pulled into Sheriff Jolley's driveway. The officer parked out front waved, and Wade waved back.

"Tell me," Katie said. "Tell me now or I won't get out of the car. You'll have to pull me out right here in front of your deputy."

"Frankie's not at your apartment, but he's been there. The only people at your place now are forensics techs, the coroner, Hank, and Agent Gross. The officer watching your apartment didn't radio in as scheduled. They got no answer when they tried to call him, so the state folks sent someone to check it out. The officer was missing. Your door was partially open. They found the deputy dead in your bed. You can't go home now because your apartment is sealed off with yellow tape."

Katie crumpled. She'd cried tonight. She'd screamed tonight. Now, she simply folded like a paper doll. She'd threatened to make Wade force her from his car. He didn't actually pull her out, but he almost lifted her and carried her into his house. Inside, he offered her Tylenol.

"I should have asked that doctor to give you a prescription for Valium or Xanax."

"No," Katie whimpered. "Just hold me."

Occasionally, time plays tricks on human beings. Neither of them could have even guessed how long they sat on the couch with Wade holding Katie. She'd cry for a while, then settle down. Once he even thought she was asleep, but she began sobbing again. Finally, she became silent for what seemed a long time to Wade. Katie lifted her face to his.

"Make love to me," she said softly.

Wade was flabbergasted. It was the last thing he'd expected her to say.

"I c-couldn't," he stuttered.

"Why? I thought you wanted me."

"I do, but . . ."

"Who cares if it's appropriate?"

"No, it's not that. Making love to you now would be like raping you. It would be taking advantage of you. Taking advantage of your grief for Samantha and your emotional reaction to this hell Barker's created."

"It would make me stop thinking," Katie said firmly. "Every time I close my eyes, I see Samantha lying there. Even with my eyes open, I see her. I hear her crying about that bastard." The tears were back. "Oh, God, Wade, why didn't I get help for her? She had no one but me, and all I did was tell her to eat and to write her lesson plans."

"You were her friend. I wasn't as close to the situation as you, and even I didn't see how bad her true condition was until tonight."

"Make me stop thinking about it. Make me forget for now. I've wanted you since almost the first time I met you. Now I not only want you, I need you."

"I can't take advantage of you like this, Katie."

"Do it for me this time, and the next time can be whenever you choose."

Katie pulled slightly back from him and unbuttoned her shirt. Wade's heart thumped and skidded in his chest. Desire washed over him totally and completely, and his blood surged. Wade Jolley was more stressed than he could ever remember being in his life, and a woman he desperately wanted was virtually begging him to take her.

Against his highly ethical instincts, Wade slipped his hand beneath her unbuttoned shirt and cupped a full, firm breast. Through the sheer fabric, his fingers felt the hardest nipple he'd ever touched. Katie reached behind her back. Wade heard the familiar snap of a clasp and slid the smooth satin out of the way as she slipped the shirt off completely, arched her back, and lifted an exquisite breast to his kiss like an offering to the gods.

Many times, Wade Jolley had pictured himself undressing Katie Wray, but instead she undressed him right there on the couch with an urgency that made Wade feel more wanted than he'd ever felt in his life. Their mating wasn't rough sex, but it wasn't the sweet, gentle experience Wade had fantasized. There was a frantic quality as though Katie couldn't get enough of him, touch enough of him, taste enough of him. But, even though frenzied, their bodies were in perfect coordination. It seemed that all he had to do was think of a position, and this woman moved automatically as though she could read his mind.

Later, Katie nudged him. "Go back to work, Wade," she said calmly. "Tomorrow I'll call Marc and offer to help plan Samantha's services. I'm going to sleep now." That's what she said, but when he came out of the shower in a fresh uniform, Katie still lay on the couch.

"Wade," she said, "I feel a little too grown up right now to sleep in Jennie's room. Can I sleep in your bed?"

Shug moaned. Anyone hearing him wouldn't have known if the sound was pain or pleasure, but it didn't matter. No one was listening.

Success!

Shug's brain was working again. The intelligence that had impressed his teachers and made his mother so proud before his troubles had switched back on. He'd located Samantha, the teacher friend who had called Maggie once last summer looking for her sister. He'd decided to follow her, hoping this would eventually lead him to Maggie.

There wasn't any "eventually" involved. The little blond bitch had been in an accident that took her to the hospital, and staking out the hospital had led to seeing Maggie, one of the women who looked just like his seventh-grade teacher, the one who'd been so impressed with his looks and his intelligence. The one who'd loved his poems.

Thinking had also led him to the perfect hideout. He'd remembered another event from the summer and a place of privacy with the perfect spot to put Janice's body. Of course, he hadn't left all of Janice at his hideout. He'd taken everything but part of her torso, her legs, and her head to the parking lot at the school. He'd put them in the trunk of that Mercedes that Maggie drove now.

Actually, he'd put them in the bass case with all the fingers and left the case for Maggie to discover after she found those two CDs he'd put on the front seat. He'd taken a chance going to buy those recordings, but as he'd begun to think clearly again, begun to be smart again, he'd grown less worried about being in public. Screw the law. Shug knew he was too damned smart to get caught.

Linda Pearson was Tennessee Linda for the night. In her mind, the loud music blared and the rhythm was solid. As they always said all those years ago on *American Bandstand*, "a great dance beat!" Her body was, in those old words of Bob Seger, "way up firm and high." No flab in her taut young stomach. Hair: a thick, lustrous mane that invited touch. Her facial muscles had not yet been repeatedly pummeled, and her nose had never been broken. Her features were fine and perfectly symmetrical.

The music played on, and the beautiful young girl danced and danced and danced. The heavy bass line thudded in her chest and found its way out through her feet. She did the twist and the mashed potato. She knew all the latest steps, and she did them well. Between dances, she was back at the table for more Jack Daniel's from the bottle in the bag. This was South Carolina before free-pour liquor, even before mini-bottles.

This was Linda's youth, when rock 'n' roll was younger than she was. If she danced enough and drank enough, she wouldn't care what Mama said to her when she arrived home past her curfew. Sometimes, not always, but sometimes, she could dance enough and drink enough not to care what Daddy did if he was awake and Mama asleep when she finally came home.

Tonight there was no Mama talking to her. Tonight there was no Daddy touching her. Tonight was before Bert had even appeared in her life. There were no cries of, "No, no, please, no!" in the big old house on Oak Street. There was no "Linda Louise" echoing in her head. There was no "Lindy Lou, are you awake?" whispering through her mind. There was just music and Jack Daniel's. The sleeping woman on the love seat smiled.

Katie awoke in Wade's bed. She knew where she was immediately, but it took a few minutes for the reality of Samantha's death to replay through her consciousness. "It doesn't seem possible," Katie thought. "I was there, but I still can't believe she's left us. I can't believe she won't call me laughing one minute and crying the next."

She considered calling Marc to talk with him about Sam's funeral, but the thought of having to speak to the mouse to get to Marc dictated a cup of coffee first. Katie half expected to see Wade sitting at the kitchen counter eating Pop Tarts, but instead there was a note from him. "Katie, I don't know when I'll be back, but Corley's out front. Use the transmitter if you need him or want to reach me. I'll call you later." Beneath the scrawled "Wade" at the bottom was, "I wish I could be with you today. I'm so sorry about Samantha." A few spaces below that was, "Still stunned by the beautiful way such a horrible night ended."

After her second cup of coffee, Katie called Marc's house. He answered the telephone, so she didn't have to speak to the mouse. "Katie, I can't believe Sam's dead," Marc repeated Katie's own thoughts to her. "I feel guilty one minute and want to go out and kill that guy she was with the next."

"I know," Katie said, "I have the same thoughts." She paused and took another sip of coffee. "I know it's your legal right to make all the arrangements," she continued, "but I'd like to help however I can."

Marc answered, "I haven't been to sleep all night. I know my head's not clear, but I was thinking a memorial service here in Tanner and then taking her back to North Carolina to be buried near her parents and her Aunt Sadie."

"I think that's what she would want. Is there anything I can do to help?"

"Samantha was so private sometimes. Katie, I don't remember her ever talking about anyone she worked with except you. I know you were her closest friend. I'd thought about calling and asking you to pick out a dress for her. I want her to have something new. When we were together, she hardly ever bought herself any clothes." Marc's voice broke. "Don't worry about the cost. I'm doing pretty well now."

"You know teachers all have state life insurance."

"Yes, and I'll check on that for funeral expenses, but I want to pay for the dress myself. I guess you'd know what size and everything."

"Yeah," Katie answered sadly. "She's a size two."

Knowing she'd have to talk to Wade before she could leave his house to go shop, Katie refused Marc's offer to bring her a check. She told him she'd buy something, take it by the funeral home, and settle with him later. In the living room, she noticed that all the couch cushions were back in place and the clothing she'd left on the floor last night was neatly folded on a chair.

"Wonder what he thinks of me today?" she questioned herself. "Oh, Katie," her mind answered, "don't be stupid. He might think the timing was strange, but what happened on that sofa last night was destined from the morning he walked into the school media center.

When the phone rang, Katie assumed it would be Wade. Even glancing down at the caller ID, which said Samantha Branham, she expected it to be the sheriff. Or maybe Marc had gone over there. The last voice she expected to hear was the one that said softly, "Maggie May?"

"Frankie?"

"Yes, it's me, Maggie."

"This isn't Maggie. I'm Katie, her sister. Where's Maggie?"

"What difference does a name make? I have lots of names. Frederick Franklin Barker, AKA Sugar Baby or Shug. You look like Maggie to me. I'm calling from your little blond teacher friend's apartment. I wanted to tell you how sorry I am about what happened to her."

"How do you know about it? Is it in the papers today?"

"I haven't seen the papers. I know because I was following her last night. Don't get jealous, Maggie. She was much too thin for me. I was following her, hoping she'd lead me to you, and she did."

"I'm Katie, not Maggie."

"You can't fool me, and even if you're Katie, you're all teachers, and I have this thing about teachers."

"Maggie's not a teacher. She didn't finish college. Actually, she hardly ever works."

"Then she lied to me, but it doesn't matter. I saw you last night at the hospital. You really looked good in those jeans, and I like that blue shirt." Katie glanced over at the shirt neatly folded on the chair.

"How'd you get into Samantha's apartment?"

"I have ways. You may be older and better educated

than me, Maggie, but in some ways, I'm a lot smarter. What's her cat's name?"

"Wookiee, but I told you I'm not Maggie. I'm Katie. Where's Maggie?"

"Don't argue with me!" Frankie's voice filled with rage, and Katie decided she'd best just go along with his idea that she was her sister.

"No, Frankie, I won't argue." Katie thought that if she could draw Frankie to her, Corley could capture him. If she could turn the transmitter on so Corley could overhear the conversation, he would call for the sheriff and backup enforcement.

"Why don't you come over here? We can talk," she said.

"I've done some really bad stuff, Maggie, but you know me. You know I'm not really bad. Inside, I'm a good, smart boy. "

"I don't think I know you at all." The minute the words escaped Katie's lips, she knew she'd made a mistake.

"Don't say that." He was angry again. "You told me you loved me just like my middle-school teacher did. Now you say you're not even Maggie."

"Okay, I'll be Maggie. Are you okay? Come over here and I'll hold you just like at Paris Mountain."

"No, I'm not okay at all. I need help. I need my meds."

"Turn yourself in. The sheriff will see that you get your medicine."

"They'll shoot me, Maggie. If I turn myself in, I'll be committing suicide by cop."

"No, Frankie. The sheriff is a friend of mine. He won't shoot you. He'll help you get out of this mess."

"The cops didn't do a damned thing to help me when I was a kid. Why would I trust them now? And you! You said you loved me, but now you're shacked up with the sheriff."

"I'm not living with the sheriff."

"Hiding out from me? Didn't work. I found you."

"The sheriff thinks you want to hurt me."

"No, Maggie, he thinks I want to kill you." His next words were tender. "But he doesn't know I love you."

"The caller ID shows Samantha's name. Stay there. I'll call the sheriff. He'll come for you and get you some help."

"You don't understand, Maggie. I killed a state law man last night. You haven't been outside. There's more cops in this town right now than at a strippers' convention."

Katie looked at the transmitter across the room. She reached, but the cord on the phone was too short. If only she'd answered the call on the portable.

"Do you know where I put the dead cop, Maggie? I put him in your bed, a present for you, but you didn't go home to find him."

"Why would you leave me that kind of gift, Frankie?"

Frankie began singing. The familiar "Maggie May" words sounded strange because he didn't sing in key. He was only vaguely near the tune.

> All I needed was a friend to lend a guiding hand
> But you turned into a lover, and mother,
> What a lover, you wore me out
> All you did was wreck my bed, and in the morning,
> You kicked me in the head
> Oh, Maggie, I couldn't have tried anymore
> You led me away from home cause you didn't
>   wanna be alone

You stole my heart, I couldn't leave you if I tried.

"I know the song," Katie said. "I asked why you killed the man at my apartment."

Barker continued singing, but made up his own words to answer her: "Because you kicked me out of your home, and I know you well enough to know . . . you don't like to sleep alone."

"Frankie, listen to me. You need help. You have to turn yourself in. The sheriff will protect you. Nobody will hurt you."

Silence. Then Katie heard him crying again.

"Frankie, remember the day when Maggie held you at Paris Mountain? Maggie told me about that. I can hold you like she did, and I'll make sure the sheriff doesn't let anyone hurt you."

"You'll hold me again?" He sounded like a little boy.

"I'll hold you and protect you. I'll take care of you, Frankie."

"That's what teachers are supposed to do. They should look out for kids and not ever hurt them."

"That's right."

"You know my real name's Fred, but I'd rather be Frankie. My mama named me Fred, but she called me Sugar or Shug." He sniffled. "I hurt her, Maggie. I hurt my mama with what I did. She couldn't bear it, and she left me. She left me for good."

"You're my Frankie now, and I'll be your Maggie May. Come to me, Frankie. Let me hold you."

"I'm on the way, Maggie."

Katie held the telephone receiver to her ear, waiting for the sound of the dial tone. Instead she heard a thud as though Frankie had dropped his handset onto a surface.

Jamming her finger repeatedly against the disconnect on Wade's phone, Katie didn't want Frankie to over-hear her warn Corley on the transmitter, but since Frankie had initiated the call into Wade's line, Katie was unable to disconnect it. She looked down at herself in the sheriff's T-shirt. She peeled it off and slipped into the jeans and denim shirt lying folded on the chair.

Katie stepped out on the front porch with the transmitter in her hand. "Detective Corley," she said into the mouthpiece. No response. "Detective Corley?" Still no answer. She walked toward the patrol car parked on the street. She was barefooted, but the Centipede grass was like walking on plush, green carpet. She could see Corley sitting in the patrol car. Was he asleep on duty?

"Detective Corley? Detective Corley?" Katie spoke his name right up to the moment she leaned into the open driver's-side window and saw the ragged red hole in his chest. Instinctively, she reached through the window and pressed her fingertips against the carotid artery in his neck. Nothing. The flesh was hard and cold against her hand. She'd seen Wade use his car radio. She was reaching across Corley's body for his radio when a hand clasped across her mouth and an arm wrapped around her waist from behind.

"No, Maggie," Shug whispered in her ear as he pulled her away from the patrol car and shoved her into the passenger side of Samantha's Hyundai, which he'd pulled up beside the patrol car and left running. He slipped his hand off her mouth and plastered a piece of gray duct tape over her lips. "I took care of the deputy before I called you. In fact, a long time ago." He pulled her arms in front of her and wrapped the duct tape around her wrists, binding them tightly together.

"You seemed to think I was calling from the skinny blonde's apartment, but I called from her cell here." He held up Samantha's pink phone, then crawled across Katie to get to the driver's seat. In moments, they were traveling down the road away from the sheriff's house and the haven it represented for Katie.

"Don't worry. I'm not keeping you like this. I want you to hold me. I need to feel your arms around me. I'll take the tape off when we get where we're going. I don't want you to change your mind and try to scream or get out of the car." Frankie's voice was calm. He drove on streets that were unfamiliar to Katie and soon they passed right by Sam's apartment complex. Katie hadn't realized it was so close to the sheriff's house.

"Yes," Frankie continued, nodding toward the entrance to Sam's place. "I'm really sorry about what happened to your friend. I admit she crossed my mind because of the teacher thing, but she wasn't my type." He laughed. "You said the cat's name was Wookiee. It wouldn't leave me alone, so I strangled it. Does that surprise you?" He laughed, louder and longer this time.

"I'll bet you wondered about the first body," Barker said after his crazed laughter. "Let me tell you, Maggie, I thought I'd met myself another Maggie May in the middle of the night. Carly looked fine and came on to me like you wouldn't believe right there in the store where you and I met. The problem was I didn't have anywhere in town to take my new friend, and Carly told me she'd just come down for a day on the coast and didn't have a room either. I could have rented a motel room. I had money, but instead, we went parking like a couple of teenagers.

"She followed me over to the burned-out church and got into my car." Frankie grinned. "You never saw my car, did you, Maggie? Anyway, each time I tried to touch Carly, she squirmed away until finally she told me she was really a he waiting for a sex change operation." His voice rose and intensified. "Do you know how that made me feel? You put me out and then I'm parked like a kid with no place to go and the woman I chose to replace you turns out to be a man. I got nothing against gay people, but that wasn't what I wanted. I wanted you, but you dumped me.

"Carly kept saying he wasn't gay. He said he was a woman trapped in a man's body. When I tried to explain, he started bitching at me just like you teachers are always telling people what to do. I just lost it. I had the gun I stole from your place. When he got mad and said he was going back to his car, I shot him. He turned to get out of the car and I let him have it right in the back of the head. I didn't mean to, Maggie. He just kept bitching and bitching and I shot him over and over in the back of the head."

Frankie drove silently with tears streaming down his cheeks. Katie couldn't believe that no one noticed the two of them riding through town. They passed police cars of all kinds, but no one seemed to pay attention to the Hyundai. Frankie sniffled again, then continued his story, "I knew I didn't need to leave any way for them to identify Carly, so I cut off his fingers. His face was gone. I thought if I got rid of his fingerprints, I'd be in the clear. I took the rest of his clothes off so if they ever connected me to the crime, no one would know he'd been wearing women's clothes. My car was a mess, so I just left it and took his. Of course, I had to ditch it yesterday after they identified him."

Frankie pulled the Hyundai over and parked on the curb of Elm Street beside a wooded section. He reached across and grasped Katie's hands. He pulled her out his side of the car. Katie stumbled on the sidewalk, but no one was on the street and no one saw the young man push a gagged and bound, barefooted woman through a break in the old fence surrounding the trees.

"Don't be frightened, Maggie. I'm just taking you where we can have some privacy. You know, I always say I don't pedal backwards and I've never been into reruns, but I may make an exception in your case. I wasn't through loving you, Maggie. I wasn't through, and you just put me out with no thought at all for my feelings."

Katie tried to move her head back and forth to show him she disagreed. "If he'll take the tape off my mouth, I can try to talk him into giving himself up," she thought. "At worst, I could scream."

Frankie yanked Katie behind him through the trees so quickly she lost all sense of direction. They seemed to twist around and occasionally to turn back. "I think we've been by here before," Katie thought as they passed an especially large oak tree. "If he'll just take the tape off my mouth when we get where we're going, I can talk to him. I can reason with him." All of a sudden, Katie felt like she was choking, and the gag scared her as much as stumbling through the woods with a serial killer.

CHAPTER 19

LINDA PEARSON WENT OUT early that morning and had already eaten her daily waffle at the Downtown Diner. She had no conscious memory of last night's dream. She only knew she felt good and had been hungry from the moment she stood up from the love seat. She'd even "made" her bed, which consisted of nothing more than shaking the pillows and putting them back in place neatly. The heat had let up a little, and it was a beautiful morning with just a touch of autumn in the air.

As Tennessee Linda entered the front gate and stepped on the veranda, she looked again at the railings all cleared of kudzu. Today she remembered cutting away the vine, and she entered the front door filled with pride at what she'd accomplished.

Linda Louise, why'd you leave so early without turning the television on for your Daddy?

"I thought he was still sleeping, Mama."

Don't lie to me, child. You knew your daddy wasn't asleep. You just didn't want to be bothered with your poor old daddy. After all we did for you when you had your trouble. You should be a little more thoughtful.

"Mama, my trouble, as you call it, is over. You tried to help me, but I paid the price, and it's over. Why don't we just not talk about it anymore? I came back to Tanner to talk to Daddy about *his* problem, and when I got here, he cheated me out of being able to confront him. All those years the counselors kept telling me I needed closure, and when I came home, it was too late."

Linda Louise, I don't know what you're talking about. You can't blame your daddy for the stroke getting him.

"No, Mama, but I can blame him for what he did to me!"

If you're going to start with those lies you used to tell me when you were a little girl, I'm just not going to listen to you. I'll just go away.

"Good, Mama. You never listened to me anyway!"

Linda paused. Her mother didn't answer. Linda was having a good day, and it would be better if Mama left her alone. Sometimes Mama could turn an otherwise good day into a hard one for Linda. She'd already eaten, and it was too early to go to the Shop & Save or to Amick's for the evening shopping.

Several options crossed Linda's mind. She could watch television with Daddy. She could work crossword puzzles or, even better, go buy some new crossword books. She could go out back and work on the kudzu covering the garage. She looked down at herself. She could even clean herself up again, but she didn't feel quite that good, and she wasn't nearly so dirty as she'd been the day she cut away the kudzu. The memory brought back pride.

Linda decided to do something she rarely even considered. She would clean the house. She was dusting furniture when she became aware of a squeaking sound and footsteps. Daddy had started walking again. She could hear him in the back, and she turned on the television hoping the sound of it would lure him back into his chair so her good day could stay that way.

After what seemed like they'd tromped through woods forever, Frankie pulled Katie into a clearing with a building. It was obvious to Katie that this was the back of a large old house. He opened the door and shoved her into a dark, dusty hallway. Katie prayed silently. "Now that we're here, wherever it is, let him take the gag off. Please, God, make him take the gag off so I can talk to him."

Katie wondered if she were in shock. She didn't feel the fear she thought she should. She was gagged and being dragged into a strange house by a known murderer. She knew a lot of what Frankie had done to the teachers, but the two killings most real to her were John Doe and Corley. She couldn't relate the corpse she'd seen on the gurney to anyone named Carly or Carlton. She'd seen poor John Doe lying nude on that hard metal table, so naked he didn't even have a face or fingertips, and he would always be "John Doe" to her. Corley was much more real. Of all Frankie's victims, the deputy was the only one she'd known personally. "I didn't really like him, but he died because he was trying to protect me," she thought.

"Move, damn it!" Frankie snapped at her, and Katie realized that her thoughts had taken her away from the real situation and she'd stopped walking. "I need to stay with it. I have to watch and think every minute. What if I get loose and can't get out of this house because I wasn't paying attention?" Katie told herself.

Frankie jerked her through a door, then pushed her onto the floor in a tiny room filled with sheet-covered furniture. Dust clouded around them. "We must be in an abandoned house," thought Katie, "but there are no big, empty houses downtown." Frankie lowered himself beside her, but he didn't remove any of the duct tape. Instead, he pulled the roll from his pocket and wrapped a long piece around her ankles, cutting the tape off with a switchblade knife.

"Well, check out those pretty pink toenails," he crooned. "You never polished them for me. I've been thinking about this ever since the morning I left your house," he said. "All of it, everything I've done was only because I wanted you."

"No!" Katie screamed inside her head. "Maggie isn't to blame for what you've done. Oh, God, make him take the gag off. Let me talk to him."

"Just look at you," Frankie spat out the words and grabbed her by the shoulders, turning her to face him. He moved in close to her face. Katie knew that the man who held her captive was the same person her sister had lived with all summer. Had Maggie ever seen his eyes so cold and hard?

"You're arguing with me right now. Just like a teacher. Always got to tell people what to do! You're doing it to me right now while you can't even open your mouth."

Katie shivered with fright, and tears filled her eyes.

Immediately, Frankie changed right in front of her. He dropped the tape and knife on the floor. He put his arms around her and pulled her close to his chest. "Maybe he'll forget the knife," she thought. "If he takes the tape off my hands, I can get the knife. No, he'll use the knife to cut the tape if he takes it off."

"Maggie? Maggie May?" He sang in that off-key voice, as though he were comforting a baby.

"Is this how he talks to his two little girls?" Katie questioned in her head. "Wonder what kind of father he is?"

"Don't cry. I'll hold you. I'll comfort you like you used to comfort me." He hugged her tight against him and rubbed her back. The hands were those of a stranger, and Katie had to fight hard not to cringe from his touch. He pressed his lips against her neck and blew gently, then moved to her ear, and recited softly, "You made a first-class fool out of me. I'm as blind as a fool can be. Maggie, I couldn't leave you if I tried."

Every muscle in Katie's body tensed. "Oh, God, no!" she thought. "It's foreplay!" Katie quickly felt a change in the tightness of his arms wrapped around her. She consciously fought to relax.

"That's better, Maggie. For a minute, I thought you didn't want me anymore. He moved a hand around from her back and touched her breast through the shirt pocket. "No bra?" He laughed softly. "Every time I tried to get you to go out braless, you told me women almost forty don't do that. I even remember the little story you told about me about your mother. Remember that story, Maggie? You said she told you to get up on the morning

314

of your fortieth birthday, take off all your clothes, and stand in front of the mirror. You said she told you that if you stood there long enough, you'd see everything droop. We used to laugh when you told me that story, and I'd assure you that nothing of yours will ever sag at all."

He cupped his hand over her through the shirt. He lifted the blue denim, and leaned forward. Frankie's tongue made little circles around the same nipple she'd offered so willingly to Wade just the night before. Though she tried hard not to, Katie shuddered in revulsion. She feared this would anger him, but Frankie thought she was trembling with excitement.

"This is Frankie," he whispered softly. "I know exactly what Maggie May likes." He unbuttoned her shirt and spread it wide, placed one hand on each breast, and pushed them together to the center of her chest. He bent forward and rapidly flicked his tongue from one nipple to the other, then looked up at her. Katie recognized the expression he now wore—rage.

"What's the matter, bitch? I've been gone almost two weeks. You should be begging for me to do what you call pleasuring you, and your nipples aren't even hard! You've been fucking somebody since I left! Who? That sheriff you're living with? You're telling me to give myself up to a man who's banging my woman?"

Katie tried to remember everything she'd ever read about not becoming a murder victim. None of it seemed to apply to her situation, but every instinct told her the only way to get out of this was to make Frankie think she wanted him. Frantically, she shook her head no and brought her bound hands up to the tape over her mouth.

"You want the tape off? Is that what you want? Why?

So you can tell me more lies or so you can tell me to go away again? Guess what? You can't tell me what to do anymore. I'm not a little boy. I'm a grown man. And teacher or not, nobody tells me what to do anymore. I thought you were different from the rest of them."

"Tears worked on him. Oh, God, let me cry," Katie thought. The mental prayer wasn't necessary because, though Katie wasn't aware of them, tears already flowed down her face. She continued to shake her head and point to her tape-covered mouth. Frankie made another of his sudden changes and reverted to a tender tone. "Oh, I know what you want. Maggie May likes kissing. You want the tape off so you can kiss me and tease me. What was your euphemism for a blow job? You want to taste me. That's what you want, isn't it?" He grinned.

Katie shook her head up and down while her mind told her, "If I have to do that, I'll throw up."

"Sorry, Maggie. I don't trust you anymore. Besides, I learned a new song for you. Did you like the presents I put in your car? I know you already had the CDs, but I wanted to have something gift-wrapped, and what I left for you in your trunk would've upset the wrapping ladies at the mall too much. Remember how I used to ask you not to play Janis Joplin? Well, I'm over that. See, there was a Janice in my past, but I took care of her. Actually, I left you Janis in the front seat and Janice in the trunk."

Frankie laughed frantically. Katie had read the word "maniacal," many times, but never used it. It described his laughter. "Crazy!" she thought. "He's crazy and I must be going crazy too. I'm at the mercy of a killer, and I'm thinking about vocabulary." Frankie pulled her shirt back together and patiently buttoned it. "We've got all the time in the world. You're mine forever, Maggie. I never had to force you to do anything, and you don't have to be afraid. I won't force you now. I know you too well. I can make you want me so bad you'll beg me to bang you."

Barker leaned close to her ear. Katie could smell him. She had to fight not to gag at his sweat and body odor. He began talking softly. "Maggie, I loved you, and you used me, then threw me away like a piece of shitty toilet paper."

Frankie grabbed her wrists. The pain was unbearable. His grip was like a vise. "I taught Janice a lesson. I may have to teach you one, too. That's what you teachers like, isn't it? Lessons. Always telling people what to do. He pulled her to a standing position and started moving. Katie stumbled and fell. She hit her face on the floor. Blood gushed from her nose down over the tape covering her mouth.

"Oh, no, Maggie, don't bleed." He sounded sincerely concerned. "I'm sorry. I forgot about your feet." He lifted her in his arms and gently sat her back against the wall. He looked around the dark room, pulled a sheet off an antique chair, and tenderly wiped the blood from her face with the edge of the dusty cloth. Then he gently pinched the bridge of her nose. "That's what to do for a nosebleed, isn't it, Teacher?" Katie nodded her head up and down

"Damn! Damn! Damn! Not you, Corley!" Sheriff Jolley gasped when he looked into the deputy's car. He didn't need to reach in and check for a pulse as Katie had done. Wade had seen enough dead people to recognize rigor mortis immediately. He never slowed down but ran into the house.

He screeched, "Katie! Katie! Katie!" but Wade Jolley knew there'd be no answer. He expected to find her corpse in his bed, but instead, he found only rumpled covers. The only thing different in the house was a T-shirt lying on the floor by the couch. In his heart and mind, Wade had known he wouldn't find Katie alive at his house when he'd failed to raise Corley on the radio. The tee on the floor and Katie's jeans and denim shirt missing from the chair told him how she was dressed. Her shoes by the couch meant she'd left in a hurry.

"Be still, Daddy. Come back and get in your chair and be still. Stop that walking." Linda scolded as she wiped off the countertops.

Linda Louise, your daddy is sitting in his chair watching television. What's your problem now?

"Would you please shut up? Can't the two of you let me have one good day every once in a while?"

Linda Louise, don't you tell me to shut up. Your daddy and I did the best we could for you. Always! We did the best we could for you, and I get tired of listening to you complain. We didn't make you drink like a fish all through school. We didn't make you run off with Bert. We didn't make you stay with him. And when you murdered your husband, we stood by you. Who sent you cigarettes every week the whole time you were in jail? Who brought you home here to live when they let you out? Knowing I was dying with cancer and your daddy was hardly more than a vegetable from his stroke. Who did all that for you, Linda Louise? So don't you tell me to shut up!

"You did! You did! You did! You did all that for me, but your nagging and Daddy's abuse made me a drunk and made me run off with Bert. You brought me home to live, all right! You brought me home to take care of both of you. I did, I took care of both of you. Then I buried both of you, and you still won't shut up and leave me alone!" She looked over her shoulder. "And he won't be still!"

I won't have you telling me to shut up!

"Shut the fuck up then!"

Linda Louise, you will not use the f-word in my house. Do you understand? Your daddy never even said that word.

"Hell, no, Daddy never said that word. He didn't need to say it. He was doing it! Doing it to a little girl whose Mama just told her to hush every time she tried to tell her what Daddy did when Mama went off or went to sleep."

I won't listen to that. You know I won't listen to that.

"Then go away and don't listen. I'll say it again . . . fuck, fuck, fuck. How do you like that? I can say the truth now. Do you want to hear the truth?"

Linda Louise, I will not listen! I will not listen!

"You never would, but I'm going to say it anyway! My daddy fucked me! There! I said it. I finally said it out loud. He did it over and over, so I can say it over and over. My daddy fucked me! What do you think of that, Mommie Dearest?"

There was no answer, not even in Linda's head. She turned back to the countertops, and after she'd finished scrubbing them, she began wiping the cabinet doors.

When Katie's nose stopped bleeding, Frankie spit on another corner of the sheet and used the moistened edge to wipe the tears and blood from her face.

"That should upset me, but it doesn't," she thought. "I can think of lots worse things he could do than rub a little spit on me. So much worse that it would be a blessing if he just stood up, spit on me, and walked away."

"Now, Teacher, I'm going to teach you a lesson. It won't be the same lesson I taught Janice because I love you. I never loved Janice. I just liked her, but, Maggie, I honest to God, love you.

Once more, Frankie tried to pull Katie up onto her feet, then looked down again and laughed as he shoved her back to a sitting position and picked up the knife. This time, Katie noticed that it wasn't a regular pocketknife. She'd never seen a real switchblade, but she recognized it from movies.

"You're staring at my knife. Do you like it, Maggie? That's one of the things I kept in my instrument case. Of course, now I have to buy a new case. I ruined mine, and I doubt your sheriff friend would give it back to me anyway."

He used the knife to cut the tape between her ankles. "There. That will make it easier for you to walk, but don't think you can outrun me." He pulled her up and stood her in front of him so close that his nose touched hers. "What would your mother tell you to do now, Maggie? You know, I did love you all summer, but you're not exactly perfect. I got tired of you always knowing which movie you wanted to see. I got tired of you always telling me which restaurant we'd go to. Sometimes you really pissed me off, but I loved you anyway. You know one of the reasons I loved you more than the others? You never tried to tell me what to do in bed. You let me be the man."

Barker paused, then began pulling her out the door and down the hall. "And you let me drive your car sometimes," he said. "Bet you thought I really got off driving that new Fusion. You should have gotten your sheriff friend to let you see my car. And you picked up most of the bills all summer. I could've done that. You only let me pay once in a while. Teachers always want to be in control. Maggie, I've got more money right now in my checking account than you make in a whole year. Compliments of my good old dad. He's the CEO of an electronics company, and he sends me whatever I want just so long as I don't go to Florida."

Katie's insides shook so bad she thought they would disintegrate and explode into little shards at any minute. "How could I have thought I could reason with him?" her mind questioned. "Wade was right. Frankie's crazy and he's evil, and he's going to kill me." Her thoughts stopped when Frankie turned around and kicked her to make her walk faster.

The hall was dark and dusty. "Maybe he's taking me back to the car," Katie hoped. "If we go driving, one of the sheriff's men or SLED agents may see the car and recognize us."

Frankie didn't take her to the street. He didn't even take her back to the door. He led her into a dust-laden bedroom and jerked the cover sheet off the bed. He pushed her onto the bare mattress, leaned over, and pressed his nose against hers. "Don't worry. I'm not going to rape you. At least, I don't think I am. Later, you'll beg me, and we'll make love, or at least I'll pleasure you, and you can pleasure me. I won't have to rape you, Maggie, but first I have some business to take care of. You're going to take a nap while I'm gone."

Barker cut the tape from between Katie's wrists, and she had a quick thought of hitting him, but he was busy yanking first one arm, then the other up toward the top of the old mahogany four-poster. He used more duct tape to strap each of her arms to opposite sides of the headboard.

Standing at the door, Frankie said, "I'll take the tape off your mouth when I get back, Maggie, and we can talk." He smiled. "You look good lying there. That's one game you didn't want to play with me. Maybe you'll decide you like it." He winked and closed the door behind him.

Tennessee Linda was determined to have a good day. She'd finished wiping down the kitchen and straightening up the parlor. She'd even bagged all the beer cans and set the trash bags on the front porch. She decided to complete her housecleaning before going shopping for the evening. She thought she could do her night shopping at the Shop & Save instead of Amick's. Daddy persisted in walking around in the back, but Mama had been silent for hours.

Linda had finished scouring the toilet in the half bath she usually used when she realized that if she dared to go through the back hall and clean the whole bathroom off that corridor, she would have cleaned all the parts of the house she lived in. Linda again felt the pride she'd known the day she cut the kudzu off the porch railings. She opened the pantry door and looked at herself in the mirror.

The Linda who gazed back at her wasn't anywhere near her sixties, and she didn't have a mass of tangled gray hair cascading over her face and shoulders. She was the young, beautiful girl who'd danced through last night's dreams. She could clean that back bathroom even if Daddy was walking around back there. If he tried to touch her, this time she'd tell the police instead of Mama.

CHAPTER 20

TIED TO THE BED, Katie listened to the screams. She didn't recognize the voice, and she had no idea that the noise came from the full bathroom in the same house where she was bound helplessly waiting for Barker to return—the same bathroom that Tennessee Linda had convinced herself it would be safe to clean. Katie asked herself, "Who does Frankie have now? What's he doing to her to make her yell like that? What will he do to me when he gets back?"

Hank wasn't a touchy-feely kind of man, but he had his arm across his old friend's shoulders. "Wade, he didn't kill Katie when he found her. He's got her somewhere. We'll find both of them!" he tried to console.

"Damn it, Hank. I've screwed this case up in every

direction. I think I'm in love with Katie. I can't deal with finding her in the trunk of a car."

"You HAVE to deal with the case, Wade. We need you. Your caller ID showed a call from Samantha Branham's cell phone. She's dead. The officer following her last night says her car was parked in front of her place when Campbell picked her up. It's gone, so we know what Barker is traveling in now — that old Hyundai."

"Hallucination," Tennessee Linda said when she stopped screaming. "Hallucination. That's all it is--hallucination." She looked down into the claw-footed bathtub at the bloody water. The legs and torso floated there — dark and bloated. She glanced over at the toilet. Wide-open glassy eyes stared from the head in there. The mouth gaped with its swollen tongue protruding and almost as dark as the long strands of hair swirling around the head in the water.

"Hallucination," Linda repeated. "Hallucination, like Mama talking and Daddy walking after I buried both of them in Tanner Cemetery." She knew the cure for hallucinations. Linda went back to the front of the house, retrieved her ATM card from the kitchen, and walked briskly out the front door toward Amick's Package Store.

Katie lay all afternoon in forced silence in the dark bedroom. The screaming had stopped. "Whatever he did to her is over," she thought. "He'll be back in here for me any minute." Frankie had told her he was leaving her to sleep. Katie thought she'd never sleep again unless it was her final, eternal rest. Her thoughts bounced around. Tears streamed down her face when she thought of poor Samantha. She'd planned to ask Wade to let her go out to buy Samantha a burial outfit.

"Who'll buy me a dress to be buried in?" she wondered. "My mama and daddy are both dead." Then she cried as she imagined the heartbreak it would have brought her mother if she'd been alive to know that both Maggie and Katie were missing. How terrible for your daughter to be found tied to a bed, raped, mutilated, and murdered in some old, abandoned house. What if nobody ever found either of them? She cried — silent, bitter, fearful tears.

"Where am I anyway?" Katie wondered. She'd never noticed the woods on Elm Street. I guess if I ever saw them, I thought it was some kind of park. When's he coming back? What did he do to that woman?" Then Katie had a horrible thought almost, but not quite, more horrible than Frankie killing her. "What if he doesn't come back? What if he leaves me to die a slow, horrible death from starvation?" She pictured herself wasting away to a skeleton even smaller than Samantha. That brought more tears for Sam as well as for herself.

Linda Louise, what are you doing with that Jack Daniel's? It's not even near nine o'clock yet!

"Mama, I told you to shut the fuck up."

Miraculously, it worked. There wasn't another word from Mama. Linda sat at the table and looked at the bottle of whiskey in front of her. Maybe, just maybe, if she began drinking now, she could go in the back of the house and prove to herself that what she saw in the bathroom was hallucination. There was no way some strange woman had drowned in the toilet. Linda shook her head at that ridiculous thought. Whoever that was in the bathroom certainly hadn't drowned in the toilet. She'd been dead before part of her wound up in the tub and her head in the toilet. The whole thing had to be Linda's mind playing tricks on her. After all, that room had been a chamber of horrors for Lindy Lou for as long as she could remember. Maybe what she'd seen in the bathroom was a manifestation of the past.

"We had a report of Samantha's black Hyundai over on Elm Street," Wade told Hank, "but when we got there, it was gone. Where the hell is that son of a bitch?" He looked over at Gross. "You're the big-shot FBI man. You've profiled him. Where's he keeping her?"

"Take it easy, Wade," Hank cautioned his old friend. "There's some good news. Police in Orlando have located Maggie."

"Is she alive?"

"She's fine. Barker started acting so strange that Maggie left the state in Katie's Fusion. He'd told her he couldn't go to Florida, so that's where she went. She was scared Barker would find her if she notified anyone where she is, but with these killings going nationwide on television, she reported in and wanted to know if her sister is okay. We advised her to stay where she is until we find Barker."

"It's a fine time for her to get concerned. That's exactly what I want to know. Where's Katie, Agent Gross? You had all the answers. Where is she?"

"Don't confuse me with your chubby psychic. You should have let me lure this killer in."

"And then I'd know she's dead." Jolley snapped in a tone as hateful and unprofessional as his expression.

"Being rude to the FBI isn't helping us find Katie," Hank said.

"It's okay, Chief. I knew this man had a personal interest in the Wray woman the first time I ever met him. Let him vent his feelings. I worked with an officer whose wife was the victim once. It's best to let him say what's on his mind. It may even give us some ideas."

"We had Katie hidden," Wade said. "He got her anyway, and you wanted me to use her as bait."

"If you'd followed my suggestion and used her to pull him in, you would have had more control over the situation. That's why we use proactive techniques — for control. You probably would have caught him by now."

For one instant, Jolley considered decking the FBI agent, but then his senses returned. "I'm going to hit the streets. I know that Hyundai. I might spot it before another officer just looking for a car by description will."

Katie's eyes were closed when the bedroom door opened. For just a moment, she thought the man standing there was Wade. Then her eyes adjusted to the dimness, and her conscious mind caught up with her. Frankie Barker.

"Maggie May, I've decided to teach you a lesson that a teacher taught me long ago." He laughed. "I thought about pleasuring you before your lesson, but I'll bet your mother taught you to eat your meal before dessert since she had so many other gems of wisdom. I think it's better if you learn your lesson first. Sex can be our dessert, Maggie. Like doughnuts were this summer. Did you cook for the sheriff? You never cooked for me. It was pizza and doughnuts all summer."

"Knowing Maggie, I'm not surprised," Katie thought.

"We'll have our lesson," Frankie continued. "Then you'll be begging me to pleasure you. You'll even beg to pleasure me. That's your word, Maggie. Pleasure! You had so many little euphemisms. Are you surprised I know that word? I had lots of teachers in my life. They taught me all kinds of things including the word 'euphemism.' That's how you talk, Maggie. You talk in euphemisms, just like that first teacher did. She told me I was special. She showed me how to make her feel good. She had different euphemisms from you. She told me to 'do' her and then she taught me how. Your word is 'pleasured,' and you want to 'taste' me."

Icy fingers of fear shot through Katie's body as Frankie cut the tape holding her to the bed and jerked her into an upright position. He kicked her in the shin. "Now walk, Teacher," he grumbled. "We're going outside for your lesson. Did your sheriff friend share my new poem with you? I wrote a poem for a young lady I met in a teacher store. She was younger than you, Maggie. Does that make you jealous? Don't let it. I made her beg all afternoon, but she wasn't half as good as you. Of course, she wasn't begging for pleasure. She wanted me to stop."

Grasping her hands behind her, Frankie forced Katie to walk in front of him. They went down the hall and out the door they'd entered. When she stumbled, Frankie kicked her leg. Katie was surprised that it was almost dusk. She had no idea what time it was or what day, but the full moon was rising in the gray sky. "How bad will a full moon make a full-fledged lunatic?" she thought.

"Teacher, Teacher, little slut, how I want to shut you up," Frankie chanted. "Always bossing me around, now my gun will put you down." He leaned forward and whispered, "Don't worry, Maggie. That was someone else's poem. I may make up a new one for you. Then you could have two 'Teacher, Teacher' poems because I love you. Even if you have to pass away, I don't think I'll kill you with a gun. How do you like the euphemism 'pass away,' Maggie? It means die."

Frankie pushed Katie over to an old oak tree with a bench facing away from the house. He shoved her to the other side of the tree and forced her back against it. Then he pulled her arms behind her around the tree and taped her wrists together again.

"At least I'm outside," she thought. "If I die tied to a tree out here, there's more chance of someone finding me than if I die inside that abandoned house."

"Is the tape too tight, Maggie? I don't want to hurt you. At least, not yet. There's a whole lot for us to do before I hurt you. Well, I mean before I hurt you bad."

Frankie stepped back and picked up a long duffel bag with a sporting goods logo on the side. A smaller produce sack remained on the ground. He opened the larger bag and pulled out a bow and quiver of arrows. "Do you remember the story of William Tell, Maggie? He was forced to shoot an apple off his son's head. A teacher told me that story when I was just a little boy. I went home and cried all night because I didn't want my daddy to shoot an arrow at me. Teachers shouldn't tell little kids stories like that. It scares them."

He picked up an arrow and pulled back the bowstring. "I've got razor-sharp broadheads on these arrows, Maggie. They're the kind you use to kill deer. My daddy took me hunting one time. I threw up when I saw the dead deer. My daddy and his friends laughed at me." Frankie laughed. "Let me take a practice shot. I'm not a hunter at heart. You teachers made me into one."

Barker turned and fired the arrow at a mimosa tree. It buried into the tree trunk. Frankie grinned at Katie. "Oh, no, Maggie. My bad. I was aiming to shoot over your head. If that had been you, it would have hit you right in the gut. You don't mind me saying you have a gut, do you? I'll bet you call it your tummy."

He put the bow and arrow on the ground and walked up to Katie. He pulled the switchblade from his pocket and pressed the knife against her throat. "I could forget the lesson and just dress you out right here like a deer. I wonder how long a woman lives if she's gutted alive? Of course, I'd have to take the tape off your mouth for that because I'd want to hear what you'd say. Nobody would pay any attention if you scream back here. People are used to hearing screams come out of this house."

The blade touched Katie's neck with just enough pressure to cause a thin trickle of blood. "Or I could just cut your throat, Maggie. I could cut your throat and hang you from a tree to watch you bleed to death, but I loved you, so I won't do that."

"He's not saying he loves me anymore," Katie thought. "He's changed it to past tense. He'll kill me now."

"But I went to the market to buy everything I needed for your lesson. It'd be a shame to waste all that effort." He picked up the bag and pulled out an apple. "An apple for the teacher, Maggie. Isn't Frankie a good boy? He's got an apple for his favorite teacher." He put the apple on Katie's head. It fell off. "Stop shaking, Maggie. I swear to God, if you don't be still, you'll wish you had. Keep this apple up there." He put the apple back on top of her head, and miraculously, Katie controlled her trembling enough that the apple stayed put.

Frankie picked up the bow and arrow and counted the paces as he backed away. At twenty, he stopped. He placed another arrow in the bow, pulled back the string, and shot. Katie felt the arrow whiz over her head as it pierced the tree trunk. The apple tumbled to the ground.

"Well," Frankie said, "I missed. Didn't hit you or the apple." He bent and picked up a piece of the shattered fruit from the ground. "Too bad. This apple's shot to hell, Maggie. Just like our relationship, don't you think?" He tossed it back on the ground. "Don't worry, Maggie. I bought a whole bag."

Every time Frankie put a new apple on Katie's head, he decreased the number of steps back and hit the tree above her head. The apple fell off each time. When he'd put Katie through this torture six times, there were six arrows stuck in the tree above her head. He backed up fourteen steps. Katie's head shook so violently that the apple fell off before he shot the arrow. Frankie ran up and slapped her face. Hard.

"Teachers played games with me all my life. Bossed me around, then broke my mother's heart when that first bitch did what she did to me. Men called me a 'lucky boy' because she was pretty." Frankie spat out the words. "She didn't even go to jail. Now we're playing my game, Teacher. You stand still or you'll wish you had." Frankie replaced the apple on her head. Stood there. Looked at her a moment.

"What you got in your pocket, Teacher?" he asked and put his hand in the chest pocket of her shirt. The tops of his fingers rubbed her breast through the fabric. He pulled his hand out of the pocket and began backing up, counting as he stepped. At fourteen paces, he shot the arrow directly through the apple and impaled part of it to the tree as pieces tumbled to the ground.

"Didn't think I could do it, did you, Teacher? You didn't know I took archery lessons along with dancing and everything else before my problem."

Katie barely heard his words. She wet herself. The dampness warmed her jeans, then quickly began to cool. Frankie walked up and looked down at the dark spot on her pants. "Did the teacher pee in her britches? Little boys do that when teachers don't let them go. Did you know that, Maggie May? Have you ever told a little boy he couldn't be excused, and he pissed himself?"

Katie frantically tried to shake her head no. He put his hand on her stomach and began sliding it down to the crotch of her pants, but he stopped before reaching the damp spot. Frankie stood there with his hand pressed against the pit of her abdomen. "Don't worry, Maggie. I won't laugh at you. We'll clean you up later. When I take the tape off your mouth, I'll take you inside and give you a nice bath. I'm sorry I don't have any bath oil, but I've already filled the tub with water and put something in it for you."

Linda stared at the bottle of Jack Daniel's. She held the bottle cap in one hand and an old Yogi Bear jelly glass in the other.

Linda Louise, what do you think you're doing? Have you been drinking all afternoon?

"No, but I'm going to start drinking soon. I'm having hallucinations."

What's new about that? Linda Louise, you know you have hallucinations almost every day.

"Yes, Mama, but these are different from keeping you and Daddy here with me. There's a woman in the bathroom. A dead woman. All cut up. Mama, is it me?"

Don't be ridiculous, Linda Louise. You're not dead.

"Are you sure, Mama? Maybe Bert murdered me."

Honey, Bert didn't kill you. You're not dead. Linda Louise, I can nag you, but that won't kill you. No matter what you think, I can't nag you to death. Bert and your daddy are both dead. Neither of them can ever hurt you again.

"Mama, you just said Daddy can't hurt me again. You would never believe he ever hurt me. Every time I tried to talk to you about Daddy, you just told me he loved me."

Linda Louise, I guess I knew all along what he did. I was so scared I couldn't support us that I didn't do anything about it. Women of my generation didn't work. I wouldn't have had any way to even feed you. When you were just a baby, I should have murdered your daddy like you killed Bert. I know you can't forgive me, but I wish I'd told you this before I died. I wish I'd told you when I could hug you. I wish I'd told you when I could have told you how beautiful you were before your daddy and Bert did what they did to you. Now it's too late.

"It's not too late, Mama. I hear you. You believed me! You were just scared. Mama, I can understand being too afraid to do anything."

There wasn't any answer. "Mama, I'll prove it's just an hallucination. That's not me in the bathroom. I'm going in there again. It'll be gone now."

Tennessee Linda screwed the cap back on the Jack Daniel's. She carried the bottle and glass into the kitchen and put them on the counter, and then she walked into the back hall and slowly opened the bathroom door. Dark hair floated around the head in the toilet, and Linda knew it was real and it was someone else. Her screams pierced the air like Frankie's arrows. Katie heard them through her fear. How could Frankie be hurting someone else when he was here torturing her?

Shrieks sliced into the air just as Sheriff Jolley passed the Pearson place. He shrugged. Unlike Katie, he recognized the voice—Tennessee Linda. It was no secret to him that Ms. Pearson frequently screamed and cried in the night. He circled the long block that encompassed the pathetic acreage left of the Pearson place. Suddenly, the sheriff remembered Ms. Pearson saying her father was walking in the rear of the house. What if Ms. Pearson had heard a *living* person in the back?

Wade's concentration on that memory almost made him overlook the car. In the dark, beneath the shade of the trees, he almost missed the black Hyundai, but when he realized what he'd seen from the corner of his eye, he curbed the Taurus sharply and was out the door before the engine stopped. Wade didn't look for a break in the fence. He went over it.

Running toward the sound of a woman's screaming voice wasn't conducive to thought, but the memory of Linda telling him her daddy had been walking pounded in his mind. What if she'd been hearing Barker? What if he'd taken Katie to the Pearson place and now he was hurting Linda? Oh, God, what if Linda was screaming because she'd found Katie's body?

As Wade rushed through the trees and brush, Frankie pulled out the switchblade again. He pressed it hard against Katie's throat, bringing blood from a different line of pressure. "Maggie, you know you'll have to die when this is over, don't you? What difference does it make when you die?"

He lifted the knife to her face and drew it lightly from beneath her right eye to the bottom of her jawline. He didn't cut her deeply, just enough to bring blood. "Now you have to match, don't you? Remember when you used to put on eyebrow pencil and you'd ask me if both sides matched? Well, Teacher, I want you to match." He drew the knife from beneath her left eye down her cheek. Katie felt trickles on both sides. Tears and blood mixed as they streamed down her face.

Linda Pearson stopped screaming. She wasn't having hallucinations. Those bloody, swollen body parts weren't herself in the bathroom. She ran out the back door in terror and stopped in her tracks at the sight of Frankie and Katie in the moonlight. Frankie had his back to her. Katie was tied to the tree facing the house, but Katie could see nothing through her tears and fear.

Linda grasped the situation immediately. If Linda Pearson understood anything at all, she understood being bound and helpless.

Frankie reached into the bag and pulled out his last apple. He put it on top of Katie's head, then took it off. He put his hand in her shirt pocket again and rubbed his fingers back and forth. "All I ever had to do was look at you and you wanted me. Look at that. I'm touching you and nothing's happening." He pinched her nipple through the fabric, then twisted hard.

"You're not ever going to beg me. You're too proud for that. You're too much of a teacher for that. Too much of a boss telling everyone what to do. I'm going to shoot one more apple, Maggie. I'm going to put a steel-tipped arrow right through one more apple. Guess where I'm going to put the apple, Maggie?" He twisted again. Took his hand out of her pocket and balled up his fist. Frankie slugged Katie in the stomach twice while Linda Pearson scrambled around in the kudzu in front of the garage. She knew she'd left the hatchet there. Where was it now? Why couldn't she find it?

"That's what it feels like, Maggie. That's what it feels like when someone you love sends you away. That's what it felt like when my teacher taught me to love her, made me touch her, then denied me when my parents found out. I was only in the seventh grade. It felt good. I did what she told me to do. It hurts when someone throws you away."

Frankie dropped the knife on the ground and pulled a gun from the produce bag. "Don't worry, Maggie. I've got a silencer on it." He thumbed the safety off and stepped close to Katie's face. "Why don't you close your eyes and make this easier for me, Maggie? After all, I did love you. You ought to make it easier for me. You caused it all." He pulled out the front of Maggie's shirt pocket and tried to force the apple into it. "I'm going to put a bullet right through one more apple, Maggie. You know where I'm going to put that apple, Maggie? I'm going to put it in your pocket . . . "

The sheriff reached the clearing just in time to see Linda Pearson leap onto Barker's back like a demon. At first, he couldn't understand what she was screaming, but Katie understood every word. "No, you won't, you goddamned motherfucker! You won't put anything in her pocket!"

As Wade ran toward them, Frankie pushed the old woman off and pointed the gun straight at her. Linda grabbed the knife from the ground. She came up, driving the blade directly into Barker's belly. It looked like a death blow to Jolley, but Barker straightened up and re-aimed the gun point-blank at Linda Pearson.

With strength dormant throughout a lifetime of abuse, she twisted the young man's hands to turn the gun toward himself. Then, and Katie and Wade both saw it clearly, she pressed her hands over Barker's trigger finger and forced him to fire the gun directly into his own chest. No doubt this time. It was a heart shot. A death shot. Barker crumpled.

Tennessee Linda released her clenched fingers off Barker's hand and collapsed on top of him. She looked around with a dazed expression and rolled herself to the ground beside the body.

Jolley bent over the elderly lady covered in blood. "Are you okay?" he asked.

"I will be," Linda answered breathlessly.

"Let me help you up," the sheriff suggested and reached his hand out to Linda.

"No, I can get up. Just give me a minute to catch my breath. You help Teacher Girl."

Jolley ripped the tape from Katie's mouth. He pulled out his pocketknife and began cutting Katie free.

Linda braced herself with her elbows and pushed herself to her hands and knees, then stood.

As Katie rubbed her arms and wrists briskly, Jolley felt Barker's carotid though he knew there would be no pulse. Then he pressed the button to activate his radio. "Headquarters . . . one, two, one . . . My location is behind the old Pearson place on Oak Street. I've got a 10-52 and a 10-40. Locate Gross, Legrand, and Coroner Hawkins and send them here with a crime scene unit." He paused, then added, "10-4."

Tennessee Linda looked around as though she were lost, then her eyes settled on Katie. She stepped over to Katie and gently ran one finger down the bleeding cuts on her face. "Come in the house with me, Teacher Girl. I'll clean those up for you." She looked down at Katie's damp jeans. "I'll give you some dry pants too. I did that to myself just the other night."

"Can I go in with her?" Katie asked the sheriff.

"I've already called for an ambulance," Jolley replied.

"I think you need a hearse, not an ambulance," Tennessee Linda said matter-of-factly and kicked Barker in the ribs with her toe.

"The ambulance is for Katie," Jolley answered.

Katie looked at him. "Let her help me. I'm not hurt bad. I want to go in with her."

"There's something inside you need to see anyway," Linda told the sheriff. She turned to lead them around the house, bypassing the back door.

"We'll be right in," Jolley told her and caught Katie by the hand. "Get a damp cloth for her face if you will, Ms. Pearson," he added. "We'll be there in just a minute."

"Okay," Linda replied. "I know all about first aid. I studied it because I wanted to be a teacher." She continued walking toward the house.

"She saved my life!" Katie blurted. "Tennessee Linda saved my life. She shot Frankie. She stabbed him and shot him!"

"No, she didn't," Wade said quietly but emphatically. "That's why I sent her in first, so our stories will match. Ms. Pearson dropped the knife. Frankie fell on it, and the gun discharged as he fell."

"No, he didn't Wade. Linda shot him."

"Her fingerprints won't be on that gun. Not the way she had her fingers over his. He fell on his gun."

"Why? She'll be a hero when this hits the news."

"She doesn't need the attention she'd get as a hero."

"Wade, she's not all that shy. She talks to the waitress at the Downtown Diner. She even let Samantha drive her home from the grocery store one day when it was raining. Linda Pearson saved my life."

"I know that, and it's why Barker fell on his knife and gun. The limelight would bring too many people into Ms. Pearson's life. They'll look too closely at her. She spent over twenty years doing time for killing her husband who abused her damned near daily. If he'd been a banker or a mechanic, she'd have walked free. There was medical proof of what all he'd done to her, but because he was a cop, they shut that poor woman up for years.

"She's just a little 'tetched' as my grandma would say because of it. Now this cop, or sheriff if you want to be exact, isn't willing to hurt that woman. I don't want people noticing Linda Pearson any more than they already do. They'll want to lock her up again."

The back door opened, and Linda stepped out. She'd changed her clothes, but there was still a smudge of blood across her cheek. She headed toward Katie and Wade holding out a cloth so wet that it dripped. Katie looked up at Wade. Hand in hand, they walked toward Tennessee Linda.

"Frankie Barker fell on the knife and the gun went off," Sheriff Jolley said.

"Really?" Linda questioned with a wide-eyed, childlike expression.

"That's what happened," Katie answered.

Linda began dabbing at Katie's cuts with the wet cloth. Water dripped down the denim shirt. Linda turned her questioning gaze from the sheriff to the teacher. She squeezed the excess water from the cloth, then looked at each of them again.

The old woman shook her head up and down, though her expression remained puzzled.

Together, the sheriff and the teacher said, "Barker fell."

"Yes, he fell," Linda Pearson agreed.

Then she smiled.

ABOUT THE AUTHOR

Fran Rizer's fiction, published in the USA and Canada, has been read worldwide. She won a Porter Fleming Award in Fiction, and her first six novels were Callie Parrish mysteries, which were nominated for SIBA, Edgar, Agatha Christie, and other awards. She is a featured author on the SCETV series, *A Literary Tour of South Carolina,* an instructional program offered to all South Carolina public schools. Rizer lives in South Carolina near her two sons and grandson. Readers are invited to correspond with her directly through email at franrizer@gmail.com, visit with her at FranRizer.com, see her book trailers on YouTube, and like or friend her on Facebook.